Praise for book

It is the first I have read by D̶ seeking out "Clipped". A ̶ Acaster Author of Torc of Moonlight, The Bull at the Gate and Hostage of the Heart

This book grabbed me from the start and kept me hooked until the last page. An outstanding read in every way - Emily Braden - Book blogger

A direct unconventional writing style from a promising new author from Hull (City of Culture 2017). Looking forward to the new book - Mick Murphy

Terrific Book. Daniel Birch has certainly taken his time and has created a masterpiece. If you enjoy a great story, you won't be disappointed. 5 stars doesn't even come close. - Joseph Graziano

Great read - slick writing - careful and loving characterisation for all participants, even the most minor ones - raw atmospherics, and most of all great story –telling. What is not surprising about Danny's writing is that it draws in people who would not otherwise be tempted to pick up a book. What is perhaps more surprising is how many other writers on Night Reading and elsewhere really appreciate his work. Danny seems to have an extraordinarily wide appeal. - Tim Hewtson Author and founder of Taylor Street Publishing.

Once I had picked it up I couldn't put it down and was sad to see the last page. The sense of mystery that permeates each chapter makes me hunger for answers. This is a wonderful quality in a novel – Jordan Renault

Daniel Birch

The Gravedigger

© 2014, DANIEL BIRCH

(dbirch10@hotmail.co.uk)

(dbirch.co.uk)

ALL RIGHTS RESERVED. This book contains material protected under International Copyright Laws. Any unauthorized reprint or use of this material is prohibited. No part of this book may be reproduced or transmitted in any form or by any means, electronic or mechanical, including photocopying, recording, or by any information storage and retrieval system without express written permission from the author.

If you do, I will look for you, I will find you…

And I *will* kill you.

For Carly

Love is giving someone the power to destroy you and trusting them not too.

I would like to say a big thank you to all my family and friends for their support and to all those who I haven't had the pleasure of meeting yet who have supported me, thank you, I really hope you enjoy the book.

Thank you to Scott Paffley (www.ibloo.co.uk) who has done a great job with my website dbirch.co.uk as well as helping me with the design of the book cover.

I would also like to say a special thank you to Kristian Wealsby (kwealsby@gmail.com) and Darren Rogers. The original artwork for the front cover of this book was done by Kristian Wealsby and I'm sincerely grateful Kristian, I know it took you a considerable amount of time and I appreciate it. The photography and effects of the cover were done by Darren Rogers (d_rogers_ocular@hotmail.com), to you too Darren, I'm really grateful.

Thank you to Carly Allen for editing the book, I know it must have been a nightmare! It is great to think that over two years ago you listened to me waffle on about an idea about this book, which I thought I couldn't pull off, and now it's here. I think it just shows sometimes no matter how much ideas may seem out of touch in your own mind, share them with a friend, and they might just have substance…

I have to give a mention to The Hillbilly Troupe (www.hillbillytroupe.com), whose music I listened to for a well-deserved break when writing this book.

Take care.

The Gravedigger

By

DANIEL BIRCH

The year was 1892 in Barnes, London, England. It was a leap year and could be remembered for a great many number of notable affairs such as Sir Arthur Conan Doyle's first publication of The Adventures of Sherlock Holmes, or perhaps the birth of Liverpool Football Club, and it was even the year that the first electric light bulb in Bulgaria was used at the Plovdiv Fair.

What a great year indeed!

However, it is not always the extravagant news we hear which tells the greater story.

Sometimes we hear tales of love and adventure which make our hearts skip a beat, but sometimes, every now and then, we hear whispers of an unsettling nature, murky tales which keep us awake when everything gets dark. Some call such stories 'black legends', some call them 'night fictions', designed to scare us.

Whichever way you slice it, such tales can still capture us in a gripping hand in which we feel it almost our duty to pass the story to the next person, to the next person, and so on.

The story I am about to share with you has two sides, one light and one dark, to which one has a greater proportion.

Ultimately, that matter is something which only you can decide…

CHAPTER 1

While many wrongly doubted the man's overall level of intelligence, there was certainly no question that he was dedicated to his work.

As such, when it fell to him to assume the mantle of his late father as the gravedigger of Barnes Cemetery, William Rathbone devoted his life to his work.

William's father, the late David Rathbone had been well known in the town of Barnes, London.

Well known indeed…

His reputation was one born from fear, for David was a bitter old man with a disturbing appearance. Many said that he was merely a poor man who had suffered some affliction which had left him only one working eye, the other remained concealed behind a black eye patch. Others however, told tales of a more sinister nature…

It is said in those parts that David Rathbone, of Barnes Common, London, was in fact in league with Lucifer, the Devil to you or I, and that if a raven landed on the plot of land on the morning of a burial, it was a sign that the Devil wanted the soul of the deceased. In such cases, David would mark the soil inside the empty grave by drawing the Devil's star on the spot where the coffin was to be laid.

Once this was done, it is said that the deceased would be bound to Hell.

Of course this was just town chatter, or was it?

Many say that the wickedness of the late David Rathbone began on the day his wife, Ellen Rathbone, died, giving birth to their first and only son, William.

The cause of death however, was in fact suicide. She was bleeding internally, and the physician claimed there was nothing more he could do. Last Rites were said, but Ellen lay screaming for days, the blood continuing to seep out of her. David, although be-sodden with the inevitable outcome of the trauma, had no real belief in gods, had no real belief in demons. His wife, Ellen, whom he did love ever so dearly, begged him for the pain to stop, for him to help her die, so he left her with a dose of morphine, one that was too much for any human to endure, she took it, and ended her own life.

When the news that Ellen had taken her own life filtered through Barnes, even her dear friends refused to turn up for her burial, for in God's eyes she was damned, her soul was now enlisted to Satan.

They say on the morning of Ellen's interment, the devil appeared to David as a raven, giving him the option, either to let Ellen's soul be bound to the eternal torments of Hell or to become a soul collector as and when required, all he had to do was draw a star…

So a star he apparently drew, over and over again.

But of course this was just town chatter, or was it?

Who was to know whether the chatter of the folk of Barnes was just idle gossip; a mere smear in the face of a poor man with one eye?

He was a cheap target for jokes and horrid tales, and with each year that passed, the wicked taunts continued; that much was a fact.

What was also a fact is that after Ellen died, he became a mean man. So mean that he blamed his infant son for Ellen's death. He brought William up on his own; he refused the young lad any education, and was determined that the boy would live a life of misery.

Once William was of working age, which was around seven years old, David beat William every other day.

He constantly reminded William of the fact that he killed his mother, something which William believed because it was instilled in him from infancy.

William often wondered what it would be like to have a mother, or even a nice father, but luckily for William, when his father was busy or out of the way, he made friends with Reverend Fanshaw or Father Fanshaw as many knew him. Father Fanshaw was in charge of the cemetery and it was he who took it upon himself to teach William to read.

And read William did. He enjoyed reading so much that after a while, the good Father Fanshaw taught William to write, albeit in a simple kind of way but he had learned to write nevertheless.

On a few occasions David caught William reading, William would pretend not to understand the words and would use the excuse he was just looking at pictures, but his father would beat him for it anyway. Over the years William became toughened to the beatings and grew up to be a tall, handsome, strong man.

Williams's looks definitely came from his mother, his strength from his father which was a result of hours upon hours and days upon days, years upon years of doing the tasks associated with this work as a gravedigger. Grave preparation included locating and marking the grave site; removing the sod and excavating soil by hand and shovel; placing and removing boards, struts and matting; and covering excavated soil. Funeral preparation tasks included positioning the casket, which was lowered by a rope, erecting canopies and arranging chairs. Post funeral activities involved lowering caskets, back filling dirt and positioning headstones.

There were a vast number of ground-keeping tasks associated with his job. Some included, cutting grass, removing dead flowers and debris from graves, pruning shrubs and trimming trees. In order to complete these jobs, William had to be both strong and dedicated.

William was without a doubt, the best gravedigger Barnes had ever seen. Better than his father ever was, he spent hour after hour making the graves look both pretty and respectful.

It was something he couldn't do before his father died, but when David passed away William made sure he would make the graveyard look the best it could, such was the high standard of his work that people of a high standing would travel from neighbouring parts of London to bury loved ones there.

Father Fanshaw felt it obvious that William should take his late father's role, though felt maybe due to the high demand of work involved that William would need a hand, but William preferred to work alone.

He lived in small quarters which had been converted from an old barn when he was younger by his father. It wasn't much, but to William, it was home.

The good Father often worried about William, as he rarely ventured out into the world beyond the cemetery gates, when asked about the fact, William would simply respond 'this is my world' and go back to his work.

It was the conclusion of Father Fanshaw that due to the years of abuse at the hands of his late father, William was damaged in some way, and maybe, when all was said and done, it was best for William to be away from other people. At least in the graveyard William was safe.

An unfortunate actuality, of which the good Father was aware, was that on the scarce occasion when William did leave the grounds, people of the town would subject him to the same torment his later father suffered; he was sometimes called 'Devil's son' and 'Satan spawn.' They even made up new names for poor William such as 'Mother killer' and 'Death man' but they used one name more than any other…

Dead talker

CHAPTER 2

All but one of the names that William was subject to being called were so far from the truth, for there was not a more gentle man in London.

The name 'Dead Talker' was given to William because it was said that when nobody could see him, he would talk to the graves.

Some would say that he was going mad; some would say that he was indeed mad already, and some would even say that William was carrying on his father's evil work with Lucifer.

However it was also said, that William did, and could in fact, communicate with the dead.

Of course this was just town chatter, or was it?

By the time William turned 30 years of age he had become a master in his art, and on one particular rainy morning he got to test his skills, for he had been requested to prepare a grave for a more affluent member of the community than normal…

April 21st, 1892, Barnes, London

After accumulating his tools in an old sack, William advanced to the bottom of the graveyard, for this was where the most space existed. After all, to cater for the likes of such a family would take the greatest of care and William had to make sure he had enough room to manoeuvre.

He laid his tools on the ground, by his feet, and removed his long black overcoat. Sure, it was raining, but William knew that good old hard work was the order of the day, so he rolled up his sleeves and got to it.

After many an hour digging, the rain finally ceased.

Looking up to the sky William wiped his wet face and decided to take a small break.

Having left an empty cup on a nearby headstone, William was pleased to see it had filled with the morning rain.

He was glad the rain was good for something apart from softening the ground so the dig was less demanding.

Having taken a sip from his cup, William reached into his coat which was also draped over the headstone, and pulled out his pipe which still had some tobacco stuffed inside; he lit it and took a satisfying puff.

The sun was beginning to rear its head through the clouds above and William smiled to himself.

What a lovely day!

It was at that moment his tranquillity was breached.

'Hey, yes you, do you mind? This is no park bench sir!'

Turning to the grave William sighed 'Oh, not you again. Look Mr Higgingsly, I have told you before, many times, that I mean no disrespect sir, it's just if I put my coat on the ground then it will get wetter still, or dirty!'

'Well *I* have told *you*, also on numerous occasions, dear sir that this is my grave, and I do not take lightly to people using it as a place to hang, of all things, a coat!'

Taking the coat off the headstone, along with the cup, William reluctantly agreed to Mr Higgingsly's request 'That's fine sir, I have done as you have asked, I was just taking a quick break, just having a sip of water, well rain water in fact and enjoying a quick puff on my pipe. If I have offended you I am sorry.'

'Bloody right too, I'd say,' added Mr Higgingsly. 'So, who are you committing to the earth now?'

William put his pipe away in his coat and placed it in a nearby wheelbarrow with his now empty cup 'What business is it of yours who I bury?'

'Well excuse me, sir; let me remind you of the fact I am indeed a resident here, it is of the utmost importance who is buried here, for whoever you are burying is going to be my new neighbour'

Chuckling aloud, William walked away, climbed into the hole he had begun to dig and carried on digging, but Mr Higgingsly would not leave it alone.

'Excuse me! If you think your silence on the matter will shut me up then think again sir, I will not shut up just because you choose to ignore me!'

William carried on, with a smug smile 'Well Mr Higgingsly, I *do* have all day, so rant all you want'

'All *day*? You say you have all *day*? Well I have forever! Beat that!'

Sticking his spade in the mud and leaving it standing upright, William ceased for a moment and looked over to Mr Higgingsly's grave 'You do have a point actually. If you must know sir, the poor chap who has recently died is a certain Lord Fenwick, and I do hear that the man was only recently married, which I'm sure you will agree, is a crying shame.'

'Lord Fenwick you say? I do seem to recall the name…ah, yes indeed, I knew of the man. A well-to-do kind of chap I must say. Well-liked among his kind too, I must add; known for his kind ways and good amount of benevolence towards people less fortunate than himself. Good to his workers, apparently. Yes indeed, I'm sure he will make a rather good neighbour.'

'How did you know him then, Higgingsly?' asked William as he got back to his digging.

'Well, as a former landlord in these parts sir, I did tend to mix with those of a high calibre.'

'Really? Or are you just saying this to try and impress me, Higgingsly?'

'I would say maybe a little of both' Higgingsly sniggered.

'So, how is everyone today? I have been rather busy getting things ready for this chap, so I haven't had much chance to do my rounds yet'

Higgingsly's grave fell silent.

William stopped digging and turned to Higgingsly's grave 'Did you hear me?'

There was no answer.

'Oh no, so what's going on? You always do this. You do realise though, that by saying nothing you are in fact saying everything, what's wrong and with whom?'

Again, there was no answer.

Continuing his work William made a mental note to do his rounds and find out what was going on. William knew something wasn't right, because Higgingsly was most definitely a talker, and when he was quiet then something was usually going on.

'Right, if that's how you want it, I won't ask again, but I can't help if you don't tell me what's wrong.'

Higgingsly spoke up again 'I want to but I can't. Dead man's code you see. We don't interfere with each other and we don't get involved with problems unless asked directly. We are in eternal sleep are we not?'

William laughed. 'You could have fooled me; you talk more than I do!'

CHAPTER 3

After readying the grave site for the burial later that week, William thought it best that he got to the bottom of the problem, if there was one, so he did his rounds.

The 'rounds' William had referred to consisted of him going to the various graves and making sure everything, and everyone was happy, or as happy as one could be if one were, as in these cases, dead.

So, pottering along to each grave William rearranged flowers and cleared each grave of old leaves that had scattered in the afternoon's breeze. He also chatted to those who seemed in need of some human dialogue. William would talk about what the weather was like and also things he knew which were going on in the world, it gave some of them comfort. William would pay extra attention to those who didn't get many visitors, 'The Forgotten', he called them, and occasionally he would write a letter to such loved ones anonymously to remind them of the fact that a visit was indeed due.

Some took the bait, some didn't, but for those that did it would always cheer William up that he was able to provide some sort of service for those that couldn't do it themselves.

The letters he wrote were not his own words, he would ask the sender to say exactly what they wanted written, so there would be a personal touch. William would always hand deliver too, so there were no postmarks.

Being almost a third of the way through his rounds, William came to one of his favourite residents, Maureen Templeby.

As William approached Maureen's grave he heard her crying 'Oh Maureen, whatever is the matter, dear?'

'So you don't know either? Nobody cares I tell you, nobody!'

Pausing for a second, William wondered what could have possibly set poor Maureen off.

'Er, I'm ever so sorry Mrs Templeby, but what is the matter? Has one of the others been upsetting you?'

'Look around, William! It's obvious!'

Looking around the immediate area William couldn't see anything which he thought could cause distress.

'I'm at a loss, but if you want to talk I am here.'

'My headstone!'

'What about it?'

'Read it!'

William read it out…

'Maureen Templeby, loving mother to John, David and Paul, devoted wife to Arthur, born 21st April 1803, passed in her sleep on…'

'You see!'

William stopped reading, he still didn't get what had upset her and he stayed quiet, deep in thought as he studied the gravestone.

'Oh heaven forbid William! It's my birthday!'

William sighed 'Oh Maureen, it is indeed! Though my maths is not very good. So how old would you have been today?'

'89! I would have been 89 years old!'

'Well Maureen, although you can't have a birthday brandy, I can talk by your grave later if you like, read you the local newspaper?'

'Oh William, how sweet you are. But I fear it will still not lift me. Twenty years since I passed, my dear boys used to visit me often, then just little John, and now even he doesn't come. Adding to such indignity there are some around here who have been teasing me about my plight'

'Really? And who might that be Maureen? I would have words with such people if you were to point me in the right direction'

'Dead man's code, William' she sighed.

'Oh you lot and your bloody codes! Come on, give me a clue?'

'Well I won't say any names, but if he were around you would have to keep guard of your watch…'

Shaking his head William walked off briskly 'Pickpocket Sam, the little bugger!'

'Oh please don't tell him I told you William, I really don't want to be secluded from the others!'

'You didn't tell me, don't worry, your code is still intact.'

As he approached pickpocket Sam's grave he could hear Sam whistling.

'Good day William, and how may I help you today? Ha-ha.'

Pickpocket Sam was killed when he was just fourteen years old, he had stolen the watch of a rich man during broad daylight and was chased by a local policeman. Unfortunately for Sam, he ran

16

into the path of an oncoming horse and cart which was going at a decent speed. Sam died from his injuries after hitting his head hard on the ground.

'What have you been up to?' snapped William, who was determined to resolve the matter quickly.

'Up to? Me?' chuckled Sam 'What can I be up to, I ask ya William? I'm dead!'

'Don't play smart with me, young one. What have you been saying to poor Maureen? It's her birthday you know? Fancy upsetting her on her birthday!'

'Oh I am sorry William. I just get bored with this whole dead game, ya' see. Be nice to get some new people in here. I was just saying I bet her people had forgotten about her and no point wasting time on the living 'cos they are not interested in us anymore. Makes sense though, doesn't it? Still, I never meant to set the old lass off!'

'Well, set her off you did. Right, I'm going inside to prepare a little surprise for her, in the meantime, you apologise, right?'

'Will do sir, surely will.'

All the dead in the graveyard knew not to cross William, for he was the only link each of them had with outside world and if he wanted to, he could make their existence even worse than it was.

Just as the souls in the graveyard had their 'Dead man's code', William had rules too, and if they were broken he would try and sort the problem out, if they kept offending, then he would hand down certain punishments.

If such punishments did not have an effect, then he took more drastic measures.

Such measures had only been used a handful of times. *Such measures were only used when William encountered the worst kind of soul…*

An *evil* soul…

CHAPTER 4

William never really knew how he came to hear the dead. He had never actually seen a ghost but could hear them clear as day, wherever he went.

He spoke of it only to one person and that was Father Fanshaw, who on listening to William's claims, didn't offer any kind of explanation, nor did he dismiss it. The good Father simply expressed his view that some people had a 'dark gift' and those that did should not look upon themselves as dark, but look upon themselves as a messenger for good.

William liked that idea.

Forming his own hypothesis on his unusual dark gift, William was of the opinion that because he planted the flowers and spoke to the dead, that in some way that kept them alive.

As mentioned earlier, every once in a while William 'got a bad one', that's how he put it. It was testament to the man that he would always try and reason with the bad spirit but, like the living that are bad, some cannot be reasoned with.

Some men just like evil, they enjoy it.

The general consensus was if they were evil in life, then it was credible that the spirit would be evil in death.

The way William dealt with such a sinister spectre was a well-planned ceremony.

The ghosts of Barnes Cemetery gave this ceremony a name, and it stuck through the years.

They called it 'The Last Rites.'

The ceremony involved all the spirits unanimously agreeing to ignore the bad spirit, to try and forget they existed. William would then read out passages from The Bible, and cover the grave in holy water; it was very much like an exorcism. William would then put dead flowers, dead twigs and weeds around the grave. He would also remind everyone, including himself that no grave is there at all.

William and the ghosts believed that it was because of such disconnection with the bad spirit that all ties to the world were severed, and the soul was gone forever.

William had only performed the last rite ritual a few times, and while it had worked on the bad souls he had encountered, he never took the view that his way was the ultimate panacea.

On the rare occasion that William was forced to perform such a deed, he still felt sad. For William, The Last Rite was the very *last* option.

William never liked to argue, with the living or the dead and he always thought it best he held a good forbearance. But sometimes he just had to act, if not for himself, then for the good of his little community.

It was imperative he was the one who imbued the community with calm.

CHAPTER 5

Even though the lady was in mourning and dressed as such, it was plain to see to all the assemblage that she was the most becoming of young women.

She tried the best she could with her well-wishing visitors; after all, appearances in her world meant everything. But the more she tried the more desultory she seemed to be in her manner towards people.

This was to be expected of course, for what pain is greater than that of a loved one lost?

Lady Anne Elizabeth Fenwick, widow of the recently deceased Lord Fenwick was 25 years of age. Although wise beyond her years, Lady Anne, known to her closest friends as Lizzy, still displayed a beauty that captivated those who surrounded her. So much so that even her late husband felt he just *had* to be with her.

Her shoulder-length black hair looked as smooth as silk, her lips as red as a rose and her skin so delicate and unblemished, one could have been forgiven for gazing longer than one should.

Lord Fenwick and Lady Anne were married only three months before his untimely death. She felt the loss, and felt it deeply, for he was a kind man at heart, but the truth of the matter was that she was in fact pushed into marrying him by her father, who was a friend of Lord Fenwick.

She agreed to marry him for her father's sake, but little did she know that Lord Fenwick had no intention of being a "proper" husband; that was made clear to her the night of her wedding.

It came as a huge relief to her that she did not have to endure the duty that was expected of most women on the night of a wedding, and in Lady Anne's case, her betrothed was more than 40 years her senior. She was not attracted to him one bit but had resigned herself to the fact that she was doing her family a favour.

She was so pleased to sit down with Lord Fenwick on the night of her wedding and have a deep discussion of what was expected in her new role as Lady of the manor. He said that it was mostly for appearances and that he would not want or expect anything of a sexual nature because he still loved his late wife, but he wanted to be good friends and he wanted female companionship.

Lady Anne was more than happy to oblige, for it was a far better outlook than she had first thought.

At first it was hard to settle in. Lady Anne was from a middle-class background and she tried to alter her speech as best she could, as well as her demeanour. Growing up, she was a strong and assertive girl, though always being reminded about a woman's place. With her father she could almost get away with such things, but as a Lord's wife there were certain obligations which had to be followed.

Such obligations, coupled with having no real friends around her, gave Lady Anne a feeling of being trapped in a world from which there was no escape.

She knew she would never want for anything, for if she so desired she could have almost anything.

The manor was beautiful, her clothes were the finest in town, her horses were well looked after, yet something was always missing. She felt out of place, like she didn't belong, and at times she felt like a prisoner in the manor; a lonely, empty soul who ghosted through a life with no meaning.

It was the day before the funeral.

Lady Anne stood with perfect poise in the centre of the kitchen where some of the Lord's closest aristocratic associates had come to visit her to pay their respects.

The more plebeian inhabitants of Barnes who were going to pay their respects would turn up on the day of the ceremony and stand at the back, of course. Today though, was more of an upper class social gathering for those closest to Lord Fenwick.

As Lady Anne moved around the room and consorted with the different people, she couldn't help feel somewhat befuddled by what she thought was obvious simulation of regret by some of her late husband's closer 'friends'.

She appreciated the sentiment, though did not welcome fraudulence when it came to feelings.

Lady Anne loved her husband dearly. Though it was on a platonic level; it was love, nevertheless.

It seemed some of the visitors had come just to be seen, like one of the Lord's ever-so-extravagant ballroom parties. Lady Anne knew what her late husband would have said. 'Bloody fraudsters' he would call them behind their backs. They would both giggle and mock various well-to-dos in private.

But regrettably for Lady Anne, this was how things were, and what was expected of her.

It was her duty to keep up appearances.

CHAPTER 6

Of the abundant spurious socialites who were in attendance on the day Lady Anne welcomed such guests to Woodworth Manor, one particular parasite made her feel more uneasy than most.

The worm wriggled around the room in his typical exuberant fashion. The guests were magnetized by his clever repartee; such was his ability to articulate a proper conversation.

Lady Anne, however, was unmoved by his fake allure and remained sternly distant from his numerous attempts to befriend her. She knew, had always known in fact, that his public displays of allegiance to Lord Fenwick were nothing more than conniving manoeuvres to facilitate some other dark scheme.

The worm had a name, and it too ended in Fenwick; but he was no Lord.

Patrick Fenwick was the younger brother of the late Lord, and was a solicitor of high esteem in London.

Many wondered why Patrick would bother to practise such a stressful career, for he did not need the money.

So why? Why the need to climb the ladder to success when one was fortunate already and had the financial foundations for a life which had no need for such efforts?

There were many reasons, one of which was power.

For the power his labour gave him in the legal profession was such that he could shape things as he saw fit. He marvelled at the idea of being a man of such stature. Being held in such regard and never one to be modest, Patrick liked to use his title and credentials to get what he wanted.

One of the things he despised about his brother was that Lord Fenwick was truly loved by people, a gentleman of the truest sort.

Patrick was also of the opinion, that Lady Fenwick should not be entitled to the manor (following the briefest of marriages) but unfortunately for Patrick, Lord Fenwick had made a will which named Lady Fenwick the sole beneficiary to all of his assets, as he had never fathered a child in either marriage.

Approaching Lady Anne stealthily through the assembled visitors, Patrick appeared before her with a sly grin as he removed his hat.

'Good day to you Anne, of course you know how deeply I am hurting right now; my brother was so, so dear to me'

Her eyebrows raised, Lady Anne replied 'Thank you Patrick, he was so-*so* dear to all of us. I'm sure you would agree and, as his widow, I would quietly remind you that it may be better, for appearances' sake, to address me as *Lady* Anne. In the interest of appearances as I say'

Through almost gritted teeth Patrick answered 'Yes, yes, appearances of course, *Lady Anne.*'

He hated that he was obliged to agree.

CHAPTER 7

Every night he slept; every night they called his name and every night he lay, he had a deep feeling of impending darkness.

The voices were subtle, but the message was obvious.

Something, someone, some sinister force seemed to want to pull him away from his mortality. As if they were whispering him away from his life.

These dreams, or as William saw them, nightmares, were regular. Although the setting was usually different, the grim and frightening elements were the same.

On this night, inside his nightmare, William was walking; there was a fog which blanketed the ground and acted as a cloak to the voices of the dark unknown. William had no idea of any destination, and folded his arms as he walked whilst clasping his hands underneath his armpits to try and feel warmer. He saw his own breath in the air join the peculiar shapes of the dark night's fog.

The fog seemed to take horrifying shapes at first. They reminded William of numerous faces in pain. He wanted to close his eyes but was afraid if he did that something may attack him. He felt in imminent danger as he walked on.

Trying to close his ears to the sounds of the night did no good either, for it seemed like the voices were so close that the lips which spoke were almost touching his ears.

'Come William,' a hollowed voice called. 'Come to us,' called another. The voices were a mix of male and female but William couldn't recognise them.

He felt an irresistible pull towards somewhere unknown amidst the foggy environment, but he didn't want to go; it seemed his legs wouldn't listen to his head and he kept on walking even though he was gripped by an increasing state of dread.

The fog thinned before him, he could make something out now, his legs taking him on a journey he did not freely choose. He was cold, and the cold increased in the air as the fog seemed to push his body to its menacing destination.

William was at his journey's end, his shock and fear wriggled through his body in collaboration to deny what lay ahead.

'A grave?' William screamed. 'Why? It isn't my time! No!' he cried.

His body moved itself uncontrollably closer, his feet were positioned on the edge of the grave; he saw the headstone.

It read 'William Rathbone, Mother Murderer.'

Sobbing tears of sincere despair William apologized as he cried 'But I didn't mean it, I was just a baby. Oh Mother, dear Mother, please forgive me'

He felt dizzy as he looked down at an empty casket wide open; it looked like it had a mind of its own as it stayed ajar, readying itself for its eternal inhabitant.

As his faint feeling grew, his balance decreased, his legs wobbled and his body fell into the coffin. William screamed as the coffin slowly started to shut, his screams getting duller as the coffin lid started to close, narrowing the light out inch by inch.

'No, no, no, please!' he screamed, but it was too late.

The coffin finally shut. William was now in a crypt of darkness, his screams unheard, his body underground, and his soul unloved.

'Oh why, do I suffer such torment?' he asked as he began to accept his fate. 'Why?'

Just as William thought his heart was about to stop he heard a voice…

'William? William? Are you alright in there?' the familiar muffled voice enquired.

He opened his eyes, his eyeballs shot to the left and right of his surroundings, was he alright? Was he alive? Then he noticed the light!

'The light!' William cried. For he was sure he was dead!

He noticed he had been sweating in his bed from the nightmare as the voice outside continued to call.

William half opened the door to see Father Fanshaw standing with a perplexed look on his face.

'Oh good, you are alright, I heard some rather strange noises coming from your room dear boy, just thought I would make sure you were alright. I apologise if I have disturbed you, it is unlike you to take a sleep in the mid-afternoon though, William.'

William sniggered slightly 'Oh please feel free to disturb me whenever you feel like it! Yes, it is strange for me to sleep at such an hour, I had been digging from the crack of dawn, and was in need of a small break; seems I overslept. I do have a few things to attend to, so I will be up and about in five minutes or so'.

'Glad to hear it' claimed the good Father who then walked off in his typical unassuming way.

After shutting the door, William felt his heartbeat return to something like normal, he breathed in deeply and grabbed his coat and gloves. He shook his head and looked around the room and smiled…

'Close one.'

CHAPTER 8

It was very rare that William let his face be seen before the end of any funeral, he was of the opinion that families and loved ones go through enough, and seeing a gravedigger waiting in the background could add a certain level of reality to it all.

If only they knew what *he* knew.

If only.

William looked at the extravagant headstone that had been put together for the late Lord Fenwick; it seemed it was met with satisfaction by his late wife. William had received a nod from Father Fanshaw earlier as the people had turned up, which meant that all was satisfactory. William was never 'proud' of his work. There was a huge sense of pride and discipline in trying to make the deceased's new home look respectable, but William still thought it sad that he had been dealt such a grim hand in life.

He looked in awe at the lords and ladies in attendance at the most recent addition to William's little community.

What beautiful garments they wore, how their skin seemed more polished than most, how their teeth seemed whiter, how their eyes seemed to shine more brightly than other humans in the area.

Maybe it was the money, maybe the feeling of self-importance?

Still, whatever their reasons for looking so good, William knew the inevitable; they would all die just the same as anyone.

At night, when it was dark and William was in the safety of his room, away from the voices, he often wondered what it would be like to lead a normal life.

A normal life.

What was that anyway? William thought.

Was normal being mean to people? Was normal rushing around trying to get more than the next man? Was normal cheating on the woman you have taken a vow to be true to? Beating her when she expresses a view different from your own?

That kind of 'normal', William had come to learn, was sadly all-too-evident in the community of Barnes.

Men full of greed, anger, and lust. If this was normal, William felt some sense of relief that he fell into the category of abnormal, for if normal was so ugly and wicked, he was happy to be the freak.

As his eyes scanned the attendees of the service, there was one who looked different from the others.

William was hidden behind Mr Higgingsly's headstone; his head peered out further as he looked at her, and she seemed genuinely upset.

'*How peculiar!*' thought William.

'Oh you *do* get weirder every day William!' remarked Mr Higgingsly.

'Shush! Keep it down will you sir, I'm trying to be nosey,' whispered William.

Mr Higgingsly seemed rather bothered. 'Well I would say you are succeeding sir. But may I remind you of the fact that this here space, this little bit of wretched land you shuffle on, belongs to, and is occupied by ME! Would you walk through someone's living room? Would you do that? No I didn't think so sir, it's just the same you know, here I am laid in my eternal sleep and I have your bloody big feet shuffling above me, really William, you should know better, in fact…'

'Oh really Mr Higgingsly will you shut it! Lord, have mercy! If you never complained I swear you would be silent! Now hush!'

William moved his feet from the area of Mr Higgingsly, and moved to another headstone. It was that of Peggy Robertson. Old Peggy, as she was known, was lovely, but she didn't talk that much. She had only died a few months back; she was the late wife of a local police constable, Mr Robertson.

'I hope you don't mind, Peggy,' asked William as he stood crouched behind her headstone 'It's just I'm quite intrigued.'

'Smitten more like,' remarked Old Peggy

'Mrs Robertson! I am merely watching the proceedings, making sure my work is well received,'

'Hmm, indeed' chuckled Old Peggy as William gazed at the woman who was crying over the late Lord Fenwick's coffin.

He noticed the gentleness of her eyes as the tears rolled down her face like rain on a window. He noticed her hair which danced with the wind, as black as her dress. He noticed her soft hands which fidgeted whilst trying to be still, he noticed her grief, her sadness.

He noticed her.

He could see she looked true, kind and lovely.

As he stood gazing, he almost felt sad that he could not comfort her. 'Poor soul,' he thought and then he wondered how nice it must be to have one so lovely grieve for you, but also how sad it must be to lose the same.

'William!' a voice in the background shouted.

'William! William!'

It was Mr Higgingsly…

'Oh for the last time sir, what?' William snapped.

'Did I ever tell you about *my* funeral?'

William put his hand on his own forehead 'No sir,' William sighed, 'go on…tell me…'

CHAPTER 9

April 30th, 1892, Barnes Cemetery, Barnes, London

She closed her eyes and listened to Father Fanshaw's words, she could feel the unusual warm wind around her hair and face, she could smell the lovely flowers by her late husband's side, and she could feel her own tears running down her face like paint on a wall.

The good Reverend spoke softly in his delivery of the prayer…

'We give them back to Thee, dear Lord, who gavest them to us.

Yet as Thou dost not lose them in giving,

So we have not lost them by their return.

Not as the world giveth, givest Thou,

O Lover of Souls,

What Thou gavest, Thou takest not away,

For what is thine is ours always if we are Thine.

And Life is eternal and Love is immortal,

And death is only a horizon,

And a horizon is nothing save the limit of our sight.'

Though the words of Father Fanshaw were kind and gentle, they did not bring Lady Anne comfort.

'O Lover of souls?' she thought 'How could there be such a person when her dear friend had been taken.

She felt conflicted, guilty even. The guilt was because she felt that she had lost a friend. A *good* friend.

But why was it she didn't feel like she had lost her husband? It was driving her crazy, and she felt so bad because of this. She knew it was a fact between her and Lord Fenwick that they were in fact 'friends.' But nobody else knew that.

Still, she did love him after a fashion. So were her feelings wrong? Was she cruel and mean that she didn't love him in a different way? Was she bound by social pressure and want for a better standing just like so many of the people who latched on to her late love like leeches for the sake of appearances?

She wasn't sure of anything anymore. Who was she? What should she do now?

She needed time to think things over; time to study herself, time to find herself, time to make things right.

She felt the world had her in a grip from which there was no escape.

How could she face people? How could she look them in the eye?

Did she even know the word *love*? Had she ever really felt it? Could the love between two friends be the same as two who loved each other as a real man and wife?

The fact was she had always been a lonely soul, she yearned for real love and though her marriage was based on some sort of love, her heart hungered for the feeling which was yet unknown to her, and so she felt she was sinning from within as her very soul searched for what would never be hers.

As she stood in her torment she opened her eyes and looked around. She could see Patrick near her giving the fake impression of a caring brother in grief, when in actual fact he was something far from such.

She looked at a few of the late Lord's 'friends', whom she saw right through; men such as the local Judge who thought he was royalty of some kind; men such as the landlords who preyed upon the poor for rents which were as high as their opinions of themselves.

There were a few good ones though, those such as Constable Robertson who could never be bribed, and of course the man in front of her, Father Fanshaw, as honest a man as one could find.

As her eyes wandered the graveyard, she saw someone in the distance, about 25 or 30 yards away.

'What on earth is he doing?' She thought to herself.

She tried to stay focused on the proceedings but then she saw him again, a man, crouched behind a headstone in the distance.

He seemed to be talking, but to whom?

She thought it odd indeed but then reminded herself why she was here.

But then she looked again.

Who on earth was he talking to?

Lady Anne thought that maybe the odd man had a dog nearby, or maybe a small child with him.

She continued to look discreetly as Patrick watched her in suspicion at her wandering eyes.

She saw the man stand and point at the grave which he stood over, he was pointing at it, arguing with it, it seemed.

'What an odd man indeed' she thought. 'Cruel in fact, for who lays harsh words to the dead?'

What sort of person does such a thing?

The actions of the odd man tempted Lady Anne to have words with him.

Should she? On such a day! It angered her that the man would be disrespectful to whoever lay at rest.

But perhaps the man was stricken with grief? What then?

Who was she to say how a person should handle personal grief and loss, for she knew the pain the man could have been in more than most.

Whatever the reasons for this strange behaviour, she felt bound to find out once the proceedings were done with.

She noticed he looked poor, by his old, tatty, long, black coat; it had holes in it which were even obvious from the distance she stood at. She noticed his old boots lacked polish and she noticed his long scraggy hair which was as black as hers. She also noticed he looked sad.

She had noticed him indeed…

CHAPTER 10

William tried to listen to Mr Higgingsly's tale, as he now talked of his past love, but was in fact trying to hurry him along, for he wanted to turn his attention back to the proceedings which he had been watching.

Or was it he wanted to turn his attentions back to her? His mind was spinning with questions about her; who was she? Where did she come from? For he had never seen her before, after all, Barnes was a small town.

'Well Sir, she really did, does sound like a very special lady, that much is clear, but if you would be so kind as to excuse me, I have to pay attention to the late Lord's funeral as I must know everything is satisfactory, you see and you of all people know about my attention to detail'

Mr Higgingsly's voice seemed had a hint of presumptuousness about it, 'That's fine *William*, proceed, if you *must*, but I would say someone else needs your ...*attention.*'

Growing tired of Mr Higgingsly's brashness, William stood sternly looking down at Mr Higgingsly's grave 'Oh really sir, you can become quite the bore!'

As William turned away, he jumped slightly for he didn't know anybody had been standing there.

She jumped too.

'Oh, oh, ma'am, I apologise, for I did not know you were there, forgive me if I startled you,' William said nervously as he bowed his head in greeting.

Lady Anne smiled ever-so-slightly. 'Really sir, there is no apology needed, for it is *I* who startled you I think. So please sir, forgive *my* intrusion'

'Intrusion?' William asked 'Er, no ma'am, I … er, I was just tidying up the graves you see,' William said as he moved some mud with his boot on Mr Higgingsly's grave.

Her smile became wider, as did William's eyes. He tried to hide the fact he had just been talking to the grave which they both now stood near.

'It seems tidy already sir. A loved one of yours I take it?'

'Er, no ma'am. Oh, it's just I put him there'

'What?!' snapped Lady Anne in horror.

'Oh no, not like that ma'am. Like, I laid him there, er, no, what's the word I struggle to find? I mean, I dig them you see, the graves ma'am. I dig them.'

'So you're the gravedigger?'

'Yes ma'am, yes indeed. I do the digging, the arranging you know'

Standing there awkwardly, William felt flustered, not knowing what to say, she was even more beautiful up close.

'Well done, William,' laughed Mr Higgingsly, 'you really are quite the romantic, ha-ha!'

William bit his own lip and kicked some mud over Mr Higgingsly's grave 'Shush!' he whispered as Lady Anne's eyes wandered around.

She looked back to William 'I beg your pardon?'

'Oh nothing, ma'am, I sometimes talk to myself you see'

She looked confused and tilted her head slightly as she spoke 'Is *that* what you were doing earlier? At first I thought, well, it looked to me like you were talking to someone, or even, preposterous as it may sound, talking to this here grave.'

'Oh ma'am no, no. I am afraid it is just my silly ways, forgive me if I caused any offence, none was meant in any way'

'None taken sir, and please, calling me 'ma'am' is like putting a whale in a pond, it doesn't fit. My name is Lady Anne, but I prefer Anne, just don't tell anybody,' she said, smiling.

She didn't know what it was, but the man before her seemed strange and different; happy but sad, confident but afraid, intelligent and uneducated at the same time, *how could this be?*

She noticed his dark eyes, his broad shoulders, huge hands; he looked scared of her, how could this huge, over 6ft man be scared of her?

Standing there awkwardly, Lady Anne felt flustered, not knowing what to say, for he was even more interesting up close.

'So Anne, I have never seen you around here, do you live in Barnes?'

'I do sir, the manor. I am here today because of my husband's passing I am afraid to say'

'Oh forgive me, Anne; I am sorry for your loss'.

'Thank you' Anne said softly as she looked him up and down, all too aware of the fact he felt as uncomfortable as she did.

'Well I must get back, sir. It was a pleasure meeting you' Anne nearly turned to walk away as William spoke.

She stopped and looked at him; he smiled, ever-so-slightly…

'William, my name's William, Anne, Calling me sir is like putting a whale in a pond, it doesn't fit.' He smiled.

'William,' she said as she nodded.

She smiled and turned away and walked back to the crowd of people with whom she had come.

Now they had met.

Who was to know what would happen?

Like the tree that falls in the wind, like the water that overfills the rivers, like the crops that dry in the sun, some things in life are just out of our control, and sometimes, just sometimes, we are helpless to our fate. It is like an unknown force pulls us in a direction we know we shouldn't go, yet our feet do not cease, and when we get there, no matter how wrong people say we are, we know we are home.

CHAPTER 11

As Lady Anne got back to the crowd of mourners she felt Patrick's disdain as his eyes looked her up and down, then seemed to search her eyes for any wrong doing so he could attach himself to it.

'Enjoy your chat?' He remarked.

She gave him the very same look back with her reply. 'I did as a matter of fact Patrick. I was complimenting the man on the arrangements, you see *he* did all this, and I think you would agree what a grand job the man has made of it? So yes, I offered gratitude Patrick; one hasn't forgotten manners has one? Or do I need to suggest you do the same?'

Patrick smiled; he loved the forced politeness to their conversations, but loved even more the undertone.

They were in a silent war, a war yet to see first blood.

'On the contrary, I was indeed going to make that my next port of call *Lady* Anne.'

'Well I am sure you will be as charming as only you *can* be.' Lady Anne smiled.

Patrick made his way to the other side of the graveyard. He spotted William, who was in the middle of re-arranging some flowers.

William noticed a pair of boots on the ground; his eyes travelled upwards and saw a man standing before him.

He was dressed in the finest of suits and had a screwed-up little plump face, which didn't look pleasing to the eye at all.

Mr Higgingsly commented straight away 'Oh my William, who is this spineless little ogre?'

William looked down to the grave with contempt.

'I was just saying,' added Mr Higgingsly.

'Good day to you, sir.' William smiled and offered his hand to Patrick.

Patrick looked at William's hand; it was covered with mud.

'Er, I don't think so, boy,' muttered Patrick whose look of disgust was all too apparent.

'Oh it's alright.' William smiled 'I am always covered in mud sir, it's alright, I forgive you.'

'I didn't ask for your forgiveness, boy.'

William moved his hand back by his side and looked to the ground. 'Sorry if I have offended you, sir.'

'Sorry? Your very presence offends me, boy. But what offends me more is the like of some graveyard swine making advances to a recently widowed lady of my family, I mean, how dare you, how dare you?'

'Sir, we were just talking…'

Patrick moved closer to William as he interrupted 'Talking? About what, I ask? What could the likes of *you* possibly talk to her about? What thoroughly engaging conversation could a peasant such as you dare to offer?'

William was stunned. 'But I ...'

'Speak up, halfwit!' shouted Patrick.

'I...I offered Anne my deepest regrets sir...for her loss, for you I offer the same sir, I mean no offence'

In a quick instant Patrick slapped both sides of William's face, left then right. 'YOU! How dare you? It's *Lady* to you, boy, *Lady Anne*!'

'Don't, please don't,' warned William with a look of impending danger.

'William! Don't you take that from the fiend!' shouted Mr Higgingsly.

William ignored the voice of his friend.

Patrick laughed 'Don't? Don't what? Do you know who I am? Don't answer, let me tell you, boy. I... Patrick Fenwick, was, am, the younger brother of the late Lord Fenwick, and I currently practise as a solicitor in these parts as well as other parts of London. I have friends, you might say. Offend me if you dare, offend me at your peril. *Offend me*, and I would have you hanged from the highest, tightest noose in England, you mud-soaked vermin! Now if I so much as see you LOOK at Lady Fenwick in a way that displeases me, you will see the full extent of my wrath. Do you understand? Boy?'

'Oh William, if I had bones this man would feel a kick, right to the shins!' added Mr Higgingsly.

Patrick then kicked the flowers that William had just arranged and smiled.

'I understand sir, forgive me' replied William who dared not look Patrick in the face.

'No I will not, now get your sorry-self back to your mud, peasant pig'

'Yes sir,' replied William who turned and looked away.

William felt himself in a grip of fear; he couldn't understand how he could have offended the man so much.

Mr Higgingsly was not impressed 'Well, I must say William, if that had been me, if….Oooo! I am seething William! Seething, I tell you. Pistols at dawn I'd say, pistols indeed!'

'He gone?' asked William, who dared not look round to see.

'Yes, gone he has, but seriously William! Run back over there! Sort him out!'

William stood to his feet and walked away with his head down.

Perhaps the rude man was right; perhaps he was out of turn, speaking to a widow.

But they were just talking, weren't they?

Anyways what could the likes of William offer the likes of a Lady?

William walked to the back of the graveyard to calm down, for the mean man, Patrick Fenwick, had certainly scared him.

William could still hear Mr Higgingsly screaming to him as he walked away…

'Pistols at dawn, William! Pistols at dawn!'

CHAPTER 12

William felt down, he sat for a while beyond the east wall of the cemetery where there were a bunch of unmarked graves. William always felt bad for the people who were buried there and figured they can't have paid the fee required to have a nice message written on the stone. There were a few stones with unfinished writing on them, one with 'To the beloved…', one with 'To my darling…', and then there was another, which William didn't understand.

'Is it a foreign language of some sort?' thought William as he read the words on the head stone again for the hundredth time.

Mortuus est Momentaneum.

William loved how it sounded, it even made him smile. It was strange how the quietest part of the graveyard always made him feel better! So much better he decided to go for a stroll!

As he strode around the graveyard, he heard Old Peggy calling him, 'William, William!'

Sighing, William walked over 'Hello Peggy, you alright there?'

'Isn't me I'm worried about William. Look, I know you are sad William, I know you can't handle conflict very well, I can see it in you, but I can also see you have a good heart, you *are not* your father, remember that. You are a good man.'

Looking up to the evening sky William breathed in deeply, trying not to cry. 'Thank you, Peggy'

'Don't you worry, lad. You know you really shouldn't be around us dead folk. You should be out there, with the living.'

'I know, but it's my home, Peggy'

'Oh dear, no talking to you is there, William? I tell you what; I have a job for you.'

'What, Peggy?'

'Something you forgot' asked Peggy.

He looked bemused 'Forgot? Why, I don't think so Peggy, I have cleared the leaves, watered flowers…er…'

'Oh dear William, I will re-word that, is there some… *one*, you have forgotten? Because let me tell you from experience, he will be feeling quite confused right now!'

Williams's eyes lit up 'Oh dear! Lord Fenwick! How could I forget?'

William ran across the graveyard to Lord Fenwick's grave as Peggy chuckled.

As he approached the grave, William could hear whistling, it was coming from the grave.

William stood by the headstone and then knelt down before the fresh flowers which were a mix of wreaths and bunches in all different colours.

William coughed to make his presence known.

'Hello Lord Fenwick sir, are you alright? My name is William.'

Lord Fenwick was as confused as Peggy said he would be. 'Oh, talking to me are you? Where are you?'

'I am just here, stood above your grave, sir.'

'My what? So I am dead? Oh my!'

'I am sorry to break it to you Sir, but yes, in a way you are, in living terms at least.'

'Living terms? I just thought I was dreaming or locked in the dark somewhere but … oh, yes … now I remember, oh yes. Oh dear. So what am I? A ghost? How positively fabulous! Can I haunt people? Knock things over? Oh my! Hang on, why can't I see you? Is this it? Oh no!'

Interrupting Lord Fenwick in his panic, William attempted to calm him down and give him the run down on what seemed to be the way of things.

'Please sir, please, calm down. The way of things seems to be that you can see, not far, just around the area of … well, the graveyard, but beyond the graveyard seems out of reach for the residents here. It's better than nothing, sir, I suppose; you have me to talk to every day at least, and the others.'

Lord Fenwick stayed quiet for a few seconds, as did William.

'Yes, yes. It is better than nothing. So how long does this last, dear William?'

'I don't know. Some of you go, wherever you go. Some of you stay here for years, forever, who knows? All I do know is I've heard the voices since I was a boy and some of you have been talking to me for over twenty years'

'Oh my word, William. So how was my funeral? I can't remember it.'

'It was extremely well attended, sir and people mourned for you and wept. You really did have people who loved you, sir. Not one bad word said. Your arrangements, as you should be able to see, are quite luxurious to say the least, no expense spared, sir.'

'Oh dear ... and Lady Anne? Did you meet her - my late wife?'

'I did, sir - a very charming lady indeed; one who loved you dearly I would say, sir'

'Ah. I can see you like her.'

'But sir we just talked ... I swear, I never ...'

'My goodness William, it seems I can read you. Oh, how interesting…'

'Lord Fenwick please! That really is quite rude, sir'

Just as Lord Fenwick laughed at his new found ability, another voice came into the conversation.

'Er, excuse me sir, yes you!' Shouted Mr Higgingsly

'Who's there?' asked Lord Fenwick.

'It is I, Mr Higgingsly as I am known, a resident here for many years and a well-respected resident too I might add'

'Oh how do you do, sir?'

'Yes, yes very well thank you, for a dead man. Look enough of the pleasantries, you don't peek without asking; it is ... well… rude sir'

'Peek?'

'Yes peek! That's what we call it. Now that you're dead, you have a few gifts, more of which we may explain to you at a later date. The one which comes quickest is the gift of peeking, into people. If they come close enough we can see into them, see their thoughts'

'I know it's positively brilliant I must say Mr ...er ...'

'Higgingsly! And as I said, it's frowned upon to do so without permission or due cause, so Lord or no Lord, I think you owe William here an apology'

William smiled. 'Really, it's alright Lord Fenwick you're new and …'

'It's not alright William; rules are rules.' interrupted Mr Higgingsly.

'Oh I do apologise, and to you sir or any I have offended. It is just a lot to take in; it is the day of my funeral though so I think I could be forgiven….'

'Indeed, indeed sir.' answered Mr Higgingsly.

'So how do I …see? How do I look around here? Am I a ghost? Can people see me in some weird misty form, because I see nothing at the moment?'

William looked at Mr Higgingsly's grave, then back at Lord Fenwick's 'Thank you sir, I will take it from here. Right then Lord Fenwick, you have to trust me, and you have to concentrate, can you do that for me?'

'Yes, William. Does it hurt?'

William smiled 'That's one thing you never have to worry about ever again, dear sir; trust me. It doesn't hurt, just listen to my words as I speak, then follow me as I walk with your mind, your ears, your eyes, your heart, your whole being…'

'Oh, but William I'm dead, I don't have eyes or ears or a heart for that matter!'

'So how do you hear me now, sir? How do you talk? You have no tongue'

'Ooh, it seems I don't…'

'So trust me, sir, because you don't need eyes to see, ears to hear, or a heart to love - all this I *know*'

'Right, I trust you. Now what William?'

'I want you to pretend Lord Fenwick … pretend you have eyes, think, deeply picture it, your own face, your eyes…you got it?'

'Yes, yes sir I think I do! Now what?'

'Listen to me, imagine following my voice like you are blind in the night. I walk left, you walk left as I speak; I walk right, you walk right as I speak. Let the words guide you, follow them … now, can you remember the smell of roast beef?'

'What? Well, yes I can …'

'Remember it, follow the smell. I have some here you see, can you smell it?'

'YES! Yes I can, William!'

'Now sir, open your eyes! NOW!'

'Oh my! Oh my William! I can see! Ooh, look at my flowers! Hello, everyone! Pleased to meet you! Actually, I like this, how exciting!'

'You are probably the first person I have ever met who thinks so, Lord Fenwick, but I am glad it worked, it sometimes takes days, weeks even! Please forgive if all don't reply to your greetings, you see some people choose to talk at different times of the day.'

'Oh, no problem, William … oh, and I have to ask, where is the roast beef?'

'Ha-ha, you all ask that at first. I have none sir, it is a way of getting your mind working again. It seems we don't forget smells that easily, so I use it as a way of luring you in, with the ladies I use flowers, with men, either whisky or roast beef! Now obviously you couldn't *really* smell the roast beef, but somehow your mind was tricked into thinking you could, now you know it was a trick I am afraid to say you will rarely be able to smell again.'

'Well sir! You are indeed a great man to know! Thank you! I will still try to smell though sir, if I have done it once, I can do it again I'd say'

Mr Higgingsly couldn't help himself. 'Yes, yes, how exciting, welcome to Deadville!'

William couldn't help but giggle at Mr Higgingsly 'Sir! Must you?'

CHAPTER 13

It was a particularly quiet night; William lay in bed. It had been an eventful day, for making conversation with people with a pulse was a rather challenging task.

As he closed his eyes, William thought of her. He pictured her beautiful face and he smiled the faintest of smiles. He looked around his room, he almost felt like he was doing something wrong and started to battle with his own thoughts, thoughts which were reminding William who he was, what he did for a living, but more importantly who she was ... she would never be seen with the likes of him!

But surely, dreams cannot be forbidden? We all have dreams after all. Closing his eyes and defying his own tormenting brain, William concentrated on the lovely first meeting between himself and Lady Anne.

But these are only thoughts, surely I am doing no wrong, surely I can think what I like? I mean no harm!

He loved the way she smiled as if she didn't want to. He loved her bright eyes and he loved her kind ways, yet also loved the obvious class with which she carried herself.

'What lovely thoughts to fall to sleep to,' thought William as he turned to his side, hoping to dream some lovely dream for a change.

Perhaps he would dream of Lady Anne tonight? He really hoped so.

Picturing her in his mind, her hair waving in the wind, her kind smile trying not to smile, her eyes bright and full of life, made

William feel so relaxed, and then just as he almost drifted off to a place where things were lovely, he heard a sound.

What the…?

Something wasn't right…

Something, or someone, was making a noise outside.

William held his breath for a few seconds; his ears were alert, and searching for the source of the mysterious noise.

It was coming from outside, leaves were rustling, footsteps were shuffling, something seemed to be moving, or then again, was it *someone*?

William looked at the old silver pocket watch which he always placed inside his work boots before bed; it read 1.35 am.

Who could be outside at such a time?

Knowing that nobody ever visited the graveyard at such an hour, William had only one thought as to who could be outside … grave robbers!

Trying to be as quiet as he could, William put on his black trousers and old work boots. He knew he had to be careful, for grave robbers were a dangerous bunch, famed for their brutal attacks when challenged. It was rare they ever were challenged though, as they mostly worked at night, preying on the helpless dead and scavenging whatever they could get their hands on.

Father Fanshaw had even told William once that an old friend at a church in Yorkshire was stabbed trying to fend off grave robbers; they were dangerous, wretched thieves of the lowest order.

Tying his long hair back, William looked around his room for something he could use as a weapon. He couldn't seem to find anything suitable, but then, in the corner of his eye, he spotted something.

There was a letter opener, it was like a miniature knife and very sharp. Picking it up and waving it side to side, William readied himself for the fiends.

Maybe in the dark they would think it was a blade? Maybe, just maybe, it would scare them off, never to return.

As William made his way outside he turned the door handle ever so slightly, the door knob was prone to making the occasional squeak sometimes.

'Please don't squeak, door. Please don't squeak,' thought William as he turned it fully and edged the door open a touch.

The doorknob seemed to have listened to William's pleas, as did the door itself as William opened it silently.

He put one foot outside, looking across the thick grey mist, which seemed to cover the graveyard and headstones in some sort of eerie blanket. The night was as still and calm as the corpses that lay beneath the mud. William looked up past the mist and could see the moon shining through it for a brief moment.

He gathered his courage and took soft steps forward towards the direction of the strange noises, noises that were getting louder as William approached.

William then heard a familiar voice. It was rare for the souls to speak late at night, even for the regular talkers, it was normal for them to rest at night, just as living folk did.

But this night wasn't normal, and an *abnormal* act was taking place, an act which would disturb even the most villainous sinner.

The familiar voice whispered to William, 'William, help.' William couldn't reply, but he knew the voice, it was Old Peggy, and the fiends were scavenging around her place of rest.

Old Peggy sensed Williams's presence though, and she knew what was coming.

William laid eyes on the perpetrators for the first time as he made his way through the graveyard's late night mist. He thought that they were even lower than the lowest of men; they were the foul shadows of men; the dark, desperate kind whose morals and codes were lower than that of the vermin which scoured the filthy sewers. They were worse than rats.

They didn't see William coming. There were three men, if you could call them such and all were removing dirt with their hands and trying to get into Old Peggy's coffin.

Trying to be as quiet as possible, William snuck up from behind; Old Peggy had been right in her thoughts…

They didn't see William coming…

CHAPTER 14

'Stop right there you awful beings, stop right there, I am armed and I have alerted the neighbours who are running for the Policemen!'

William stood in the cold dead night. He thought that maybe he should have just attacked them, that maybe they may have seen through his bluff by the fright on his face and the goose-bumps on his naked arms.

He was scared and confused as to what to do but he knew one thing for sure, he wasn't about to let the thieves run away with any of Old Peggy's things.

All of the men shot to their feet, they gazed upon William from foot to head, as if sizing him up like boxers before the bell. William towered above all three of the men with his huge muscular frame, and to most people, William was an intimidating figure with such a size and cold dark looks.

But these men were not the sort to be deterred; these kinds of men loved trouble, loved a good fight, and even loved a good murder, especially when the odds were in their favour.

One of the men started to laugh in a whispery fashion like a witch, he bared his teeth as he spoke and William felt revolted at the blackness of the rotting, crooked fangs. The man was tall and thin, but looked like the leader of the group as he spoke with authority.

'You better back off. There are three of us, and we could kill you easy, easy says I!'

The vile man's two accomplices each brought out weapons and spread out in a circular fashion in an attempt to surround William. The man to William's left was a scraggy little man dressed in attire so full of holes he must have been a beggar by day, and he pulled out a small silver pocket knife. Then, almost at the same time, the man to William's right, who was quite chubby for a thief, it had to be said, threw his striped flat cap on the ground and pulled out a barber's razor, which seemed to shine brightly, even in the dead of the night.

Not responding to the man, William swung the sharp knife-like letter opener side to side as a warning 'I am warning you, the police will be on their way!'

The razor-wielding man looked at his leader who was stood in the middle of the three 'Perhaps we should leg it, boss? He says the police are coming, they'll bloody hang us if they catch us this time; hang us, they will!'

'Shut it, you!' barked the leader as he turned his attention back to William. The man smiled with his awful teeth as he spoke slowly through his evil-looking mouth. He too pulled out a razor with one hand as he threw an old sack to the ground. It looked full; William presumed full of things he had scavenged from the graves.

'The Police you say? Hmm, well if indeed there is police on the way, then surely, you would have taken the time to realise that the only policeman who could possibly turn up at this time of night, in this part of town, would be the old bobby Mr Robertson? And knowing for a fact that man lives at least twenty minutes from here, well, I would say, sir, that we have just enough time to kill you, then get away with the things we have already acquired on this fine night'.

Stepping back just a few paces, William's eyes went from the chubby man to the scraggy man then back to the middle where the leader slowly crept forward.

He could feel his own heart beating, and the cold night mist wrapping itself round his exposed chest, for he was only dressed in trousers and boots.

He could see they were edging closer, so William tried one last time to make the men see reason 'I have no wish to fight you men, please, just drop the things you steal from the dead. It is the worst of sins … the things you take were given in sorrow, from the heart and soul. Neither you nor I should even dare touch, never mind take them. They are the possessions of the passed souls. Please, leave them here for me to re-bury; it is wrong the thing you do, wrong I say, as wrong as can be!'

As he finished his sentence, William heard Old Peggy. 'Oh William, it is of no matter now; please, do not lose your life for such things, for your life is more precious than such.'

William looked at Old Peggy's grave. 'Be quiet, my dear. I will not let them take what is yours'

The three men paused for a second; the little scraggy man looked to the chubby one. It's him…'

The chubby man paused too. 'What? Who? Who is it?'

The scraggy man talked louder, '*The dead talker,*' he then pointed to the headstone, which bore Peggy's name. 'Look.'

The leader of the men laughed and shook his head 'So you're the *one,* eh? The one they call the dead talker?' He looked at the faces of his sidekicks sternly. 'It's rubbish, old wives' tales I tell thee, he isn't no dead talker, but in a minute he might be, because he'll be dead himself!'

Old Peggy couldn't help herself. 'Oh dear William, maybe this was a bad idea!'

But William still stood, adamant in his belief.

'Go on then,' barked the leader at his two accomplices, as they closed their circle of danger around William.

Poor William had nowhere to go. Sure, he could have run … but William just would not let them take what they were trying to. It just wasn't right, and if it meant his life, then that's what it meant.

'This is your last chance,' William whispered. 'Please, drop the things and leave.'

All the men giggled like schoolboys at William's bold statement, finding it both amusing and absurd, given William's predicament.

But they did not know William; they did not know William at all…

The chubby man was the first to make the mistake; he swung his razor at William, who leapt back quickly like a cat from a tree and swiped the razor from the chubby thief's hand. The man's eyes filled with impending doom as William lifted him off the ground with one hand around his throat.

The chubby man could feel his neck being crushed in William's grip, which was like a python crushing its prey. He gasped for some sort of breath as he wiggled his legs in mid-air, pleading with his eyes for forgiveness from William.

Sensing the man's imminent submission, William showed mercy to the fat thief and lessened his grip whilst lowering him to the ground. As he did so, he felt a sharp pain in his back, then more pain in his shoulder.

Turning quickly, William pushed the little scraggy man who hit Peggy's headstone and fell to the earth, William noticed the little scraggy man quivering as he lay in fear, then he noticed man's knife wasn't there; but where was the leader?

The question was soon answered as the leader of the thieves appeared before him; he slashed William once across the chest, twice, then a third time, William winced as the razor cut deep into his bare flesh. Then to make matters worse, William fell backwards and hit his head on a headstone.

William felt dizzy and his head hurt as he lay there, vulnerable to the wishes of the evil men, he saw them walking towards him but he couldn't move, all sound seemed muffled apart from one thing - Old Peggy's voice.

'Shush, it'll be all right dear boy, it'll be all right, dear William. Close your eyes, close your eyes.'

He couldn't help it; it was like his eyes had made up their own mind; he could faintly see the men almost upon him when his eyes closed…

CHAPTER 15

When he closed his eyes it had been dark, and when he opened them, it was darker.

Dazed, confused, frightened and frail, William rose to his feet, but his wounds no longer hurt.

Everything was black around him, like the lights had gone out in the world and the blackness had taken over everything. There was no path to follow but his feet were grounded nevertheless, which meant he could walk. There was no sky, not in front nor behind, he couldn't see his own body but he could feel it. William used his hands to feel his wounds but they were no longer there.

There was no blood as his fingers felt dry and his old wounds bore no pain.

Where was he?

Was he alive, was he dead? How was he to know? All William could feel was his own heart beating and his own breath panting in panic.

'Hello?' he shouted, unsure of whether or not he wanted an answer. 'Hello?' he tried again, but to no avail.

Wherever he was, he was alone it seemed, with not even an echo from his own voice to keep him company.

Should he wait, perhaps to wake up if it indeed it was a dream, or should he move?

William went with the latter, he couldn't just wait, wherever he was or wasn't, he needed to move. He figured being alone in the dark staying still was a bleak prospect, at least if he ventured forth he would keep busy, perhaps find some light.

He walked forward slowly, and he noticed there was no sound. No whistling wind, no patter of rain and no echoes of his footsteps as he slowly moved into the unknown blackness.

He walked and walked and walked, he felt so alone and the further he walked the more alone he felt. There was a strange feeling rising within him, it was a feeling of dread.

But where did the dread come from, what was waiting ahead? Was there some awful climax in waiting? Some terrible taste of something so bad his very soul felt it was trying to warn him?

Whatever was coming, William knew it was bad.

He kept walking, there was no choice, it was as if, as he walked, everything behind him disappeared; he had to move forward, forward, forward.

One step after another he strode, into the darkest darkness. The mystical, moody, black cloak of fear seemed to be wrapped around his very being.

Then, there was light - very faint at first. William walked faster in hope of it getting lighter still. It seemed to work at first because William could make out his own old boots, his legs, and then he held out his arms and wiggled his fingers as he started to make out his own body.

Finally, some light!

But that was as light as it would get. At least he could see something now though and just as he began to wonder where he was, he recognised a door.

The door was but ten paces from his feet, 'I know this,' William thought.

And know it he should, for it was the door of his quarters at the church. He walked into the room. It was as it should be mostly, and the spades were near the front door, his long black coat hung from the handle of his sweeping brush, which was in its usual home when William slept.

But what was different?

As he ventured further in he heard voices, a number of voices, they came from within his quarters! Who was there?

He peeked around the corner from the entrance; people were gathered around his bed!

What on earth were they doing? These were his private quarters, what a cheek!

Noticing Father Fanshaw first was easy as he always wore a long white bed gown at night with a little white sleeping hat that William had always found amusing, and then besides Father Fanshaw, was a man dressed in black.

It was the policeman! Mr Robertson!

As William got to them he began to speak, 'Oh, thank the Lord. I have had the strangest of nights I tell you, did the robbers flee? Were they caught? I can give good description if needed and…'

Then it hit him, they couldn't hear him, there was another man sitting on the bed, in front of Mr Robertson and Father Fanshaw; he had a stethoscope and looked to be treating someone.

William walked around the bed, just to see if anyone could see him, he waved his hands in front of all of them. 'Hello, hello it's me! Can you not see me, can you not hear me?'

He listened to them talk but he couldn't hear them properly, their mouths moved slowly and their words sounded distorted like he was hearing them from another room.

What was going on?

Looking at Mr Robertson, Father Fanshaw and then the Doctor, William wondered why they all looked so concerned. The answer to his question came as William looked at the bed.

He looked from the bottom of the bed all the way up. 'This is my bed, my sheets…' then he realised the boots on the body were his too, as were the trousers, then as he looked up to the shirtless, bloodied body on the bed he saw that the face was his too.

He stood, frozen in time, was he dead?

Standing in his room with a sense of total bewilderment, another sound entered the mix, but this sound was clearer.

Clear as day.

William could hear a cry, crying, someone was in tears. Someone was absolutely beside themselves.

'Who could be so upset?' thought William.

Seeing someone upset always made William feel sad; he would always try and do whatever he could to make such a person feel better. He left Father Fanshaw, Mr Robertson and Doctor and his own battered body on the bed.

The crying came from the corner of the room, it was a child's cry, William crouched, and he could see a small child huddled in the corner of the room, just next to his father's old wooden chair.

The boy cried as if his heart were broken, sobbing tears which sounded inconsolable.

'Child, do not fear,' William whispered as he reached out his hands, 'Please child, come, I mean you no harm, let me help you.'

Still the child did not move.

On his knees now, William shuffled forward to the child slowly. He could see it was a little boy by the old flat-cap and knee length shorts he wore. His naked knees were cut and bruised.

As William got right next to the boy, he noticed the hands which the boy held over his face were bruised and cut.

'Oh dear my boy, have you had an accident? Please, let me help you.'

William gently moved the boy's hands with his own and leaned closer; he couldn't see the boy's face as he seemed to be hiding in pure fear, shaking like a leaf.

'There-there boy, I can help you. I mean you no harm. It will be alright, my name is William'

The boy looked up slowly; the corner of the room was quite dark but William could make out that he had grey and purple bruised eyes, with dried blood smeared all over his face, it was evident he had been beaten badly. William looked at the boy's face and was horrified that someone could do this to a child, to anyone. Then as the boy lifted his face up fully, William jumped back, out of the way.

'What? No, God no!' screamed William.

It was the first time in a long time that William had felt like this, the feeling gripping him had been a feeling which had been absent in his life for what seemed like an eternity.

William realised the little boy was him, the little boy his father had beaten *over and over*, the terrified child who was bound to the darkness.

The dreaded feeling from the past had returned, and it was fear…

Pure fear.

CHAPTER 16

Standing over the bed with his hand resting on Father Fanshaw's shoulder in an attempt to comfort him, Mr Robertson asked the question that Father Fanshaw dare not ask.

'Is he going to make it Doctor?'

Pulling the sheets up to the middle of Williams's chest the Doctor rose to his feet and rolled his sleeves back down. He walked off a few feet to a bowl of water and washed William's blood off his hands, dried them, and took off his glasses for a moment as he wiped his brow.

'It's hard to say, sir. *Should* he make it? No. William has sustained significant trauma by way of a knife wound to his back, as well as numerous deep lacerations to his chest as you can see. If that wasn't enough, the poor chap has endured a sizeable blow to the head, probably by falling and hitting his head, as I do not feel a man could strike such a blow. I have stitched the wounds on his back and chest, as well as the deep gash on the back of his head. *Can* he make it? Absolutely, but I fear with the *damage* this man has taken, it is very unlikely indeed. And with each hour he sleeps, the likelihood of him waking decreases. He is in what we call a coma, a deep sleep if you will, and from here on I am of the opinion that his life now lies in God's hands, for mine can do no more for him.'

Marking the sign of the cross on his own chest, Father Fanshaw sighed in concern, he then wrapped a crucifix around William's left hand.

'God be with you, my boy.' Father Fanshaw then ushered Mr Robertson forward, as well as the Doctor. 'Kneel' Father Fanshaw whispered.

The doctor and the policeman did as Father Fanshaw asked, and knelt either side of him as he began his prayer for William.

'O God, the strength of the weak and the comfort of sufferers: Mercifully accept our prayers, and grant to your servant William the help of your power, that his sickness may be turned into health, and our sorrow into joy; through Jesus Christ our Lord. Amen.'

The three men rose to their feet. Mr Robertson stood firm, and tipped his hat slightly 'I will be going now Father, Doctor, keep me informed of William's condition, I will make my enquiries, see if I can find the dogs who did this. If he wakes, be sure to send word. Goodbye.'

The Doctor left not long after Mr Robertson, but Father Fanshaw would not leave William's bedside.

As the good Reverend watched over William, he noticed how much William was sweating and patted his head with a damp cloth.

'There, there, my son. Be calm, relax, let the illness leave your body; let the Lord heal you.'

William continued to moan and groan through the night. Father Fanshaw thought this must be a good sign, for it at least showed some life in the man. He tried not to fall asleep, his head kept nodding forward only for him to wake suddenly as it did over and over. He felt disgusted with himself for nearly falling asleep while he waited by William's side.

But Father Fanshaw was an old man, and not in years had he been up at such an hour, with such incident too, and as the minutes ticked away, his eyelids grew heavier, his head nodded forward, again and again, then the nod turned into a nap, the nap, to sleep.

CHAPTER 17

On his way out of the church Mr Robertson grabbed one of Williams shovels which was stood against a wall. He felt it of the upmost importance to tidy the grave of his late dear wife, he couldn't leave it disturbed and in ruin. Afterwards it was his plan to get to the police station and speak to his men about the grave robbers and William's attack. Walking at speed to try and warm himself from the night's cold, he suddenly caught a glimpse in his mind of a day he had been trying to bury deep within.

The day he lost Peggy, his wife of over 30 years.

'Dear Peggy,' he thought as he walked along, but then he stopped, he looked around the empty but misty graveyard and thought of the day he placed flowers at her grave and said farewell.

Casting his mind back to that day made him shiver; his bottom lip quivered, he looked around again, as if it would be a sign of weakness to go see her. He fought such thoughts and wondered what harm he would do just nipping over for a few minutes.

Once beside her grave, he crumbled. All the old emotion he had felt came swinging back at him like a hammer to the heart; his tears felt cold as they rushed down his face like icy rain. He fell to his knees.

'My love, my dearest love, how I miss you so' he cried as he shovelled some of the removed soil back into its place.

Though he didn't know it, Old Peggy was right there with him, and though he couldn't hear her either, she was talking right back to him too.

'Oh my darling husband, my beautiful man, don't cry my love.' She wished she could reach out a hand and touch him one last time; she wished she could throw her arms around him; she wished she could ease his pain.

She wished.

Mr Robertson thought back to happy times as he kept on tidying the area around Peggy's grave. He remembered the meals she had cooked when he returned home late at night after working long hours chasing crooks, and how perfectly she cooked the meat. He remembered how excited she was when he took her on her first carriage ride and how she teased him every time she beat him at 'Bridge', her favourite card game. The thought of her laughing and teasing made him smile a smile that was the truest smile he'd had for a very long time.

He smiled at Peggy's headstone, he was shaking. 'You know my love I still often recollect the midday strolls we shared on hot summer days. You remember?'

He paused for a second and cried.

Peggy felt so happy he had remembered those days. 'I remember my love, you were just starting out back then and used to sneak off to meet me for a walk and a picnic. Oh how I loved them so, I used to look forward to it'

'Oh, my dearest wife,' Mr Robertson continued 'I loved to meet you during the day, it broke the day up and made me realise what I had to look forward to when I got home.'

He looked around the graveyard and sighed. 'But now, the only time I can meet you is here, in this place, and it breaks my heart. The only gift I can bring you is flowers. You know you used to say *pray*, pray for this person, pray for that person. *Why* I ask my love? Why? Why pray for *anybody*? For what is the use in praying when the man I pray to took you from me? And if that is the case, I have to say my love that I do not want to know him.'

Poor Old Peggy felt much sorrow seeing her beloved husband being bound by such conflict within him. She concentrated, hard. She saw deep inside her husband's thoughts and heart and decided she had to try. She concentrated harder than ever, she got into his thoughts; she saw the deep chasm of sorrow he was carrying around every day.

She knew she had to intervene, she knew the only gift she now possessed on the other side had to be used.

She talked as she tried to heal his mind. He couldn't hear her, but felt in a state of slight unconsciousness as she did what she knew she must...

'Oh my love, please don't think like that, death happens, sad and tragic as it may be, but it does. We will be together again, my love. But for now you have more life to live, more things to do. It was just my time, that's all, but I will be waiting for you, and when that time comes I will feel your touch once again and we can walk on together in heaven as we did on those warm sunny days. Don't grieve for me any more my love; don't walk with such a heavy heart. Remember me with smiles, and remember me with laughs. Now when I cease to talk in a few seconds, you will stand to your feet, as the proud strong man I married, and you will live my dear husband. I love you, always have, and always will. Goodbye, my love.'

As Mr Robertson opened his eyes he felt strange, like he had fallen asleep while awake somehow. He quickly reached into his jacket to look at his pocket watch; he had only been of absent mind for a few minutes, if that.

'Must have been nodding off,' he said to himself. He looked at Peggy's headstone; he smiled at it. 'Well Peggy, looks like I tidied that up well, it will do for now I guess. I will have to go though as your old man has bad men to find, see you soon.'

He hurried off out of the graveyard placed the shovel against a wall, and as he headed off he felt better than before. He didn't remember crying and he didn't remember his heart breaking. Peggy had done something to him - he didn't know what she had done, nor did he remember what he had said to her, but she had done something.

Whatever she had done, he felt better. He had a drive; a drive to catch the criminals once and for all who were doing the grave robbing in the area.

Back at the grave, Old Peggy had mixed emotions. Mr Higgingsly offered comfort in a way only he could.

'Hey, Old Peggy, you know you did well there. A good thing you have done, a really good thing'

Old Peggy stayed quiet.

'Hey, what? What's going on?' added Lord Fenwick, who, being new to the supernatural world, was unsure about what had transpired.

'Mr Fenwick, it really isn't your business. We have much to show you, tell you, teach you. Much that can't be explained until you have gotten used to how things are first. Yesterday, you couldn't even see, now you can. You have to crawl before you can walk, one thing at a time I'd say, sir'

'Oh, I understand Mr Higgingsly, I do. It's just all this which is going on around me is so mysterious! I just wondered what she did to him, or what happened."

'Oh Peggy,' sighed Mr Higgingsly 'Do you want to explain to our newly deceased inquisitive buffoon what you did? Or do you want me to tell him to shut it?'

Peggy sighed too. 'Nothing to explain really sirs, nothing much at all. A sad thing, it has to be said, but something I had to do…for the time being at least.'

Lord Fenwick couldn't help himself 'What dear Peggy? What did you have to do?

She thought of her husband, she remembered the day he put the ring on her finger and she felt happy…

'Say goodbye.'

CHAPTER 18

Shuffling back in terror, William felt a sudden shock that seem to grip his body like a vice. He couldn't move, he shook and closed his eyes 'Where the hell am I? Am I alive or dead? Oh Lord, please help me!'

Pausing for the briefest of moments, William decided to try and control his erratic breathing in an attempt to calm down.

Everything seemed to be calm. William wondered if he opened his eyes if things would go back to normal.

Would the boy, the younger version of himself be gone? He hoped the haunting was over and decided to open his eyes ever so slowly. As he did he squinted at the light. The sun shone as bright as he had ever seen it, he looked around; things looked more familiar.

He was in the graveyard, lying on the grass on the south side.

I'm home!

But something seemed different ... there weren't as many graves. As William stood and walked slowly around, in no given direction, he observed the different head stones and noticed that Mr Higgingsly wasn't there, nor was Old Peggy!

Where have they gone? thought William, who was now getting more confused by the minute.

He strode forwards and heard a familiar sound, a sound which he recognised instantly…

Digging.

But who was digging? After all, only *he* did the digging in this grave yard so who would dare to dig in his place?

Following the sound like a dog to a whistle, William gained sight of the man from about 30 yards away, though he could only see him from behind.

The man wore the same long dark coat he did, and seemed to dig rather quickly. The man didn't seem to be careful in his work either and just flung the dirt over his shoulder with no concern about the mess he was making.

'Excuse me, sir,' shouted William. 'What is the meaning of this?'

The man didn't stop digging, William was only 10 or so yards away, perhaps he hadn't heard William?

William raised his voice as he got closer 'Sir, did you not hear me? I said excuse me, I think we might have words!'

Again the man did not respond, and continued to dig frantically, with dirt being flung everywhere.

Getting irate was a very rare occurrence for William, even when he was a lad and the kids teased him, William rarely retaliated, but one thing that could get a rise out of William with certainty was messing with his graveyard.

Right behind the man now, William stood tall and shouted at the top of his voice 'Right, sir. I demand that you stop; stop at once I say!'

Surprisingly, the man did as instructed.

William wasn't used to giving orders, or even shouting for that matter, but when it came to matters such as this, well ... he just had to act.

Calming his voice to a lower tone, William now wished to question the man.

'Now sir, if you would be so gracious, would you please face me and explain what you are doing digging here? This is in fact private land; one does not just turn up and start digging. Please, turn and face me sir, explain your actions.'

The man in front of William lowered his spade to his side and stood quiet; William felt cold, something wasn't right. There was no wind, there was hardly any sound, and he could feel his heart beating quickly.

'Turn sir; who are you and what are you doing I say?'

In what seemed like an instant the man turned and while doing so swung the spade through the air, like a knight with his sword, the spade was aimed for William's head.

Luckily, William ducked and the spade narrowly missed him. The man, who was now off balance, was vulnerable, so William took his shot. William kicked the man's legs away from under him and the man fell. Quickly, William mounted him and sat above him, raising his own fists in the air like a hammer about to strike a nail. William screamed as he brought down the blow in what seemed like slow motion, as his fist came down William looked at the man's face.

Williams's eyes opened so wide he feared they might pop out; his fist stopped about a centimetre away from the man's motionless face.

He could have killed the man with such a blow.

There was complete silence as William and the man looked at each other.

The man was not scared or pleading for his life - he was not saying anything at all; he just looked straight into Williams's eyes, as if he could see into his very soul.

This man was not a stranger…

This man was William's father.

CHAPTER 19

The following morning was a wet morning indeed, and Father Fanshaw looked out of the window as he poured himself a glass of water and watched the never-ending raindrops hit the ground; it was as depressing as it was monotonous.

Feeling full of woe at William's misfortune, the Reverend had partaken of a light breakfast in an attempt to gain some strength, for it had been a long night. Then he wandered back to the bedside where he sat and held William's hand.

'Oh my poor William, my poor, poor William. You really do seem to have the lion's share of bad luck, dear boy. I remember you as a boy - quiet, kind, obedient, content. But one thing I can never remember is when you were truly happy.'

Pausing for a few seconds, the Reverend had an awful feeling which he had felt before; it was one of guilt which he couldn't help feel. He had never actually witnessed William's father beating him, but he should have known. Sure, he had an inclination, but when he asked about various bruises William had from week to week, William's father would just say he got the bruises fooling around. The Reverend felt guilty he had been somewhat ignorant of the abuse William had undoubtedly suffered, and couldn't help but wonder if that abuse had made William the way he was.

'Oh William, I am sorry you know, deeply sorry. I feel I should have challenged your father; I really should have. Perhaps dear boy, if I had, you would have lived a more normal type of life, not spending your time with an old Reverend, digging graves and keeping yourself locked away from the rest of the world.'

Placing William's hand carefully back on the bed, Father Fanshaw stood over William and placed his hand on his cheek.

'Please, get better, please.'

Just as the Reverend finished his words he heard a knock at the door.

He looked left and right in bewilderment, for who would call so early in the day? Quickly moving to the nearest mirror in the hallway the Reverend checked his appearance and tidied his thin grey hair a little, then set off for the door.

As he opened the door he smiled to see Mr Robertson, his favourite policeman, with what looked like some official police papers folded under his arm. He wondered if there had been some development on the case of William's attackers. But then the Reverend's eyes strayed right a little, and he realised Mr Robertson had some company. He had seen this lady before, but his memory was such these days that her identity escaped him.

With the broadest of smiles the Reverend greeted them. 'Oh hello, good morning; please excuse my appearance but I have been up most of the night watching William. Please come in, both of you, please do come in.'

Mr Robertson stood with his usual composed look of discipline and seriousness and introduced the lady at his side.

'I am sorry for the early call, Father, but I was on my way to let you know there are a few suspects, there have been some similar instances you see, and we have a few names to run by you ... William too if he wakes of course. As I entered the front gates, I bumped into this dear little thing...'

The lady smiled and held out her hand to the Reverend. 'It's Lady Fenwick, Father, but please, just call me Anne.'

'Oh of course, dear Lady Fenwick! Oh my dear, I remember you now. Oh I do hope you are coping alright. Such hard times for you I am sure.'

She smiled a comforting smile. 'Hard times for us all I'd say'

'Indeed' added Mr Robertson.

The Reverend nodded with reluctance. 'Yes, yes,' he agreed 'I'm sure the officer filled you in on the dreadful events of last night?'

'Yes, most dreadful, I cannot comprehend someone doing such things, *stealing* from the dead? Then to add insult to said indignity, they beat the man who challenges them? Ghastly, just ghastly, while truly unforgivable I might add.'

'It is, as you say, quite the crime of cowards and fiends my Lady, yet I have to say, and please don't take this the wrong way dear Officer, my only concern at the moment is for William; that is all I am focusing on.'

Both Lady Anne and Mr Robertson nodded in agreement.

Father Fanshaw stood fiddling with his own hands for a second in silence. 'I would offer you some tea, but it seems after last night I have no more left. I have to venture into the town today for some more, oh and food and some other bits; it's just, I didn't want to leave poor William alone.'

Lady Anne smiled 'Tell me what you need dear Reverend, I will go and get it for you.'

'Well dear, that really is lovely, a lovely gesture indeed, but I get certain rates you see, being a man of the cloth and all. This job does have some perks, but it requires me to buy the goods in person. A few blessings here and there make me some good savings I might say.'

'Well usually I would offer to stay, but as you will appreciate I have an investigation to conduct' sighed Mr Robertson.

'Oh, I know dear sir, I understand' smiled the Reverend.

'I'll stay with him,' Lady Anne interrupted. 'It really is no trouble, no trouble at all."

CHAPTER 20

Everything was dark, everything was peaceful. *Everything* made no sense whatsoever.

As he lay conscious of the fact that he had no idea whether he was dead or alive, William realised he was lying on the grass in the graveyard. He looked up above to the midnight blue sky, the trees' branches which intruded on the view looked like black veins in the sky.

This made William wonder, 'is everything alive? Is everything dead? What is alive?'

He thought that if alive is what his life had been so far then perhaps he was better off dead, for what had he achieved? Who had he touched? Who had he loved? Who had loved him?

It was then that he began to cry; he cried so hard.

Feeling an overwhelming sense of worthlessness, he thought that he didn't deserve to be alive. He had witnessed so many beautiful souls who had passed, leaving so much love behind, so many people to mourn and ache for their return.

But who would mourn him?

Nobody.

Nobody cared, and that was a fact William now faced. He didn't blame anyone, this was his own doing; he knew he had separated himself from the grasps of real life, real friends, and real love.

He never really gave himself a fair chance, he just cowered away, to be unseen by the mortals. That way, nobody could hurt him. Nobody could mock him, nobody would be left disappointed.

It started to rain, he felt the raindrops hit him and it brought him comfort. He lay there, welcoming the rain as it soaked him. He hoped the rain would fall so hard it would drown him; he had had enough of everything.

Everything was horrible, everything was vile; *everything* was just so damn pointless.

It began to thunder; loud cracks shook the trees as if they themselves were afraid. But the noise didn't scare William, he welcomed it. He lay in awe as he watched the lightning accompany the thunder in what was like a symphony of the gods themselves.

He hoped the bloodcurdling lightning would strike him.

PLEASE…

It wasn't that he yearned for some sort of torturous pain; he just wanted to feel something, anything.

He listened to the fierce thunder and closed his eyes again, he prayed for it all to end.

Life had no meaning; that was clear now.

The thunder stopped, the rain did too.

'Perhaps this is it,' William thought. He was calm; he was ready, for in his mind he was dead already.

He heard a voice he could not place…

It was a soft voice, it whispered through the air like an arrow…

William…

He listened again, had he been mistaken?

William…

'Who was calling to him?' he wondered.

He tried to open his eyes but he couldn't. He heard mixed noises and tried to get up, but he couldn't. He felt mixed pains; he tried to speak …but he couldn't find any words.

He cried in confusion, what was happening?

William, the voice repeated.

He knew the voice; it was the voice of an angel whose name he would never forget.

His eyes opened slightly. He couldn't make much out at first. He was being held down, by whom?

'William, come back William,' the voice said.

His eyes opened, and the angel stood before him.

He found words from his tongue, but the only words he could find were those of her name 'Lady Anne?'

She smiled at him, her dark hair tied back, her lips as red as roses, her eyes more beautiful than any sacred stone man could find.

He was still crying as he tried to sit up. 'Lady Anne? I…, why are you here? Am I dead?'

'Now-now William, rest,' she said softly as she eased him back into a lying position.

He was scared. 'But am I dead? Am I dead, Lady Anne?'

She moved her fingers through his hair softly, then patted a warm, damp cloth over his forehead and held his cheek in her palm.

'You're not dead, sweet William, you are very much alive; Very, very much alive; and I am so happy about that, I must say. Now rest William, rest.'

William couldn't believe it; he didn't want to rest. He had been away for what seemed like far too long.

Everything was lighter now; everything was peaceful; everything was looking a lot better indeed.

'*Everything*, that's what she is,' thought William as he watched her smiling at him.

At *HIM!*

Usually when a girl smiled in William's direction he found that it was always aimed at the man behind him.

But not today.

This smile…was all his.

CHAPTER 21

May 4th 1892

So, William was alive. But not only in the sense which we all take for granted - he felt alive, truly alive. He had a feeling stirring deep within the darkest corridors of the place he had kept hidden and secret from every other living person since he could remember, the place where he kept glimmers of a hope he dare not hope, a dream he could never dream, a feeling he dare not speak of, for he would never witness it or ever understand it. But the feelings were there nevertheless, like they are in us all.

And where do we harbour such thoughts, such longing, and such hope?

In our hearts of course; and even the hardest of hearts have such feelings. William's was not such a hard heart; it was more of a fragile nature, untested by the tribulations of relationships, inexperienced to love or hate, fragile though not broken, tainted though not spoilt, apprehensive though not scared.

Hopeful, not expectant.

All in all though, William didn't know what he was feeling. He was smart enough to know it wasn't a bad feeling, or was it?

Whatever the feelings were, they were aimed at one person - that much was a certainty.

As William grew stronger day by day, the feelings grew stronger due to the presence of Lady Anne. It seemed they had found a way to talk to each other and for four days in a row she would knock on William's door at 11.30 in the morning to see how he was.

Every morning she would say something like, 'I just thought I would stop by and see how you are, William,' as if justifying her presence.

William though, saw to it he got longer with her, he drew pictures every day, painted new paintings, or found some new topic to discuss, just to keep her around for longer.

To which she seemed to have no objection.

William had a funny thought that he wished he could be ill for quite a while longer, for there would be no reason for her to come and visit once he was deemed fit to resume his responsibilities.

The thought of not seeing her as much made him sad. Thoughts … that's all he seemed to have these days. In some cases he wondered if he would be better off not having any thoughts about her at all.

No.

Of course not, for who can deny the great feeling, *that* great feeling. The one where you know something is happening between you and another; some connection has been made, some line has been crossed, some feeling has been realised, some dream you want more than anything in the world.

That feeling, the feeling they were feeling was what you or I would call…*attraction*.

I would ask you to close your eyes and think about the words I write.

Now I'm sure you may still remember. Can you remember that feeling?

Can you remember when you first saw them?

Can you remember being drawn to them? Like you just spotted them out of the crowd and you could only focus on them.

That is what I am talking about, pure, bold, raw, unexplained attraction.

Attraction makes everything stand still for a moment, suddenly everything fades into the background, and all you can hear is the beating of your heart; the person before you is all that matters, all you want.

Close your eyes and think.

But not for too long, for I have a story to tell, do I not?

William liked how he felt. He wanted to spend more time with her, to find out things about her…her hopes, her dreams.

But for Lady Anne, things were not as straightforward…

CHAPTER 22

The first steps he took since he had been injured felt good for William, he liked being back on his feet. It was late, William could see the faint shine from the street lanterns a few streets away, it made the black night feel more subtle with its yellow glow.

Walking through the grave yard barefoot, William loved the feeling of the moist grass underneath his feet, it didn't bother him that his feet felt wet; it felt nice. There was a slight chill in the air but it wasn't cold. Just a soothing calm breeze that felt like a soft breath on the neck.

A soft breath.

The thought of this made him think of her again, he smiled as he pictured her in his mind, her smile, her touch, her hair, her voice.

'Stop it!' he thought to himself as he shook his head and continued to walk.

Just as he passed Mr Higgingsly's grave he heard Mr Higgingsly's voice, he smiled as he heard it; it had been a while.

'Stop what?' asked Mr Higgingsly.

'Oh, nice to see you too sir. Yes, I'm fine, thank you for asking!'

The voice chuckled and coughed, as only Mr Higgingsly's did. 'Well, my boy that was in fact going to be my next line, but you preceded me before I had chance to offer such niceties. So, if you will allow me to retort, or in this case conclude, I would like to say that on speaking with the other residents, I would like to offer, not just mine, but the whole residents' eternal gratitude for what you did, dear William. You were brave, you were noble, and you were the man we already knew you were, it is criminal what happened to you. The injuries you sustained, the whole ordeal, was just horrible. I for one will feel I owe you a debt for the way you look after us. Now I know I cannot do much, given my current predicament. But if there is anything I ever *can* do, then please, just ask.'

William couldn't believe it, to say he was taken aback was an understatement. He took a deep breath. Mr Higgingsly's words were so comforting to him, the very fact that they all understood how deeply he felt about his protection of their graves made William feel appreciated in a way he was not accustomed to.

William sat by Mr Higgingsly's grave, cross-legged. He put his hands together and felt his own bruised face; he took in a breath of the fresh night air and relaxed.

'Well sir, it warms my heart for you to say such kind things, things which, for the most part I have never fully realised. But in fact, I do care so much about the preservation of all of your places of rest. It is something I feel most strongly about, and I will not, will never, see such places tarnished by the hands of low, unlawful fiends … if it means my life, then I will defend them with such'

William heard a sniffle.

'Are you alright, sir? It was not my intention to upset you, just to convey gratitude at your words.'

'I am alright; I felt a little choked up, William if I am honest. Which is strange as I have never been one to show much emotion, it must be this being dead thing, most strange. Moving on, err… I was just thinking about what you said.'

'Which part sir?'

'The part when you said if it meant your life, which got me thinking about…your life.'

'And?'

'Well sir, as much as it pains me to say, and please don't think I want rid of you, but what are you doing with your life William? I mean really? You are spending your time looking after us, the dead. But yet your contact with the living world is minimal. We have all been praying you know, me, Old Peggy, Lord Fenwick even the young swine, after we heard the news that you had come around, we talked about you at length'

William smiled. 'Oh you did, did you? And what was all that about, can I ask?'

'Well sir, it dawned upon me and the others, that you need to realise that there is a whole different life out there for you. There really is, young sir. You are still young, polite, well spoken…'

'But Mr Higgingsly, I have no education, no skills, no prospects, I cannot even seem to be in others' presence without them getting scared or repulsed by me'.

'William-William-William, this is all in your head, boy. You are not the scared little boy your father bullied. You are a fine young man, and you are a man of the finest quality I might add. You say you cannot socialise with the living, but what of the fine lady who was by your bedside as you lay these past days? You know she wasn't forced here, William; she came of her own free will. Free will, William. You say you have no prospects young boy, but you have choices don't you? Please believe me when I say, while you can choose you can change.'

CHAPTER 23

May 9th, 1892, Barnes Town Centre, Barnes, London

Walking the cobbled streets of Barnes on a Wednesday was always pleasing to Lady Anne, for Wednesday was the famous 'Foreign Market' day, and how she loved it.

Sure, there was a market every day in Barnes, but Foreign Market day was always the best for anyone looking to make a purchase. The local traders didn't like the fact that the so-called foreign swine could make money on their patch. But terms were agreed nevertheless that anyone not of English origin could trade on a Wednesday only, which just so happened to be the slowest part of the week.

However, people were so bowled over by the vast range of goods that they simply saved money until the Wednesday.

There were all sorts of different things to try when shopping at the immigrants' bazaar. For men, a choice of stronger whisky and new flavoured alcoholic spirits seemed to excite many a palate. Whilst for a woman with a thirst for fashion and the money to quench it, there were dresses with elaborate V-waists, layer upon layer of fine fabrics and elegant bell sleeves, as well as the finest lace a lady could find.

For the more modest of folk, the very sight of overseas fruit left many to ponder. Bananas and mangos from distant lands were seen as trophies and some would buy such fruit as presents or gifts, for they were so colourful, so tasty and so rare.

Also rare, particularly on a Wednesday morning at 10 am, was the attendance of Patrick Fenwick at such a place. Usually, the self-professed important man of the courts was deep in session with only the most vital of matters. But as a case he was involved in had ceased for a half hour due to a witness being late, Patrick had decided to have a quick walk and a smoke on his pipe.

He also knew Lady Anne walked the cobbled paths of the foreign market on a Wednesday… a blessed convenience should they cross paths.

Which of course they did.

He fell upon her line of sight just as she had purchased some French silk. Pleased with what she had acquired, she placed the silk into a bag and walked on, and then she saw him, standing before her with a smile which she had come to loathe more and more over time.

His greeting was one of fake surprise, a fallacy of which she was all too aware.

'Of all the people to see on such a dire and irritating morning' Patrick tipped his hat 'Lady Anne.'

'Mr Fenwick' she replied 'Of all the places, whatever next? Have you not some wrong to right on this day may I ask?'

'You may indeed, and as a matter of fact I *will* right a wrong this day, I am filling time you see, awaiting a key witness to arrive in court. He is going to speak this afternoon in what is a most dreadful case, one which will see me strenuously seek a verdict of murder, for which a punishment of death by hanging should rightfully suffice'

'Murder, how awful, well I am sure you will get what you want Patrick.'

She tried not to look at him too long; his conceited ways were such that she felt uncomfortable in his company. There was an awkward silence between the two as Lady Anne wondered what the most pleasant way to say goodbye was whilst Patrick wondered how to keep her talking for a while longer.

Patrick insisted he walk with her a while, reminding Lady Anne that markets, such as the one in which she was walking, were a breeding ground for pickpockets. So she reluctantly agreed, as she had a sizeable amount on her person should she be robbed. The market was situated on a long stretch of cobbled path, at the end though, there were always Hackney coaches ready and willing to take you anywhere you wanted to go. Lady Anne loved horses, and would give the horse a carrot every now and then after her carriage ride home. Her plan was to endure Patrick until the end of the street, call a driver, and go home.

Lady Anne felt uneasy, so she decided to get Patrick to talk about his work, she figured it would be a safe subject to approach as he loved to brag and boast, and as he would inevitably waffle on she would be able to bid him good day without the questions about what she was doing and who she was spending her time with.

'So what has he done, this man who may be hanged?'

The trick worked, Patrick's ears almost stood up at the question. He straightened his collar as he spoke and tried to look important as he strode with his thick wooden cane clicking against the path as they walked.

'*May* be hanged you say? Oh my dear, you are clearly unaware of my conviction rate, bless you. I am fairly certain of conviction at this point, my final witness is the old 'nail in the coffin' shall we say?'

'But why do you need one if it is almost a matter of certainty?'

'The show! The show my dear! I like to put on a show, so there you have it.'

'But I thought the truth was paramount, as a man's life is in the balance is it not?'

'Indeed, but all need to know of such a man when the act is one of murder. The people need to know such a crime, will be met with the harshest of consequences.'

'Well, I would say death is a harsh punishment indeed. I have never witnessed a court, nor even witnessed a sentence being passed. What does the judge say? Is it as simple as 'go forth and be hung?' What happens?'

'Well aren't you the curious one? What will happen today goes a little like this: The judge will decide I am right, and the accused did in fact commit the most heinous crime of murder. Then the right honourable judge will say something like, "Thomas Miles, you stand convicted of the horrid and unnatural crime of murdering Shaun Maloney, your friend. This Court doth adjudge that you be taken back to the place from whence you came, and there to be fed on bread and water till Wednesday next, when you are to be taken to the common place of execution, and there hanged by the neck until you are dead; may God have mercy on your soul." The man was found with a pocket watch of Shaun Maloney's; we believe robbery was the motive as is often the case these days. Horrible, horrible thieves, I would stretch every one of their necks.'

'The thought makes me quiver with fear. Imagine knowing you are to be sentenced to death, how awful and barbaric.' Lady Anne was noticeably horrified.

Patrick sniggered 'What did you think happened? That we sat the offenders down and said "Look we are really sorry, but you're going to hang, anything we can do to help?" No, we are direct. Harsh words for harsh crimes which lead to harsh action. Action, which is right, just and dignified.'

'Well Patrick, to call it right and just is a matter for others to decide, but dignified? I would beg to differ, how, is stretching a man's neck until it breaks a dignified action?'

Grabbing Lady Anne's arm firmly, Patrick revealed a side to which Lady Anne was more accustomed. 'You forget your place, woman.'

Trying to pull away in vain Lady Anne asked him to let go 'Please,'

'I will release you when you learn your place. Now listen to me, listen to me very carefully, we have many things to discuss, which is why you will dine with me tomorrow evening to consult about a few things.'

Patrick noticed a few people were looking at him, he let go of her arm and smiled as if he cared somehow, Lady Anne knew he didn't, it was for the sake of her not making a fuss in public.

'I cannot I am afraid Patrick, I am otherwise engaged,' she said politely as if the grabbing of her arm did not happen.

Breathing quickly through inflamed nostrils, Patrick gritted his teeth and spoke through them. 'I am not *asking* Lady Anne…'

Looking to the ground with a sigh, she felt she had no choice 'What time?' she asked quickly.

'7 o'clock, at my house, I will have you picked up and…'

'I can make my own way there, Patrick,' Lady Anne quickly snapped before calling a carriage across.

'Ma'am,' the driver said as he tipped his hat. The driver climbed down and opened the carriage up for Lady Anne. She got in and didn't look at Patrick.

'Good day Anne.' Patrick smiled cunningly.

Lady Anne did not return the pleasantries.

CHAPTER 24

When one takes a walk in the forest all alone, one may get scared, have no feelings at all, or be enchanted by it, for William it was definitely the latter. He loved to take walks in the nearby forest. He would walk for miles. It was one of the only places he walked apart from the grounds of the grave yard. On the very rare occasion William ever did venture into town for anything, he would do so very early to try and avoid the thing that scared him: people.

At the end of his walk William would cut wood for the fire (his own and the Reverend's) and then he would place all the wood he could manage into a large old sack and drag it with sheer strength all the way home.

The task was tiresome, but worth it.

He liked being alone with his thoughts, and today his thoughts were the same as yesterday's. Thoughts of Anne…her eyes, her hair, her face and the sweet smell of jasmine whenever she was near.

William tried to snap out of his daydream as he walked, with his log cutting axe strapped to his back as his feet felt the soggy, squishy ground and the twigs breaking underneath him.

He smiled in appreciation of the forest as he gazed upon the tall, wonderful, slender trees, with knobbly trunks and branches. The green that covered the forest looked so pretty. The rustling leaves of the trees brought a kind of life to it; all that William loved.

Always looking for trees which had fallen rather than cutting one down, William found a huge tree which must have fallen in natural circumstance; such was the size of the thing.

It took hours for William to chop up some wood into manageable chunks for the fire. After completing his task he gathered it into the sack and started the long task of dragging the wood home. As he walked his eyes browsed the area as always. It seemed he always found something new to love in the woods and was always on the look-out for things he hadn't noticed before like a new plant, a new tree or even a different type of bird. What did catch his attention though was a set of paw prints on the mud.

'There aren't many wild dogs in Barnes,' thought William. Then he thought that maybe the paw prints belonged to a fox, but he realised they were too big.

William was having a good old think 'Whatever could it be? Must be a fox, a big fox perhaps?' He thought.

William stopped for a second as he heard something, but what was it? He continued to walk as he realised it was the sound of horses.

Now there are things, actions and sequences of events, if you will, in this life that some would say are pre-destined, regardless of the decisions you appear to make.

Some would call it coincidence, some would call it luck, but there are those that would call it fate. There are also those that say once you make a decision in your own mind, whether you are conscious of it or not, that the universe conspires to make it happen.

Lady Anne had certainly not made any conscious decisions for her and William to be closer or to be friends even. The same could be said for William too. None of them were pursuing the other with any definite motive.

But what did happen was that the universe did conspire, because in each of their unconscious minds, they *had* made a decision, as do we all in matters of the heart. We all know if we want that person or not, and after such a decision, the rest is just a matter of when it will happen, how it will happen, and those very thoughts, such exciting thoughts, make us crazy.

Some yards away from where William had started to drag his firewood, were the outskirts of the forest. On the outskirts of the forest was a road, and on that road, a horse and carriage.

Lady Anne felt better once she was away from Patrick. She was just taking off her gloves, as she felt a little hot, when she quickly glanced to the left window; she smiled at the forest's beauty and stared deep within it.

Then she saw something; it was moving… dragging something. Was it a body? She shouted for her driver to halt for a moment, which he did.

After quickly exiting the carriage, she moved closer to the forest, but did not venture in. She remained on the edge of it, but was now only twenty or so yards away. She looked deeper at the man and then she recognised him as her driver politely asked if she was alright.

She smiled, to herself then at the driver.

'I'm fine' Anne replied, as she watched William drag the sack of wood.

'William!' she shouted 'William!'

Pausing for a second William ceased walking and looked around, he looked to his right to see a figure in a dress waving and shouting to get his attention.

'Could it be?' William thought.

Then a huge smile spread across his face as the realisation that it was Lady Anne calling him, gripped him as he giggled. The hairs on his arms stood up and Williams felt little tingles all over his body like feathers brushing against the skin.

Dropping the wood, William tidied his hair a little by sweeping it from his face with his hands, he then brushed down his coat which had little pieces of wood stuck to it.

He walked slowly over to Lady Anne, when he reached her; her smile was as wide as his.

It made William happy, to see *her* happy.

'Good day to you, Lady Anne. Whatever brings you to these parts?' William smiled.

'Good day to you William, I have been to the foreign market in the town. I got many a bargain and am well pleased. And you, what are you doing on this rare, dry day?'

He tried not to stare at her eyes, but then fidgeted a little as he realised he was doing just that.

'Er, just been cutting wood, ma'am, for the fire. Mine and the Reverend's. I don't chop any good trees, just old ones or ones that have fallen, just dragging the wood back now.'

Lady Anne looked behind her to the carriage and bit her bottom lip as she thought.

'One second William, bear with me,' she said, smiling as she held out her index finger.

She walked off quickly towards the driver, as William waited patiently.

'What is she doing?' thought William as he tried to listen to what she was saying. He couldn't hear though, but it didn't matter because she jogged back to him after a brief chat with the driver and stood before William with a smile.

'You can come with us, William!' She said as she panted for breath.

'Excuse me, ma'am?'

'Your wood, the driver says he can secure it on the horses. We will drop you off at the church; it will be far easier than dragging it all the way home.'

'Oh ma'am, you are too kind, but I must decline, I couldn't *possibly…*'

Lady Anne interrupted, still with a huge smile on her face. 'I'll not take no for an answer William, I insist!'

'Oh, er…' William looked around, unsure of what was proper.

Lady Anne grabbed William's hand with both of hers, William flinched a little and she noticed it and held his hands softly. She noticed how rough his hands were; she saw scars on them and wondered what could have caused such injury.

'William, it is alright, quite alright for you to accept a favour from a friend. Now I am offering you help, the proper thing to do is to accept it and say, 'Thank you, Lady Anne.'

'Err…alright then, Lady Anne. Thank you. I will just go over and get the sack then.' He smiled but it was obvious to Lady Anne that William still felt uneasy. He wasn't used to help, in any way, shape or form.

He pulled his hands away but he didn't want to. It was the first time a lady, any woman, had touched him like that, in a caring friendly way. He knew she had noticed his scars and felt conscious of the fact.

He turned away from her 'Won't be a minute, Lady Anne.'

But she wasn't just going to sit and wait; she walked with him and just as she did she turned to the driver and shouted 'I will not be long, sir, just giving a helping hand.'

'Not proper for a lady, my lady,' the driver shouted.

'Not proper for you to comment I'd say, driver, now wait!' She snapped back.

'Sorry about that, William, old men and their values, honestly. As if a lady cannot even display the basic common example of decency and goodwill without it being 'improper'. So, this forest, you know it well, I take it?'

William couldn't believe Lady Anne would stop to come and talk to him. He felt honoured. He was trying not to offend her, by answering her questions as politely as he could, and as short as he could as she almost skipped along beside him to keep up with his fast-paced walk.

'Yes, Lady Anne. I have been walking these woods since I was a boy'

'That's so lovely; I imagine it to be ever so lovely to spend time around such tranquillity. The forest seems so quiet though, and maybe a little scary really. Did you play in the woods as a boy?'

'Yes ma'am. All the time and I assure you, these woods are not as quiet as you think.'

Lady Anne smiled, 'Oooo, tell me more, what lurks amongst these strange and eerie woods?'

'Nothing…everything.'

Lady Anne looked confused.

'What do you mean William?'

William stopped walking and turned to Lady Anne. He noticed her eyes staring right into his; he felt his heart beat faster as the two shared a silence for the briefest of moments.

'Can you trust me, Lady Anne?' asked William, in an almost whispered voice.

Again, she smiled at him; she knew she could trust him but could not explain why, for she hardly knew him. Something inside her knew he was decent.

'Yes, William. I can trust you.'

'Close your eyes.'

'Excuse me?'

'Close your eyes, Lady Anne.'

As she closed her eyes William moved closer to her from behind, he was not touching her, but she could feel him near … his breath on her neck.

'Can you hear it? Listen to it breathing…'

Lady Anne listened to the strange noises as she felt her senses awaken. She listened to William's words and truly listened to the sounds of the forest.

It was as if a new sense had been given to her that somehow sounds which were usually silent to her were now as loud as the town crier's call.

She smiled and even giggled a little as she heard the sounds of the forest.

'The forest is never quiet. So many sounds live in it that it would take a full year to hear them all. From the little birds that sing, to the wind and rain; from grazing deer to crispy leaves in autumn floating in the wind and squirrels foraging for nuts and berries... And even in winter, the snow brings life to the forest; you cannot help but to marvel at all its majesty. It has stood proudly way before we were here, and will do so long after we are gone.'

She opened her eyes. 'That was...'

'Different?' smiled William.

'Yes, different. I think I can agree. An understatement perhaps but one I will agree with.'

Interrupting an obvious silence, soft drops of rain fell out of the sky onto both William and Lady Anne.

She looked up to the clouds. 'Oh, I love it, William, come here; dance with me in the rain!'

Struggling to know what to do, William froze with his mouth slightly open, wondering what all the fuss was about, it was only rain after all.

But not to Lady Anne - she loved the rain; she loved the coolness on her face. It made her feel free and alive.

Seizing William's hand, like he had no say in the matter, Lady Anne put it around her waist. She grabbed the other and kept it steady in the air as she twirled William around in the rain.

'You see,' Lady Anne laughed. 'It's wonderful, isn't it?'

William tried to stay as reserved as he could, but his smile betrayed him. He had simply never done anything like this before.

'Err…I don't really know what I am doing, ma'am,' William stuttered.

'Who cares?' laughed Lady Anne. 'You're dancing with me anyway!'

They danced as the rain fell gently onto their faces. Locking eyes, they shared a smile that they both knew was real. The time seemed to stand still, like they were both untouchable as they skipped hand-in-hand along the wet forest's floor.

Coming to a halt as they both ran out of breath and nearly lost balance, the silence returned.

Lady Anne spoke first, giggling as her words came out. 'Sorry about that, I like to dance! Shall we get that wood moved and escape the rain then?'

They continued to walk. They stayed quiet for a moment, both knowing they had shared a feeling… something. Lady Anne couldn't bear to be quiet.

'So you grew up around here then, William?'

'Err yes, well, the church, ma'am. Been there my whole life'

'Really?'

'Yes, my father did the job I do before me, and then I took over when he… been doing it ever since, ma'am.'

'And your mother, William?'

Looking to his left where Lady Anne was walking beside him, William tried to avoid the question by thinking of something else to say. The trouble was, he couldn't think of anything. Lady Anne looked at him for a response. She sensed by William's reaction to the question that his mother was gone, and the subject was off limits.

'Do forgive me, William, I am ever so sorry. My mother used to say it wasn't proper of me to be always asking questions of people when newly acquainted. It's just I get excited by interesting people you see and you, William, are so very interesting!'

Looking bemused William picked up the huge sack of fire wood.

'Interesting, me?'

'Yes, you! You seem so very mysterious.'

'I assure you. ma'am, there's nothing mysterious about me; I just dig the graves, ma'am.'

'That you do and do so very well.'

There was a silence as William carried on walking with Lady Anne.

Listening to the woods, they walked towards the carriage. William glanced surreptitiously at Lady Anne from time-to-time and she in turn glanced at him. Neither was aware of the other's observation.

'So William, we are here.'

Lady Anne motioned the driver to help William with his sack of firewood. The driver secured the wood on top of one of the horses with William's help and then opened the carriage for Lady Anne and William, with a look of disdain.

They climbed in.

William felt out of place, as if he was doing something he shouldn't, but maybe he deserved such a luxury after his recent, unfortunate, events.

CHAPTER 25

Sharing a carriage back home with Lady Anne had made William so happy, and although he had tried to keep as reserved as one does when trying to make a good impression, he couldn't help but talk to her.

She was so easy to talk to.

William watched the woods pass by at speed from the carriage window and tried to think of something good to say, but no matter how hard he tried he struggled to find the words.

Lady Anne though, didn't have such trouble, but was concerned that maybe she had upset William about asking questions about his mother.

'So William, I do apologise again about the question about your mother, and I apologise if I was intrusive. If you ever needed someone to listen I would be more than happy to. But, in the hope of not irritating you further, I was going to ask about the rest of your family? Tell all, do you have any brothers or sisters?'

Shaking his head, William answered, 'Not much to tell, Lady Anne.'

'Lizzy,' she laughed. 'Remember, my closest friends call me Lizzy, being called Lady Anne is more appearances, a habit I fear I will never become accustomed to.'

Smiling as if he was trying not to, William took a mental note. 'Lizzy, so I am your friend Lizzy?'

She smiled back. 'Yes, indeed you are, William, a true gentleman if ever there was one.'

Holding out his large hand, William noticed how Lizzy didn't break eye contact as she shook his hand 'Pleased to meet your acquaintance Lizzy'.

'You too William, you too' Lizzy smiled.

Once they had got back to the church, William turned to Lizzy and thanked her for her kindness and bowed his head. Lizzy laughed a little and shook her head.

'You are done with me then, William? Is that it?'

William looked at her with a vacant expression.

'I wondered if you might show me around, William.'

'Around here?' William asked politely.

'Yes.'

'Not much to see, Lizzy, I'm afraid. You don't want to be spending your time here my lady.'

'I do as a matter of fact and, as my late husband is buried here, I would like you to walk me round the place'

'Well…I…er…'

'I won't take no for an answer.' Lizzy smiled.

After he had taken the wood indoors, William took Lizzy for a walk around the grounds. Lizzy's driver waited at the front of the church as instructed, and started to smoke his pipe while doing so.

The driver did not look impressed.

'Don't think he likes me,' William said with a smile as he and Lizzy started to walk the grounds.

'I wouldn't worry yourself, William, I don't think he likes anybody'

The two laughed. William could feel his walls coming down, he felt like the barriers he had built over the years to protect himself were melting slowly with every word she spoke.

But Lizzy could feel it too, like there was something about this man, something she could not explain, but whatever that something was, it was pulling her closer and closer.

They walked and talked in the light of the midday sun. Lizzy made easy conversation about the town, society and her father teaching her to ride a horse. William listened like a child to a bedtime story.

It all seemed to be going so well, the perfect afternoon even, and then it became apparent they were not alone…

'Hello?'

William closed his eyes for a second, ignoring the voice.

'Shall we walk this way Lizzy?' asked William as he gestured for them to take another route away from Mr Higgingsly's grave.

'Oh yes, if you like,' replied Lizzy, who had not spotted William's concern.

'So William, I would like to thank you again for the work done on my late husband's…'

'Not at all ma'am,' interrupted William, 'It is all part of the service'

'Still, there was such effort involved, the flowers, the service, everything was so lovely.'

'You suffered a great loss, Lizzy, it was the least we could do.'

The voice would not go away.

'Hey, excuse me? Oh my word, William, she's come here, with you! A positive sign indeed!'

Lizzy looked confused as she noticed William smile into the air.

'William?' she asked, befuddled.

'Sorry, Lady Anne, er… Lizzy. I … er… I thought I was going to sneeze!'

'Must be all the pollen from these wonderful flowers!' She smiled.

'Indeed' smiled William as they continued to walk.

Lizzy started to talk about Lord Fenwick, how they had met, how they came to be married, and William wanted to listen to her so very much - but Mr Higgingsly just would not be quiet. Wherever they walked, his voice was ever present.

'Oh, what a tragedy! To have to marry because she thought no real love existed, to marry because of friendship. To belong to one but not to receive what a true partner should, oh Mr Fenwick, what were you doing?!'

Lord Fenwick's voice then came into the frame.

'That's LORD Fenwick, I should remind you, Higgingsly!' Lord Fenwick snapped, 'and I would bring to your attention that we were the dearest of friends. Oh my, it is good to hear her voice. I do wonder if she is wearing that beautiful jasmine perfume, I will try and smell again and see if I can catch a trace of it!'

Mr Higgingsly laughed as William shook his head in anger.

'Oh Lord Fenwick, yes, she is here indeed, in attendance with William!'

'With William? Why?'

'Why indeed?' laughed Mr Higgingsly.

'Stop it. Mr Higgingsly. Your suggestive implications will not rile me. If Lizzy has chosen company, then I would more than give blessing for that company to be that of William. A fine young man indeed.'

'Agreed Lord Fenwick, wholeheartedly. But does it not bother you that she is philandering with another man so soon? I mean your body is probably only half-rotted!'

'Bother me? Not in the slightest sir, in fact we had an agreement…'

William tried to balance listening to Lizzy as well as Lord Fenwick and Mr Higgingsly, especially about the agreement Lord Fenwick was about to disclose.

'Which was?' asked Mr Higgingsly.

'That after five years of marriage, or on the day I pass, that she should try and find a true partner, one of good kin and worthy, a man who would show her the love she so deserved. But she was always a defeatist on the matter. If she has found someone as a friend, or anything else, I encourage it. It was more of an arrangement than love; I needed to be seen as married, so did she. We were friends, so it all kind of made sense.'

Mr Higgingsly laughed, 'I fear any such hopes are premature anyway, Lord Fenwick. It is William, after all. A woman would need to give him years to pluck up the courage for a suggestion of courtship.'

Both Lord Fenwick and Mr Higgingsly laughed together like the pompous old busy bodies they were.

William ignored their collective jest and focused on Lizzy.

Lizzy smiled at William, who seemed to be somewhere distant. 'If my questions bother you William, feel no need to answer. Sometimes my inquisitive ways can be so unbecoming for a lady. For that I apologise. It is only because I find you interesting you see, I hope you can take it as a compliment.'

Trying to drown out the nearby waffling of Mr Higgingsly and Lord Fenwick was challenging, but the more William concentrated on the present the quieter their voices became.

'You do not offend me, ma'am… Anne… err … Lizzy. I just, I find it hard to talk to *most* people, about even the most trivial of things, so talking to you, when it seems so easy, is so strange. I feel myself *wanting* to tell you such things, and I cannot understand why'.

Lizzy grabbed William's hand, stopping him as he walked. William moved back ever so slightly, but she noticed and stroked his hand very softly with her fingers. She moved her other hand up to his cheek and felt his rough stubble; as she did so she smiled. 'Oh, dear William, so sweet you are. You can tell me *anything,* anything at all. Though I may not have all the answers, I will certainly listen, and if I can offer advice or help, I will surely do so, because that's what friends do, you see.'

Although he was trembling, William stayed calm. He liked the fact she had touched him; he liked the fact he could talk to her, but more than that, he liked the fact she said they were friends.

Friends.

The word friend was a word William had little experience of, and the fact he had been mentioned as such by Lizzy, made him feel very happy.

As they stared into each other's eyes for only a few seconds, a loud voice, a real one at that, echoed around the graveyard.

'Lady Anne, Lady Anne!' The voice shouted.

As William and Lizzy heard the calls the two moved apart.

From around the corner, the driver appeared; he stopped as he saw them.

'Ma'am,' he said as he threw a less then approving look at William.

It seemed Lizzy was far from impressed too. 'Driver, I thought my instructions were clear; you were to wait for me, were you not?'

'Yes ma'am, but I was under impression you needed me to drive you later. Have you forgotten? For you mentioned you were to be taken to the dinner with…'

'Yes, I am aware; it seems I have lost track of time. Now go to the carriage, William will walk with me, won't you, William?' Lizzy smiled as she motioned him to walk.

Walking with her to the carriage, William couldn't help but feel frustrated. He wished he had more time with her. He felt that they had connected somehow, like he could talk properly to her. Still, he was so grateful for the time he *had* spent with her, and that made him smile.

As they walked together to the carriage the two did not speak, William noticed her trying not to smile.

Lizzy noticed William trying not to smile.

They reached the carriage and William opened the door for her, she held her dress as she climbed in and William shut the door after her. William looked at the driver, then at the carriage, then to his own feet, he breathed in deeply, then stood firm as he attempted some type of composure.

William broke the silence, 'Thank you for the help today, Lady Anne; it is most appreciated.'

He wanted to say something different, something completely different. His lips were saying what they had to, but in his mind and his heart, he was saying 'Lizzy, don't go, please don't go.'

Looking into his eyes, Lizzy knew William had something different to say behind those tightened lips and heavy breathing.

'You are more than welcome William, I will be stopping by again soon.'

She gave him a big smile as the driver set the horses on their way.

William stood outside the graveyard, watching the carriage disappear into the distance.

Lizzy sat in the carriage; she found that she was still smiling which made her smile even more.

She had said what she *had* to, what society deemed appropriate.

But she wanted to say something different, completely different.

She breathed in deeply and closed her eyes.

She wanted to *do* something different, *completely different*.

CHAPTER 26

Rushing was something Lizzy didn't like to do. After getting home she got herself ready for the evening ahead. She really didn't want to go. She found Patrick insufferable, but she knew that she had to attend, if only for a quiet life.

Gossington Hall was Patrick's home; it had been given to him by his brother, Lord Fenwick, when Patrick became a full and proper Legal Practitioner.

Lord Fenwick had practically raised Patrick, and over the years had grown tired of his younger brother so had bought him a big home in order to be rid of him. Lord Fenwick saw it as an easy way of keeping his scheming brother out of his affairs, for he knew his brother was motivated by only two things, money and power.

There were many reasons Lord Fenwick bought Gossington Hall, one of which was that the house was huge, very impressive, and so very Patrick. Another reason was it was all the way across town, so Patrick would be further away.

The latter being the main reason if the truth be told.

Upon her arrival, Lizzy noticed the house her late husband had given to Patrick had undergone quite a few changes.

As the carriage stopped she saw Patrick standing outside his door with servants and maids behind him as if he were royalty, but the things which tickled her the most were the two half man-sized statues of lions at either side of the front door.

She found it incredibly amusing.

As Patrick helped Lizzy out of the carriage he motioned his servant to pay the driver.

'You are too kind, Patrick.' Lizzy smiled as they walked to the house; the servants made a line at either side of them as they walked indoors.

'No problem at all,' replied Patrick offering his arm for Lizzy to hold as they walked.

She didn't take it though and smiled. 'I am quite capable of walking, sir.'

He ignored her rejection and gave compliment on her perfume, 'Ah, the fragrance of a lady, jasmine?'

'Indeed it is Patrick; you have a keen nose it seems.'

'I have, though I am keener on many other things.'

They entered the house and Lizzy felt quite uneasy. She thought that if she felt this uneasy, this soon, that something wasn't right. She felt he was trying to impress her.

She pondered his intentions.

Patrick loved to talk, about very many things. In politics, Patrick had many an ally in various circles and would always name drop to look important at his many dinner parties. Then there was the judicial system, Patrick made out he knew the Law so well that he 'may as well have written it.' But then there was one subject, the most important of all, the very subject that Patrick would drop anything in the world for, the most important thing in his life, which he loved to talk about … himself.

Lizzy and Patrick sat at a decent sized table, not the main dinner table where Patrick wined and dined his guests for his stately get-togethers, but a smaller six-seated table, which was still beautiful nevertheless.

Patrick had flowers arranged in the middle of the table; there was a dim light all around the room and as the servants brought out each course, Lizzy tried to keep Patrick talking about himself as she kept a mindful eye on the clock which was situated behind him.

After they had finished their meal; they retired to a seating area which overlooked the lovely greenery for which Gossington Hall was famous and in the infant night, the trees and hills looked still and lovely, a scene to behold.

But Lizzy was not gullible and she would never be fooled. She knew by Patrick's unusual sedate mood that something was not right.

Walking up behind her while he sipped his whisky, Patrick looked at the scenery which Lizzy was looking upon.

'Don't you just love serendipity?' Patrick laughed.

'It depends,' replied Lizzy.

'On what?'

'The context.'

Patrick puffed out his chest. 'You can be most difficult, Lady Anne, but it was an innocent question. I was merely highlighting that I would have been happy with any old place when my brother offered me a home and I wanted a more modern place if I am honest, but yet, I can't feel aggrieved, I can't. After many a night looking out at that, out there, it dawned upon me that I have stumbled upon this gift of nature, and the scenery is so very beautiful, I have grown to appreciate it.'

Turning from the window and further away from Patrick, Lizzy smiled. 'Well sometimes, sir, it can be that things are good, yet we do not see it in front of our eyes. I am glad you appreciate what he did for you, *really* I am. I have to ask though Patrick, what was the meaning of all this tonight? I am sorry to dampen any mood, for that is not my intention. The hospitality and the evening as a whole are very much taken to heart. But let's be honest with each other, we have never seen eye to eye, so if this is one of your schemes, get to it, for the hour is late and I am growing tired of our false pleasantries'

With his back to Lizzy, Patrick snarled and then smiled. He turned to her and looked her straight in the eye, and then up and down.

'I have reason for you being here, that much is true. I have motives, I do. It is simple Lady Anne, you and you alone, inherited everything from my brother. Everything, from the shoes you stand in to the bed you climb into at night. All you have, all you are, all you ever will be, is down to one thing, my brother's ridiculous kindness. It is that kindness of his that appals me, and I find it hard to stomach. That he would leave everything to you, and forsake me. What kind of brother chooses a wife, and from what I could tell a fake one at that, over blood?'

Lizzy was shocked, she had known Patrick was not happy, neither with the marriage she had to Lord Fenwick nor the fact that he left everything to her, but she never imagined such a bitter statement, one so obviously intended to sting.

'Patrick, I am shocked you would say such things. Your words not only offend but wound me deeply. The fact he always looked after you, do you not *see* that? You say these things about me, about the shoes I stand in, about the things he left to me; well I assure you it was not by my doing. I was married to your brother, as you know, but how we were as a couple was and never will be any of your business. I concede our marriage might have not been the most usual, and may not have adhered to what society would say it should have been, but our friendship and closeness was real, and I never, ever, sought anything from him, Patrick. All I inherited when he passed was from his own free will. Adding to all this I struggle to comprehend the words you speak without a certain amount of contradiction, since the very walls that surround us right now were given to you in love. How dare you sir, how dare you question his intentions?'

In a sudden sharp movement Patrick threw his half empty whisky glass at the wall. Lizzy jumped up as Patrick approached her. He was close, so close she could smell the whisky on his breath.

'How dare *I*? Oh my word, you have some nerve, woman. Why *you*? Why did he have to marry *you*? Why can't you be like all the other women? Why can't you be normal, be a normal lady, do lady *things*? You could sew, gossip, read, and play instruments, drink tea with friends and attend bazaars? Why the pressing need to have an opinion in this man's world? Do you think any *man* values your opinion? A *woman's* opinion?'

Lizzy walked backwards, away from Patrick who seemed to be getting more agitated as he spoke. That fact didn't deter her though...

'I don't care what you think, Patrick, nor do I care what you say. The only thing I want to know now is what you hope to achieve by all this, what do you intend to do? Why bring me here to treat me like this? I have never wronged you, and do not wish to do so; I just want to live my life without incident'

Dropping to his knees suddenly, Patrick began to weep. His hands were over his face and his cries got louder and louder.

Lizzy looked at the door; she knew she could run, get to the carriage and go home. But that was not who Lizzy was. Horrible as he was, she couldn't leave someone distressed like that. She walked closer to him.

'Patrick, I *am* sorry if my words have caused you stress, I did not mean to upset you.'

Patrick turned to her and looked at her. 'What about me?'

Confused, Lizzy knelt down to Patrick's level.

'I don't understand, Patrick'

'Me?'

Lizzy thought Patrick had drunk too much whisky.

'Shall I call for help to get you into bed? I really think you have drunk too much Patrick'

Patrick grabbed her; she struggled and tried to get him off but he was too strong. She tried to talk but he covered her mouth with his hand, so she froze.

His face was so close to hers, he rubbed his cheek against her quivering face. He could feel her shaking, feel her fear, and he liked it.

He was in control now.

'You know, I always envied him, my big brother. Why did he get you? Why did he have all the luck? Why? You know you could be mine? I could change and if you would too, we could be together, be a *real* husband and wife, and do *real* husband and wife things. Have children, like married people should do. If we could, we could both share what I am sure my brother intended us to share. Why do you need all that you have? Why do you choose not to have children? Why choose not to be loved in a way someone could love you? I believe you could love me. It seems so foolish for us to fight, when in reality it makes perfect sense for us to be one?'

Noticing that tears were rolling down Lizzy's cheeks, Patrick let go of her.

'Anne' he said in a matter-of –fact manner, 'I'm sorry if I startled you, or if I have shocked you, but this is why I summoned you this evening. I struggle to find the words, but now I am sure you know what I want, what I need'.

Rising to her feet, Anne walked backwards until she realised she was at the wall. She tried to gather herself and be calm, when in fact every bit of sense in her was telling her to run.

'Patrick, don't ever do that to me again, ever! Now I will say this once, and let us not revisit this again. I do not, cannot, nor will not ever love you. My only feeling towards you is fear of what you may do in the face of my rejection, and fear of what you could do in the future to spite me. I do often ponder at my decision to marry for the wrong reasons … reasons which I would never go into with you. But I would never make the same mistake again, ever.'

Patrick smiled; it was as if his tears were invented solely for purposes which now were all too loud and clear.

'But Anne, oh Anne, do you really want to make an enemy of me? *Me?*'

'I do not wish to make enemies of anybody, sir.'

'But you know I always get what I want; it is true what people say about me, I do always win. And I will Anne. You can never beat me. In view of what I am sure is wrongful indecision on your part, why not trust my judgement? Or, if that is not enough, think about what is best for you? Do you really think it is safe, all alone in that big house of yours?'

'Are you threatening me, sir?'

Patrick laughed. 'Me? Never! Ha!'

Lizzy knew it was time to go, she hurried away towards the door but it was locked 'Damn!' she thought. She looked outside and could see her driver asleep at the carriage, she banged her fist on the window in an attempt to get his attention, but the driver did not wake.

She heard footsteps behind her and turned to see Patrick standing there. He had a quite visible scowl now and Lizzy was scared.

'Patrick, will you please unlock the door? The driver knows I am here and …'

'The driver?' laughed Patrick 'The driver doesn't care, all he wants is money and earlier as I nipped out of the room I paid him to stay and wait for you. I even said it may be morning when you were ready!'

'How dare you, Patrick, how dare you?' she screamed.

'Oh Anne, Lizzy, or whatever you want to be called, I know how you spent your day…'

'How?' Lizzy replied

'You spent the day, with that no good, scoundrel, that, that buffoon! Isn't he handicapped? Is it right for a lady to spend time with some handicapped town idiot? You do know that the word handicapped derived from the words 'hand –in cap'? Don't you? So I guess the two of you fit! Ha-ha!'

She was outraged and slapped him across his cheek. 'You are vile, Patrick Fenwick, vile indeed. Who, when and where I spend my time is no concern of yours. Yes, I spent time with a friend, his name is William. Yes, he is different; yes, he is quiet but he is more of a man, more of a gentleman then you will ever be. You disgust me. LET ME OUT!'

Patrick was delighted he had got Lizzy to slap him. He loved conflict and now she was shouting to be let out, it gave him the control he loved so much.

'I will let you out when I am damn good and ready woman. But know this… you *ANNE*, are no lady. You are nothing but a woman of easy virtue, not quite a prostitute yet, but still you are what we men call a philandering dollymop! I will get what is mine, eventually. I always win; you *know* I always win… everybody knows I *always* win.'

He opened the door for her and she ran out crying, Patrick laughed as the driver woke and helped her into the carriage.

'Be careful driver,' shouted Patrick as the driver started pulling away. 'She's a dollymop that one. You hear that ANNE, a dollymop.

Laughing at his own rudeness, Patrick turned to see a maid peeking from behind a wall inside the house.

'You! Come here at once! How dare you eavesdrop on your master?'

The maid walked forwards slowly, she was very young and Patrick licked his lips as she approached.

'How old are you, girl?'

She quivered and looked at the floor as she answered, 'Seventeen, sir.'

'Seventeen, you don't say? Why were you listening in on conversations above your station?'

'Sir, I… I heard a glass break so I came to see if everything was alright, then I noticed you still had company, so was waiting to clean it up. I wasn't listening sir, honest, couldn't hear from over there anyways, sir.'

'Oh you were, were you? I tell you what, *girl*; you have a clever and witty tongue in your head, my pretty young maid, why not stick it in mine and wiggle it about?'

The girl stood motionless.

Patrick looked at the ground outside. There was some horse manure scattered around the forecourt leading up to the steps of the house, Patrick huffed in disgust then smiled a wicked smile.

'Better still, *girl*, there is some unpleasantness near the front step, please get rid of it.'

CHAPTER 27

What a beautiful day it was, William noticed the sun trying its best to peek through the rain-filled clouds.

William had a busy day today; he had a lot of tasks to do, one of which was cutting some weeds which had begun to grow in the far corner of the grave yard.

After having a light breakfast, William got dressed and picked up his old gloves as he whistled his way outside. He didn't know what tune he was whistling, in fact he knew of no songs to whistle, but still, he was whistling.

It felt good; *he* felt good.

As he approached the weeds, William walked by Mr Higgingsly's grave.

'Morning, sir.'

'Well good morning, William,' Mr Higgingsly wholeheartedly replied.

Then William walked past Old Peggy's place of rest.

'Morning, Old Peggy.'

'Good morning, dear boy.'

Then past Pickpocket Sam, Maureen, then Lord Fenwick and many others.

'Morning! Morning! Morning!'

Everyone was happy.

'What a lovely day indeed,' thought William, who had now reached the wretched weeds.

And then it hit him.

'Damn!' he said out loud.

He realised he was missing his pocket knife.

William walked back to the shed but couldn't see it; He looked around his quarters but still, couldn't seem to find it.

Then it dawned on him! He must have left it in the forest. He remembered cutting some loose thin branches off the wood and putting it down on the ground when he was bagging it all up.

'Still, all is not lost,' thought William. It was promising to be a nice day, after all, especially if the sun came through the clouds. So William took a slow stroll to the woods to find his knife.

As he wandered through the woods, William smiled at the light coming through the trees. He felt as if someone, or something was saying, 'Good morning William, everything is alright.' So William nodded to the light, as if to say, 'Yes, it really is, good morning to you too.'

It was still early, and still a little bit foggy, but William liked the fog too.

His nostrils breathed in the earthy smell whilst his ears enjoyed the quietness. His skin gave slight goose bumps at the coolness and his eyes appreciated the little things such as the moss growing on the trunks of the trees. Droplets of water were dripping from large leaves and ferns, water trickled through the little creek and he could hear the sounds of birds scurrying around and the tweets from their young.

Smiling to himself, William thought that this was all amazing and as the sun broke through the trees it was as if this was the sun-dappled, ethereal beauty of God's private chapel; cool, quiet, a place of comfort and serenity.

The best thing was that apart from him, there were no humans to mess it up.

It seemed his feet had been quicker than he anticipated, as he reached the spot where he had got the wood the day before.

William looked around for his knife and after a few moments he noticed it on the ground near some twigs and leaves.

Crouching to his knees, William picked up the blade and wiped the dew off it on his leg. He was just about to put it in his pocket when he noticed the paw prints again; his eyes followed the prints, they were fresher than yesterday's, that was for sure.

As his eyes followed the paw prints past some bushes and a few trees William noticed something *beyond* the trees, something white, something bright, something moving.

Readying his blade in a mix of confusion and unease, William crept slowly *towards* the trees. A voice in his head told him he ought to be moving *away* from whatever lurked beyond the trees but something kept him moving forward.

Was it a beast of some kind, *someone*, or some ghastly wraith waiting among the willows to pounce?

As William strode forward the figure seemed to pass from sight, William breathed easy for a moment as his uneasiness alleviated. Then, unexpectedly, in a quick flash William was knocked to the ground. He had not seen it coming; it surprised him with both its grace and swiftness.

Recovering quickly, William shot up to his feet and came face to face with what had knocked him over.

William's eyes met a large white and grey mass of fur with eyes of pure ice. He felt the hairs on his neck stand on end as it raised its head and let out a loud rumble that made his body shake. The air echoed with the call of the wild as he stumbled back, whilst trying to maintain his balance. William's body shook with fear as he looked at its piercing eyes staring at him.

The beast, the creature, the wraith, was in fact, a wolf.

They circled each other, it was like the beginning of some sinister dance of death, but who would strike first, who would make the first move?

The wolf now stood in a stance of confidence; lips pulled back in a snarl, watching Williams every move.

'Come on now, boy, I don't want to hurt you my friend,' whispered William as he continued to circle the beautiful predator.

'I mean you no harm, come on boy,' continued William.

Trying to connect with the beast seemed foolish, but William could see in its eyes it was conflicted, it looked afraid, shy even. He wanted to reassure the beast he was no threat.

He got on his knees, arms far out in front of him; the wolf persisted in its engagement. William then dropped his knife close by. He looked deep into the eyes of the wolf, and he could almost feel it, like he was in sync with the creature somehow.

'I mean you no harm, boy,' William said again and offered his palm out in the air. The wolf stopped growling, still watching him though with its wary eyes. It moved forward, it was in a more normal stance now. It reached its nose out to William's hand; William felt the wetness of the nose and smiled. 'Come on, boy, I won't hurt you.'

The wolf scurried back a little, still watching him. It was as if the wolf thought he was going to be deceived somehow and all the good will of William was a mere charade.

Any thoughts that the wolf was a danger had completely vanished from William's mind. There was no way this wolf was a danger, no way in the world. Watching the beautiful beast made him giggle. The wolf was certainly more relaxed now and after five or so minutes, William was stroking it behind the ears, then across its long furry back, and then on its belly. He couldn't believe it; it was as though it were a house dog!

After playing about with the wolf for about an hour, William remembered he had to go and do his job; he had lots to do today. Feeling sad to leave his new friend, William stood up and brushed himself down, as he was covered in wolf hair.

'Well boy, I have to go,' said William with sad eyes. 'It was really great to meet you.'

William stroked the wolf's head a little playfully and started to walk.

But the wolf had other ideas.

'What? You can't come with me, boy!' laughed William who felt awful leaving but was also laughing at the way this magnificent beast had taken a liking to him.

The wolf stopped, looked up at William with eyes that said 'Don't leave me.'

'Oh, Mr Wolf! What are you doing to me?' William laughed and stopped for a second.

'Mr Wolf? No, that's no name for you is it?' William crouched down again to cuddle the wolf, and it licked his face a few times causing William to fall back on his backside.

'Hmm, I think I have a name for you, in fact, I *know* I do.'

The wolf looked at him with its beautiful fierce eyes, William smiled.

'Azrael.'

CHAPTER 28

Tuesday May 15th, Barnes Cemetery, Barnes, London

The leaden clouds moved across the sky as a quick gust of wind slapped a lock of William's black hair stingingly onto his cheek. The cold had sunk into his bones an hour ago and it looked like the weather would worsen. Still, William was used to the weather, and his spirits were high, he smiled slightly as a little tornado of leaves from green to yellow, brown to red, danced along the side of the old church. William noticed that the grey light of the day had dimmed and it would be dark in another half an hour, so he thought he'd best get his jobs done for the day.

All the weeds had been pulled, which had been William's main job for the day. In addition to his many tasks, William had even managed to do some work which was supposed to be for tomorrow. He had been ordered to dig another hole for some poor chap, apparently someone was being hanged soon and someone had footed the burial bill, which was fine by William. The only thing that concerned him was if the poor soul fitted in with the rest of the group, should he find a voice.

'Come what may,' thought William; he was getting good at letting tomorrow worry about itself. The main reason William wanted to be ahead was that if Lizzy should visit, he would have more time to talk with her.

He hoped she would visit, he really did. He yearned to see her face, her smile, her hair. He craved to hear her voice, her laugh.

Going over and above with his tasks was nothing new for William, he enjoyed doing more than he should, and during the windy day he had chatted with a few of the residents, from

Pickpocket Sam who was regretting his misdemeanours, to Old Peggy who was missing knitting, Maureen who really fancied 'a good old cuppa tea' and, of course, Mr Higgingsly, who wondered if worms had ghosts.

But it wasn't only the usual chatty spirits William checked in on, William would also try and see if some of the older residents needed anything, and yesterday's encounter with the wolf made William think about an old friend long silent.

Cyril Levy.

Cyril Levy had been a resident since William was a boy. He was one of the first William had heard, and one of the first he had helped bury, which was good for William because he was a really nice chap. William's father had made him help with the moving of the body into the coffin, and then burn Cyril's personal items.

This really saddened William, especially as a young boy. William had to make a small bonfire sometimes and burn things such as old wallets and photos. But the day William was told to burn Cyril's things, William found a book which he had kept and when he learned to read years later, he found that book mesmerizing.

William had not heard from Cyril in years and years. The two of them used to chat about a great many things. Cyril was of Jewish faith and had suffered many a grievance at the hands of people who did not understand his religion. It was maybe the ignorance of people to those who seemed different that made William and Cyril share a connection. Neither of them had ever fitted in with what folk perceived as 'normal.' Cyril would often say 'Never lose yourself William; do not change your beliefs for anybody.' This was one of many advisory quotes which William remembered throughout his life.

William felt sad that Cyril didn't speak anymore, but also in that sadness, he felt some sort of happiness that maybe, just maybe, Cyril was where he belonged now, somewhere better than here, somewhere he wouldn't be judged, where he was accepted for who he was, where he was loved.

Cyril Levy, at twenty-two years of age, was convicted of murdering a gentleman over an argument in the street. The two had bumped into one another, the so called *gentleman* said something nasty, Cyril reciprocated with an equally hasty remark, they got in a fight, the gentleman fell, hit his head and Cyril was a murderer.

That's how things were for the poor; a rich man does the same thing?

Accidental death.

A poor man does it, in this case Cyril? Guilty of murder, sentenced to death.

Cyril told William of the last sound he heard; the crack of his own neck, William always remembered that and felt ever so bad for Cyril.

So William had gone and said hello, of course there was no answer, but William told him things that had gone on over the years, about the new residents, their tales and tribulations, and of course about the main thing on his mind…

Lizzy.

CHAPTER 29

Pacing the long hallway in her home Lizzy felt slightly irritated with herself. 'What to do?' she thought as she walked backwards and forwards in indecision.

She knew what she wanted to do, she knew where she wanted to go, but more importantly, she knew *who* she wanted to see.

After deliberating her decision for almost a half hour, she sent one of her young maids outside to call her a driver to take her out as soon as possible.

Sure enough, after another ten minutes had passed, a driver turned up and knocked three slow knocks at her front door.

As she opened the door with genuine excitement of the day ahead, her look of enthusiasm was soon thwarted as she recognised the driver's face.

'Oh,' Lizzy muttered, she looked particularly bothered by the choice of driver who lowered his hat slowly and gave a sarcastic sounding 'Ma'am,' greeting.

Lizzy turned to her young maid, and ushered her away from the door, she whispered to her, 'Was there not any other driver about on the road?'

The young maid seemed genuinely apologetic, her eyes looking up at Lizzy like a puppy 'No my lady, he was the only one about; he was only around the corner and I thought you were in a rush. I will send him away and look for another one if you prefer?'

'Ah, it's alright, there'll be no need for that. Go on now, a driver's a driver after all, I will make do. Thank you.' Lizzy smiled, and then walked back to the front door where the driver who had driven her the day before waited.

She knew this man had reported to Patrick about her helping William with the wood and spending time at the church. She also knew she ran the risk of more possible future repercussions if Patrick were to enquire further.

But what was she doing wrong? The way Lizzy felt she had done nothing wrong; it was perfectly acceptable to have a friend.

'Let them talk!' she thought as she approached the mean old driver.

'You *again*, I see? Oh dear, well you may be interested to know I am in fact *again* visiting the Barnes Church, I will in fact *again* be visiting my late husband's grave and may likely, most probably in fact run into the wonderful gravedigger there, and should I do so, I will speak to him…*again*'

The driver looked befuddled 'Er…none of my business my lady, er…was just doing what the Lord told me to do.'

Lizzy moved really close to the driver, who stepped back, almost as in fear of being struck from the way Lizzy drove forward, which the driver thought most unusual for a lady 'The Lord? He is no Lord, and he has no right of supervision when it comes to me or my doings, do you understand that, *driver?*'

The driver looked submissive in his quivering stance and stuttered as he tried to answer. 'Er…yes…yes, of course, of course'

Pulling a few coins from her purse, Lizzy held them out in the air, the driver went to collect them and Lizzy snapped her hand back momentarily 'So we have an understanding then? Yes?'

'Yes, yes my lady.' The driver nodded.

Lizzy let go of the coins and the driver quickly put them in his pocket and hurried to the door of the carriage, bowing slightly as she entered. He slammed the door shut and set off, en route to William.

CHAPTER 30

After arriving at the church, Lizzy told the driver she would be taking some considerable time, and to come back to take her home at 7 o'clock that night.

'But, my lady, 7 o'clock? It will be dark then, are you sure?' asked the driver in a tone Lizzy did not appreciate.

'7 o'clock, driver and that is the end of the matter. Now go,' she instructed.

Off the driver trotted with his horses and carriage, Lizzy watched him leave in case he had decided to hang around and be nosy. She watched until the driver was way out of sight and then gave a sigh of relief, followed by a smile at the thought of the anticipated day ahead with William.

As Lizzy walked through the front gate, she took a deep breath of the chilly morning air and felt refreshed by it. Closing the gate behind her with some old rope, she turned and looked across the grave yard for any sight of William, and sure enough, about thirty yards or so away, in the far left corner of the yard, she spotted him.

William seemed to be crouching above one of the graves. Lizzy thought that he must have been tidying it up or perhaps re-arranging some flowers or something. With each step closer she could see him more clearly and as she did, she noticed he was talking.

But to whom?

Lizzy thought at first, that the Reverend may have been nearby. As she got closer she thought that really must have been the case as William was laughing now and quite hard too.

Seeing William laugh made Lizzy laugh too, it was nice to see him smiling and looking at ease. More often than not Lizzy felt that William was holding himself back when he was in her presence, like he was trying too hard to be quiet and not letting himself go, almost as if he was afraid of offending her somehow.

'Good morning there, William!' The unexpected voice came from behind William as he turned sharply to realise Lizzy was there.

'Oh my, Lizzy, I didn't even hear you coming! What a grand surprise!' said William with a huge smile that lit up his whole face. Lizzy could see William looked positively elated.

'Oh it really is great to see you, William. I hope you don't mind me turning up unannounced like this, but I thought if you needed a hand around the place then maybe I could be of service, it really is the least I could do,' smiled Lizzy.

Standing to his feet William picked up a rake which had been lying on the ground and stood beside it. Lizzy could tell he was deep in thought, but his smile gave away that he loved the idea of the two spending the day together.

'Well, it really is great to see you too, Lizzy. But the fact is that most of my tasks today are done and dusted. So I'm afraid we will have to do something else. A walk in the forest perhaps? I could show you the lake that runs by it?'

'William, that would be simply splendid,' answered Lizzy, her bright white teeth shining as she smiled.

'That's that then, sorted. I tell you what, Lizzy; I will bring an umbrella just in case we get half way down there and it decides to rain. You know what the weather's like here, predictably unpredictable! Oh, and I will leave a note for the Reverend as he has been out of town for a day; stayed at his sister's on a farm I believe. He is back this morning though, so I will just leave a quick note letting him know that everything is fine. Usually, when he has stayed at his sister's he doesn't sleep well, so comes back and sleeps most of the day! Don't tell him I told you that though, because he would tell me off.'

Lizzy looked confused whilst trying to give a polite smile. William looked at her. 'I won't be a minute,' he added and went to leave his note for the Reverend.

Pacing a few steps nearer to the graves while he went to go write his note, Lizzy looked around with curious eyes.

If the Reverend was out of town, then who was William talking to earlier?

Lizzy thought that maybe William had just been talking to himself, after all, who doesn't at some point?

She wandered slowly around the graves as she waited for William, and she couldn't help but feel sad at the many that lay in rest. The thought of the dead made her think of a poem she once heard…

Lives lived and now long past, lives that were loved, but not long do they last. Lives with a voice, touch and taste, now with nothing, oh what a waste. Lives that mattered, with drive and purpose, now gone forever, taken away from us. Lives that felt the sun and the rain, now marked by stone, it's not the same. And so we mourn, we mourn for hours, and now we meet them, to bring them flowers. Oh life, why? Why give to take? And leave us in, this eternal heartbreak.

'I'm back!' shouted William, as he hurried across the graveyard.

'So you are,' smiled Lizzy as she wiped her eyes.

'Are you upset, Lizzy?' asked William who could clearly see that she had been crying.

Taking William's arm, Lizzy nudged him slightly 'I am alright, William, now take me on this walk you have promised me.'

'I will indeed,' smiled William as he felt Lizzy's grip on his arm tighten.

The two of them walked back towards the church, Lizzy looked at William as they walked 'But the gate towards the forest is the other way, is it not William?'

'You are right, it is the other way. Now your answer to the following question will determine what we do next. The question is, do you want to know a secret?' A mischievous William said through a loveable grin.

Lizzy smiled back at him. 'Mr Rathbone, what *are* you up to, I wonder?'

Standing there, pausing as she stalled to give William his answer, Lizzy knew in her own mind there was only one answer she would ever give him and it was a resounding 'yes', but that was a fact she liked to play on, as she watched the eager anticipation in his dark eyes as he looked at her.

'So, what is your answer to be? Do you want to know the secret, or do you prefer to err on the side of caution, and not indulge in the unknown?'

Moving closer to him, Lizzy reached to William's face, he felt the warm breath on his ear as she spoke ever so quietly and ever so gently.

'Tell me William, tell me your secret.'

William moved back slightly and his eyes met hers in a gaze that could be felt, not only by the eye, but by the heart.

They held their moment, both their minds wandering to a place they yearned to explore.

Sighing in retreat, William closed his eyes for a second and re-opened them with a slight smile to see Lizzy smiling back.

They had shared a moment, a split second, an instant of connection, but it was one that William would not forget. He tried to revert back to his line of thought; it was hard to do but he nodded at Lizzy briefly and continued with his original purpose.

She watched him walk away to the tool shed which was only a few feet away; he unbolted a thick lock and unravelled a chain before he proceeded inside the shed. Lizzy heard some scuffling about and wondered what he was doing.

'Oh, William, what are you doing in there?'

As William walked out with his new friend on a chain, his secret was revealed. Lizzy's eyes scanned the large white and grey furry beast which stood before her.

'Oh my gosh!' She shouted as she stumbled back. 'William, am I mistaken? Is that not a beast … a wolf?'

William crouched down to his knees, rubbing the back of the wolf's ears and the wolf responded by rolling onto its back as William rubbed its belly.

'Fear not Lizzy, for this is my friend, my new friend. We met in the forest. In answer to your question, yes, he is a wolf, but he is no beast. He is as friendly as can be, like a house dog. I think he was lonely, in need of a friend too. Come, stroke him, he won't hurt you, I promise. Trust me.'

Lizzy walked forwards to the wolf and William and crouched down to where they were. She moved her hand towards its nose and felt the wetness of it, the wolf licked her hands, still on its back, and Lizzy joined William in rubbing its belly as it looked as happy as a little boy at play.

'I cannot believe it, William,' laughed Lizzy as she fooled around some more with the wolf. 'I cannot comprehend how you have found a *wolf*, of all things; a creature which has not been seen in these parts since I was a little girl, and brought it home! I remember my father telling stories of the woods, and *not* to go alone. I remember tales of men hunting the wolves into extinction in this area. Such a shame, such beautiful creatures, misunderstood I think. Judging by this one here at least, isn't that right, boy? Isn't that right' she laughed as she cuddled the wolf.

'Well I was still intending to go for our walk; I just figured that we could take him with us, if you did not mind, that is?'

'Mind? Of course not William. I would give you warning though, that such animals are prohibited as pets; so please, for your own sake and that of the wolf, keep it a close secret.'

'I intend to, Lizzy. I figured I would let him sleep in the tool shed and take him out during the day to the woods, let him wander a little. For food I thought I could give him my leftovers and whatever else I could find. There are always dead rabbits about here and there, so I think I will be able to keep him from being hungry.'

'I tell you what, William, after our walk. I am going to take you into town.'

Shuddering at the thought, William's concern was obvious. 'To the town? Really? For what, may I ask? I try to stay away from the town if can, my lady. Bad people say bad things, I feel most uneasy when I am there. If and when I do venture outside, I go as early as possible, to avoid the people.'

'*Outside* William, outside? Is that what you call it? We are outside now, are we not?'

'Yes but, oh it is difficult explain, Lizzy.'

'I understand, really I do. It seems to me that all this, this place, is your safe haven. That somehow, in some way this graveyard, these graves, as scary as it may be to others, is your home. Your home, your indoors, your inside. And out there, where real people roam, where real life is rife, all that *is* the outside. While you are here you are safe, with nobody to hurt you, nobody to mock you, nobody to know you. But William, there is much more than this. You deserve more. Damn those who judge, damn them all!' Lizzy smiled 'Why not just listen to the thoughts of those who care for you, those who love you, for nobody else's thoughts matter?'

The wolf sat up, and William stood to his feet, as did Lizzy.

Looking down at his own boots, William dared not look Lizzy in the eyes; his shyness returned as he prepared to lay down a truth he never thought he'd speak. 'It's just, I know it sounds like I am a coward, being so afraid of the outside world, but the truth of the fact is I am. I am not normal you see, the secret I reveal to you today with the wolf is not the only one. I have darkness in me; a darkness I fear would keep you away.'

Lizzy didn't give William the chance to bare his dark mystery, she grabbed his hands with hers, then put a finger over his lips and smiled, and she kissed him on the cheek.

'Some other time William, you have bared enough of your soul for one day. Nothing you can say will keep me away. I know you are good, William, I can see it inside of you, and I believe you judge yourself too harshly and the wrong people have spoken the wrong words in your ear. Now we will walk, with *our* new friend here, and when we return, I am taking you to the butcher's where we will buy some meat for him, and watch his little fiery eyes ignite like the street lanterns at night!'

And so they walked, they walked and talked about a great many things. It seemed the hours passed like minutes when they were in each other's company, and as the time flew like birds on a spring morning, the two of them shared thoughts, stories and common insecurities they learned were more mutual than one could have believed.

It felt comforting to both of them that they could talk openly with one another, yet William still had the itching, buried feeling of a secret yet undisclosed.

But even the thought of saying it out loud left him aghast.

He pushed such feelings as far away as he could as he gratefully accepted, enjoyed and embraced the company of Lizzy; for this was the happiest he had ever been in his whole life.

He was happy, truly happy!

She was the most beautiful girl in the world.

After walking for hours, William and Lizzy stopped deep inside the forest and sat down on the trunk of a huge fallen tree. William took the chain off Azrael and let him run free.

'Go on boy, go on Azrael,' William shouted as he relaxed his legs by sitting.

Lizzy turned to William. 'Azrael? You have given him a name?'

'Yes, indeed I have,' smiled William.

'But why one so peculiar? Why not a more traditional name such as Henry or Edward perhaps?' quizzed Lizzy.

Chuckling slightly, William loosened his boots and looked to the trees as Azrael ran deep into the forest's cloak. William could still see bits of Azrael's white fur shining through the trees as the beast ran and explored the woods.

'The name is one I read about, from a book I got from an old friend, an old friend, from an old time, a time long gone.'

Lizzy nudged William, 'Don't leave me in suspense! Go on, I am intrigued as to how you came about such a name.'

He told her about Cyril Levy and how a simple misunderstanding with a so-called gentleman led to his death by a rope from the laws of the land, in the name of an unjust justice he could never understand.

Nor ever wanted to.

He told her about the book he read which had belonged to Cyril, and which he came to own.

The book had no visible name as the front had been worn and the leather casing had peeled over time, though William believed it to be a book about some sort of mythological content, and not to be taken literally.

The characters of the book however, captured William's imagination and sometimes he would close his eyes in wonder at the things he would read.

There were stories about dragons, magic and even *death*.

The latter was what caught William's eye and his favourite character was that of Azrael. Azrael, *the Angel of Death*.

Lizzy sat focussed on William's words as he told the tale of the dark character. It was said that the name literally meant 'Whom God Helps' in an adapted form of some kind. The book referred to Azrael as the one who received the prayers of good people when they reached Heaven's gates, but he was also feared as he commanded legions of heavenly angels. Azrael was said to be the one who hunted the wicked and those unfaithful and unrepentant of their sins. He would scour the earth for the wicked, kill them and suck their souls from their bodies.

So William described all he knew of the character named Azrael, and said he gave the wolf the name because when they had met, the wolf could have killed him, but didn't. It had the power to do what it wanted, but William believed the wolf was good and sought friendship, rather than a fight, or worse. So William gave the mighty creature a mighty name, and Lizzy was in agreement that the name fitted the beast.

Such tales that William would read about Azrael and others acted as a form of escapism for him, during a time when his father beat him every other day, such tales and stories got him through somehow, but she didn't need to know that. He just liked the fact he could share the nice things with her.

Lizzy loved that William had shared the story with her; she felt William was opening up. William too, felt so happy that he could share his nice thoughts and notions, yet there were more secrets to tell, of a darker variety, but he knew that it could wait for now.

One thing at a time…

CHAPTER 31

Sunday May 21st, 1892, Barnes Cemetery, Barnes, London

It had been an eventful few weeks indeed in Barnes. Not only had William ventured out to the butcher's with Lizzy and gone into the town centre for the first time in what seemed like an age, but there had been a murder in the town. Barnes buzzed with chatter about it. Then there had been the execution of the murderer too, and the townsfolk's tongues wagged with all sorts of gossip.

And so it happened that on Wednesday 16th of May 1892, *one Thomas Miles, a human being, was found guilty of murdering Shaun Maloney, a human being, for which the punishment was death.*

It was heard in court that Thomas, at the age of 19 years, did kill the prosperous, up and coming landlord, Shaun Maloney.

It was said that Thomas owed rent, could not pay, argued with Mr Maloney and so did kill him with blows to the head of a psychotic and evil nature; to cause death was surely his only intention.

Thomas pleaded his innocence, as did his young bride-to-be, claiming he had been with her all night. But there were a few people of a more believable stature who witnessed Thomas shouting at Mr Maloney in the street that very evening. Thomas stated he was merely asking for time to pay, and then returned home without incident.

But not one was convinced of Thomas's story, nor that of his fiancée, Emma who, incidentally, was pregnant out of wedlock which was shame enough!

Who could believe such people, such beings of low moral standing?

The answer was not one person at all, and after the jury found him guilty, Thomas was taken to the gallows, and hung by the neck until he was, as the judge put it…

'*Dead, dead, dead.*'

The courts and the various legal people involved were happy with the outcome, most noticeably Mr Patrick Fenwick, who was the prosecutor in the case, claiming it was 'Good justice delivered indeed.'

That was how it went, and on the following Sunday, the 21st, Thomas Miles was buried at Barnes Cemetery, Barnes, London.

Apart from Emma, his pregnant partner, there were no others to mourn. The Reverend said some words for the boy and tried to comfort the young girl.

Afterwards she lay at the grave weeping, inconsolably.

William watched her from afar, he didn't think it his place to speak to her, but he felt so sad for the girl as it was obvious she had loved the boy dearly.

He wanted to tell her it was alright, he wanted to tell her time heals; he wanted to say the boy was in a better place.

But William knew that not to be true.

As the days passed William watched over young Thomas's grave for signs of a voice, and surely enough, about a week after being buried, Thomas's soul, found just that.

It was a young voice, a gentle voice, a voice of regret and as William later discovered a voice of great interest…

CHAPTER 32

When a new soul found their voice the other residents would try and help as much as they could. Mr Higgingsly would usually be the first to introduce himself, and then the others would follow suit. During Thomas's first day as an awakened spirit, he met Pickpocket Sam, Mr Higgingsly, and Maureen Templeby as well as Lord Fenwick and Old Peggy.

Thomas was surprisingly calm throughout the whole process and seemed to find a level of acceptance very quickly. William found this quite bizarre given the fact he had a child on the way and a young beloved whom he could now never marry.

Still, William preferred Thomas to be as he was, there was nothing worse than a new spirit riling up the old and causing fuss.

But there was something about this boy, this man, this ghoul, that William found odd. William sensed a great burden, stronger than usual.

Most of the spirits William had spoken to felt a certain deal of injustice for the way they died. 'Too soon' was a common thing said, along with 'why me?' and in Mr Higgingsly's case 'I can't believe *I* died! There is no more *me!*'

With Thomas it was his silence which spoke to William, and William thought it correct and proper that they spoke in private.

So, with that in mind, William instructed the other spirits not to listen in, and they all agreed respectfully, even the reluctant Mr Higgingsly agreed, though he was most put out to say the least, claiming, 'Nobody tells me anything anymore!'

Speaking to Thomas was a task, even for William who was used to talking to the dead. Thomas was a quietly spoken lad; he had manners, was polite and seemed so very caring.

William thought it odd this young man was capable of murder!

After a few days, and a few gentle chats with William, Thomas finally opened up, and what he said concerned William greatly.

William was due to see Lizzy; she was coming by to take Azrael to the woods. She had said the day before she had some fresh meat from the butcher's. William had accused Lizzy of spoiling Azrael, but the wolf certainly didn't mind, licking his lips whenever Lizzy turned up with a steak wrapped in brown paper.

Before William stepped outside that morning, he checked the clock and knew he had over an hour to chat to Thomas, as Lizzy was due at 10 am, the usual time. So William sat by Thomas's grave and the two chatted away, it was only a few minutes until Thomas broke down in tears, which was of no surprise at all to William.

Every spirit cries eventually, after all, they are dead.

'Now, now, Thomas, come on lad, there, there,' whispered William in comfort.

'But Emma, my unborn child, what will become of them? I did no wrong sir, I tell you I did no wrong!'

William didn't know what to say, what could he say? That in fact he had been convicted of a heinous crime known to all as murder?

No, William wouldn't say that, he didn't feel it was his place to judge, for in William's mind even if someone had done something bad, most would repent. And if they paid the ultimate price then they were surely square with the house again.

But some in the area did not have as much tact…

'No wrong? No wrong you say, well I do not take personal satisfaction from stating the obvious, young boy, but us spirits *do* talk you know. And word round the deadites is you were hanged, and hanged for murder no less. So, young man, on the current news we go by, I'd say you did plenty wrong, plenty wrong indeed!'

'Mr Higgingsly! Must you? You gave your word, I would remind you!' snapped William.

'Really, old chap,' added Lord Fenwick. 'You really can't help yourself can you?'

Mr Higgingsly huffed and puffed. 'Well excuse me for stating the obvious; once again the seeker of truth and justice is chastised for telling it as it is!'

'Keep your opinions to yourself will you? Or the seeker of…whatever you say, will find weeds and nettles planted at his grave!'

'Oh, the cheek!' shouted Mr Higgingsly.

'Quiet!' replied William.

After a few loud moments, the atmosphere became still.

'I just can't believe the way things have turned out, sir. I have failed everyone, my father's name, my unborn child and my future wife; myself,' cried Thomas. 'I am such a failure,' he added.

It was hard to know what to say to Thomas, and William knew he didn't have the answers, but what William was good at, was listening, and afterwards just being a friend. William didn't try and pretend he could solve the dead people's problems, give sound advice or unravel the afterlife's riddles, but he was a kind face in time of need, and the ghosts of Barnes cemetery loved him for it.

After Thomas had calmed down somewhat, William attempted to get him to focus on the good he had had. 'For the love of a woman is a beautiful thing,' explained William. William also mentioned to Thomas that he would live on, through his child, and tried to ask Thomas to seek comfort from the fact that a part of him would go on in the world forever.

Thomas liked the idea of that, and for the first time in days, he felt a little less depressed.

Leaving Thomas for around a half hour, William came back with some fresh flowers; he put them on Thomas's grave and sat beside the less than extravagant headstone.

William looked at the headstone and back to the mud of the earth.

'Not very good is it, I bet?' laughed Thomas

'You can see already?' asked William.

'No,' Thomas replied, 'but the rest explained it will come in time. Was I right? Is my headstone cheap and tatty?'

William brushed some dust off the headstone with his hands. 'No. Thomas, it's not that bad, not bad at all'

'William,' laughed Thomas, 'I've not known you long, but you don't strike me as a fibber. Come on William, give it to me like it is. Is it straight even, a decent stone? Oh please tell me my name is spelt right, tell me that much!'

Looking up and down at the masonry, William did give a little grin. He didn't mean anything by it; he just knew who had cut the stone because he recognised the work.

'Thing is, Thomas, oh and I sound so wicked to say it out loud. I know the work, not that it isn't satisfactory; it is, believe me, it is. But I know this must have been the work of Old man Bubbles, y'know? The one they call Bubbles Baker on Lawn Street?'

'Yes, I knew *of* him? Oh no, he was a drunk, wasn't he? Oh, please tell me Emma didn't go to him! Oh no!' Thomas laughed, even though he knew the joke was on him, literally.

'Yes, that's the one,' chuckled William. 'Thing is, as I said, *your* work is not *too* bad, but when you can see, if you don't like his work, I will re-do it for you, free of charge. But the thing which caused me to cluck, was an old mistake he made, many years ago'

'Oh, do tell William, I need a laugh!'

As he got ready to tell his story, William stuffed some old, moist tobacco into his pipe, sat back, lit it and readied his tale.

Inhaling deeply, William laughed again. 'He got this job once, a Lord from the other side of town, anyways; this fancy Lord's missus had sadly pegged it due to a bad case of the flu. Now the Lord was Lord Abbass, tradesman, merchant, self-made man, who was to be admired for his drive and success. So obviously, this man with such stature wanted a lovely headstone, befitting of his beloved wife; thing was, Bubbles liked whisky. Bubbles liked whisky so much so, he did the unthinkable. He worked whilst drunk. The rest I am sure you can imagine, the large funeral, the pretty flowers, no expense was spared. But as the Reverend was saying his piece, he read the headstone (as most Reverends do so they get the name right) to read something like 'Oh dear Mrs….and instead of Abbas, he said…Abbess!'

'Oh no! He didn't? Did he?' laughed Thomas in shock.

'He surely did Thomas, he said Mrs Abbess, and as you know, in these parts Abbess means Madame, or in other words a brothel keeper! Now it would have been an insult to any but to a Lord and Lady. Needless to say, his work kind of dwindled a little after that'

'Ha-ha!' Thomas laughed 'Oh William, you really have cheered me up!'

William also heard sniggers from further afield in the graveyard.

'Eavesdroppers!' laughed William, he knew it was Higgingsly; it was something Higgingsly would find more amusing than most.

The air became quiet again and William thought that maybe Thomas was done talking for now. William stood to his feet and prepared to leave Thomas in peace until Thomas spoke again.

'William?'

'Yes, my friend?'

'I didn't do it, you know.'

'Do what?'

'Kill that man. I didn't do it.'

'Thomas, you do not have to prove anything to me, lad.'

'But I didn't, and it's important to me, if we are to be friends for I guess what could be a while, that you know that of me, for I am not a bad man. Will you let me give you my account of events?'

'If you really want to Thomas, if it makes you feel better.'

'Well, I wouldn't say better, but the quick version was this. It weren't me sir. I can say it now, after all, they can't kill me twice can they?' laughed Thomas

'What happened was I'd gone to Mr Maloney's house that night, that much was true, couldn't afford his high rents, kept putting them up you see. So, I asked for another few days, was going to do a little boxing at the old gentlemen's club for a few bob, which would have sorted me square. But he wouldn't have it. Anyway, he was going somewhere so we squabbled from his front door out into the street. We continued to argue until I reached my house and that's where I left him. I walks in, Emma has cooked me some pie and potatoes; I sat down, ate it, and reads my new book I'd borrowed from my boss at the factory, lights my pipe, I'm set for the night. Emma had gone to bed, tired ya' see from being with child n' all. Anyways, about half before midnight, I hears' some squabbles outside. I thought it was late for such commotions, and I looked out the window. Could only see shadows though, I counted four men in all, and in the shadow of the night lanterns I could see arms swinging and blows being struck, I tell you! Me missus woke up, I tells her to get back to bed, not to worry. I goes' outside to see what the fuss was about. Goes down, and these three men were stood over another man, all with fists readied and tough faces. Well, they saw me watching; one even pulled what looked like a razor, thought I was done for! But then, one of them said something to the other two. I couldn't make out what, and luckily they ran away, ran fast away they did. Well, I couldn't leave a poor chap all hurt on the floor, so I goes over, rolls the man over, and who is it but Mr Maloney! Now, we didn't get on, for that was no secret, but I didn't wish the man dead, by any means! I panicked a little because I know nothing of nursing and such, I shouted out 'Police, get the police, get a doctor!' A few neighbours down the street opened their windows, sees me with Mr Maloney. Now I know how it must have looked, but then they shouted', 'Police, Police!' Surely enough the Police came to the scene, I had blood on my hands, was out of breath. They blamed me for it. Neighbours said they saw me arguing over my rent affairs, for them lazy coppers it was enough of a motive. I then get the noose.'

'Oh my goodness, Thomas, that is awful!' gasped William 'Did you tell the police?'

'Well, I was going to, I made a statement when they pulled me in, a copper called Harvey brought me some legal people in, and this legal man, some Mr Fenwick or whatever, says I couldn't say that, to retract my statement, says to listen to him or they would kill me, kill my wife after she'd given birth and put my child in the orphanage. He said not to mention the three men, to stay quiet, plead guilty to manslaughter and that I would do a year or two! He did me like a kipper! Never expected the death penalty! So that legal man Fenwick did my statement, I signed it like a numpty and crank! My neck got stretched good and proper! That, William, is the whole and honest truth!'

Facing the air, with his eyes closed, deep in thought, William felt unsettled. 'You say there were three men, Thomas?'

'Three sir, indeed'

'What did they look like? Can you recollect?'

Thomas was quiet for a moment as he tried to remember the fateful night, then it came to him 'There was a large man, fat I'd even say. He was the one who pulled the razor, had a hat on, a cap even.'

Shaking his head, William interrupted Thomas's flow 'The cap, any sort of pattern on it?'

'Err, maybe, it was dark ya 'see, if it was it was like lines or something'

'Stripes?' asked William.

'Yes! Like stripes, how do you know, William?'

'Wait Thomas; please go on for a minute'

'Right then, the other man was small, scruffy, looked like his clothes didn't quite fit him, like one of them beggars on Old Dagger Lane, you know the type?'

'I do, Thomas, and the other?'

'Tall, skinny man, when he spoke to the other two the light from the street lanterns briefly lit his face and as he spoke I could see he had a dark mouth, like there was no white on his teeth, looked quite scary really'

Thomas's description made William feel sick, he was shocked and the words had such impact he began to feel dizzy.

'William? William, are you there?' asked Thomas who at his early stage of deadness could not yet see beyond the grave.

Panting a little, as if in sudden panic, William tried to speak through his own erratic breaths, 'I....I....'

'What's up, William? Whatever is the matter?'

'I... I think I know of the men whom you describe'

'Know of them, how?'

'The tall man with black teeth, the fat man with cap and razor, the untidy man with baggy clothes. They are the fiends who attacked me in the graveyard! Left me within an inch of my life. Damn grave robbers they are!'

'Oh my word, William, what if they're the same men? They are roaming the streets, perhaps even doing more bad! What will you do, William? You have to do something!'

Composing himself as his breathing calmed down, William stood to his feet. It was nearly time for Lizzy to come. 'I have to think about this, Thomas, *we* will have to talk about this some more. Then, if we are beyond doubt, I will take it to the police.'

'But William, please be careful, for I fear that this trio of evil are protected somehow, and I fear the police could be the ones doing so!'

'Fear not, Thomas, for if I bring this to attention, it will be to the only policeman I trust, a true and kind man of virtue, incapable of corruption'

'Well, forgive me for being uneasy, William, but my current predicament makes me unable to share your trust in the police. Are you sure?'

'Yes, this policeman is the best. Mr Robertson would have no part in such plots. We will revisit this conversation soon; I have to go.'

'All right, William, bye!'

'Bye, Thomas,' said William as he strode away.

CHAPTER 33

In light of what Thomas proclaimed, William felt a burden he aimed to ease. Deciding to have a quick puff on his pipe, William pushed the thoughts of the last hour to the back of his mind.

The last thing he wanted to do was spoil his time with Lizzy.

His mind rattled with theories about what Thomas had said, though he would not forget about the issues, the man had paid with his life, perhaps for a crime he did not commit.

Was he innocent? Could it be? William had flashbacks to the men who attacked him. Was it the same three? If so, then why did Patrick want to protect them? Was it all just a simple coincidence?

Or maybe it was something more sinister?

As he inhaled his pipe, William turned his mind to sweeter things and as he did with closed eyes he saw her face clearly in his mind's eye, her beauty was unabated, her eyes unmatched, her hair unmistakable. He loved the moments when he could close his eyes in peace and think of her, and wait for her in sweet anticipation.

Just as he savoured his gratifying thoughts, a scent breached the thick cloud of tobacco smoke and made its way to William's nose.

It was the most polite of invasions, as William breathed the scent deep down into his lungs, he realised the origin of the magnificent aroma, as hollow footsteps could be heard approaching.

It was jasmine.

It was Lizzy.

Rushing out of his quarters, William met Lizzy at the door; she was smiling like a Cheshire cat as her eyes met his. She stopped as she saw him and then she stood straight and proper.

'Well, good morning, dear William,' she said politely.

'Good morning, Lizzy,' William replied.

Lizzy noticed William's fingers fidgeting; William placed his hands in his pockets.

'Well, William, today I have a surprise for you.'

His eyes opening wide, William could not hide his smile, he tried to, but failed miserably.

'A surprise? For me? How have I earned such a treat?'

'You do not have to earn such William; I do it because I want to. Now, can I tear you away from your work for a few hours?'

Looking around from left to right around the graveyard, William tried to think of an excuse not to venture outside the gates.

But William's normal feelings of trepidation towards venturing out betrayed him, as another part of his being so desperately wanted to be with her.

Stuttering in indecision, William took a stand.

Why not go outside? Why not follow one's heart? Why not be happy?

William smiled as he saw Lizzy anxiously await his answer. 'Yes, why not? After all, I started work early again and I do not have any new…well, I've no digging to be done.'

'Then it is settled' smiled Lizzy, 'although I do have a further proposal.'

'Which is?'

'I wondered, in the most subtle sense of the word, if you would care to leave a day a week open? Now, I am well aware you have your work and also I am aware that to have enough time is awfully vital, but I just thought that if we had the time to spend together we could really have the most wonderful of times. Adding to which, I think I owe you, William.'

Taken aback, William's eyebrows raised at Lizzy's words. 'Owe me? How?'

'You have shown me so many lovely things, as they are meant to be seen, the forest in all its majestic glory. You have introduced me to Azrael, the most magnificent of pets any could dare to play with! But most of all, you have brought into my life a friend, a voice, a presence. You William, you are the greatest gift of all.'

William was positively stunned.

He moved towards her, he could see her tremble as he did so, he held out his arm.

She took it.

CHAPTER 34

After the day of Lizzy's proposal, it came to be that Wednesday of every week was a pencilled in day for William and Lizzy to spend time together.

As the weeks passed, so did a month, and then two.

Every day they weren't together seemed to drag so much, and when Wednesday came, both would wake with the joyous spring of a child on Christmas morning.

A blessed time for them both it had been, and yet deep inside William, a need was developing, he wanted to see her more. More and more and more.

Lizzy's feeling echoed William's and as the weeks progressed, so did her needs as a woman. She looked at William in a way she dared not confess.

Did he feel the same? Were his intentions solely those of friendship?

Or something more?

Did he feel the love that was undoubtedly building inside her fragile heart?

They both felt the same, but they equally dared not put purpose to their feelings as they both feared the outcome.

It was as if their love would be outlawed, forbidden, cast out with the wrongs of the wrongdoers!

The days they spent together had been marvellous. They took turns in deciding where they spent their time. One week, Lizzy would come to William, and the other week, William would go to Lizzy's house. They did a variety of things. William would take Lizzy out with Azrael to the forest; they strolled in perfect harmony as they would watch Azrael run around. Lizzy would find a small branch from a tree and have Azrael play 'fetch' like a house dog. Azrael loved to play, it was as if he didn't know what animal he was, and it made both William and Lizzy laugh at how a beast with such power could be so tame and lovingly loyal. Once they had played and ran and laughed, they would stop and enjoy a small picnic, if the weather permitted, they did this every other week, and it never got old.

The time at Lizzy's consisted of other activities.

One day, Lizzy introduced William to the game of chess. As a lady she was never expected to play, but Lizzy's father taught her, being a man of a modern mind and wanting to make sure Lizzy developed a strong mind of her own.

Her father's plan most definitely worked.

Lizzy explained all there was to know, and on the first day of teaching chess to William she went through the basics. William hung on her words, loving the concept of a game he never knew existed.

She looked at him sternly; the pieces were all laid out in proper position. 'William, never forget that the king is the most important piece in the game. Although he can only move one space at a time, if your king is captured, you lose the game.'

William nodded.

Lizzy moved her fingers to another piece. 'The queen is also a very important piece in the game. She can move any way she wants, as many spaces as she wants, which makes her a favourite piece amongst chess players. The queen represents herself in the game. The bishop can move diagonally. The bishop represents the church and religion and is located on either side of the king and the queen. Then you have the knight which is another self-representing piece. The knights can move in an L-shape. The knight piece is actually that of a horse's head, because that's what knights rode. In medieval times, knights weren't poor, as you may think. On the contrary, only the highly educated and wealthy men could become a knight. At the end of the second row, there stands the castle, which represents the castle's walls, which protect the king, queen, bishop, and knights. The pawns represent the serfs, or peasants, who had to pay money to live on the king's land. Although they aren't really there to "protect," they stand in the front row, kind of like cannon-fodder!'

William scratched his chin; he looked up to Lizzy and smiled.

She smiled back, 'Understand?'

'William bit his lip slightly with a befuddled look. 'Er…'

Lizzy laughed. 'Look, dear William, the way to play is to think you are controlling a medieval battle. 'PROTECT THE KING'!'

They both laughed, and as the weeks passed by quickly, William's ability grew stronger as Lizzy taught him the various *do's* and *don'ts* of the chessboard.

As well as chess, Lizzy had a huge passion for music, and it was a passion she *had* to share with William.

July 26th, Woodworth Manor, Barnes, London

Pulling up the collar of his coat to protect himself from the rain, William couldn't believe it was July and muttered such as he walked up the steps of Woodworth Manor's front entrance. He shook the rain off himself like a wet dog, then, carefully, he took off his jacket as he entered the porch way, just near the huge wooden front door.

William also removed his hat and brushed his long black hair backwards from his face. The hat had not kept much rain off him, as his hair was still wet; he shook it to try and dry it a little, then he wiped his wet hands on his trouser legs.

Just as William was about to use the huge knocker to alert Lizzy, the door opened, smile met smile as Lizzy and William's eyes met.

'Oh, William, do come in!' laughed Lizzy as she noticed the rain outside. 'I should have had a driver come and pick you up. Here give me your coat and I shall dry it by the fire, can you believe the rain? The clouds, it is so dark for this time in the morning. I have been cold these last few days; have had to have some firewood brought in, in July! Fancy that!'

She was as happy as ever, and William loved to see her so.

Following Lizzy into the warm fire-lit room, William wondered what was on the agenda for the day, not that he cared; he just loved the time they spent together and thought of every day with her as a true blessing. It was still early, just before 10 o'clock and William smiled at the thought of another great day ahead. 'So Lizzy, what are we doing today? Some more chess? Some more lawn tennis maybe? Although I can't say it's the weather for it and I am still not wearing them white clothes you tried to make me wear last time! Or perhaps a book? You choose!'

After hanging William's coat over a small metal rack near the fire, Lizzy returned with a cheeky grin.

'No,' said Lizzy, her head rose as if cross, William knew she was playing as she stormed out of the room, her grin betraying her playful deceit.

'No?' William laughed as he followed Lizzy out of the room and down the hallway into another big room, one which he had not been in before. He looked around the room which was lit by scattered candles... There was not much in the room apart from the candles, two small chairs nearby, and something under a huge sheet. William watched the candle flames flicker as he noticed a window near the covered object was open, and the draft from the window chilled the air.

Lizzy looked really excited, William could tell she had something up her sleeve by her failure to hide her smile.

'Why are we *here*, do I hear you ask?' she smiled

'I didn't,' laughed William.

'You were certainly about to!'

'All right then, I was. Why are we *here*, Lizzy?'

Lizzy walked towards the window where the sheet was covering the object it was hiding.

'We are *here*, dear William, because today I have for you, another treat! Something splendid and I do really *think* you will love it, I do really *hope*, you love it!'

Puzzled by Lizzy's imminent surprise, William merely stood buoyantly, wondering what was feeding Lizzy's colossal enthusiasm.

Standing in front of the object in a perfect poise, Lizzy looked almost regal to William and he again thought …

'I must be the luckiest man in this world, to be spending time with her'

'Are you ready William?' she asked

'I am ready Lizzy; at least, I think I am!'

'Are you sure? Because now, I introduce to you, my favourite item in the house. If all were to burn into ruin and I could but save one single item, it would be this…'

Pulling back the off-white coloured sheet Lizzy revealed something that made William's eyes widen.

'Is that, what I think it is?'

'It certainly is!' shrieked Lizzy as she ran her hands across it. 'This is my D'Almaine cottage piano!'

'Oh Lizzy, it certainly is beautiful! How long have you had it? Do you play?'

'I do indeed, William, I love to play. I received it from my father as a present. He came by it in 1852, I believe, and from what I am told, but not supposed to know, he won it in a card game! Imagine that! Come and see it, William.'

William looked at the beautiful piano, his eyes scouring the details from the wonderfully crafted hexagonal wooden legs to the pretty flower patterns on the piano lid.

'I love the flowers on the lid,' remarked William, 'Very pretty, very well done'

'The lid is known as the 'Fall', William, and on the inside of the fall there are flowers too; my father said the flowers reminded him of me.'

'He sounds like a man who was well informed.' smiled William.

Lizzy bit her lip, trying her very best not to look ecstatic at William's hinted compliment.

Taking one of the vacant seats at the piano, Lizzy opened the fall and brushed her fingers against the keys with her eyes closed, she kept them closed as she spoke...

'William, I want you to sit by me in the empty chair. I am going to play a piece for you, the name of the piece I will reveal in a minute, but before I do, know that this is a piece of magnificence.'

As Lizzy instructed, William took the seat just behind her. He wasn't too close, but he was close enough to smell the jasmine perfume she wore, close enough to smell her hair, close enough to feel her hair on his face when the draft from the window blew it close as he closed his eyes.

Lizzy breathed in deeply and sighed as she remembered her late father playing the same piece she was about to play for William.

'This piece William, is Beethoven, you may have heard of him. I love the starting part in particular. If you close your eyes and imagine, it seems to lead you, as if one is to embark on a new road. I have so many thoughts on the piece, and sometimes they change with time. When my father died I hated this piece as I thought it mimicked the toll bell, as if it were tolling the end of a day, the end of a life. The story of this piece goes that Beethoven was taking a walk at dusk, when he heard a piano playing, it was his own composition. He peered into a window of a poor house. Inside, a young teenage blind girl was struggling at her piano. A man (her father I believe) was fixing some old shoes next to her. The girl commented how hard it was to play the piece, and wished to hear Beethoven himself play it. The shoemaker agreed, but sadly said they didn't have enough money for it. His heart aching, Beethoven pitied them so much, he walked in and they let him play it for them. While he was playing, the girl sat by the window. A cool breeze blew in and blew out the candle. The girl was beautiful in the moonlight, like a marble statue, and Beethoven was moved, and suddenly began to compose the piece I am about to play. He composed as he played, and the man and girl were caught in this breath-taking music. He left quickly when he was finished, and it wasn't until after he had left that the two people in the house realized who he was. Beethoven then went home and wrote the piece down.'

Readying her fingers to play, Lizzy turned slightly to look at William; his eyes were closed and he was smiling, this made her happy, he was absorbing her words and she loved it.

'This piece, William, is the Moonlight Sonata'

She started to play the piece and William kept his eyes closed as his ears accepted the beautiful music, and as he consumed the thought of his most recent times with Lizzy. It was as if the Sonata itself was a budding romance in the first movement, and reminded him of the feelings he felt since he met her; feelings of a fresh love in a place where the world seemed perfect; A place, where the two of them could live in a world of their own and live by the rules of love as they knew them.

He imagined the love blossoming as the second movement came. As if the two of them were feeling something, something that could only be described as a higher level of love.

As he listened, his heart raced as he thought of feelings of a physical nature which mingled with romance and thoughts so sweet they were almost overpowering.

William's imagination ran wild and as the third movement came, he felt sad as his worst fears surfaced. He imagined the romance turning sour, filled with conflicting emotions. He thought of the horrible man, Patrick, the people in the town who mocked him, the excuses of mean people, arguments, jealousy, emotions going wild, and finally the graves with souls long forgotten.

As Lizzy finished the piece she turned to William, she touched his hands with hers, then she moved her right hand to his face. The wind and rain from outside blew fiercely through the open window, and one after another the candles started to blow out.

William opened his eyes; he felt her touch before he saw it, he looked at her, her eyes cried tears, but they were not tears of sadness. He then realised, as she wiped his face with her hands that he had been crying too.

The moment was one of sheer beauty, and William looked deep into Lizzy's eyes and nodded as she tilted her head with a lovely sincere smile.

'It, er…kind of got to me I think. But Lizzy, that…was…beautiful. Thank you'

'Thank you William, I knew you would love it,' answered Lizzy, as she rushed off behind him to wipe her eyes; she tried to deflect the thoughts she was having by continuing to talk about the music. 'The presto agitato is quite the most anxious piece of music I've ever heard - the anxiety, frustration and simmering anger is almost palpable. I'd say, wouldn't you agree?'

'I would Lizzy, I would indeed.' William stood up; he could still feel his heart racing. He wanted to grab her, to kiss her, but he knew if he did he could undo all the good that had transpired between them, for surely she did not feel the same?

But what if she did? What if he was wrong? His mind was like two separate entities, one side representing his heart arguing the 'for' and the other side representing his mind arguing the 'against', almost like William's thoughts were in a courtroom, and he was on trial.

He looked at Lizzy, she had turned to him, her eyes still red but her cheeks now rid of tears after she had wiped them away.

William nodded to her again and had a deep thought…

'If I was on trial for my feelings, then I'd be guilty, as guilty as one could ever be, guilty of loving you.'

CHAPTER 35

August 4th, Barnes Police Station, Barnes, London.

Constable Henry Ravensdale was a man criminals feared in Barnes. His frame of 6 feet 4 inches made most who dared to oppose him think twice.

He was mean, nasty, crude and his patience was as short as his police truncheon. The strength of the club was not to be underestimated though, as one hard strike from a man as large as Ravensdale could crack a skull with ease.

It had been a trying day, and Ravensdale was ready for some food once he got home. An hour earlier he had arrested a pickpocket in the market square, catching him red-handed.

After catching the 'little toe-rag' as he called such, he gave him a few good hits across the legs as punishment, so hard that the young man, of around fifteen years of age, could hardly walk, so Ravensdale dragged him through the streets, booked him, and threw him in the station's holding cell, ready for court the following day.

Ravensdale joked with a few other policemen in the front entrance of the station, commenting on how funny it was to see the criminal cry. As the policemen laughed at Ravensdale, who was equally feared by his peers, Constable Robertson walked up, with a face as stern as a judge.

'Who, arrested the boy thief?' asked Mr Robertson as he looked around from left to right, awaiting an answer. 'I repeat, who arrested the boy thief?'

After lifting his eyebrows to his colleagues, Ravensdale turned to Mr Robertson and shrugged his huge shoulders. 'Me, why?'

'Why? Do you realise that the boy has legs as black and blue as the uniforms we wear? He can hardly walk!'

Ravensdale sniggered. 'So? Boy's a thief, shouldn't have ran. I'd have given him more than that if I could; I tell you that for nothing!'

Mr Robertson moved closer to Ravensdale 'You, I expect better from. You are a police constable. To set an example, *not* to go around clubbing people in the middle of a street, no less, in front of good people, in front of women, children even! You should be ashamed of yourself man'

'Whose side are you on? I beat him, yes, what is all the fuss?'

Mr Robertson had grown tired of men of the law like Ravensdale and those like him in his station. He liked to make examples of such men who abused their power.

Pointing to the front door of the station, Mr Robertson had had enough. 'Home, now. Do not come in tomorrow, a one day's pay loss too.'

'What? A day's pay! Oh, I can't believe this!'

'Make that two days' pay, then you can think about what you did. If you still don't see the wrong you did, don't come back at all.' barked Mr Robertson.

Slamming the thick wooden door on his way out made the other men who were present jump, and Mr Robertson noticed he had the full attention of his constables.

'Let that be a warning to *all*. We are the police, not criminals, not bullies, police. Let this be a reminder of how NOT to act. For the next man I catch doing such deeds will not be met with as much leniency. Now I don't like deducting a day's pay from any man, but this was not the first time. He must learn or he must leave. It is as simple as that.'

Mr Robertson walked away from the men who had hurried back to work after his warning. His intention was to check on the boy again, to see if the swelling had gone down on his legs when out of the blue, a voice called.

'Oh er…Constable Robertson, may I have words?'

After turning to see who was talking to him, Mr Robertson couldn't hide his disappointment.

'Ah, you, what can I do for you, *sir*?'

With his ever-present detestable grin, Patrick Fenwick exhibited his yellowy-white, tobacco-stained teeth to Mr Robertson.

'Mr Robertson, is that any way to treat a good friend, a fellow man of the law even?'

Giving a tired fake laugh, Mr Robertson was in no mood for Patrick's usual ear pollution. 'Sir, it is late in the hour, and I have much to do, as I am sure you can appreciate, what, may I do for you?'

Walking towards Mr Robertson, Patrick placed his arm on Mr Robertson's shoulder in a rough fashion, as if they were long lost friends 'Oh, my old favourite bobby! I am here on behalf of the courts, sir. Slow week this week, seems people are behaving themselves!'

'Oh, and we can't have that now, can we? Imagine that eh? People are committing less crime, means we may be doing something well after all! A good thing I'd say?'

Gripping Mr Robertson's shoulder more tightly, Patrick didn't seem to take to Mr Robertson's sarcasm. 'Well, of course that would be wonderful, if it were true. But there are some people, not me of course, but some people, maybe people down at the court house who don't think that, you see. There are also some who think that, dare I say it? Criminals are getting off with 'harsh warnings' then are being freed to roam the streets. Then there are *some* that think that maybe, well, of course this would be absurd, but maybe, the police are not doing their jobs properly? Of course, *I* couldn't believe such nonsense but if such nonsense were true, and let's say, certain people got wind of it, maybe a judge or a councillor perhaps, then maybe, *just maybe*, the funding could be cut here, men would lose their jobs for heaven's sake! How awful would that *be*?'

Mr Robertson reached up and grabbed Patrick's arm; it was stiff so he pushed it off with force. 'Are you threatening me, Patrick?'

Patrick smiled at Mr Robertson and headed for the door as he pulled an elegant silver pipe out of his jacket. 'Not at all sir, I am just sharing some thoughts; that's all, my good man, nothing doing here, eh? Well, I will be off, farewell to you!'

'Farewell to you too!' Mr Robertson shouted 'Oh, I would so like to shove that posh pipe right up his…'

Mr Robertson drew looks of disapproval from his men as he stormed off back to work, because when all was said and done, Patrick Fenwick was a powerful man. They knew it, Mr Robertson knew it, but worst of all, Patrick Fenwick knew it too.

As Patrick got outside and into the street, he prepared for his overdue smoke. So after stuffing some tobacco into his patterned silver pipe, he positioned it to his craving chops and prepared for a good old smoke.

But then, disaster, he had left his matches at the courthouse!

'Oh, of all the rotting luck of a beggar!' Patrick said out loud, all the time his eyes scouring for the sight of someone smoking.

Then, a saviour appeared, it seemed a man, a policeman no less, was enjoying the sweetness of his pipe, a sweetness Patrick desired, and needed so very much.

As he trotted over in a brisk fashion, Patrick was blunt with his greeting; he *needed* that smoke!

Patrick got close and tilted his pipe in the man's direction. 'Ah sir, could you do me the honour?'

'Why can't you just come over and talk to me, Fenwick?'

Patrick made hard eyes at the man, 'Shush, I do not want to arouse any suspicion. I saw you storming off earlier as I entered the station, problems?'

'Yes, there are problems. That too-good, know-it-all, codswallop boss of mine. Telling me who I can-and-can't arrest, who I can-and-can't hit. I mean for heaven's sake, I thought we were supposed to *fight* crime?'

Breathing in his first puff of his pipe, Patrick felt at ease again. 'Ah, magic! Oh, you were saying, Ravensdale?'

'That old wet wellington; he is always having words with me, I am sick of it, I tell you.'

'Do not worry yourself with such things, Harvey. You see, you should think of me as the conductor who *controls* the orchestra, managing speed, dynamics and instructing each instrumental section when to enter, and so forth. You are part of that orchestra. All you have to do is wait for my command and then we will fall into sweet synchronisation and let great things happen'

Ravensdale looked unmoved. 'You say these things, like things will improve for me, but when? I am arresting more and more, doing my best to fill the courts, but sometimes old man Robertson will let them go! He questions my judgement!'

Patrick looked around the busy streets at people coming and going from place to place. 'Rats, aren't they? All of them, busy, busy rats. I hate rats, they mess good things up. I think we have a rat, in that station, messing up our plans. It will be dealt with in time, I assure you. What about our other friends? Are they doing as asked?'

'As always sir, although they need payment for their latest…outing.'

Reaching into his pocket, Patrick bustled around and pulled out an old brass pocket watch 'Here, you know I will not give them straight money. So give this to one…'

Patrick handed over the watch and continued the fumbling around in his deep coat pockets with the pipe hanging out of his mouth

'Give these to the other one,' Patrick added as he handed over some gloves. 'Proper deerskin dress gloves they are, should fetch a decent price'

Ravensdale placed the items inside his jacket above his belt and shielded them with one arm 'What about the other one, sir. You can't give two out of three, you know what they are like, argue like kids they do!'

'Oh, hang on a minute,' snapped Patrick as he puffed on the last bit of tobacco from his pipe 'Here, here you go' he snarled 'that good enough? Nothing else for a month now, these leeches are bleeding me dry!'

'Oh Fenwick, they'll fight over that for sure,' Ravensdale laughed as he looked over the pipe Patrick had parted with.

'I have another pipe, not to worry, a better one at that. Just make sure they do as I ask'

Ravensdale nodded. 'What for this month? Any more landlords need 'retiring'? Or some more treasure hunts at the graveyard, perhaps?'

'No, but I do have some more needs in the case of my late brother's wife.'

'You want her watched again?'

'Yes, more closely than before, I want to know where she is, with whom she speaks, everything.'

'Is that it, sir?'

'One more thing, do you know of that imbecile, the one who digs the graves?'

'The weird one sir? Don't like him, he makes my skin crawl, no good he is'

'That's him. I want you to keep an eye on him. Keep your beady eyes on him, will you Ravensdale?'

Ravensdale smiled mischievously…

'It's done.'

CHAPTER 36

Disorientated, disarrayed and in disbelief, William staggered to his bare feet. He looked down to see he had no shoes on, the cold and icy cobbled path beneath his feet made it hard to keep balance.

William only had his work trousers on, he folded his arms to try and shield himself from the night's wintry winds.

Examining his immediate environment with frenzied eyes, William knew that something in the ambience was not right. He knew from past transgressions that this was a dream, a nightmare even, but he had been through this before, and it dawned upon him that surely in any dream, any nightmare, one could not be truly hurt? With a fresh sense of confidence, William walked forwards to face any potential terrors that lay ahead…

I can handle this

But could he? That was the question…

For who was to know what he would face, who was to know what lay ahead?

Who was to know, *who* was waiting for him?

As he walked he tried to keep his mind sharp. 'Just a dream, just a dream,' he repeatedly reminded himself as he trudged through the icy-cold, mist-filled, cobbled streets, but then something registered in William's mind…

'I *know* these streets!' shouted William and as he did he heard his own echo travel with the wind.

But where was he? The cobbled streets were common in Barnes, so he could be anywhere. But as he continued to walk, he noticed a concerning trend with the cobbly path…

It was getting thinner…

'Oh no,' William thought; he tried to turn but the path was getting thinner behind him too, so he carried on, maybe he could outrun it!

It was getting thinner…

'What the hell?' he screamed as the path shrunk before his eyes, but it was not the path he was most worried about … it was the hard brick walls which lined the path that scared him, for he may be crushed!

It was getting thinner…

'What the hell is happening to me?' William screamed as he slipped on the ice covered surface. He slammed hard and fast to the ground; he cried and didn't feel he had the strength to move on, when suddenly as if by magic, some miracle even, the walls and path had stopped closing in on him!

'Oh thank you, thank you!' William sighed with mix of some leftover panic and new found relief.

Catching his breath, he got up and looked around; it was so very quiet…

Too quiet...

'Oh no,' William thought, he somehow knew it wasn't going to be that easy; nothing ever was in his life. He had a sense of impending doom, a doom which in some way or other, was

CHAPTER 36

Disorientated, disarrayed and in disbelief, William staggered to his bare feet. He looked down to see he had no shoes on, the cold and icy cobbled path beneath his feet made it hard to keep balance.

William only had his work trousers on, he folded his arms to try and shield himself from the night's wintry winds.

Examining his immediate environment with frenzied eyes, William knew that something in the ambience was not right. He knew from past transgressions that this was a dream, a nightmare even, but he had been through this before, and it dawned upon him that surely in any dream, any nightmare, one could not be truly hurt? With a fresh sense of confidence, William walked forwards to face any potential terrors that lay ahead…

I can handle this

But could he? That was the question…

For who was to know what he would face, who was to know what lay ahead?

Who was to know, *who* was waiting for him?

As he walked he tried to keep his mind sharp. 'Just a dream, just a dream,' he repeatedly reminded himself as he trudged through the icy-cold, mist-filled, cobbled streets, but then something registered in William's mind…

'I *know* these streets!' shouted William and as he did he heard his own echo travel with the wind.

But where was he? The cobbled streets were common in Barnes, so he could be anywhere. But as he continued to walk, he noticed a concerning trend with the cobbly path…

It was getting thinner…

'Oh no,' William thought; he tried to turn but the path was getting thinner behind him too, so he carried on, maybe he could outrun it!

It was getting thinner…

'What the hell?' he screamed as the path shrunk before his eyes, but it was not the path he was most worried about … it was the hard brick walls which lined the path that scared him, for he may be crushed!

It was getting thinner…

'What the hell is happening to me?' William screamed as he slipped on the ice covered surface. He slammed hard and fast to the ground; he cried and didn't feel he had the strength to move on, when suddenly as if by magic, some miracle even, the walls and path had stopped closing in on him!

'Oh thank you, thank you!' William sighed with mix of some leftover panic and new found relief.

Catching his breath, he got up and looked around; it was so very quiet…

Too quiet…

'Oh no,' William thought, he somehow knew it wasn't going to be that easy; nothing ever was in his life. He had a sense of impending doom, a doom which in some way or other, was destined to unmask itself sooner rather than later. The thing which angered William was, why wait?

Why can't doom just be brave enough and meet him head on?

Why can't doom be man enough to just come out with it?

Why can't doom stop playing games, finish this once and for all?

After stopping to catch a breath, William looked around again, the menacing mist had cleared somewhat, and he thought he recognised where he was; he didn't like it.

He was at an old lane, but it had shrunk from what he remembered it to be, his mind, he thought, more-than-likely altering it into some creepy dark alley just to make it scarier.

There it stood, long dark and menacing, it was an old walkway built many years ago, and was as cold as it was uninviting. It was like some monster's mouth just waiting to consume anyone who dared to enter it. William couldn't see the far end as it had been blocked off by a grey and white mist. This lane was horrible, it had a presence of unspeakable terror, and as William felt the feeling of dread enter his mind, his very being, he remembered the name of the old lane…

Dagger Lane…

There was a story about someone being attacked and murdered in the lane for the pittance in their pocket, but no one knew for sure as it had allegedly happened many years ago. Other macabre stories surrounded the dark alley but over the years these stories had become more horrific so the real story was lost, but it was fair to say most people avoided this lowly and unwelcoming place.

William felt things were getting stranger by the minute. For one, in his other dreams it was rare he saw any type of ground, rare to sense smell, but as he walked the cobbles of old Dagger Lane, he could smell stale urine and faeces and things scuttled underfoot as he carefully trod. The walls seemed to run with slime which covered the brickwork. No one liked the lane, the dark alley, whatever the hell it was. No one used the alley except for the brave and the foolhardy, for you never knew what lay in its depths.

William walked on.

Dark, dingy and dripping with unseen dangers, derelict buildings formed the alleyway that didn't seem to have an end.

Scuttling vermin held claim to this place, for it was their domain.

But still he walked and walked, his legs growing weary, his feet cold, his arms riddled with goose bumps, his hair blowing against the wind.

Then suddenly, William saw the mist clearing towards the end of the alley, a shadowy shape seemed to form.

What was it? Who was it? William readied himself. 'Come on then, I'm ready,' he thought and clenched his fists in irritation.

He was sick of this, sick of the fear, sick of his own mind playing tricks on him; sick of a past he was unsure of, sick of being held hostage to fears that he wasn't responsible for. He wanted to confront it, challenge it…beat it.

But nothing could prepare him for what he saw, and as he ran towards the shadow he began to make the shape out, it became clearer to him. As it did his fists unclenched and his feet stopped running. He skidded on the iced surface and slipped, falling on his backside.

The mist had cleared fully now and a figure stood before him, she wore a fancy dress but it wasn't made of any fabric a man could make, it was like a white vapour surrounding her body.

William didn't recognise her face but felt warmed by her presence. She was beautiful and William felt soothed as it seemed she almost glided towards him.

The mysterious figure reached out her hand to William who was on the ground looking up at her in sheer amazement. Her hand touched his face; it was like nothing he had ever felt.

The touch was warm and comforting, as if it was some sort of blessing. He let his head go limp as she held his head in her arms, he looked at her eyes as she smiled at him, and William felt there was something about her, there was a feeling of instant love, a feeling of love unconditional, and a feeling of love absolute.

A mother's love.

He knew … she knew.

He knew that she knew he knew, and smiled so very widely.

A mother's love.

'So this is what it feels like' William thought.

The ice from the ground didn't seem to be cold now. The wind stopped, the fear disappeared and the lady in front of him smiled as she helped William to his feet.

Now on his feet, William kept hold of her hand and looked adoringly at her.

'Mother? Could it be?'

'Yes' she answered in a sweet soft voice. 'I am here, but William, I have always been here, in your heart.' She smiled as she touched his bare chest with her fingertips.

'But where have you been? I have searched for you in my dreams; I want to know so much dear mother. Was it my fault you died? Am I cursed? Why am I so different? Why do I feel a criminal for falling in love? Why am so strange?'

'I am wherever love is, my son. We will have our time, do not worry about me and do not worry for the dead. Worry for the living. I have come to you to show you truths, truths which you need to know before he comes again, you know who I mean'.

'Father,' nodded William.

William's mother looked at him with a sorrowful gaze. 'Yes, but we can't help him now, son. Now, we don't have much time. You have a gift, not a curse, it is a gift. Always trust your gut, for it is an extra sense you have, like an animal senses danger, you do too. I will show you another gift you have son, now you have to trust me.'

William watched his mother place her flat palm on the middle of his chest; he felt a strange sensation like he was going dizzy and a he swayed a little to the right, then to the left.

'Oh, er…mother, I don't feel right'

'It's alright son, it is your first time. What I am doing is showing you something, a naked truth, a part of me; my life, how things were, what happened. You have this gift too. It works more than words; it shows you into my soul, it shows real truth, through my eyes. Now relax and submit, for no harm will come to you…'

A feeling swept over William as he felt his mother's hand on his heart. He felt anxious but yet he was unafraid. He knew he was in some sort of dream, but yet his eyes were wide open, and for the first time since he could remember, this was a dream from which he did not want to wake.

His eyes stayed fixed on her face, for he did not want to forget it. He had never had any sort of idea what his mother looked like and he wanted to keep the visual memory locked deep inside for when he woke.

His eyes tried to stay open, but they couldn't. She smiled at him and nodded. 'It's alright son, close your eyes, feel me, see through my eyes.'

In what seemed like an instant, his eyes were closed. It felt like he was hovering in some unthinkable realm, somewhere incomprehensible; where bright colours made his eyes squint until all of a sudden, it was like he had awoken…

But he hadn't.

As William adjusted all he could do was see. Was this how the ghosts of the graveyard felt? Was this how they saw things?

His view was distorted at first, then things seemed to clear as he realised he was watching over a number of people he did not recognise.

It looked like some sort of party. He felt like he was floating but he could neither see nor feel his body.

'How wonderfully odd!' thought William.

As his eyes scanned the room, he realised the house he was in was a house you could find almost anywhere among the common parts of Barnes.

People were happy, laughing and talking loudly, William even felt happy just watching them but then all of a sudden, he saw her face. It was his mother!

She was standing near a man playing the fiddle. She was with another woman engaged in what looked like an agreeable conversation when her eyes made an abrupt turn to the far corner of the room where a man William recognised was smiling at her. He was a good-looking chap, and he tipped his hat to William's mother, to which she responded by doing a curtsy.

It was William's father, but he looked completely different. He looked kind; he looked full of life…

He looked happy.

Just as William was getting used to the jovial setting, he felt dizzy again. The colours returned and he felt he was being pulled somehow; his vision blurred again, then… His eyes readjusted and he was somewhere completely different.

He observed his mother riding a horse with his father riding beside her. They laughed and joked as the ride got faster into a full gallop, his mother's hair blowing in the wind, and then his father's hat falling off as the speed of the ride intensified.

He went dizzy again and, as before, William was whisked away somehow to another place in time.

As he waited for his eyes to gain focus, he felt elated to see his mother having happy times; it made him feel absolutely overjoyed.

The visions came one after another now, and William saw his mother getting ready for her wedding. His mother's beauty was without question, and she shone like a star in the white dress she wore, but there was something William couldn't believe, and that was how the handsome man from the party was his father, he looked like such a nice chap.

Where did that man go? What happened to him?

The last visions William saw were not as pleasant. He saw his father arguing with another man and being told there was no work. He saw his mother with a baby bump and his father getting stressed because there was no money.

Then came the visions of his father digging graves, whilst also fighting in the pubs in illegal boxing matches … some he won, some he lost, and as he fought each week, his face became more and more unrecognisable.

Then came the hardest vision, his father screaming as the doctors told him the bad news.

His wife was dying, but there was some salvation, he had a son.

'I don't want it!' he screamed 'I want her, where is she?' he cried.

It saddened William to think of the pain his father must have felt, and although it was to his own detriment, he almost understood why his father had held him in such contempt.

Watching his mother beg for the pain to stop as she screamed in blood-soaked sheets, watching his father beg the doctors for help, to be told there wasn't any, made William feel a sorrow he had never known. Then as David gave her a bottle of something to drink, he watched as his mother mouthed the words 'Thank you,' to her husband before she slipped away.

The very last vision was as haunting as William had ever dreamt or seen.

His father, David, was in the graveyard, which was now William's graveyard, he had walked beyond the east wall, where the unmarked graves were kept.

He saw a familiar headstone, the one where he always felt peace. His father screamed to the sky 'Why?' and thunder echoed around the graveyard. David then carved letters in the headstone, and the words read something that William had read a thousand times...

Mortuus est Momentaneum

But what did it mean?

Then William saw his father surrounded by ravens, as if they were his friends and, shortly after, he saw his father drawing stars on the soil of new graves...

Then, the images stopped... William opened his eyes, he was in his mother's arms again.

Shaking like a leaf, William was in a state of panic 'Mother? What the ... oh my, I feel lost for words!'

'It is alright son, be calm,' she said softly as she stroked his hair. William calmed down and they sat cross-legged at the end of the dark lane together.

He had so many questions, so many feelings, but it was as if he and his mother's minds were connected and she told him things before he asked.

She told him David had been a good man, but had become obsessed with money, gambling and how others would see them. She said David wanted a higher social standing and did not want to want for anything. The biggest problem David had was his temper, and it became so bad that nobody would take him on for a job, so things got harder and harder.

It came to light that, after she died, David thought her soul was damned and he went mad over it. He made a deal with some dark force, a bargain of some kind, that if he did the Devil's work, her soul would be saved. But she had been a good person in life, and she told William that she was happy and David had been tricked by the forces of evil.

She also told William how she never regretted anything and that David had a good heart, it had just been twisted by grief.

She said sorry to William for dying, adding that she wished she could have been a mother to him. This made William cry and he responded by telling her they would have their time someday.

They hugged and William felt like he was at home in her arms.

Then just as they broke the hug, a dark mist filled the lane. The warm feeling William felt vanished, replaced by a sudden cold rush of wind. The lane filled with rats and William shot to his feet, kicking them. 'Go away!' he shouted.

He felt his mother's hands grab his arm, 'William he is coming! I do not have much time so listen to me. Do not be scared of love, for love can never be wrong, follow your heart my son and you will find treasures which can't be put into words. You deserve it, it is there for you. You just have to take it. Good and bad is down to choice my son. Be yourself; do not let the world twist you as it did your father. Love, live and be free, be *you.*'

She smiled and whispered. 'I love you, son.' as she started to disappear, William felt her grip on his arm loosen. 'Mother!' he screamed. 'I love you, mother, I will never forget you!'

She was gone, William stood as the black mist surrounded him like smoke on a fire. William felt angry that something had disturbed such a moment with the mother he had never met and there was only ever going to be one culprit…

His father.

This wasn't just a dream; this wasn't just a nightmare, this was something more. So real to his soul that it was a whole new category which he could not fathom.

This was his personal chimera, a torment of the very darkest kind.

CHAPTER 37

He appeared like a magician in a grand theatre, his presence developing through thick black mist, rats scurrying around him like obedient pets.

'Hello…son,' he smiled.

Looking at his father's twisted, evil face in pity, William approached, devoid of fear.

'Father, I won't look at you with fear any more. I know what happened; you were tricked, the love you had for my mother was used against you, you are not bad, you aren't!'

David's eyes were as dark as the night around them, but William could tell he was conflicted, he could tell his real father was in there somewhere, trying to get out.

'Boy, don't test me'

'But father, why do you torment me?'

Shaking his head as if he was shaking something off himself, David's eyes became lighter 'William, my son, I don't have much time. I am damned, you can't help me.'

'Father, are you in Hell?'

'I don't think so, I think I am somewhere in between, for who knows? But I know you are in danger'

'Danger, how?'

'The love you so desperately covet; the love which cannot be yours; it will only bring you closer to me, my son. To succumb to love is to succumb to evil. It is doomed; you will end up like me, twisted and tormented forever!'

'But father, I *love* her. What wrong can that cause, whom do I offend?'

David's eyes went dark again, 'You offend all! She is a widow, she is a lady, she is beyond your standing, it will never be accepted, you are low … you are nothing! Dig the graves and know your place, mother murderer!'

'But father, I know the truth,' cried William. He then walked towards his father who looked filled with hate, he touched his father's arms and his own hand began to burn, but he did not let go.

'Father, there is good in you, fight it!'

David's eyes went lighter again, and William saw what looked like a tear, but as it fell it sizzled on his cheek. 'You see, boy? The part of me which fights is destroyed every time' Even a tear cannot hide; it is hunted down, found and destroyed by the heat of Hell's fury. My fate is decided, yours is not. You can lead a simple life, William, but a dark path awaits you, I plead with you now to not follow your doomed quest for love; it will only lead to pain…son. I can help you no more.'

William kept hold of his father's arm, and ignored the fact that his hand was burning, his flesh turning bright red and starting to peel like cooked meat. 'But father…' William shouted as he ignored the pain and as he did, the evil eyes of the demon within his father took over again, and David turned away from William and disappeared back into the dark mist.

As his father disappeared, William grabbed his own hand in pain. It was burned very badly, and then as he held his hand he woke, he felt his movement restricted.

'What the hell… Where the hell am I?'

Focusing his eyes just in front him, William realised he was boxed in somewhere. He struggled and shifted his body from left to right, right to left, but there wasn't much room to manoeuvre.

Agitation set in as his mind couldn't seem to register where he was. It was so dark, but whatever he was lying on was padded, his body was laid out, horizontal, it was almost as if he were laid…

In a coffin!

'HELP! HELP!' William yelled at the top of his voice. He pushed and punched over and over until he made a dent in the thick hollow wood, his knuckles hurt as he hit with all his might and doing so made him almost out of breath. Finally, after almost feeling like he had broken his hand, a decent crack appeared and William used both his hands to pry the lid off, he sat upright and looked about.

It was a coffin!

Getting out as quickly as he could, William rose to his feet, he was dressed extremely well, better than he had ever dressed in his life, with a suit that would have probably cost more than all his clothes put together!

Regaining his breath and composure, he wondered what else lie in wait for him on this dark journey, for it truly was the nightmare to end all nightmares.

He screamed in defiance 'What next, what have you got for me?'

Whatever was feeding the nightmare, duly answered.

There was a tap on William's shoulder. Spinning around rapidly his eyes fixed on a man before him. The man was the same size as him but his head was looking down to the floor so William couldn't see his face.

'Who are you, then?' asked William with a certain amount of leisure. He was getting fed up of this, and his usual fear was now reducing with each challenge the nightmare brought forth.

'I said, who *are* you?' asked William confidently.

The man lifted his head and fixed a scowl on William.

He recognised the man; he had seen this face every day, all his life...

It was William, or at least some other version!

'Who are you? You are not me! You are an imposter! A dark imposter, I say!'

He felt delirious, crazed, unsure and extremely angry.

He clasped his fingers together to make a fist, a fist that could cause pain if thrown, a fist that wanted to cause damage, a fist with intent.

He hit the imposter with the hardest hit he had ever thrown.

Was this the bad version of himself? Was it his mind's way of telling him he was his own enemy?

He was past caring, and as his fist of fury flew through the air like an archer's arrow, it hit the intended target with a ferocious impact that literally smashed the imposter to pieces! William looked on in surprise as his brutal blow went straight through the figure, and as his fist finished by his side, the pieces of the figure turned into something, some *things.*

The *things* were bats, and the little vexatious critters flapped around the air. As William slapped them off they turned to fire. But there were too many and, as he hit them, their flames began to engulf him, but he didn't know what else to do. His legs were alight. William danced in dismay, he couldn't think straight at all and as if that wasn't bad enough he felt a terrible pain in his leg, as if teeth had sunk into his flesh so deep the teeth had scratched his bone! He closed his eyes, just wishing the pain to go away, wishing for this nightmare to end as he heard strange noises and evil laughter all around.

'Why?' he screamed. Then, as if someone had heard his pleas, as if someone were watching over him, everything went quiet.

Almost quiet anyway, he could hear heavy breathing, and he could still feel some pain in his leg.

Opening his eyes, he realised he was in his own quarters, he shot upright and gasped for air, his bed sheets were soaked with sweat. Then, as he calmed down and used his eyes, his saviour was revealed to him, as was the answer to the heavy breathing.

William never thought he would feel so happy to see those wild eyes.

'Oh Azrael! Azrael! My friend! You saved me, boy! You saved me, for sure!' William shouted as he hugged his furry companion. Azrael licked William's face and rolled over onto his stomach.

William looked at his leg and there were teeth marks all right. The injury wasn't too bad though and after covering the wound up William felt fine. He played with Azrael for a while and talked as he did.

'How did you know, boy? How did you know? Are you my guardian angel?' laughed William. He realised Azrael had snuck in as he had left his door ajar since the nights had been hot lately. William smiled as he thought he must be the only person on earth who could feel so excited that a wolf had crept onto his bed!

Recollecting the night's events William thought back to his audience with both his parents. His mind was all over the place, who was right and who was wrong?

Should he follow love like his mother told him? Or should he stay safe, away from potential darkness like his father had warned? Could his father be tricking him maybe? Wanting William to lead a dull life absent of love so he too became a twisted, tormented old man? Or was his mother naïve; was she thinking everything was simple and ended happily ever after?

What would he do? What *could* he do?

There was something that William *couldn't* do, and that was to ignore the greatest feeling he had ever felt in his life. No way was he going to turn his back on Lizzy, especially on the word of his father.

Owning his own feelings made William feel strong minded, he was in love, and that was a fact he would never ignore, never turn his back on.

Ever.

CHAPTER 38

The creation of an evil plan took time, even for the most cunning of plotters. So when Patrick Fenwick finally thought of some terrible tactics, he was more than eager to put them in place.

Staying up most of the night was an oddity for Patrick. Most nights he was in his bed way before 10 o'clock and slept soundly without disturbance all the way through to 6 am, which was his daily waking time.

Having searched his whole brain for possibilities, having explored many different scenarios, Patrick had his scheme set in stone within his own psyche.

Over the last few weeks Patrick had deployed a few sets of eyes to watch events he took an interest in. To have people do his dirty work gave Patrick a quiet satisfaction that always seemed to remind him he was more important than the average man.

So as the reports came back to Patrick, it was evident that over a period of time, Lady Anne Fenwick, the widow of his late brother, had been spending time with the gravedigger at Barnes cemetery. Patrick didn't like it, he did not like it one bit!

Measures had to be taken, they just had to be. After all, who was she to think she could drag his name down by potentially being seen with such offal? Who was she to think she could spend time with whom she pleased?

More importantly, who was *he* to think he could get close to a lady, a *lady*!

No, no, no! Patrick wasn't having this. His spies told him of Lady Anne and the gravedigger taking long walks together; his spies told him Lady Anne actually invited the gravedigger into his brother's house.

Into his brother's house! Outrageous!

She had to stop; the gravedigger had to stop. *It all* had to stop.

So what were Patrick's options? He had tried to warn Lady Anne, he really had tried, but how many attempts would it take? He could maybe try once more? Try the softer approach perhaps? And what of the fiend, the town idiot, the town creep, the town scum? What could he do to this gravedigger? What could possibly keep him away from stock higher than his station? His family had already perished, so Patrick knew he didn't have that angle to explore, he owned nothing, and so stripping him of possessions wasn't a viable option. So what could he do?

He needed rid of this *gravedigger*...

Decisions, decisions...

What could he do? Whenever a complicated case was placed upon Patrick's lap, he had a system, his own system which he configured many years ago. You see, as a young man of the courts, back when he was just learning his trade, Patrick would read, read and read. He would read so much his eyes felt like they were going to melt in his head. The funny thing about that fact was sometimes he would read so much material, so many books, he still couldn't find what he was looking for. It was like the answers were lost in some secret embedded code he could not understand.

Until one day, it came to him.

A very unique epiphany was realised, and it was the most simple of methods.

The revelation changed Patrick's whole approach to his work. He still read his books, he still explored the many theories, but when a case was complicated, he found that the easiest way of solving it was to break the problem down to its simplest form. After he learned how to master his system, his success rate was so high he was the talk of the town. He also applied his theories to other aspects of his life, and he gained over and over.

He didn't need a title to know he was a lord, but yet how he craved one.

So having racked his brains for solutions, having tried to be reasonable, there was only one thing to do.

He had to simplify matters, he had to solve the problem of Lady Anne and the gravedigger for the whole mess had started to grieve him greatly.

He broke down the difficulty, made it a basic problem.

Question: Two people - one problem, how do you solve it?

Answer: Take one of the people away.

Problem solved.

CHAPTER 39

Walking with a spring in his step down the old cobbled streets of Barnes, Patrick felt positively pleased.

He walked past the town's librarian who was an old fat lady named Polly whom Patrick would usually never acknowledge, but today was different. He was so happy and wanted to share it with everyone and so he tipped his hat to Polly. 'Morning, my beautiful Polly,' he laughed. She returned an anxious smile and carried on down the street with some books under her arms.

Then he passed some children who had spotted Patrick approaching and stopped their hop skip and jumps so Patrick could walk by, but instead of his usual kicks at their bottoms, Patrick smiled. 'Play! Play, young children! Ha-ha.'

As he walked he felt a feeling he hadn't felt in a long time, an old song popped into his head and he smiled as he tried to remember the words.

'Got it!' he thought as he first whistled the tune, then the words came and he sang them without a care in the world.

'Of all the girls that are so smart

There's none like pretty Sally;

She is the darling of my heart,

And she lives in our alley.

There is no lady in the land

Is half as sweet as Sally;

She is the darling of my heart,

And she lives in our alley'

He continued the song as he walked; he remembered it was a song by a man named Henry Carey who from what he could remember was supposed to have died at the age of 56 by hanging himself in his home. 'What a pity,' thought Patrick as he realised he had reached his destination.

He still had the tune in his head, but he put it to the back of his mind, today after all, was business. Things were going to be done.

Things, *needed* to be done.

He looked at the front doors of the town's Police station and giggled a sarcastic cackle. It boggled him as to how people could trust the idiots who donned the badge; did they not know if it weren't for the likes of *him* these imbeciles wouldn't be able to tie their own shoes?

A quick puff on the pipe was in order before his entrance. Preparing for his smoke was always a nice, therapeutic practice for Patrick; he stuffed the pipe with his favourite tobacco which was Ogden's famous St James Empire Blend. Oh, how Patrick loved the smell; he read the label which depicted that the tobacco was "exquisite, cool and fragrant". 'What more could a man want in a smoke?' thought Patrick as he lit the pipe and inhaled his pleasing treat.

Puffing away on his pipe as he watched the inhabitants of Barnes go about their merry business was a funny thing; he looked at the poor people shuffling from one place to another, tatty, unkempt and unclean. An old man walked by and coughed near Patrick who stepped back out of the cough's course.

'Excuse me, sir,' the old man apologised.

The very thought of the man's germs infecting him made Patrick's lip curl and he snarled as he noticed the old man had coughed up blood into an old, stained handkerchief.

'No, I won't excuse you,' barked Patrick.

The old man hurried off, looking frightened.

'You disease spreading rat! Die around your own dwellings, not in public where others may catch your afflictions'

Just as Patrick finished shouting his abuse, Constable Harvey appeared from the station's doors.

'Ah, making friends I see. One of your friends, is he?' Harvey mocked.

Not looking amused at all, Patrick snapped at Harvey too 'How dare you, you gong-farming mutton shunter!'

'I say sir, quite the mood you seem to be in, I was only making a joke, and no offence was meant.'

'Well you do cause offence. They *all* do, these people, these insects, these riddling little rodents, all shuffling around looking for a piece of mouldy cheese to chew on. I *hate* them.'

Harvey could see Patrick was upset, so he invited him into the station for a cup of tea.

Patrick obliged and they walked into the station together.

'Get the tea on, boy,' instructed Patrick as they glided in the station past the main reception.

'I was going to get someone to do it for us … thought we may have business, sir?' said Harvey as he took Patrick's coat.

'Oh, we will, but not yet. Today I seek the other man from whom you take orders, the delightful Mr Robertson.'

Harvey took Patrick to the office in which Mr Robertson worked. It was a small office, and as Patrick walked into the room he sniggered at the humble surroundings of Barnes's chief policeman.

There was a little wooden table, one of the legs had come off and was balanced by some old books. There were ring marks from old cups of tea on the surface, and dust; the dust was everywhere!

Mr Robertson's face changed when he saw Patrick walk in. His glasses rested halfway between his nose and his eyes as he had been reading a book with his feet resting on a small bookshelf.

Pulling his feet off the bookshelf and fixing his glasses back on his face, Mr Robertson straightened himself up when he saw it was Patrick.

'Ah, Patrick Fenwick, to what do I owe the pleasure? You have to understand, I was reading some er…was busy researching, I was.'

Noticing the book's title from the side as it was laid on the table Patrick smiled, 'Yes, evidently.'

Harvey walked into the room with two cups and a pot of tea. Patrick motioned him to pour the tea into the cups on the old wooden table, which Harvey did. Then Patrick whispered, 'Leave us.' And Harvey did as instructed.

Mr Robertson felt embarrassed; he had not been working as he should have been. He had been taking a quick break, and the title of the book laid out his little lie for Patrick to see.

'Jules Gabriel Verne's 'Around the World in 80 Days', eh? A fantastic novel I'm sure you will agree, Mr Robertson,' laughed Patrick as he dusted a chair down and sat leisurely like he was at home.

Not intimidated by Patrick one bit, Mr Robertson sipped his hot tea and smiled. 'I haven't read it all yet; some rather odd names I'd say, but the story seems an intriguing one. I am mostly reading because of my wife. She loved her books she did, so in some way I feel like I have to read her type of books, it reminds me of her giggling, it does.'

'How thoughtfully sweet! Yes, I was well aware of her passing, a sad thing indeed. You say the characters names are odd? I find them pleasing to the ear? I am particularly fond of Phileas Fogg, a wonderful name I think for a wonderful character.'

'Well, like I said, Fenwick, haven't read it all yet. So what brings you here today?'

'Ah, yes. I guess I best get to it. Business, what else?'

'But what business do we have?'

Patrick smiled. He brought out a clipping from a newspaper he had had stashed in his pocket and placed it onto the table in Mr Robertson's line of vision.

He slurped his tea loudly from the cup before he spoke. 'Murders, there have been murders! I have a friend in Kensington, another policeman; Harking is his name, who, you may be aware, is out of town. Now, as I'm also sure you are aware, we have more than enough policemen here to manage. So I wondered... my friend wondered, if you could help with the investigation. It would only be for a couple of days. You would just go down there and see if you could make anything of their evidence. They have a few suspects, but they really would desire an outsider's point of view. When approached by him, I could think of no other so abundantly qualified as you, sir.'

Examining the news report of the paper through his brown thick rimmed glasses Mr Robertson nodded as he hummed in agreement.

Looking up to Patrick, Mr Robertson sat up straight. 'But, you really think they need help?'

'Oh, so very much sir, you would be such a help, and you would receive a nice little bonus from the appreciative police station of Kensington, another week's wage in fact!'

Mr Robertson smiled, it was the first time he had ever smiled at Patrick, but why not? He had been presented with a real job, a *real* challenge, and the bonus of a trip out of town and another week's wage in the pay-packet did nothing but add to the attraction.

Offering out his hand outstretched across the old wooden table, Mr Robertson thought he was doing a good thing. 'It seems I am in agreement, Mr Fenwick.'

Accepting Mr Robertson's hand, Patrick shook it with a teeth-baring smile. 'Superb indeed, I will make the arrangements for later this day. I will have one of my finest drivers take you there and back.'

'So soon?'

'Murders wait for no man, constable, as I know you will agree. The fiend of Kensington must be caught swiftly before widespread panic ensues.'

'If it is to be, I will go and pack a bag then,' Mr Robertson said as he stood to his feet and gathered a few books, not least his novel by Jules Gabriel Verne.

'For the coach drive obviously,' smiled Mr Robertson as he saw Patrick was watching him.

'Do as you do, sir. As aforementioned, I have a particular fondness of Phileas Fogg. I would also add that I think I share certain similarities with the character. He, like me, is driven, he like me, adventurous!'

Mr Robertson gave a small fake laugh 'Well, I must get ready, what time is the driver to call for me?'

'Oh, around 4pm this day sir, I would also like a report of your findings upon your return. Would that be agreeable?'

'No problem sir. Bye,' said Mr Robertson as he left quickly.

Viewing Mr Robertson's pesky office with a general disregard, Patrick fancied another smoke.

So he lit up his pipe again and smoked contentedly, that was until he heard shuffling outside the office door.

'Just come in, Harvey, instead of waiting there like a fool,' Patrick sarcastically muttered as he exhaled some smoke.

He assumed correctly and Harvey walked in. 'Are you all right Patrick? You said we have business too, didn't you, where is he going? Out of town?'

'Oh Harvey, you wouldn't have been eavesdropping would you?'

'Er…no, just outside doing some bits and bobs that's all, got good hearing, I can't help that Patrick, all I heard was something about Phileas Fogg, that's all, honest.'

'Ah yes the good old Fogg, ha-ha. Cracking tale, really it is. I could be Phileas Fogg, I could. Exploring the world and its wonders, but what role would you play I wonder? Ah I've got it! You could be my sidekick, my Jean Passepartout, my humble servant! Ha-ha!'

Harvey didn't react, he just watched Patrick enjoy his pipe as Patrick started to sing.

'My master and the neighbours all

Make gave of me and Sally,

And, but for her, I'd better be

A slave and row a galley;

But when my seven long years are out,

O, then I'll marry Sally;

O, then we'll wed, and then we'll bed

But not in our alley!'

CHAPTER 40

She had told William the day before she might be late for their daily meeting, as she had to venture into the town. Unbeknown to William though, Lizzy was planning a surprise.

Having spent a lot of time with William in recent weeks, Lizzy had wondered how it must have felt for him, being alone nearly all his life. She also noticed a distinct lack of possessions, not that he cared.

One particular day when William had taken her to the forest, she noticed the panic in William's eyes when Azrael had run out of sight. He had stood and whistled and called until Azrael came trotting back and Lizzy thought of a gift which could have helped in that type of instant, she also noticed he liked to look beyond the trees, to the large hilly mountains beyond the forest.

The gift was one tailored for William, she had ordered it a week ago and even had William's initials imprinted on it.

WR

'Thank you so much sir, it is perfect!' Lizzy said happily as she handed over the money to the shopkeeper.

It was a fine, 6 inch Brass Telescope, and now William could look far and beyond at whatever he chose.

Trotting out of the shop with an air of satisfaction, Lizzy's agreeable mood was dampened by the sight of a familiar swine.

Patrick.

'Ah, a sight for sore eyes you are indeed. Good morning to you, Lady Anne, looking as pleasing as ever. Radiant. *Chatoyant,* even.'

In no mood for Patrick, Lizzy tried to hurry by him as quickly as she could and as she did she told him what she thought. 'Really Patrick, your false adulations are not clever, in fact they are a bore, so if you wouldn't mind I have places I need to be.'

'Yes, I am sure you do,' laughed Patrick as she brushed by him. 'With people you need to see, no doubt?'

Stopping in her tracks, she knew what he meant; she knew to whom he referred. Turning half around, Lizzy tilted her head, as the look of disdain became all too obvious.

Patrick approached her with smugness, as if he knew something, as if had won a battle where the first shot had not yet been fired.

'We need to talk, *Lizzy'*

'I haven't long Patrick, so where? Where can we talk away from detecting prying ears?'

Patrick lit his pipe and held out his arm for Lizzy to take. She shook her head, appalled by the notion, but Patrick gave evil eyes and warned, 'You will need a man's company where we are to walk, take my arm, now.'

Lizzy did as Patrick instructed, but only for self-preservation. They walked in pure silence and Lizzy wondered where they were going, but deep inside she knew whatever Patrick wanted to say was sensitive, otherwise why the secretive route to privacy?

There could only be one thing this was about…

William.

CHAPTER 41

They walked for about ten minutes, but to Lizzy it seemed like forever; she desperately wanted to know what all this was about. She guessed he must have known about her and William's meetings; that much was obvious. So what now? Another warning on how she should be living maybe? Or perhaps it was just another attempt by Patrick to woo her? She really hoped it wasn't the latter.

Lizzy didn't like where they seemed to be headed. She looked around the streets and saw beggars and thieves scouring her with their eyes. She noticed little alleyways off the street they were on, where provocative women shouted at men walking by, trying to entice them by showing some leg.

Lizzy kept her eyes ahead. 'It will be alright, it will be alright,' she told herself over and over in her mind.

They stopped just near a stand where a man was selling what looked like half rotten apples and oranges; Patrick threw the man a coin and put a finger to his lips. The man nodded. Patrick turned to Lizzy. 'Now we talk, woman.'

'Oh, woman, now is it? I've gone from lady to Lizzy to woman, all in a half hour.'

'You know where we are? I could call you a lot worse and no person would turn an eyelid.'

Lizzy's eyes hurriedly took in the surroundings; it was not very pleasant, the air was thick with smells she did not recognise, and a grim aura seemed to hang over every person she saw. Rubbish spilled over the gutter, and rats squeaked menacingly in the dark alleys. Although she knew this was a bad part of town, the fact was there had been many twists and turns along the way, so the truth was; she wasn't quite sure where they were at all.

'I give up, where *are* we Patrick?'

Lighting up the new wooden pipe he had bought from a man on the market, Patrick took in a puff and blew the smoke in her face 'They call it Flapperfold Lane, a place where the people are as unsavoury as the drainage systems. They walk by you now, but don't be fooled, if I left your company they would ravage you like a cooked dinner.'

'And you would do that, Patrick? You would leave me to these beings? Surely even you wouldn't do such a thing?'

'You had better believe I would, Lizzy. I would, I say again. I speak to you to tell you the truth, the real truth. I speak to you because you were once family, once of worth to the name Fenwick, once of worth to me. If you had not been my brother's wife I would have washed my hands of you long ago.'

Shaking her head, Lizzy spoke softly 'To be honest, Patrick that prospect sounds more than appealing, for if I never had contact with you again it would be fine by me. We don't seem to have kind words to say to each other, so in light of that, why do we speak at all? Is it not more sensible to let bygones be bygones and move forward? Instead of this constant conflict we find ourselves in whenever we cross paths?'

'That is a valid point indeed,' Patrick smiled as he continued with his pipe, 'but enough idle queries. I brought you here to tell you something, something which may shed light on a character that has a past as murky as the streets in which we stand. You see I have been doing some digging these past weeks, collecting information on certain things, certain people even.'

'William, you are talking about William, aren't you? You don't understand! He is a true gentleman, and possibly the loveliest person I have ever met. Untouched by greed and social standing, not needful of possessions or hungry for power and he is, more importantly, a real and true friend.'

'Ah Lizzy, I think it is you who do not understand. This man, this *gravedigger*, is dangerous. Dangerous to you, dangerous to me, dangerous, dare I say it, to all. Did you know what people called him when he used to travel to town? Do you wonder why he doesn't like to be around people, why a man who in his thirties is not married yet and settled down, or at least looking to be? They call him 'dead talker', Lizzy. 'Dead talker', amongst many other names. Let me see…' smiled Patrick as he pulled out a bit of paper from his pocket and started to read from it.

'Dead talker, mother murderer, freak, devil boy, Rathbone the corpse lover, William Satan spawn, and the list goes on. Do you not wonder why all these names have been shouted at William? Do you not think there is *any* truth in them? The man is disturbed, twisted and I would even go so far as to say he is not entirely well in the head.'

Lizzy felt a build-up of tears, but she would not let them go, not in front of him, no way! How dare he? How dare he speak of William in such a way?

She wasn't scared of Patrick, not any more. She could see straight through the vile excuse of a man and prepared a piece of her mind as she tensed her face at him.

'You, Patrick, are a horrible man. Yet the continuance of your plots and schemes never cease to surprise me. With each week that goes by so does another attempt for you to cause malice in another's life. How *awful* you are. I don't think I speak out of turn when I mention your face is so *twisted* with hate it reminds me of a squashed frog. Your very appearance repulses me; you have without doubt the same repugnant sensibilities of one of the excrement throwing baboons in London Zoo. I would think many may consider it to be an act of bravery just for you to look in the mirror every morning. Everything about you is a fiction; you are not a real man, just a pathetic projection of something your mind so desperately wants to be. You may be rich Patrick, you may have power. But without love, a delight you will never know, you are truly the poorest and weakest man there will ever be. Now I would bid you good day, but I can't even do that, so *bad* day Patrick, I hope you have a really *bad* day!'

Lizzy fled quickly away from Patrick, her tears could hide no longer and as she held her dress and attempted to run through the dirty pathways of Flapperfold Lane. She was frightened by the way she was being looked at; she was, without doubt, a target for thieves. She quickly looked behind her and was at least relieved to see Patrick was not in pursuit.

Then, up ahead, relief. Lizzy spotted a policeman walking the streets at a slow pace.

'Sir- Sir! Please help me!' Lizzy cried.

The young policeman quickly jogged to her. 'Ma'am, are you alright?'

'Oh dear sir, I fear not. I seemed to have gotten lost, taken a wrong turn somehow, could you please escort me back to the safety of the town centre I wonder?'

'The policeman smiled broadly, puffing his chest out as he took Lizzy's arm. 'Oh dear ma'am, you did take a wrong turn. Quite unsavoury these parts are. But fear not, I will get you to safety.'

The panic now in abeyance, Lizzy's heartbeat returned to something like normal. As she walked with the kind policeman she listened to his witty chatter but she only wanted to see William, he was all that was on her mind.

The time for tip toeing around was over, she had to speak with him, about Patrick, about the lies Patrick told, about her own feelings!

About love.

CHAPTER 42

Sitting cross-legged beyond the east wall, William felt relaxed as he looked at what he knew now, was his mother's grave. As he sat peacefully, he closed his eyes and remembered her face from the dream and he would never forget it.

He opened his eyes, and looked at the words on her headstone.

Mortuus est Momentaneum.

He thought of asking Lizzy what it meant. He also thought that one day soon, he could put another word on the headstone. It didn't need to be anything fancy; he just thought of one word, and that word was 'Mother.'

The thought of it made him feel warm inside.

As he stood and walked across the graveyard, William heard the voices of the passed chatting away, it seemed they were lively this morning, but the funniest voice of them all came from his old friend Mr Higgingsly, for he was singing…

'O for the look of those big blue eyes

Seeming to plead and speak

The parted lips and the deep-drawn sighs,

The blush on kissen cheek!'

William gave a quiet cackle at Mr Higgingsly's singing voice as he noticed the birds fly away from the graveyard.

Perhaps they had heard the tune too?

'Mr Higgingsly, what a good mood you seem to be in. Though I fear the birds don't appreciate your golden voice.'

'Mock me all you want young sir, for today I am in good spirits... hey, do you get it? Good spirits! Ha-ha!'

A shake of the head by William was accompanied by a true smile at his ghostly friend's happiness.

'So what raises the mood in you, I wonder sir?' asked William, who wasn't used to his friend being as jovial as he was.

'Tell him Old Peggy, Peggy? Maureen? Lord Fenwick? Anybody?'

Old Peggy laughed and was joined by Maureen, pickpocket Sam, Lord Fenwick and even a few other ghouls who didn't usually join in on the everyday chitter-chatter.

Mr Higgingsly piped up, annoyed by their laughs. 'Oh you may all laugh, but it's true I tell you, true as the ground in which we lie!'

Sighing, as he halted his walk, William stood above Mr Higgingsly's grave. 'I am at a loss, my friend, please explain.'

William then heard Old Peggy trying to talk, but she stammered and stuttered from laughing hysterically 'Oh William, he has truly lost it now, he-he!'

Then Maureen found voice, also in a fit of giggles. 'Ask him, William. Ask him, please! We just want to hear him say it again!'

'Ask him what, Maureen? Will somebody *please* explain?' asked William, who was now also sniggering without even knowing what he was sniggering *at*.

'He has a new gift it seems,' added Lord Fenwick. 'Ask him, ask him what it is.'

'Well, I don't see why that is so funny, for you all have some sort of a gift to be even speaking like you are. Go on, then old boy, what is your new found gift?' smiled William as he patted Mr Higgingsly's head stone.

Giving a loud clearing of the throat, Mr Higgingsly readied his announcement to William '*I*, do have a new gift William, I *really* do. The gift which I have wondrously received is that of smell! I can smell things, I say!'

A loud rapture of joint laughter echoed through the graveyard which William thought sounded like the birds in the morning.

William tried to stay composed. 'Well, if you say it sir, I believe you believe it. Though may I remind you that you once mocked poor Lord Fenwick for claiming the same? That being said, you are many things, but a liar I don't believe is one of them. It is hard to comprehend I have to say, for you have no nose. But if you can, you can, so good for you, sir!'

Old Peggy continued her laughter as she interrupted. 'Don't be fooled, its complete codswallop! If you are in doubt, ask him what he could smell this morning.'

'Go on then sir, what *could* you smell this morning?' asked a curious William.

'Sausages!' screamed Sam the pickpocket. 'He could smell sausages, ha-ha!'

'He is a sausage!' added Lord Fenwick.

'That is not all though,' Mr Higgingsly said defensively. 'I could also smell the pee on my grave from that beast of yours, William.

Which leads me to ask, should you really be letting a wolf roam the grounds so casually?'

Also laughing along, William tried sedating his humour. 'Oh sir, I do not 'let him roam around' as you say, I keep him in the tool shed and occasionally let him free to do his business, but I stand with him. The only time he roams free is when I take him to the forest.'

'Well tell him to stop peeing on my dwellings,' barked Mr Higgingsly.

William buttoned his coat, the morning air was getting chilly and it had started to drizzle. He looked down to Mr Higgingsly's grave and smiled. 'Look, I believe you sir. We will talk about this later, for it looks like the heavens are about to open up.'

He looked up to the sky as he continued. 'Yes, there is going to be much rain, I think, Now you all talk nice, I will see you all later and have a good chat and tell you about my …'

All of a sudden there was a silence, a sudden, astounding, loud silence.

A smell of jasmine filled the air

William looked in front of him to see Lizzy standing in the rain; she was crying, but staring straight at him.

He stood in front of her; he felt naked, speechless, his mouth was open and he searched for words but they wouldn't come out.

She looked at his eyes which looked as wet as the rain which fell. She gave a nervous smile as she bit her bottom lip with nerves.

'Oh, William…''

CHAPTER 43

As the thunderous rain attacked her face and body, she ran across the fields which led to the forest. She focused on the tall trees ahead of her and tried to sprint a bit quicker as she held the bottom of her dress. Her shoes pounded heavily across the boggy ground causing the mud to splash up her legs, she winced at the squelching of the mud under her feet. She realised she was soaking wet, but it didn't matter, she couldn't possibly get any wetter than she was.

Closing in on the forest, she hoped William was alright. He looked so upset with himself, but why? She knew whatever the reason she would understand.

So what if he talked to the graves? So what if he found some sort of sanctuary in that? Was that so wrong? Lizzy could understand why he did so, as human beings were becoming harder and harder to trust by the day.

Why did he run away? Why couldn't he talk to her?

Lizzy's mind asked a bunch of questions as she found herself deep in the forest, the rain pouring down as hard as hailstones.

She spun around as she called his name.

'William!'

But the only answer came from the blowing rain and winds, crashing into the trees around her.

'William!'

Still, there was no reply.

Why was he scared? How could he be scared of her, the only person in the world who could ever understand him?

'William! Don't do this to me, I beg you!' she cried as she fell to her knees. She sobbed hard as her knees sunk into the mud below her. Her hand gripped some twigs on the soaked forest floor and she wept like she never had before. Her tears joined the rain as it fell without remorse.

The pitter-patter of the rain was as loud on the leaves beside her as it was on her windows at home. She closed her eyes and wished for William's presence. 'Please, come to me, William.'

Just as she wished for him, just as she begged from her heart for his attendance, a twig snapped nearby.

'Could it be?' she asked herself.

Slowly daring to open her eyes, she lifted her eyelids slightly in a desperate hope of William's appearance.

Her eyes first registered the brown of the mud, then the trees which surrounded her like a watchful crowd. As she lifted her head she saw black...

Black boots...

She knew these boots, she couldn't wait one second more as she lifted her head and as she did a hand reached down to her, a big, strong hand.

She knew these hands.

Taking the hand, she hoisted herself up to see a face in front of her.

She knew the face...

It was the face of the man she loved.

She reached out and touched his face, then ran her fingers through his long, black, thick, wet hair.

William looked at her in sorrow. 'I am so sorry, I am sorry, my love.'

Locked in an embrace as their arms wrapped around each other, William cradled Lizzy's head as she tilted it back.

The downpour persisted … not that they cared. Their eyes were fixed on each other's, their breathing erratic, their hearts thrashing against their chests like a victorious set of war drums, their touch, gentle as silence itself.

His lips met hers and as they did, there was an explosion of intense emotion that neither had ever known a kiss could contain. The spellbinding electric currents that passed between them were like a fire that could never be extinguished.

As they temporarily ceased their loving touch, they looked at each other in sheer amazement, both smiling as the kiss refreshed the very air in their lungs.

Something extraordinary had materialised, something heavenly, something majestic.

It was love, pure and mighty, unquestionable love.

CHAPTER 44

The rain had stopped, but the wind remained. No longer cruel and violent, the strange relaxing zephyr blew through his hair as he sat behind her on the hills beyond the forest. They faced towards the sun as it briefly broke the clouds, and for once the world was silent. Neither of them felt anxious, stressed or worried. They felt like they could sit there for eternity, just digesting the beautiful scenery with a childlike fascination.

Turning to her, William thought it was time to open his heart, to tell her everything, absolutely everything.

Lizzy beat him to his first words. 'I have always been afraid of this.'

William sensed what she was talking about but asked the question anyway 'Afraid of what?'

'This… giving my heart away, feeling complete and utter love for another person. But not anymore, I love how I feel William, I love it so much.'

He couldn't hide his delight as the words he never thought he'd hear came from her mouth. 'I was scared too, Lizzy, scared of everything, my dreams, my reality, my past, my present and my future. I was scared of people, of life itself. But most of all I was scared of not being able to tell you how I felt, how I feel, and if I never did I wouldn't ever feel real love in my life. It is a notion I dared not even dream throughout my whole life, until I met you. But now I feel it grip my soul so tight that nothing, not a hundred men or more could stop me loving you. No man, no Patrick, no laws, not anything. My love is *mighty,* Lizzy. Mighty, true and pure and it has given me reason to live my life.'

She gripped his hand in hers as her eyes filled with tears of overwhelming joy.

'We live in a cruel world, Lizzy, a world where people chatter, and oh how they will chatter.' William smiled.

'Let them chatter.' Lizzy smiled back.

'As you know, Lizzy, it seems to be that people are more concerned about what they own, where they stand and how they are seen instead of the important things. Everything is about what's proper. Well I am not proper, Lizzy. Never have been and I never will be I guess. But I love you, Lizzy, and if there is such a thing as good honest love, then that is what I have, that is what I promise to you. It is real, so real, so…'

'Proper?' Lizzy smiled.

They smiled together and then they kissed.

Lizzy asked about the events which led to William running away.

He did not have to hide anymore, so he told her…

He told her the whole thing. He told her about the dreams, about his mother, his father, his dark and saddened past.

Nothing was left out, William explained about the voices, and how for years when he was younger he felt he was going mad.

He didn't know what was stranger, the fact he was telling her all this, knowing that most people would think he was crazy and run away faster than they could say 'lunatic,' or the fact she genuinely seemed to believe him. Either way, it felt comforting to know he could tell her anything.

Lizzy didn't ask many questions about the incident, why should she? She loved him regardless. She didn't regard the whole thing as impossible *or* possible; William believed it, so it was good enough for her.

After all, what *is* real?

The hours rolled by like minutes and William asked if Lizzy wanted to stay at the church for some dinner. She agreed; she was sick of hiding their love. She wanted to celebrate it. They didn't want to leave as they sat in a mellow harmony.

Their love felt completely untouchable, impregnable.

Invincible

CHAPTER 45

Have you ever heard of the word 'enlightenment'? I am sure you have, it is described in the Oxford English Dictionary as 'the action of enlightening or the state of being enlightened.' Perhaps there was a better word to describe how the two of them felt as they finished their supper and talked for hours upon hours about life and love, but they could not think of it.

'Awakening' - now there is a word. Defined as 'an act of waking from sleep' or 'becoming suddenly aware of something'.

Had they both been asleep for these many years? In which case, they were truly aware now. Funny, isn't it? How love can resurrect one's true soul? How it can almost shield two beings from anything outside the vicinity of each other's touch.

The night had been a lovely experience, the start of many they hoped. William desperately wanted Lizzy to stay with him a while longer but she couldn't, even if she wanted to.

She explained she had to get back to her house, not for the wonder of her maids about where she was or the chance of any prying eyes' suspicion, but to freshen up and prepare for the next day ahead. She had another musical day in store for William.

His very first piano lesson was set.

He was excited at the prospect and walked her through the graveyard on the way to the main gates of the cemetery.

Just as they passed some of the graves, a voice spoke, it was soft, but William heard it.

'Hello?' the voice asked.

It was Lord Fenwick; did he know Lizzy was here?

William wondered if he should ignore the voice.

He couldn't, the day had been about truth after all, Lizzy had accepted him for who he was.

He had to show her, he owed it to her.

'One minute, Lizzy,' William said as he softly stopped her by taking her arm. 'I have to show you something, come with me.'

'What's the matter, my love?' she asked as they walked only a few steps to where Lord Fenwick was buried.

'Do you trust me?' William asked.

'Of course I trust you' she replied 'that will never be in question.'

He gently smiled at her. 'Then trust me, for there is something you must see, someone, with whom you must speak.'

She didn't seem at all frightened, and why should she have been? She trusted him unconditionally.

Focusing completely on William, she didn't realise which grave she was near. William heard Lord Fenwick's voice again and whispered, 'Give me a minute, old boy,' Lizzy gave William a look of confusion.

Placing his hand over her heart, William looked deep into Lizzy's eyes 'Trust me, my love, close your eyes.'

She did as William asked and as she did she automatically felt different, like she was floating somehow, like she was in a dream.

It was pleasant, but all she could do was hear, she couldn't see anything at all, but she wasn't scared. She just wondered what was going on, all the while aware of the fact she was safe in William's arms.

The first thing she heard was William's voice. 'Lizzy, are you alright dear?'

His voice was as clear as could be. 'Yes, yes, William I am quite fine. Where are we, what is this?'

'This, Lizzy, is my gift. This is how I see without seeing, now, somebody wants to talk to you. I will be here, you are still in my arms, but I will keep out of your conversation, for it is a private matter for you and someone past. Over to you, sir…'

Waiting for something to happen, Lizzy called out 'Hello?'

'Hello, Lizzy,' a familiar voice said.

She was lost for words, she knew full well who was speaking to her; the voice was one from the past, and a friendly one at that.

'Oh my word! Oh my goodness gracious, it is you! Oh my dear friend, I would ask how you are but I'm not sure it would be appropriate given the circumstances.'

'It is I, your friend. Do not worry Lizzy, I am quite alright. I have made new friends here, who are all so very interesting in their own right; apart from the sausage next door but we won't get into that. I wanted to speak with you, Lizzy. I wanted to speak from the heart.'

'Go on,' Lizzy said, wondering if he would be mad at her love for William, which she assumed he knew of.

'The arrangement we had … we should have never done it. It was all my fault, you were a friend in a time when I needed one, and I pressured you into marrying me. I know you never loved me in that way and I could never love another that way too after my wife. But you must see, it was for friendship and marriage should be about love, dear girl. Now this man who holds you in his arms, he loves you. I can read people you see, a rather handy gift I could have done with in my business days, let me tell you. But yes, back to what I was saying, this man, William. He is a very fine lad, and I know you love him too. As for that no-good brother of mine, ignore all he says, he always wanted you for himself. Stay clear of such men, such evil-doers. Follow your heart, Lizzy, for when it skips a beat for someone, it is never wrong. Be together, be happy. I will always cherish our time as friends, and I will hope to hear of further good news about the two of you over the years! Hey, you could even get married here, one day in the future perhaps, but if you did I could be here! How amazing would that be?'

Another voice piped up. 'Oh for god's sake, stop rattling on would you? Some of us are trying to sleep!'

'Sorry Lizzy,' whispered Lord Fenwick. 'That's the one I was talking about, old sausage face!' Ha-ha. Right, I will be going now, you take care my dear! Toodle-oo!'

Lizzy's eyes opened and she saw William before her. He was laughing at her obvious amazement.

'I don't believe it, William! I mean, I do but, oh my goodness gracious!'

'Are you glad I showed you? I thought it was important.'

'It was, so important. I never doubted your gift, but to witness it like that, to hear a voice from the other side, well, it is an experience I will never forget. It is good to know he is alright too.'

'He is fine, and I will always look after him while I work here.' William smiled.

'A question though, William?' asked Lizzy

'Anything,' William replied

'Who is 'sausage face'?'

'Oh Lizzy, that is a story that can wait,' laughed William as he took her hand and they walked slowly to the main gates of the cemetery.

Together they waited in the fading evening's light for a driver to pass, and after a short while one did. Lizzy motioned the driver to come over to them, which he did. William helped her into the carriage and once seated she gave him her hand to kiss as she said farewell.

'Till tomorrow then?' William grinned.

Her attempt at being reserved was let down by her glaring cheerfulness, her white teeth shining at him in a full and wonderful smile.

The driver looked back as he readied his whip. 'You ready to go?'

'Aye, driver,' answered William, and as the carriage set off he mouthed the words 'I love you.'

She laughed loudly and blew him a kiss as she mouthed back at him, 'I love you too.'

William laughed even louder than Lizzy, in fact it was the loudest he had laughed in years.

He couldn't wait to see her again. 'Only a few more hours,' he thought as he walked back through the graveyard. He stopped at the tool shed, and opened it to find Azrael sound asleep. Not wanting to wake him, William tried to shut the door quietly but as he did it creaked and Azrael's eyes quickly opened. Azrael gave a few short woofs and William re-opened the door and whispered, 'Shush boy, don't want people to know you're here do you?' Azrael trotted over to William and licked his hands then playfully knocked William to his knees as he jumped and wriggled, his fur surrounding William's head like a warm blanket.

'Come on, lad, you can sleep in my room tonight,' William said as he led his furry friend out of the shed and into his quarters. William kicked his shoes off and threw off his shirt and then jumped on the bed. He tapped his own legs with his hand and Azrael responded by jumping up on the bed. William stretched out, his head on the pillow, as he snuggled his friend, Azrael.

He drifted away to sleep thinking of Lizzy and the unbelievable day that had passed.

He was in love, he had found love!

CHAPTER 46

Often when he got scared as a child, the Reverend would come and comfort him. William's father never helped, so the Reverend always seemed to fill in when and where he could. He would give William various lessons on trying to control his fear. Sometimes it worked, sometimes it didn't. One of the lessons William always tried to remember, was for when he heard things go bump in the night.

William had heard a few sounds outside; he tried to remember what the Reverend had said about all humans' primary sense being sight. And when that is taken away, the brain panics, which in turn creates panic all over the body. A picture of the dark is formed in the mind, so that whenever you see a dark place after that, your brain panics again, because it knows that it will lose the primary sense. People tend to pay much more attention to their hearing in the dark, because of lack of sight. Therefore, the strange noises heard are actually always there, it's just they sound more prominent because the mind is more alert.

William missed his long chats with Father Fanshaw; they simply didn't seem to have time for each other these days. It seemed when the Reverend was free William was with Lizzy, and when William was free the Reverend was out of town, which the Reverend often was to visit various people. He was an important man after all. William hadn't seen the Reverend in days, so figured he was on another one of his trips out of town. 'I am going to make time for him,' thought William as he noticed Azrael's paw move.

He looked at Azrael's wet nose and beautiful cuddly face, he was fast asleep. 'Some guard dog,' thought William as he stroked Azrael's fur. Then William thought it was good that Azrael was asleep for it would only be trouble if he *did* bark. William looked at his clock on the wall; it was ten past three in the morning.

He breathed in deeply as he told himself he was foolish to be frightened by silly sounds of the night. He turned to his side, trying to shove Azrael aside a little as he was doing his best to take over the bed.

'Lazy mutt,' thought William as he cuddled his face into Azrael's fur.

Just as William felt in a place of complete warm comfort, Azrael shot out of the bed and to the door. William jumped back, startled at the sudden movement. He knew Azrael was fast, but not *that* fast.

'What's wrong boy?' William asked, he even waited for a response then it suddenly dawned upon him that he should be the one taking a look outside. His memory revisited the aftermath of the last time the graveyard had late night visitors, and it made him wary of taking a look.

This time William figured he would at least put a shirt on, and as he did so his mind was spilt.

Should he go outside? Should he investigate the creepy sounds of the night?

Biting his bottom lip with a nagging curiosity, William figured lightning surely would not strike twice; that perhaps it was an animal; maybe a fox trapped in the grounds and needing to be let out through the gate. He had a quick look around his room for a weapon, and then William saw a hammer which he had left in his room earlier that day to fix a hook to his door on which he would hang his coat.

Picking the heavy hammer up, William felt it would be much more useful should any foes be in waiting.

William hit the air with the hammer three times in practice; just in case he needed to use it, he told himself he was being silly, for surely nothing was outside.

'Come on, lad, don't be a scaredy-cat.'

Gathering all his courage (and of course gripping his hammer tight) William tip-toed outside into the night's latest challenge.

But what was out there waiting for him? An innocent animal? A simple, unlocked gate, clanging in the wind? Or some dreaded trespassers like before?

Continuing his hushed footsteps as he moved forward towards the graves, William was at least pleased that the night's air was free of mist, which meant it less likely he could be surprised. His eyes wandered the graveyard for any possible abnormalities, any sign of something that didn't fit.

Everything seemed fine to William as he dared to breathe in relief. Lowering his hammer as he strode the soft grass of Deadville, William looked ahead and noticed the front gates were indeed open.

Now, William would usually think what most people would in such a situation; the thing was…

He specifically remembered shutting the gates; he remembered the rough rust on the handle as he closed it tight shut.

No animal could stand up and open a gate which was chest height, no wind could unfasten a latch and lift so as to open.

So what, or *who* did?

His heightened sense of caution returning, William raised his right arm with the hammer again, looking left and right as he walked towards the gate. He was going to shut it again. As he got not a few feet away, he heard a noise again. He quickly turned and swung the hammer in the air.

He thought he briefly saw a shadow appear then disappear within seconds. Was it *his* shadow though? Or was his frightful mind playing tricks on him? For once he thought he could really use some help from his ghostly friends, but there was none. Their voices were silent tonight; were they afraid like he? Or had they abandoned him in his hour of need?

'I hear you,' William said sternly. 'I am about to lock the gates, if you leave now I will not alert the police, but go now, in peace, please. For this is a place of rest!'

There was an answer, but it didn't come through words. It came in the form of three shadows which William gradually watched grow bigger as they advanced towards him.

Then as a faint yellow light from the only lit street lantern just outside the graveyard caught the advancing shadows, William's eyes widened in shuddering recognition.

Once again, they circled.

Once again, they were armed.

Once again, it was them, the wrongdoers, the grave robbers, the very same attackers as before!

Each of the dastardly trio showed their hand for William to see.

They wanted him to see

The tall and twiggy man smiled and bared his black-as-tar teeth as he patted what looked like a policeman's truncheon with his hand. 'We meet again,' he laughed.

The jelly-bellied bruiser with the unmistakable striped cap flicked his razor ready for service with a death-seeking hungry smile. 'Evening,' he nodded.

Then the third of the trio, the small scruffy rat-faced devil opened up his pocket knife with what looked like purpose.

William knew what he faced; he had to hide his fear, deep down inside where they could not see it. 'I have no riches, men, nothing to bring you fortune.'

The tall, underweight man laughed loudly and then put a finger across his own lips. 'Hush, I will tell you a secret. We are not here to steal.'

Having figured that part out for himself already, William deserted his usual caution. 'That's quite alright, gentlemen. I know it's me you want. But I actually do have something for you.'

The fat man laughed, 'Yeah, what would that be then, freak?'

William raised the gift he intended to deliver to them high into the shiny moonlight. They saw it; and William saw that they saw it.

He wanted them to see it.

The tall, scraggy man shook his head. 'Why don't you just let us be on with it, you fool? We promise it won't hurt, then again, it might, but not for long! I tell you what, we can make a deal, if you die without fuss, we promise to treat your dear lady friend with the upmost respect when we visit her next. Lady Anne, is it?

I've never killed a lady before, should be fun, but don't worry we will pay her some extra attention if she is as pretty as they say!'

The men had William's full attention, and for the first time since he could remember, he was angry.

'Don't you dare say her name, don't you dare. You don't get to say her name. Your fight is with me, not her. She has done you no harm.'

'Neither have you gravedigger, never-the-less you must die, and that's just the way it is.'

The fat man laughed as he saw William's eyes flicker from one man to the next. 'Look at him, he's scared stiff! Ha-ha! Aw here kitty-kitty, come to me, I have something for you,' he mocked as he twizzled his razor between his fingers.

'What do you think you can do gravedigger?' the scruffy man added. 'There are three of us, one of you!'

Gritting his teeth, William answered. 'There is nothing even a hundred of you could do when it comes to protecting her. You are all dead, the three of you…and that's just the way it is.'

CHAPTER 47

William was aware he needed to be wary of his form of attack, to not rush in, to not over-extend his thrust when swinging, to not be blind-sided.

Three different men.

Three different weapons.

Three different problems.

There were three of them but they were not rushing to attack William, and William hoped they would back off, and somehow see that there was no way he would give in, no way he was going down without a fight, no way they were ever going to hurt Lizzy.

The black-toothed man was evidently growing impatient as he looked inside his jacket at an old brass pocket watch. 'What you waiting for? We haven't all night, get him!' he barked at his two sidekicks.

The potbellied man swung his razor from left-to-right and right-to-left erratically, 'Come on, come on, you freak,' he whispered as he taunted William. But William stood unruffled; clutching his hammer like it was the key to life itself. Then the second man, the messy miniature, seemed to find some guts and walked towards William with his pocket knife in the air. Until finally, the scrawny grotesque man, the third of the bunch, joined his fellow criminals to do what they were there to do.

Taking the night's air deeply into his lungs, William knew he had to strike right, had to strike perfectly, he played three moves out in his head like the chess game Lizzy had taught him and then her words entered his mind from memory of the first day she introduced the game to him.

'William, never forget that the King is the most important piece in the game. Although he can only move one space at a time, if your King is captured, you lose the game.'

It was if she had known, it was as if her inner voice had found him somehow to protect him.

William exhaled slowly, he blocked out the men's taunts as they closed in, he only focused on Lizzy's words from that day…

'William, the way to play is to think you are controlling a medieval battle. PROTECT THE KING.'

The battle was most certainly commencing, and the enemy was closing in, but tonight…

William was the King.

They were almost upon him now, but still William waited. Timing was crucial; he wanted the moment to be absolutely perfect.

He *had* to do this, if he didn't, he was dead, it was that simple. The last time they nearly killed him, and William simply couldn't afford to take any chances.

It was kill or be killed.

'One step more, just one step more,' he thought.

As the fat man's foot landed in the mud near William, William looked at the overweight dimwit and fastened his grip on his hammer.

There were numerous blows thrown in the quick melee that followed, but only three mattered. With three dull thuds it was all over, it had promised to be so much more. William expected some hard-fought, desperate battle for his life, but what transpired was much simpler.

A quick and efficient sequence of specific movements conjured up from a game of chess with Lizzy, the little delicate pieces replaced by a knife, a bat, a razor … and William's hammer.

Dropping his instrument of death and falling to his knees, William's relief was replaced by a new problem as three dead bodies bludgeoned and bloodied were spread out on the grass, all of which were as still and cold as the night which surrounded him.

Feeling suspended in some deep-seated apprehension, William had no idea what to do. He shuffled forward slowly, first to the tall man's body. William poked him with a finger and quickly shuffled back, there was no response.

William then shuffled towards the fat man. There was a huge dent in the fat man's forehead and William was smart enough to know he was dead.

Then it was to the third, the small scruffy one. William looked over the man for signs of life but there were none. All there was a huge crater in what was once a face, William winced a little as he saw how the nose and part of the middle bit of face had become inverted by the thunderous strike of the hammer.

'Oh dear,' said William out loud as he closed the man's eyes with his fingers. He then realised he had blood on his hands from touching the bodies, so he wiped his wet bloodied hands on his shirt.

Struggling to find a suitable plan of action, William thought the best possible thing would be to tell the truth, to get the police and tell them what had happened. But then, as if by some magical telepathy, William heard what sounded like the whistles of the police.

The sound of the whistles was unmistakable, only the police used them!

'Oh, thank goodness,' thought William as his hopes turned into reality. He saw dark uniformed men running towards him, the whistles still blowing loud and clear.

'Thank god! I am so glad you are here, these men, these men…'

It all seemed to happen so fast. William couldn't even finish his sentence as the police knocked him to the floor and pulled his arms behind his back in the most severe of fashions. There were a crowd of police now, and as they pulled out their thick polished police truncheons and started to beat him, he couldn't help but feel aggrieved at the fact that they were messing up the graves nearby.

A tear came down William's face, though it was not one of fright, neither was it one of the pain his body was feeling as they beat his back and legs with their thick wooden problem solvers.

It was a tear of sadness, a sadness that came because it seemed they had already made up their minds.

He was already guilty.

Trying to speak as the beating slowed down, William whispered to one of the policemen, 'I am sorry, but they attacked me sir, I had no choice.'

'Shut it, you devil worshiping scum!' said one of the policeman who then knelt down to William's eye level. 'Pick him up,' the man shouted to one of his colleagues.

Feeling intense pain as they pulled his long black hair back to raise him from the ground, William noticed all the blood on his own shirt.

Things didn't look good at all.

The policeman in front of him put the truncheon under his chin and pushed back as another policeman held William's head. William could hardly breathe but didn't want to make a fuss. He thought it would be better to pass out than to complain, he was hurt enough already.

'Now you listen here, you grave-digging pig. *You* have killed three innocent men. Three men, visiting loved ones, you absolute swine, you *will* pay. Oh yes, you *will* pay. They will rush this through for sure won't they lads?'

Feeling another blow, this time to the head, William's body fell to the ground. It was like everything was in slow motion as he saw what looked like maybe eight or nine policeman all around him with weapons in their hands, laughing and smiling like they had caught the world's worst criminal. His head hit the grass. 'I'm sorry, my friends,' William whispered to the grass, hoping his friends of Deadville could hear him. 'I'm so sorry.'

'Hear that?' One of the policemen shouted 'He's saying he's sorry! Practically admitted it, he has!'

As all the feet moved around his eyes William wondered if this was what drunk felt like. He remembered his father lying on the floor many-a-time during his youth when his eyes would be open but he couldn't seem to move. William's eyes gradually began to close, but then he saw a really polished pair of boots in front of his face. The boots bent slightly and were followed by knees, then a face that leaned in next to his.

He recognised the face, and even though he was drowsy and hurt, William knew he was done for.

'I told you gravedigger,' the face said quietly as the other men shouted and caused commotions in the background.

'I told you, but you wouldn't obey. Now, you are mine.'

Another voice shouted loudly nearby and William tried to see who it was, but his head was being forced into the ground by someone.

'He has a wolf sir, a wolf I say, it's watching from the bush up ahead … another proof of his weirdness! What shall we do?'

The familiar face in front of William smiled 'Kill it'

William cried out and tried to get up. 'No! It is gentle! Azrael run! Run for your life, forget me!'

The face then vanished as William felt a huge thud across his head as he heard Azrael howl so loud it echoed like the church bells.

His eyes were now well and truly closed…and soaked with tears.

CHAPTER 48

'So this is what an army man must feel like,' smiled Patrick Fenwick as he stuffed some tobacco into his pipe.

'Excuse me, sir?' Constable Ravensdale asked.

'You know, when an army general or something makes a plan for his enemy and wins. Everything carried out so very, very perfectly. It is quite the satisfying feeling, let me tell you.'

Ravensdale shouted a few instructions to the men nearby as they dragged William's beaten body away. 'Yes, take him to the station, no, not the hospital, the station, he's a criminal, he doesn't have the right to treatment, if he dies he dies.' He then re-focused on Patrick. 'Sorry sir, you were saying?'

Patrick nodded and laughed. 'Oh look at you, stressed! I was talking about how well you have done lad, served me well and I say with meaning that it shall not be forgotten. Rise quickly you shall if you let me steer you the right way. Now, enjoy a smoke with me, a victory smoke we shall call it!'

After accepting a small amount of tobacco from Patrick, Ravensdale stuffed his own pipe and lit it. He inhaled deeply and turned to his ally. 'Not quite the victory yet though, sir, is it?'

'Why not?'

'Well, he is alive isn't he?'

Almost choking because of inhaling too hard, Patrick patted his own chest and laughed at Ravensdale's words 'Yes, I'll give you that, the man yet breathes air, but for how long my friend? Do you not think I will have this rushed through? Do you not think that *I, the* Patrick Fenwick, the *true* lord of Barnes, hold persuasions beyond any man's temptation? Huh? You have to ask yourself, young one, how long have I planned this? How thorough do you think the man with *the* best conviction rate this-side-of-London has been? Well, in answer to my own question, I have taken the most very special care. I have spoken to my judge, yes *my* judge, his right honourable Judge Stanbury'

'Stanbury? Really, you have him? Now that is a feat in itself!' laughed Ravensdale.

'Well, I do have my ways of turning even the most stubborn of characters. I explained this gravedigger was a fiend, a devil worshipper etcetera-etcetera, and that it was thought the man was planning murders. I sought a warrant for his arrest but the judge would not sign it, he said without any good evidence nothing would stand up in court. So I showed him one of these…'

'Oh my word!' Ravensdale shouted as he saw what Patrick pulled out of his jacket 'That is one very fine pistol indeed!'

'The finest' Patrick smiled as he held it out in front for Ravensdale to look over 'You see this very dandy piece of lethal equipment is in fact a 16 bore Galton, William IV percussion conversion of a 1796 Dragoon Pistol, needless to say, an undeniably rare piece. Galton were a prestigious family who lived at Barr Hall and later purchased Warley Hall Estate, you know which one, it's the big one on the other side of town with the viewing gardens. Anyway the Galton family were prominent gun-makers, with a gun works in Smethwick. Now I found out, through many a discreet enquiry I will add, that Judge Stanbury has been after this very piece for his notorious pistol collection. The thing is there are only a few in circulation, and a few weeks ago, I happened to find a gun merchant who had two pairs. Judge Stanbury found this information out too, but I bought them before he could. Apparently he was most displeased. So when I saw him at the courts I asked him ever so graciously that if I could present to him such evidence of the gravedigger's wrongdoing, would his justice be swift, and just. He paused for a few moments, then when he saw a perfectly polished wooden box with none other than the 16 bore Galton itself staring at him, with the promise of *his* name engraved on it ... well he gave the most pleasing of responses'

Ravensdale laughed hard 'I bet he did; oh you, sir, are a schemer indeed!'

'You better believe it.' laughed Patrick 'Play your cards right, and you can have one of those too, Ravensdale'

'Really? Oh sir, that would be so wonderful, I have always wanted such a prestigious weapon'

Blowing out the dregs of his pipe, Patrick put his pistol away inside his long jacket. 'Get the evidence ready, have it written good and proper, so there is no doubt to the guilt of the fiend, then the rewards you shall reap.'

'It shall be done,' snapped Ravensdale as he jogged off full of glee.

Looking around the graveyard Patrick felt so good, so happy that another who had defied him was going to be nothing but another forgotten nobody.

'One down, one to go,' he smiled as he walked out of the graveyard. He then let out a little chuckle as he noticed all the headstones on his way out. He even saw his brother's and snarled at it.

Then he thought of William, beaten, bruised and defeated. 'The next grave he'll be near is his own, as he's laid in it.' The thought of this made him so excited; he just had to share the news, and who better to share it with than his former sister in law…Lizzy.

CHAPTER 49

There were always things that bothered Constable Robertson about the police station of Barnes, for Robertson was somewhat of a perfectionist. It was his belief that the police under his command should always be looking for ways to improve, but he had seen some bad habits recently, and Robertson blamed himself for not being the authoritarian he maybe could have been. His concerns were underlined more so by spending time with another set of policemen on his trip to Kensington. The case he had gone to help with had been very interesting and after giving his own theories he left the Kensington Police Station to return home but did so with a sense of renewed optimism that he could get his station running like theirs. He wanted more men, men who could do the job, but most of all men who were right for the job.

On entering the station which was like a home to him now, Robertson was pleased to see bodies buzzing around. Everyone seemed so busy; Robertson looked at it in two ways.

One, it was good to see everyone working for a change, and two – something bad had happened. He feared the latter.

Even though he had only been out of town a day and a half, Robertson wanted to have a meeting with his men. For he had learned many times before, that in one day in Barnes, many things could happen. Before being brought up to speed on current events though, Robertson wanted to outline the men's duties, to give his men a stark reminder of what it was to be a member of the police. To do a proper duty for the crown and more importantly the good people of the community. He thought it would be good just to reaffirm some purpose.

As he stood at the reception area watching all the men walking in many different directions, Robertson picked up the bell on the front table, which was supposed to be manned at all times.

It wasn't.

The sign near the bell said 'Ring for assistance.' Robertson rang the bell, once, twice, three times. He shook his head and put his large satchel down on the floor and then straightened his jacket which was buttoned right to the top. He prepared his voice by coughing a little, and then let loose.

'GENTLEMEN! MAY I HAVE YOUR ATTENTION PLEASE?'

The many that could see him stopped dead in their tracks like a bunch of disturbed mice around a block of cheese.

They all looked, knowing that when Robertson raised his voice that full attention was demanded.

'A meeting in the incident room is required, spread the word. All officers currently in the station are required to attend. You have five minutes.'

After a few moments of chairs being shuffled around so everyone could see, Robertson stood at the front of the room. He looked at the dozen or so men in uniform looking up at him, all with the 'Am I in trouble?' expression on their faces.

'I am sure you are all aware I have been away for a day or so attending to important business. While that is a separate issue, it has come to light by watching the good officers of Kensington that standards here have been slipping. It stops now. Now let me remind you all of a few things. This is not aimed at all, I know some of you do your duty to the absolute best of your abilities, but there are others, who do not. So here goes… a good policeman is somebody people believe they can talk to and not be afraid of, and who is excellent at his job. He should not have a short temperament, and should be sympathetic at all times, although still being professional. We're an essential part of the community and no job should ever be beneath us. Our work is based in, around and for the local communities. That's why it's important we respect the culture and beliefs of others, whatever their status, to gain respect from them. As police, we have to show respect to all, yes-even the old naggers, yes- even the sometimes silly, young, irritable teenagers and also lest we forget, the criminals. We should not stand out as a bold figure of authority that nobody would like to speak to. We should be the opposite, Standing up for the common man, for when they need assistance, or just a re-assuring word from a figure of authority that can protect them, and their co-inhabitants. Now I want each and every one of you to write the following down.'

Each man in attendance quickly opened up various little notebooks and held their pens in their hands, waiting for Robertson's words as he walked around the room, making sure they were all doing as he asked.

'We need to be honest, my fellow law enforcers, mature and socially aware. We need to be assertive, for I have seen some of you that can quiver in front of men who intimidate. Do not let them do so, stand your ground! It is hugely important we be effective communicators after all, if we can't talk to people, our job cannot be done. I want you to remember to be sympathetic and tactful, I heard just a few weeks ago that a man from this station went round to deliver news of old farmer Stephenson's passing to his wife. Now bear in mind, this poor old chap was crushed under a carriage of firewood. His old dear was distraught as could be expected. Then, after delivering the grave news, he proceeded to pester the daughter of the farmer when he left the house, and even pinched her bottom as the new widow looked out the window! Pinched her bottom he did!'

There was a snigger at the back of the room and Robertson's head shot up like a dear hearing a twig snap.

'Who laughed?' he shouted. 'Which dim-witted, no-good prat thought that was funny?'

'Sorry sir,' a man said while making it plain and obvious he was not, his smile doing its best to conceal itself but failing miserably.

'Constable Ravensdale, why am I not surprised? You are on thin ice boy, don't make me crack it, I warn you now, take notice of these words because things are going to change around here!'

'I'm sorry, sir' Ravensdale said with an unconcerned look on his face.

'Yeah, you look it. We'll chat after this, all right?'

'Sir' Ravensdale nodded reluctantly.

As I was saying before I was so rudely interrupted, sensitivity, men … it is so important. Now, I know we are all men, and while our blood runs red we will have urges, but you have them somewhere else, not on duty! Be decisive with good judgement, very important, none of this, 'Oooo I don't know what to do,' malarkey, use your head for Lord's sake! I want every man here to want to better his skills, year on year, and you will be pleased to learn that I will be developing certain training exercises once a year, with a written test so you had better be reading those books men, for a good policeman is happy to study and learn. I know I am, even in one day away from here I learned new things; you are never too old or too experienced to try new things. It helps, trust me. Now I know you have a hard job, and it's damn hard some days. You get insults; people look at you funny, but you have to stay disciplined lads, it's the job. Saying that also brings me to personal safety, if a guy is too big, go and get another to help you, do not try the impossible, although you do know that you must be prepared physically and emotionality to deal with everything we are faced with. Now I would like to think I am a good policeman, I really would and I am not saying I do not make mistakes. We all do. Just use that judgement, men, use it well. I have to admit, even I sometimes let some offenders away, if they are sorry for their actions and I can tell they won't do it again, I have also built some valued relationships with members of our little community, most of whom I know by their first names. I also stop off at many old people's houses, and have a chat with them. It makes them feel like they have a 'friend' they can trust. Makes them feel part of the community, like they too have a voice, and they really do, so use them and respect them.'

Robertson looked around the room and smiled. 'That is all, return to your duties. Thank you, men.'

Most of the men scurried off to do their various jobs. There was a lot of huffing and puffing but Robertson expected that, he just hoped the words sunk in. That somehow, some of them would take notice and make Barnes a better and safer place to be.

Always wanting to keep his finger on the pulse, Robertson walked around the station; he browsed random police files on desks, and asked random policemen how they were doing. In most cases, things seemed to be running as smoothly as he expected in his absence. He had not left anyone in charge so-to-say; however there were a few more senior men of longer service that seemed to have kept the place in a relatively decent state.

After fixing himself a cup of tea and reading through some old case notes, Robertson spent much of the morning signing various documents and checking correct forms had been filled in for various cases. Such was the importance of paperwork more and more in the so-called modern age. Throughout the morning Robertson read through a whole bunch of petty cases such as the new pickpocket schemers who seemed to be operating in the market, the prostitutes sneaking their way into the centre of town and so on. All the issues needed addressing, but would be done quite easily.

It seemed like the hours had flown by for Robertson, then, upon more casual browsing, Robertson found something which caught his attention like a fish on a hook.

'Hammer attack in Barnes cemetery,' the file read. Robertson quickly flicked open the file in complete surprise. It was dated from the day before, three dead, perpetrator in custody, full confession, and court appearance tomorrow.

'Tomorrow?' thought Robertson, 'Why so soon?'

Why had nobody told him? Surely this was the most important case at the moment? And why had the file been put at the bottom of his pile of papers, especially as it was dated from only the day before?

Something didn't sit right, not at all. All the intuition of a policeman of many years said this was not what it seemed.

And so he read on…

Three men, all innocently visiting graves, attacked by a thug with a hammer.

But why? And by whom?

He read on…

The man in custody was a William Rathbone, a loner and gravedigger at the cemetery.

'What?' Robertson said out loud, 'Not possible!'

He looked at the signature of the officer in charge of the scene. The signature made Robertson bite his bottom lip.

'Ravensdale, you idiot!' thought Robertson as he searched the notes for evidence of a solid nature. 'Why do you push for a sentence without a thorough investigation?'

The evidence seemed as sound as could be. Ravensdale had a confession, witnessed by as many as three officers it seemed. But William was no murderer, Robertson was sure of it; he had to get to the bottom of this, he just *had* to. Then two words on the bottom of one of the pages hit Robertson like the deadly hammer in the case.

Two little words made so many questions ring in Robertson's head. The words formed a name and the name was Patrick Fenwick.

Patrick Fenwick was the lead prosecutor in the case, and without a doubt in Robertson's mind, this had to be more than coincidence.

CHAPTER 50

Awakening after what seemed like a long time asleep; William wiped his eyes and looked around. The place was filthier than a pig sty. His eyes stared at the thick, black iron bars and the realisation of where he was hit like a brick.

There were all different types of smells, none of which were pleasant. He could smell waste of every variety. There was a smell of some sort of cleaning fluid that men, who were mopping the floors outside, were using. They walked by as they mopped and one of them gave William a damning glare. But the worst smell William inhaled, worse than any could imagine, was the one most of us couldn't register. The kind of smell only someone with a special gift could trace.

It was the smell of fear, and it riddled the walls and floors like rats riddled the sewers.

The noise level varied. It had seemed quiet in the morning but William expected it to get more rowdy as the day grew. The worst noise for William was the echoing clang of metal doors opening and closing in the corridors.

He examined his own body as he lifted his blood-stained shirt. There were bruises and cuts and William felt some ribs move which were obviously broken.

But it wasn't the physical pain which made William's eyes fill again; it was the thought of Lizzy. It was mid-morning and they would have been due to meet by now. What would she think? Would she know of his plight? Would she believe him?

Deep down, William knew she would. He knew that she knew that he would never ever lie to her. He hoped he was all right. As his tears ran down his cheeks, he wondered about his other friend, Azrael. William hoped he got away. He could remember the last thunderous howls before he was knocked unconscious, and his heart begged that they were not the last.

Just as William wiped his eyes for what seemed like the millionth time, his ear picked up a different sound.

Loud hollow footsteps bounced off the cells walls, followed by insults thrown by others imprisoned at whoever was walking the corridor.

'Let me out, ya pig!' and 'You damn horrible peeler!' were but a few thrown the way of the mystery walker. The footsteps got closer and closer still. They got so close William turned towards the bars to see who might pass as the sound of the steps came to a halt, William looked up at a face he knew could be trusted, a face that always spread warmth and truth.

Constable Robertson.

William dragged himself to the bars and got as close as he could, he was still on his knees, and unable to walk due to the beating the police had given his legs the night before.

'Oh dear sir, I am so glad to see you. Oh lord, where do I begin? You must help me, sir, for it was not my fault! Lizzy, dear Lizzy you must protect her for I fear she is in grave danger, there are men who want us dead, dead I say!'

Crouching to William's level, Robertson halted William's speech. 'Stop, hush-hush, William. Please calm down, boy. I do not have much time if I am to act swiftly, I need to know as much as you can tell me, with as much detail, and as fast as you possibly can. Can you do that for me?'

Trying to control his consternation, William spoke as quickly and as clearly as he could, reliving the events of the night before.

He spoke of the three men, and that without doubt they were the grave robbers from before. He spoke about their appearance, the weapons they had in their hands, and he spoke of their intentions, to kill him and then to go and kill Lady Anne. William spoke of Patrick Fenwick's obsession with his and Lady Anne's love, and how it seemed to offend Patrick to the point he would do anything to stop it.

Robertson knew something hadn't been right. He knew it in the pit of his stomach. As he looked at William's beaten body and blood-stained shirt he felt a genuine sympathy for the man, and it was that sympathy which made it all the harder to tell William he was due in court the next day.

'I don't care sir, all I care about is that she is looked after, protected even, for she is the only important thing right now,' William said quietly.

Robertson knew these weren't the words of a guilty man … no way in Hell. Robertson had seen guilty men, plenty of them, and not once had any been concerned for anything other than their own well-being. He knew he had to get to the bottom of things, and fast.

Taking William's hand, Robertson's words oozed with intent as he spoke to William with fiery eyes. 'William, you must hold on, hold on, dear boy. I will do what I can, but I fear Fenwick has a plan in place, and I also fear his corruption has spilled into others , others of an even higher status, to get all this in place so quickly. Fear not for Lady Anne, for I promise I will take every care of her, I will do this myself. I will see the Reverend too and together, God-willing, we can unravel this series of bitter happenings once and for all and unmask the full truth. I will have one of my most trusted men watch you too, and have a doctor come and tend to your wounds.'

Robertson stood quickly. 'Rest, William, I will return.'

Holding his gratitude inside along with tears of relief, William tensed his face so the tears didn't fall. 'Thank you,' he whispered with a nod.

William heard Robertson run down the corridor and shout at somebody. 'Nobody comes in or out of here without *MY* permission!' Then he heard someone else shout 'Yes, sir.' as the door clanged shut.

He had never been one for praying, but William clasped his hands together as tight as he could.

'Please, please look after her, if there is any fairness left in the world, please look after her.'

CHAPTER 51

Rushing around was not the typical way Robertson operated. He always believed it was better to take his time, gather things at a manageable pace, for the reason of undoubted clarity. But there was no time to be as careful as usual, the time involved was a luxury he could ill afford, for a man's life hung in the balance.

The first point of call was Woodworth Manor. Lady Anne needed to be alerted. Her welfare was paramount for a promise he intended to keep. Finding a driver when he needed one was always a chore. During the day he would always see plenty of them nagging for work, at every corner. It was typical that when he was desperate for a driver, none were to be seen.

'Damn and blast!' Robertson said out loud, which made a few people who walked by look at him with contempt. But he didn't care; he needed the driver, not in half an hour not in ten minutes but *right now*!

Robertson jogged the street in hope to clap eyes on an empty carriage, and then about twenty yards away Robertson could see a well-dressed and obviously well-to-do couple getting into a carriage, the driver holding the door open for them. Now Robertson was never one for abusing his position, never one to use his job to get what he needed, but today was different, and by hook or by crook he would use whatever he could to get things done.

Anything.

Blowing his police whistle as loud as he could, Robertson ran down the street towards the driver and carriage. The door was shut now and he could see the driver readying his horses to set off. He ran as fast as his legs could carry him, all the while blowing his whistle as the people who walked the streets stopped to look and nose in on a possible drama. His cheeks puffed out and were as red as a robin's chest as he gave one big final blow on the whistle to alert the driver. He spat the whistle out and shouted, 'You there, driver, STOP! STOP NOW!'

The driver's head turned with an expression as if to say, 'Who, me?' and Robertson nodded as if he read his mind. 'Yes, you!'

The driver halted his horses and got off. 'What is the matter, old boy? These people in trouble?'

Robertson stopped for a second as he got his breath back, panting and puffing as he did. He wasn't used to this much exercise.

'Oh, Jesus' he said as some air began to fill his lungs again. 'No, these people are not in trouble, nor are you. I need a ride.'

'But, sir,' the driver responded 'These people were here first, surely you of all people know its first come first served and I…'

'I don't care,' Robertson interrupted, 'You have to excuse my rudeness but my usual manners aren't a priority at this time.'

There was no way Robertson was waiting for the driver to make up his mind so Robertson did it for him; he approached the carriage where the couple where situated and opened the door. 'Apologies, but you must vacate the carriage.'

'Pardon?' The man said while his lady friend held his arm in disbelief. 'Why? What is the meaning of this?'

'Vacate the carriage,' Robertson repeated. 'I shall not ask again.'

The couple stepped out while the man continued his grievance but Robertson paid no attention, instead he signalled the driver to get back to his horse, which he did as the man proceeded to demand an explanation for their unfortunate eviction.

'Go driver, Woodworth Manor, make it fast,' Robertson shouted.

The driver set off and gathered a good speed.

As the carriage moved at speed down the busy, cobbled streets, Robertson racked his brain for answers to questions that were coming to him minute-by-minute.

The right questions needed to be asked, but more importantly, the right questions needed to be answered.

CHAPTER 52

He told the driver to wait and that he would be paid a handsome sum if he were to give a full service for the day. The driver gratefully accepted and waited outside Woodworth Manor as Robertson rushed towards the front doors.

Banging his hands against the door like a monkey in a cage Robertson desperately hoped she was home.

'Lady Anne, Lady Anne Fenwick, are you home?' he shouted.

The large wooden doors opened and Robertson was surprised to see Father Fanshaw already there.

'Er…good day, dear father, I am here to see Lady Anne, is she here?' asked Robertson quietly.

Looking full of woe, Father Fanshaw nodded and took hold of Robertson's arm. 'Hello Constable, I wanted to talk to you, I returned early this morning to hear the news. Now, before you go inside, please be aware that the good Lady is distraught with the awful events which have transpired. I have been waiting for her to calm down somewhat, but she is overcome with emotion at William's predicament'

Putting his arm around Reverend Fanshaw and keeping his voice down, Robertson was curious as to how Lady Anne came to hear of the news. Reverend Fanshaw explained that she was visited by none other than her brother-in-law, Mr Patrick Fenwick, accompanied by a policeman. He explained that it had been brought to their attention, that William killed three men in cold blood and that he was not allowed any visitors whatsoever until it was determined what the sentence would be.

Robertson was stunned.

Why had Fenwick delivered the news, accompanied by an officer, why? Which officer?

Robertson had his theories, but that's all they were. He needed proof, cast iron proof.

As he walked with Father Fanshaw into the house he prepared himself for Lady Anne's understandable anguish.

'Lady Anne,' Robertson said softly as he approached her. She sat at her piano with her head in her hands.

She looked up, her face awash with tears for the man she loved. 'Mr Robertson, what have they done? You have to understand, he is no murderer! They won't even let me see him! They say he may hang! I can't bear it, I just can't!'

'Steady girl, come on,' Robertson said softly as he cradled her in his arms. 'I don't believe he is capable of murder either my lady, not our William. He's a wee bit strange at times, I'll give him that, but the lad's no killer. What he did, if he did it, he must have done in self-defence. The thing I have to do now, my dear, is clear his name; find out the truth about what's been going on. I need to find the connections, my dear, and the little pieces that will link all this together somehow. Now I know that brother–in-law of yours is involved, but why? Why would he want William in jail, or worse? What is his grievance with the lad? Why would he benefit from him being out the picture? Who are his confidants? How does he keep them loyal? Oh yes my lady, many a question needs an answer, but with your help, and yours too my good Reverend, I am certain we can find out, and clear that poor lad's name.'

Lizzy wiped her eyes with her lilac silk handkerchief. 'However I can help, sir, whatever you need to know! Though I am told he will attend court tomorrow for questioning; if that information is correct will you have time to do all this? Will I be able to see him? Can you please allow me to see him? I beg you.'

'Now- now,' Robertson said as he patted Lizzy's arm. 'I will get you to him; it will be very late though, and I must tell you to come with Father Fanshaw here, for William is indeed not allowed any visitors apart from either legal or from the church for the time being. So nobody must know you are coming. I suggest you mask your appearance with a robe or something which I'm sure Father Fanshaw can provide, am I right dear Reverend?'

Father Fanshaw smiled, 'Of course, sir, I have just the thing.'

Lizzy nodded at Robertson. 'Thank you, sir, thank you. I know you are a man of rules so to break them for me, for William, is much appreciated.'

Mr Robertson stood up and moved Lizzy's hair away from her face with his hand. He smiled at her and she tried to smile back as he looked into her eyes. 'It is no problem for me to help, Lady Anne. Someone somewhere is breaking *all* the rules, doing what they've done, so I guess it's time I broke a few.'

Both Father Fanshaw and Lizzy thanked Robertson again as he explained to them he had to go to the scene of the crime.

Something was amiss…

He could feel it in his bones.

CHAPTER 53

It was now late afternoon; time had ticked by ever-so-slowly for William as he desperately waited for Robertson's return. Folding his arms in an attempt to keep warm in the damp, cold cells, William heard feet approaching and shuffled forward to the bars of his cell in a hope of seeing who was coming.

Was it Constable Robertson? Had he found out the truth? William dared to dream of release; he dared to imagine Lizzy waiting for him. He longed to feel her warm embrace again; he yearned to hug her so close he could smell her sweet jasmine perfume…

He ached to see her smile.

Loud feet grew closer to William, and he thought he could see a policeman's uniform, he heard the jangle of keys!

Surely this must be it, this must be his release!

As his eyes settled on the men in front of the cell door, his heart felt heavy, it was not who he had hoped for. Maybe Robertson was busy, maybe these men would set him free?

One of the policemen opened the iron-barred cell door; it creaked loudly. The policeman shouted at William. 'On yer feet, scumbag!'

Confused, William shuffled backwards away from the two policemen. 'But I, I can't walk properly, sir.'

'You'll never walk again if yer don't get up, scumbag. Now I'll give you to the count of three – one, two…'

Right on the three, William got up. His legs really hurt and he moaned in pain. One of the policemen grabbed him and pulled him out of the cell, the other shut the cell door behind him.

The policeman who spoke stood in front of William and smiled at him. 'Now, murderer, we have to take you to the courts, so we need to take precautions.'

'But sir, I thought, I was told … I was not at court until tomorrow?'

'Well, you thought wrong, didn't you? Now shut it, you rodent. Keep yer head still,' the policeman barked.

All of a sudden everything went dark; they had placed a black cloth bag over his head. He kept getting pushed forward, and then pulled by the chains around his wrists. He was so scared that he would not see Lizzy again and his mind buzzed with questions.

Where were they taking him? What would his fate be?

The policemen who escorted him made jokes and he felt the occasional boot up his behind, which meant to hurry up, but he found it hard as his legs really did hurt.

'What's the matter? You scared of the dark?' one of the policemen laughed.

William really wanted to say something back, but felt it necessary to stay silent, but that did not stop his mind answering back.

I love the dark you fools, for I have lived in it all my life, I embrace it.

After walking for around five minutes, William felt the cobbles of the street underneath his feet; he heard the sound of click-clacking horse's feet edging towards him. Being told to wait, William did as instructed and tried to stay balanced as his legs ached. The hood over his head made sure he could not see a thing, but one thing it didn't stop was his smell and William's nostrils twitched as he took in a deep aroma that smelt like wood chips, then dust, hay maybe, all mixed together with the lingering scent of sweat.

He knew the smell, it was the horses, and as the click-clacking stopped William heard a creak and then he was pushed inside what must have been a carriage.

After some shuffling around, the sound of the click-clacking began again and William braced himself as the rocky ride to the courts began.

CHAPTER 54

'All rise,' a policeman shouted from the front of the courtroom.

William could see now, the men beside him holding his arms had removed the hood as they entered the court building. His eyes wandered the large, open room with the many rows of benches and a podium at the front. The Judge walked in regally with his scarlet robe hanging to the floor as he took his seat behind the podium, while the jury were seated silently on the benches next to the podium. There were other people around, but the room wasn't full by any means. It was quite a relief to William that it wasn't full. He remembered Thomas from the graveyard saying that people shouted all sorts of abuse at him when he was in court, and some people even spat at him!

How disgusting!

'Please be seated,' asked the Judge and everybody took their seats.

William had been introduced to his legal counsel, just five minutes before the hearing; the barrister was called Reginald Walker; he had a rather strong essence of whisky on him, which didn't breed confidence in William at all. William guessed the man would have been in his late fifties; he was overweight and quite bald.

Barrister Walker hardly asked William any questions, just instructed him to speak when he was spoken to and to keep his mouth shut or face *grave consequences.*

People whispered and ruffled papers, everyone seemed such busy little bees until Judge Stanbury coughed to his left and a policeman acknowledged it meant the Judge was ready to proceed.

'Silence in court,' the policeman shouted.

The Judge hit his gavel hard three times and looked up at everyone in front him.

'Good morning all, now I think it best to proceed. This is case docket number WR847701, in the matter of William Rathbone. Present in the court room are the defendant and his counsel, the prosecutor, and the witnesses from this heinous crime. The jury also attend here today, and I shall give you further instructions as to what will be expected of you when called to do so. I would remind the court that *all* persons are innocent until proven guilty. You have the option to plead not guilty, or guilty, William Rathbone. In the matter of William Rathbone who is charged with three counts of the murders of Henry Jones, a human being, as well as George Dobblesbury, a human being and lastly Frank Redding, again a human being. It is stated you murdered these persons in cold blood with this weapon, which was obtained by our good men of the police.'

William felt cold as he saw the judge raise the bloody hammer in the air.

The Judge stared right through William and it made him feel like he was hated. William looked at the square black cap which the judge was wearing on top of his white wig. It reminded William of a teacher he buried long ago who wanted to be buried wearing one.

'Please step forward,' instructed the judge.

William slowly moved forward but found it hard due to the shackles around his ankles as well as the pain in his legs.

The judge picked up a large book, William wasn't sure what it was until the judge spoke, and then he realised it was the bible.

'William Rathbone, please raise your right hand. Do you solemnly swear to tell the truth and nothing but the truth?'

William did as was asked, he wasn't entirely sure what he believed with regards to the bible, but he played along anyway, his right hand in the air. 'I do.'

'Mr William Rathbone, you are charged with three murders, how do you plead?'

'Not guilty, sir,' William said softly.

The Judge leant forward to William. 'In my courtroom, if I ask you to speak then you will address me as your Honour, do I make myself *clear*?'

'Yes, your honour.' William nodded.

'Right then,' the Judge shouted as he leaned back in his chair. 'If the prosecution would like to start us off and present its case then that would be grand.'

Patrick Fenwick stood in his gown with his wig neatly placed on top of his head. 'Good morning, your honour. I feel this will be quite straightforward and, without sounding over-confident, I believe that when I have finished speaking, all will be clear to the court, and we will be able to put this to bed. This is as simple a case as could be.'

Patrick Fenwick gave a dramatic performance as William watched on in horror. Fenwick walked across the room and spoke of events as he wanted people to perceive them. On a few occasions Fenwick even approached William up close, shouting and damning him with every breath he could muster. Fenwick explained that the police were alerted by a member of the general public at a late hour, that a man was screaming abuse and threatening to kill some men who were visiting a friend's grave and that when the policeman came to investigate the disturbance, William stood over them smiling, with his hammer and rubbing their blood over himself while licking the blood off the hammer. The small number of people who were in the court gasped in disbelief as Fenwick conveyed his fiction. This was what Fenwick excelled in, he was quite the orator, using his gritted teeth and mimicking his hand as a hammer to add further weight to the version of events which all pointed to an inevitable conclusion.

Barrister Walker didn't do much at all when it was his turn to speak, William was shocked to hear him read out a few sentences in his defence which were immediately shot down by the prosecution. Barrister Walker then sat down as William stared at him. 'Is that it?' William asked. Barrister Walker looked with a blank expression, but William was having none of it.

William couldn't believe he was just expected to sit and say nothing, so against the usual court etiquette, he stood up and spoke. 'Er…your honour,' he said quietly.

'Yes,' snapped the judge.

'Can I please be allowed to speak?'

The judge looked at Barrister Walker. 'Your client's doing your work for you now, eh?' He then focused his eyes back on William. 'Go on then, make it quick, if you must.'

'Sir, I have heard many lies here today,' the courtroom gasped at William's claims, for Fenwick was a respected man of the courts and to have such things said against him was a great insult.

Judge Stanbury hit his gavel twice as he stared at William in disgust. 'Silence people. You, William Rathbone, forget your place. This is a court boy; we rely on facts, if you have none then be seated.'

'But I do sir, this man, Patrick Fenwick, has wanted me away from this town, or worse. He is riddled with an obsession to do me wrong. The men you say I 'murdered' were all vicious thieves; they had attacked me once before you see.'

Fenwick clapped his hands. 'So he admits to killing them, and yet he pled 'not guilty'. Well, is there anything *really* more we have to say! The man lies to the court, *as well* as admitting to murders!'

'Silence Fenwick, let him speak for now,' interrupted the judge.

'Yes, I struck them once each with the hammer. Yes, my intent was grave. I will admit that. But had these men not attacked me before, nearly killing me, I might add, I may have used a force of an inferior variety. As things stood on that night, they came at me with weapons, a knife, a razor and a bat; they came at me and while doing so, threatened to kill the woman I love. It was 'kill or be killed' sir, what could I do?'

Raising his arms in the air vividly, and then pointing to William, Fenwick spoke loud and clear for all to hear. 'Please, enough with the elaborate attempts to save your skin! Judge, I beg of you, do away with this jury, we do not need them, the confession is clear, for all to hear! Surely we do not need to drag this out further? Surely we have a responsibility to the families of the dearly departed to deliver a swift and proper justice? Surely we can't sit here and stomach these awful fabrications this fiend in trying to shove down our throats with his poisoned tongue?'

Hitting his gavel again the judge demanded order.

'I have to say, Barrister Walker, that in light of your client's crystal clear confession in front of the court today, that I am left with no alternative than to move speedily to sentencing. That is, unless you have anything to add?'

'No, your honour,' Barrister Walker answered as William sighed in defeat.

The judge looked at Fenwick 'Anything further?'

Fenwick turned to William and his mouth smiled ever-so-slightly. 'Yes judge, just to add that this man should be punished with the full extent of the law.'

'How predictable,' muttered William.

Fenwick raised his voice in retaliation. 'You see your honour? No respect for the court, for your honour, for me, and even for the dead he so brutally bludgeoned with a hammer. Oh yes, William Rathbone, you will receive justice!'

Looking at the judge William pleaded once more to be heard. 'Please your honour, this is so wrong, I am not a malicious man!'

'Oh yes, I am sure you are an honest, law abiding, charming individual,' Fenwick mocked.

Turning to Fenwick, William moved his arms but the shackles on his wrists stopped him moving any further. He looked down to his wrists then back to Fenwick. 'Thank you Barrister Fenwick. If I weren't under oath, I'd return the compliment.'

Fenwick laughed, 'Do I really have to say any more, your honour?'

The judge hit his gavel again. 'Silence to all.'

The courtroom fell silent as everyone waited for the judge to speak. The judge loved this part; he loved the way the people would look at him, awaiting his verdict. He loved the power.

'William Rathbone, step forward,' the judge instructed.

William shuffled forward, his eyes fixed on Judge Stanbury's face. William hoped for mercy, he hoped that someone would rush into the court to his rescue. He wondered if Lizzy was all right, he wondered where she was. He wondered if Constable Robertson was taking care of her, and if he had found any evidence that could help, he wondered if he was already doomed as the judge proceeded to his verdict.

'You, William Rathbone have confessed to the murder of three persons in front of this court. It is my decision that I carry out sentencing immediately.' The judge cleared his throat and sat up straight, his voice echoed off the courtroom walls as he read off a piece of paper he held in his hand.

'Therefore, William Rathbone you stand convicted of the horrid and unnatural crime of murdering Henry Jones, a human being, as well as George Dobblesbury, a human being and Frank Redding, again a human being. This Court doth adjudge that you be taken back to the place from whence you came, and there to be fed on bread and water till tomorrow morning at ten o'clock, when you are to be taken to the common place of execution, and there hanged by the neck until you are dead; agreeable to an Act of Parliament in this case made and provided; and may the good God Almighty have mercy on your soul.'

The judge hit the gavel again thunderously, as the few people who were in the court cheered. William turned to Fenwick as the policemen, who were either side of him, dragged him away. He looked at the pleasure in Patrick Fenwick's eyes and shouted at him, 'How could you? You call this justice? This is a farce!'

The judge continued his condemnation as William's face filled with pure dread. 'Take him out, out of these honoured courts, to the place where he will die! Let his punishment be a lesson to the wicked, let us forget this man, and strike him from our hearts so he truly dies, forever!'

Fenwick laughed and nodded at the judge's blast and then at William, as William was pushed and pulled gradually out of the court.

'You will receive justice one day, Patrick. It will come. By my hand or another, it will come. Sooner or later truth will hunt you down.'

'Be sure to make an appointment,' Fenwick laughed as William's screaming continued into the long halls of the court.

Fenwick breathed a sigh of relief.

It was done; his foe was going to die.

A good day's work indeed.

CHAPTER 55

A cool shudder crept up his spine and his eyes flickered around nervously. As they wandered the cell walls he thought he could see weird shapes that looked like creepy faces within the damp and smelly brickwork. Flickers of light seemed to randomly sneak in every now and again through what must have been a window down the hall. They moved slowly past the bars in William's cell. The tiny, dim portions of light fed the haunting shadows on the walls. Realisation had set in now for William and he knew he was completely alone in the dark.

Alone, it was a word he thought he had cast out for good. It saddened him to know he was wrong.

He closed his eyes and listened to the wind howling outside, and it almost sounded like laughter to his panicked mind.

He said the words in his mind, 'Death sentence,' and it still hadn't quite sunk in. So they were going to kill him. A million questions attacked his brain like ants on a sugar cube…

Was his life destined to end like this? Who would ever know he existed? How would he be remembered? Would people say he was some bloodthirsty maniac like they described him in the courtroom? Whatever angle he looked at it from, it was bad.

Everything was bad.

He had been moved to a different location, Barnes Prison, the last place he would ever stay; the cold floor the last place he would ever sleep, the executioner's face, the last face he would ever see.

His eyes closed tight, his body aching, his mind shot-to-pieces. William whispered a thought in his mind, 'Kill me now, just get it over with,' and as he did, as he prayed for the end, a loud clang bounced around the prison's hallway.

The noise was an exclusive one, one which in his short experience behind bars he had come to recognise more quickly than any other. It was the opening of the gate down the hall.

William's ears pricked up as he listened to the squish-squish, tap-tap and clonk-clonk of the footsteps which got closer and closer. The sounds finally stopped...

Was it time for his death *already*? Had the night gone by in such a flash?

He dared not open his eyes, but shut them tighter, as if someone or something was trying to get in. 'Please, no!' his mind screamed, yet he stayed deadly silent, hoping his ears had betrayed him and the steps were stopping at another door, for another person.

Then all of a sudden a smell, something wonderful, something he recognised, something truly ambrosial reached his nose. William wondered how the scent could reach his nose and not his mouth and yet he could still taste it.

Jasmine, oh, the sweet smell of jasmine, which meant only one thing...

Lizzy.

He quickly opened his eyes, three figures stood at the bars. His legs still hurt but he ignored the pain and clung to the bars as he saw the three figures shuffling around in the dark.

The barred door opened, the three figures walked in quickly and quietly. William saw there was a policeman standing before him, it was Robertson, then his eyes registered Father Fanshaw, but who was the other who remained hooded? It was obvious to William it was just another religious fellow. His heart sank as he really thought he could smell Lizzy's sweet perfume. Apparently she got it from some perfume house called the Houbigant in Paris. He remembered the day she played Beethoven's Moonlight Sonata to him, he remembered her turning to him as she played, her eyes glistening.

He came back to life as Robertson clicked his fingers. 'William, oh dear William,' he said as he crouched down to where William had sat back down. 'The animals, I can't believe what has happened, they beat you didn't they, the policemen?'

'It doesn't matter,' William replied. 'All is lost now, didn't you find her? Did they get to her?' he continued with his hands over his eyes.

'William,' whispered Robertson a little louder. 'Look.'

Raising his head, William looked forward, at first he wondered what Robertson meant as his eyes saw plain-as-day Father Fanshaw holding a bible, but then the mysterious hooded figure by the Reverend's side pulled back the hood.

William was speechless as he desperately hoped his eyes were not playing tricks on him. The face he dreamt of, the face he yearned for, the face he loved, was right there in front him.

His eyes examined her in disbelief, was it really her?

It was her, it was Lizzy. She crouched down to him and ran her fingers through his hair as he cried.

She cried too as Father Fanshaw and Robertson walked outside. Robertson looked at Father Fanshaw and told him he would watch the gate. Robertson had paid the gate man a hefty figure for a full hour. In the hour Robertson wanted to tell William he was doing all he could; he had some more work to do. He wanted to tell William not to give up hope, but firstly, the time was for William and Lizzy. He wouldn't deny them their time, and being a man who believed in love, who had known love, he simply couldn't.

William placed both his hands on either side of her face and smiled as he looked at her intently. Her elegant yet strong bone structure stood out like no face he had ever seen. Her sharp, alert look was like a hunter's, and her nose was small like a button, with the tiniest couple of freckles on it, the small flaw that made it perfect. Her look was that of a real person's look, one any soul in the whole wide world could talk to and know and fall madly in love with. Her skin was smooth, but William could see where she was going to have laughter lines when she got older and even when she'd be still and concentrate on something there was always the ghost of a smile ever-present on her lips, lips as red as wine, as red as a rose, as red as blood.

Lizzy spoke first. 'My darling, oh my darling, what have they done to you?'

'Everything's alright, my love, for you are here now. As long as you are alright, I was beside myself with worry for you,' smiled William.

She kissed his face frantically and William even giggled a little as he then kissed her just as frantically back. He smelt her hair and neck, he felt her skin with his fingertips and the sensations engulfed his body with a wonderful euphoria only she could ever provide.

As they stopped their fast petting, William looked into her eyes. 'My love, my Lady Anne, my Lizzy.'

Lizzy's eyes streamed with tears as she knew all he wanted to do was reassure her at a time when most mortals would only think of themselves.

That was the man; that was *her* man, the man she deeply loved.

'I am that, William,' Lizzy replied. 'I am yours forever.'

'And I yours,' William smiled, 'though you know what is happening to me in the morning my love? You have to be strong, for me, you have to be strong.'

Together their hands slightly touched, the skin-on-skin-feeling making them both shudder as they each longed to be in a different place, a different time, a different world.

Lizzy stroked William's hair with one hand as the other stayed locked within William's fingers. 'But how *can* I be strong, William? Answer me *that*. For you have been woven into the fabric of my life. My life on earth will be meaningless without you, like a magpie without its mate, I'd be lost.'

As Lizzy spoke to William he felt her breath on his face, it was so soft and gentle, like the first ever feeling of silk on his skin.

'Lizzy my love, do not fear, please do not fear. I am not afraid of death, and if it is death I must face than I shall do it with a full heart, a loving heart, a loved heart. The best thing that has ever happened to me looks at me, weeping, right now. You will always know that my love was…is true and I shall be alright my dear, for knowing you are safe fills me with happiness. And when you play that sweet piano I shall be listening right beside you.'

Her tears flowed like a river as he spoke and Lizzy thought that perhaps he should make a run for it. 'But William they are going to hang you! Why not leave, why not run as soon as Robertson opens the gate? They will not stop you, they may even help, you could run and have your life!'

William shook his head with loving smile, 'But how can I run, how can I live, when all I love and live for is right here?'

The moment was all theirs, theirs for eternity.

Lizzy kissed William again and again and he returned the sweet kisses as they cuddled together followed by William whispering loving words into her ears.

'Listen to my heart; it beats for you, Lizzy. Please, I don't want you to mourn me; I don't want any more tears shed. I have lived, but more importantly I have *loved* – you gave me this joy. Be happy, for me, please, I beg you. For I fear it will be the only way my soul could rest. I'll talk to you, in the night, in your dreams; I will never be far away. I will be the warm blanket in the cold, the towel you dry on, the food in your mouth, the water on your lips. You will never have to move...you will never have to think...all you have to do is close your eyes... and just listen... and I promise you that you will be all right, I will always be around you.'

Lizzy held him tight as the two of them wished time would stand still; she never wanted to let him go.

'You truly are an angel, William Rathbone; my only regret is that I didn't give in to my feelings sooner. I just wish we could have confessed how we felt more quickly than we did so maybe we could have left this town and gone far, far away; it would have been heaven, my love, pure heaven.'

William opened his eyes as much as he could as he looked at her beautiful face, he didn't want to blink even, so the image of her face could be etched into his mind. 'But, you have already made me live in heaven since we met.' William then tapped his chest in the middle 'Right here.'

William felt Lizzy's breath on his chest as he held her there, and hoped, despite his predicament, that someone somewhere felt as truly happy as he felt in that moment. They were simply two people who loved each other. When they held each other as they did in that moment they felt unaffected by time, blessed by each other's presence. He had received the greatest gift of all, to love and to feel loved.

He was ready to face anything now, for nothing could ever take away this moment from his soul, nothing could ever compare. William smiled as he felt true forgiveness and a certain degree of sympathy for those who had wronged him. He didn't blame the judge; he didn't even blame Patrick Fenwick, after all, they were only men.

Only men, who had no idea what life was about, what love was about, he doubted they had ever even felt real love, but hoped someday they would.

Real love and real loss was something he knew would hit them harder than any hammer he could ever swing, because to feel real loss William knew that firstly you had to feel real love and to feel real love, you had to absolutely care about someone more than yourself, a thing he doubted they could ever do.

Throughout his time as a gravedigger, William had seen hundreds of pairs of dead eyes on hundreds of dead bodies as he placed them carefully into their last place of rest. He remembered staring at the many lifeless eyes and thinking how true the old saying was that the eyes were the windows of the soul. Some of those many souls even spoke to William; he had listened to their fears, their despair, their regrets, the wrongs which they could never right. But William counted himself lucky, because he also got to witness the good.

And the good always outshone the bad.

Witnessing people's true love for other people was one of the reasons William kept going throughout the dark years of loneliness, he hoped one day, that such a love would touch him. Even a glimmer of it would be a true gift for which he would be eternally grateful.

And now love had touched him.

The light of love had shone on him brighter than he could have ever anticipated…

It was *that* light that he would carry with him forever, in this world or the next.

CHAPTER 56

They stayed in their loving embrace as long as they could, but time's acceleration was beyond their control. The thought of the noose hadn't even entered William's mind whilst Lizzy had been with him, there was no panic, no sense of danger, no fear.

Having been soothed somewhat by William stroking his huge strong hands through her silk-like black hair, Lizzy reacted to the footsteps entering the cell as the barred door swung open.

'Oh no, can I not stay here for the night, Constable Robertson, please?' pleaded Lizzy as Robertson and Father Fanshaw walked in.

Kissing her forehead, William spoke to her gently. 'It will be alright.'

Father Fanshaw offered his hand to Lizzy. 'We need to let Constable Robertson do his job, my dear, we only have ten minutes before the guard down the hall said he would arrest us, and trust me, bribe-or-no-bribe, he will. Let us give the policeman a few moments to speak with William before we leave.'

Reluctantly accepting the Reverend's arm, Lizzy stood and smiled at William placing the long hood over her face. 'I will say goodbye before we leave.'

William nodded silently.

Sitting down beside William, with his notebook and pencil in hand, Robertson sighed and took a deep breath before speaking. 'Right then, dear William, out of respect you know I only speak the truth to you now. You do realise that I will *not* promise false hope, I will *not* sugar-coat a thing. All I will do is speak the truth; can you handle that, my dear boy?'

Giving a slight chuckle, William nodded. 'I would expect nothing less, dear sir.'

'The facts at hand are very damning of you, William, of that there is no denying. I do, nevertheless, have many questions, many avenues to explore. But whether I can do this in time for …well … tomorrow, remains to be seen. I would prepare for…well, all I would say is dear boy, if the inevitable happens please be assured that I will not rest until this whole matter is investigated thoroughly. Again, I fear I cannot do it in time for…'

William nodded in acceptance. 'I appreciate all you are doing, and are *trying* to do, sir. But the main thing for me is to make sure she is safe, and that the evil hands that plot to grab her are deterred by any means necessary.'

'Swiftly chopped at the wrist,' smiled Robertson. 'Now, the night it all happened, I am clear about the three men, what they did, how you reacted and so on, but is there anything else? Anything else at *all* you could possibly think of that could maybe cast a shadow of doubt over the prosecution's tale of events?'

'I don't think so,' William whispered. 'If there was I think I said it all in court....the little I did have opportunity to say anyway. They didn't listen sir, they didn't care. All they wanted was a conviction; they had no interest in what really happened. It was Fenwick's stage, and he played out his finest act to sickening satisfaction. Fenwick was as happy when the judge sentenced me as he was on the night they arrested me.'

Standing to his feet Robertson put his notebook and pencil back in his pocket. 'I had to ask, we don't have much, William. I will nevertheless check a few things tonight and…wait a minute…'

William's eyes snapped up to Robertson. 'What sir? What's wrong?'

Reaching for his notebook again, Robertson wet his finger as he searched for the last page he had written on. His eyes quickly flickered up and down and left-to-right on the pages, his lips moved as he read silently what he had written on the pages.

'You just said *he* was there?'

William gave Robertson an odd look. 'Who sir'?

'He! The man, Fenwick, was he there the night you were arrested?'

'Why yes sir, sat in front of my face and smiled as they beat me.'

Looking into mid-air, Robertson thought out loud. 'But why was *he* there? He had no *reason* to be there, none at all. Unless…'

'Unless what, dear sir, what are you thinking?' William asked keenly.

Robertson looked at William blankly. 'Unless someone told him something was going to happen; unless someone knew what events would occur … which begs the question, was it all a plan? Look William, we really have to go, I would warn you though, that whatever my personal thoughts on all this, we are still no closer to any sort of denouement. There is still plenty to do, so before you get to kiss the dear Lady Anne for what may be your last time, shake my hand, for I *know* you are a good man. I *know* you have looked after my late wife's grave, planting fresh flowers there whenever you have had the chance. It is not

345

unnoticed you know, and I tell you what, my Old Peggy would so love them daffodils you like to plant. Loved them she did bless her soul.'

Watching Robertson cross his chest with his finger as he said, 'Bless her soul.' made William ask questions to himself.

Could he show him?

Should he show him?

It was time to think on his feet, he didn't have time for the usual mind-wrestling; it was time to do it, time to show Robertson something special.

'Look Robertson, you have to trust me,' William snapped as he stood up.

'But I do, William, that's what I have just being saying.' Robertson said as he wondered what William was doing walking towards him.

'Oh, dear chap, er. What are you doing? Er…Lady Anne, Reverend Fanshaw?' Robertson said a little louder, as William grabbed him. Robertson couldn't push him off. 'What are you doing William, I want to help you?'

William smiled at Robertson and placed his hand over Robertson's heart. 'I want to show you something, my dear friend, something you need to see … something…you will never forget'

Before starting, William briefly glanced outside the cell's bars, both Lizzy and Father Fanshaw smiled at William.

They knew what he was doing.

In a sudden flash, Robertson found himself in a weird state of conscious unconsciousness. He gasped for air as memories from a time when he was happiest flooded his brain in an overwhelming rush.

'Oh my God,' Robertson wept as he saw Peggy's face smiling at him as if she were right in front of him. 'Oh my good Lord, Peggy, my darling, could it be you?'

Drowning in emotion, all of which was good, Robertson thought back to happy times, he remembered the meals Peggy cooked when he returned home late at night after he had been working long hours chasing crooks, and how perfectly she cooked meat. He remembered her teasing him about how bad he was at the game 'Bridge.' He saw a vision of himself and Peggy walking hand-in-hand on mid-day strolls they shared as the sun shone brightly.

Peggy looked at him, her face the same as the day they met. 'I love you, my darling. Oh how I have always loved you so. I am alright; I am in a good place.' Robertson cried as he replied 'Oh my dearest wife, I love you too; always have, always will, I have never forgotten you.'

Peggy touched his face with her hands and he actually felt her, as if she was right next to him, she smiled again and spoke softly, 'The last time you were at my grave you asked questions my dear, you seemed like your faith had been diminished, your hope as thin as the cheese you sliced for me in sandwiches.'

Robertson laughed 'You and your cheese sandwiches! But yes, after you died my love, what hope was there?'

'My love, there is always hope; never give up, on anyone… anything. Nothing is impossible. You asked me 'Why pray for anybody?' My answer to this is pray all you can, remember all you can, but do so with happiness. I made you forget me because I couldn't bear to see you sad, my love, but I know you needed some final words with me, and here they are, I love you, and I will be keeping a seat warm for you when you come and join me. But you are not ready yet, you have work to do, especially for our mutual friend.'

'William?' Robertson cried.

'He is special, my love; do all you can.'

'I will,' Robertson cried. 'I promise I will.'

Peggy started to walk backwards away from Robertson. 'I have to go now, my love. Remember my words, for we will be together again. Remember me with laughs and smiles, for that was how we lived together was it not? I love you, goodbye.'

Her face vanished as Robertson woke; he was on his knees, William steadied Robertson by placing his arms on his shoulders.

Father Fanshaw walked in and helped Robertson up. 'We really have to go, sir.'

'You, you are special William. You speak to them? In the graveyard, the dead?'

William nodded in silence.

'Thank you.' Robertson smiled. 'Thank you so much.'

'No problem at all, dear sir,' replied William.

Lizzy kissed William over and over, until Robertson had to pull her away. 'I love you, William, remember that! Don't give up hope!' she continued as Robertson pulled her back.

William stood up again and shook Robertson's hand as well as Father Fanshaw's. 'Do not worry for me, for I know it is not the end, even if it is.' He turned and looked at Father Fanshaw. 'My friend, if they do…what they intend tomorrow, please do something for me?'

'Anything,' Father Fanshaw replied 'Anything at all.'

'Would you bury me beyond the east wall? My mother rests there; hers is the one that says…er…'Mortuus est Momentaneum'

Lizzy smiled at William 'Death is momentary? How consoling.'

William's eyes lit up. 'Is that what it means? I always wondered! Right good Reverend it is settled, if I go tomorrow, to you-know-where, I want that very same message on my head stone, would you have that done for me?'

Father Fanshaw's eyes filled as he agreed, 'Yes, yes William I will.'

'Now go Father, thank you for always being there for me, you were the father I should have had,' smiled William as he then turned to Lizzy. 'Lizzy, go,' he pleaded as she clung to the bars 'Remember those words my dear, death *really is* only a moment!'

She cried as the Reverend and Robertson escorted her away.

As William heard the loud clang he dropped back to his knees.

It was safe to cry now, and it was quite acceptable to cry too.

He grabbed his ripped, blood-stained shirt and put it to his nose; it still smelled of jasmine, still smelled so lovely, smelled of her.

He ripped the shirt off his back and held it against his face, lying down on it and breathing it in as he closed his eyes in preparation for his last night on earth.

CHAPTER 57

Dropping Lizzy off at Woodworth Manor, Robertson explained to her and Father Fanshaw that he had to get on with his work for time was of the essence and it was already well into the evening.

Father Fanshaw also had some things to attend to; he wanted to make sure he was registered as William's rightful Reverend for the day ahead, so he could be by his side at the end, but he also wanted to stay with Lizzy. She *insisted* though that his business was of far more importance than her need for soothing company, and added that she would be quite fine on her own for a few hours, although she did not fancy being alone *all* of the night.

Having promised he would return as soon as he was registered, he said that he was going directly to the Prison Governor's house, but it would likely take him a few hours to get all the documentation signed and sealed.

So both Robertson and the Reverend went their separate ways.

The Reverend went east, the Constable headed west.

Robertson was heading west, *away* from the police station because he had an idea, a theory which needed exploring. He had been searching his mind over and over for answers to his riddles, one of which was why there were no weapons found on the men when William clearly said each of them was armed. Had they been left behind? It could have been the case that passers-by took them after all the commotion; that tended to happen if the policemen hadn't taken them first, which also happened too often. Or was it the fact that the weapons in question were simply not included in the report from his men?

How convenient that would have been for Fenwick.

So, if the weapons were not stolen or taken by his men, what would a schemer do with them?

Keep them for his own amusement? Surely not, for who could risk anyone recognising them? Then something hit Robertson like a kick between the legs, a question he knew could lead to somewhere!

*If I were a criminal, what would I do with the weapons? Answer – get rid of them, and where best to get rid of thing*s?

The morgue.

That was why Robertson headed west, and as his driver rode as fast as he could. Robertson ached to examine the dead men's last list of possessions at the morgue.

Robertson got out of the carriage and instructed the driver to wait for him.

Robertson noticed the driver had stopped quite a distance from the morgue and looked at him questioningly. 'You scared or something? How come you didn't drive us closer?'

Shaking his head the driver was adamant. 'Oh no, sir, sorry. Paid or not paid you won't get me near there. I will have to go one day I guess, but when I do I'll know nothing of it, but go there with air in my lungs, I will not'

'You silly old bugger,' laughed Robertson as he walked towards the main gates of the town's mortuary. 'Nothing to fear in there, old boy, everyone's dead!'

He looked at an old sign fastened onto what looked like an old farmhouse gate. It read 'Echo Meadow.'

Once he reached the main gates of the morgue Robertson saw another sign in the grounds; it was wooden and planted in the grass. 'Echo Meadow Mortuary.'

'Sounds lovely,' thought Robertson, walking as quickly as he could and breathing in the late night's air.

It took ten minutes before anybody answered Robertson's loud calls and bangs at the doors. Robertson knew it was late, but he also knew that the mortuary was *never* unmanned, so he knocked and called continuously until he got an answer.

The answer came in the shape of a little old man; he appeared with what looked like a hundred old keys on a large ring and carrying an old lantern with a candle lit inside it. Standing at only around five feet tall at best, and sporting a scruffy grey beard with old clothes, the old man explained he was only a pair of hands and that Robertson couldn't go through any potential details concerning the cause of deaths. Robertson assured him that he was not there for that reason and handed the old man a list with three names on it explaining that he only wanted to see the bodies of the three on the list. The old man knew who they were and where they were kept.

'You been lucky,' the old man said as he led Robertson inside the building and then down some dark tiled corridors.

'Why's that?' asked Robertson as he noticed how loudly his voice bounced off the long, hallowed corridors.

'These ones are getting cremated tomorrow.'

'Oh right,' answered Robertson, 'Is this the room?' he asked as the old man stopped and prepared to open a door with his keys.

'Yes, sir. Now the men will have a tag around their toes. The room is quite, er… full at the moment. A lot a people seem to be pegging it; I'm sure the ones you're after are the last three laid out on the end. I warn you though; it will smell a bit in there. I'll be outside when you're done.'

The old man passed Robertson the lantern with the candle inside still burning bright. 'Here ya go sir, don't want to be in the dark with them buggers.'

He took the lantern and took a step forward, but just before he turned the handle, Robertson turned to the old man 'What about their clothes and belongings that they came here with, where are they, sir?'

The old man pointed to the room Robertson was about to enter. 'All in there, sir. Each name tag will have a number and the row of drawers on the left of the room as you walk in you will see are numbered, they are all open, but as I say, each name matches a number, so feel free to have a look. We do get to keep the possessions, though if the families don't claim the body, sir.'

'Yes, that's fine; doesn't concern me, old boy. Right then, I will commence, thank you. I hope not to be long.' Robertson smiled as he walked in with his lantern high in the air.

Being in the police for many a year, Robertson had seen his fair share of morgues, and seen his fair share of dead bodies.

There was one thing though he never quite got used to that always made him feel weird, and that was the bodies never looked real. They just looked like big rubber dummies. In the past he had even viewed a couple of autopsies and at first thought that the actual operation would have made him feel sick, but that's not what got to him, it was the smell. The stenches in the places were overwhelming. It wasn't the smell of death, that was more like if someone left rotting meat out in the heat for a couple of days. Robertson wasn't sure what it was, but figured it was the smell of the inside of a body once it was cut open. Robertson had witnessed many a policeman lose his lunch after experiencing that smell.

As he walked past the numerous bodies, Robertson realised just how dirty it was in the place. There were stains all around and Robertson dreaded to even think what they were.

There seemed to be a lot of stainless steel. The instruments were grimly laid out on tables near the bodies' autopsy tables. There was even stainless steel sheeting on the walls. There were cheap industrial tiles on the walls and floors too, all covered in horrible dirt and looking like they hadn't been washed in years.

'Ah, finally,' Robertson said out loud as he came to the end of the row. He lowered his lantern and saw a set of odd looking toes sticking out of a plastic sheet. He read the name, and looked at the number.

'Yes, that's one of them' he said to himself as he made his way to the drawers where the possessions were kept.

He opened the first draw, there wasn't much; it looked like there was just a bundle of bloodied rags at first.

'Yes, trousers, shirt, flat striped cap of some sort, and oh…wouldn't you know it, a razor. No weapons they said? Then he saw something which made his heart skip a beat, it was like he had found treasure as he pulled it out of the drawer and brought it to the lantern's light.

'Oh my goodness,' Robertson whispered quietly.

It was an old brass pocket watch, a very familiar old brass pocket watch.

He wanted to run back to town straight away, but he needed to look through the other men's things too!

So, as quickly as he could, he matched the dead toes to the numbers, and searched each man's possessions, where he found more alarming proof of what he had known deep down all along!

Proof, finally, that Fenwick was indeed in league with the evil thugs!

CHAPTER 58

After lighting some candles she had placed on her piano, Lizzy sat on the chair and prayed, closing her eyes, and hoping somehow, her prayer would be heard.

Her palms pressed against one-another with a tension so hard it made her arms shake as the candles' flames flickered in the draft from the open windows like they were angry.

'Please hear me, please hear me,' she begged.

She composed herself as she searched her mind for how to express her feelings, for there were so many.

'Dear God, *dearest God*, this is for the one I care for, William Rathbone, I want you to relieve him from the horrid stage people have set, please bless him; find a way to help him for I fear this is my last hope. William Rathbone is always the first one to be there for anyone who needs help of any kind. He is unselfish, loving, and as pure a soul as there is. I care for him, I love him and would like to tell you that if he survives his treacherous ordeal that I will be by his side for as long as he is on this earth. Please help him, please help him, please help…for I fear nobody else will…amen.'

Her tears made their way out of her eyes, even though she tried to keep them away; her breath struggled out of her mouth even though she sat still.

Hearing loud applause, Lizzy quickly opened her eyes and spun around to see from where the noise came. Her eyes opened and met the eyes opposite her with fury.

'You! You…you!' she screamed as she picked up a candle and threw it at the intruding man who faced her.

'Bravo, Lady Anne! How touching.' Patrick Fenwick smiled as he dodged the intended missile. 'Is that any way to treat a guest?' he laughed as the candle missed him and hit the floor with a wet-like splodge as the liquefied wax stuck to the floor. 'You really need to vary your greeting, Lady Anne, for tea parties would most definitely be inappropriate if you threw candles at your guests, he-he!'

If there had been a knife around she thought she may have stabbed him; if there had been a pistol, she thought she could have shot him, but there were no such armaments at Lizzy's disposal, and if there had been, Fenwick may have been in trouble. Her eyes searched the room for any potential weapons, as Fenwick smiled his sickening smile that could test the patience of a saint. Then, out of the corner of her eye, she saw the fire poker, and her mind imagined shoving it into his fat, disgusting body.

Fenwick followed her eyes though, and with one swift move, he dispelled any attempt she would ever make for the fire poker.

'You like my pistol?' he asked as he gave her a quick side-view of it before returning the aim of it to her head. 'Quite sought after it is, by many a gentleman, it would seem. In fact, I would go so far as to say this here pistol is my new lucky charm, my new rabbit's foot!'

Lizzy stood carefully as she wondered about Fenwick's intentions, her overworked mind reeling off many possible cruel purposes.

Was he there to finish his evil game, to murder her? Or perhaps he was there for something even worse…?

Only time would tell.

'Sit down, *Lady Anne,*' Fenwick instructed, with the pistol in line with her head.

'I'm quite fine standing,' she assured him.

His hand which held the pistol shook, mirroring his lack of patience. 'I am not asking, *Anne*, sit, now!'

Doing as asked she placed herself on the floor, her legs beside her as she looked up at Fenwick in the position of power he coveted so greatly.

'You do not speak to me, Anne, from now on, unless I ask you a question. Do remember I have a pistol. The reason for my visit at this late hour is as follows. I require something, something from you. Something from you that was taken, wrongly I may add, something which is rightfully mine, my birth right I would say, my right by blood that you schemed to steal with your evil and cunning ways of a woman.'

Lizzy heightened her eyebrows in a questioning fashion as Fenwick stopped her in her tracks. 'Don't, don't do it, speak when spoken to, remember? You women, always so very keen to open your mouths, even with circumstances against you; a trait I always find quite baffling. Anyway, I digress; the purpose of my presence is simple, I want what is mine. I want Woodworth Manor; I want the whole damn estate, for which the title *Lord* would follow should you give it to me, which you will…won't you, my dear?'

Lizzy looked at Fenwick puzzled.

'Speak!' shouted Fenwick impatiently.

Giving a slight huff in the air, Lizzy shook her head. It wasn't the fact she was surprised by Fenwick's request, she merely pondered if there was ever going to be an end to his tenacity 'Why on earth, would I ever grant you a thing in this world, Patrick? Why? How could you display such *effrontery* in light of what you have done to me and the man I love?'

Baring all of his teeth with his best fake smile, he stood as straight as he could. 'Well, *Anne*, for my own personal well-being of course. Have you learnt nothing about me in all these years?'

'Never! You will never get a thing from me, you pig,' Lizzy snapped. 'You lying scheming pig!'

'Oh, your words cut me so, Anne. They really do!' he mocked, 'but moving on, I don't have much time; places to go, drink to enjoy, people to kill…whoops sorry, couldn't resist it.'

He walked closer to Lizzy, she shuddered back a little, wondering if he would shoot her with his prized pistol, he leaned in and pressed the pistol to her head.

'Do it,' she said, although in her heart she was completely sure he *could* do such a thing, and quickly thought she should have engaged her brain before opening her mouth.

'Why would I kill *you*?' Fenwick sniggered, 'Unless I had to, of course. No, your fate should not be as easy as the freak you so *scandalously* desire. Your fate, *Anne*, will be to know you have to live with the fact I bested you, for all time. You say you will *not* entertain my request, but I *know* you will. You say you would never do what I want, but again, I *know* you will. And do you know how I know? Because I, and *I alone*, hold the key to that pathetic subject's life, *Anne.*'

Her jaw dropping slightly in astonishment, Lizzy stuttered at first as her words came out. 'William? You, you could save him?'

'Indeed I can, *Anne.*' smiled Fenwick as he revelled in his stance of superiority and embraced the thought that Anne was at his mercy.

'Is this a trick?' she nervously enquired.

'No, no trick,' Fenwick assured, 'but you have to trust me. I can indeed have your dear William's sentence reduced, and would in time see it quashed. He would probably serve around thirty days until I presented my 'new evidence,' but if you do as I ask Anne, it will be done. There would be conditions too, that you and the wretched man leave my town of Barnes, a banishment of sorts… never to return! If you can agree, then we have a deal. For what is all this you have when you don't have your *love*?'

Any fraction of trust she felt in Fenwick's words disintegrated by the second before her mind had even registered the prospect.

But what choice did she have? How could she live in the knowledge that there might have been one possible escape route, one possible option to save the man she loved?

Whatever the price, she would have paid it a million times over if it resulted in the outcome she so desperately craved.

'But how can I sort something out so quickly, Patrick? Your late brother always handled such affairs. I wouldn't know where to start. Could it be done in time?'

Lowering his pistol, Fenwick gave Lizzy a caring look which made her skin crawl. 'Why it will be fine, dear Anne. You must know that fiendish as I undoubtedly am, I am not without a plan? I have foreseen all that has transpired; played my moves like a proven chess master, always one step ahead. It just so happens that I have drawn up the necessary paperwork and documents to transfer the ownership of Woodworth Manor and the title as attached to me. All you need to do, to save his life I remind you, is to go to my legal companions by the name of Manley Legal, situated next to the old watch and clock shop down the cobbled road of Bulcock Street. You know, the one owned by the old fool 'One-finger Wally' which is five minutes away from the market you browse so frequently.'

Lizzy knew the place and acknowledged the fact with a slight nod. 'Yes, I know it well.'

'Go there first thing in the morning, alone. Any attempt at any Tom-foolery will be dealt with. There will be a person nearby watching and if you enter with another, the deal is off. If you attempt anything of a fraudulent nature, there will be no second chance and again the deal will be off. But if you do as asked and if all goes through without incident, the man who will handle the transaction will signal my watchful spy, who will collect the said paperwork, and deliver it to me for my perusal. If all is as it should be, then and only then, will I have the hanging stopped. Are we clear?'

'Crystal' Sighed Lizzy. 'I will be there as early as I can. What time will he see me? I will go now if I can.'

'No, no, no! That will not be necessary; the paperwork is all drawn up, on his desk and ready. All that is needed is your signature and then it is done. He has told me he will be there for 8 am, which gives a full two hours before William's scheduled hanging, but fear not. If all is done correctly, it will go away! Is there ever an end to my benevolence?' He laughed.

Standing up, Lizzy was as cautious as she was hopeful.

She looked at him with the same disgust she felt when she looked at the pools of vomit outside the pubs in the early morning; she was reminded how faint his credibility was. 'How could I trust him?' she thought to herself. 'How could I trust one so very evidently incongruous? I hate him. I hate him. I hate him! He is without question the most insufficient pile of mortal twaddle to ever draw such undeserved breath!'

'It is settled then?' She asked politely as her brain continued to insult him.

Fenwick looked bright in the face with satisfaction as he breathed smugly. 'It certainly seems so; I would shake on it, but for the fear of diseases I might contract. You will hear from me when it is sorted, until then…'

Fenwick bowed slightly before exiting Woodworth Manor briskly.

She felt dizzy, she hoped Father Fanshaw would hurry and come to keep her company. She asked herself if she had been a fool. She pondered if she should share the details of the proposed deal with Father Fanshaw, or maybe even Constable Robertson. She worried about the many possible outcomes, but only wanted one.

William, safe and alive, that's all she wanted…and nothing else mattered.

CHAPTER 59

It felt like the busiest night of his life, and for the out-of-breath Constable Robertson, the going was only to get tougher. Having checked on Lizzy after his eerie trip to the morgue, Robertson was pleased she was not on her own. Father Fanshaw had kindheartedly decided to stay with her for the remainder of the early hours; they doubted sleep was a possibility for anyone before the dreaded day ahead.

Robertson just hoped he could change things in time. One thing was for damn certain, he would do his very best.

It was just past dawn now in Goodridge Grove, and Robertson's eyes adjusted to the light with pleasure as he walked amongst some of the most sought-after houses in Barnes.

The thought crossed his mind that not one person who lived in the area would have ever struggled for coin, or to put food on the table. They had probably never struggled at all.

He looked in awe at the fancy cottage as he checked he was at the right place. 'Stanbury Mead' the sign said. It seemed to be loose and could have done with an extra nail in it. He did a quick skip and jump over the small gate and proceeded into the garden. It was a good sized garden and Robertson wondered how the heck one would have managed to maintain it, then it came to him…

People around here didn't cut their own grass, pull up weeds or trim their hedges…they had others do it.

As he walked through the garden, a nest of birds in the magnolia tree beside him caught his eye. The pink flowers were in full bloom and Robertson's mouth twitched to a smile as he thought of a time when he and Peggy shared a picnic under such a tree, he remembered the tasty scones they brought in the picnic basket that day, all stuck together with the best butter and strawberry jam, just the thought made him hungry.

He walked past the front porch which was furnished with fancy wicker furniture surrounded by ornate vases filled with an abundance of flowers. The smell was very pleasing to Robertson and he breathed the pleasant scents several times before deciding to knock on the front door and put his serious face back on. After all, he was here to ask serious questions.

The continuous knocking on the door didn't seem to be having an effect, Robertson even walked a few steps to a nearby window and leaned over to take a look but it didn't look like anyone was coming to answer.

He knew that people were home, he had already determined it by his third knock at the door. There were keys clearly visible at the other side of the door on a nearby table; an empty lantern holder which meant somebody had taken the lantern upstairs was also a dead giveaway.

Robertson decided to increase the level of noise…

Banging even harder at the door, Robertson was of the opinion that a man of such standing as Judge Stanbury wouldn't take kindly to embarrassment, as saving face in such a neighbourhood was a high priority indeed. People in such parts didn't look favourably on scandal. So, upping the ante, Robertson called out as he continued his loud rapping at the judge's front door.

'Judge Stanbury, it is the police. The *police,* I say, I need to see Judge Stanbury. I am the police. Judge Stanbury, I need to question you! Judge Stanbury…'

Panicked feet made a noise like animals in a stampede as Robertson heard the judge shouting; first as he raced down the stairs then into the hallway and as he fumbled with his keys near the front door. He did not sound at all pleased. Robertson didn't care though; he was way past worrying about social graces and any sort of professional courtesy. A man's life hung in the balance… that was all Robertson cared about, and should there be a little bit of gossip about a judge who did not practise in the proper ways, then so be it.

Let there be gossip.

'What in heaven's name is all this about sir?' screamed the judge as he opened the door, his nightcap still hanging off his balding head.

Robertson smiled as he gave an answer, 'You, Judge. I suggest you let me in.'

Closing the door a little as Robertson stepped forward the judge's mouth screwed up. He was livid at Robertson's early morning racket. 'I most certainly will not, and I assure you I will have words with your superiors. I would remind you I have friends in high places.'

'Oh yes. The name dropping begins. Do you believe judge, that I have porridge for brain cells? Do you think I have such a low intelligence that I do not know who you are or what circles you stand in? Which leads to me to a point, it is those circles, the company you keep, which have led me to you today. We have to talk right now or, God help me, I will scream down this neighbourhood with accusations of your wrongdoings and then break down your door, and drag you through the streets for all to see. At the end of that humiliation you will be locked in a prison cell and charged with perverting the course of justice, amongst many other heinous plots. So, tea and two sugars, please.'

CHAPTER 60

In all of his years of service as a policeman, Robertson had a weapon he favoured to use above all others.

His gut.

There was a lot to be said about a gut feeling, or as many would call it 'intuition'. Initial feelings or a gut reaction to something was always a huge factor for Robertson. He wasn't so superstitious as to ignore hard evidence, but over time he found he would more-often-than-not have a feeling and in most cases, he would be right. It was like his soul telling him whether something was right or wrong and he found that if he ever went against it, things didn't feel so good.

Now Robertson had *some* evidence, and he had his gut, it was time to combine both and get the truth.

As the judge brought in a cup of tea for Robertson, little did he know that Robertson had already begun to work; his inquisitive eyes scanned the lovely room piece-by-piece to put together his jigsaw of theories.

It was amazing what secrets a person's house gives away, as if the very house whispered clues to previously unrevealed queries.

Robertson had his plan of action in mind. He had done this a million times before, and despite the warm surroundings of a beautiful home and the comforts of a snug chair and tea with two sugars, this was in fact an interrogation, and the funny thing was, the judge didn't even know it. False sense of security was always a tool which Robertson loved to use.

The judge sat down opposite Robertson who took a sip of his tea like he had all the time in the world. Of course he didn't, inside he was dying to get the matter wrapped up to try and save William.

Robertson's loud unending slurps of the tea made the judge more irritable by the second but little did the judge know that he was being observed. The judge's hands couldn't keep still as he sat cross-legged and tapped his feet as if there was some sort of musical beat. Robertson looked at him and smiled as he observed the judge cross his arms, then un-cross them, then he seemed he had a nail on his finger that was half-hanging off so proceeded to pull it off. He licked his lips and bit his bottom lip followed by deep slow breaths.

'I tell you what, judge, lovely cuppa tea. What tea is this?' Robertson asked as he noticed the judge's patience grow thinner by the minute.

''Jagglesbaggles Brew', the best tea manufacturer in England, they say,' the judge answered as he attempted to conceal his tension.

'Mmm, nice. I have always favoured the Yorkshire blend.' Robertson nodded, as his hand kept his warm cup steady. He placed the cup on the tea tray next to him, and as he did so it made a little chime.

It was time to cease the mind games and commence with business, and Robertson was as blunt as a spoon.

'So judge, it is time.'

'Time for what?' the judge asked sharply.

'Time for you to tell me all you know, and before you backtrack and dig a deeper hole, I suggest you should explore the possibility that I know all you know, and that my questions may be rhetorical. I have asked myself many-a-question over my investigations, one of which is how a judge such as yourself would be in league with a character as twisted as Patrick Fenwick?'

The judge's eyes opened fully and he took off his nightcap and sat up straight, Robertson knew he had the judge's full attention as he continued.

'Why would a man, who sits at a throne of justice, be tangled in a web of deceit? Deceit which could ultimately lead to the loss of a man's life? I mean, how terrible is that? I have evidence I would like you to see, judge.'

Robertson reached into his pockets; he pulled out three items and placed them on his knees.

'These pieces of evidence, judge, a brass pocket watch, a lovely silver patterned pipe, and some rather fashionable deerskin gloves. These items were found on dead persons; dead persons who were killed in an altercation. Now the police, who supposedly examined the bodies and the area, said the men were unarmed, yet I also found a razor, a small knife, and a bat. All of which I have placed in a secure location, I might add. Now just the matter of the weapons alone indicates that the investigation was flawed, but adding these other interesting items, we have cause to at least question the sentence, don't we? I tell you what, judge, don't answer yet; maybe this is all circumstantial? Maybe this is all some misunderstanding? Well, you see this pipe here and these gloves, and the extravagant pocket watch? Now, correct me if I am wrong, but are these not the accessories of a gentleman? Are these not items which most men, myself included, could hardly ever afford? So who could afford such items? Three out-of-work thugs whose shoes had holes in them, whose clothes were as dirty as potato sacks? Who, even before they perished smelled like badgers' bottoms? No, of course not, for these are the items of a man of stature, a man of supreme importance, for if he can afford a pipe which holds the same value as all the clothes I stand in, surely he has coin to waste?'

The judge held his head in his hands and then looked up quickly at Robertson, 'Not my items though, sir! Not mine!'

'No, I know that to be correct, sir. Not yours at all. But you do however, by the looks of it, have a lovely collection of things in this room. Let me see, ornaments, probably European by the looks of them; vases, oh what wonderful vases you keep, and the guns, sir, how does one obtain so many fine pieces?'

The judge stood and paced the room back and forth a few times before stopping in the middle of the room. 'I made a mistake, damn you! A mistake!'

'Yes, you have,' smiled Robertson, 'a *big* mistake. Now, I am in the position to save you, judge. The offer I am about to propose expires in five minutes. Firstly, you tell me everything about Fenwick, everything you know or even *think* you know. Secondly, you write a letter of pardon, immediately for William Rathbone. The man is innocent, fact! I want you to publicly state in your letter that new facts have arisen, and those facts totally exonerate William Rathbone; that he receives a full and public apology by the court. Thirdly, I want a warrant out for Patrick Fenwick's immediate arrest together with a letter of expulsion from the courts to prevent him practising law ever again. Lastly, I do not want to see your face in a court ever again. You are *old*, you have financial security, you simply step down due to 'health issues'. No one will ever be the wiser. It is a fair deal. Now, and right now, I want one answer, what will it be?'

The judge walked over to his chair and parked his fat bottom back in it. He sighed as he looked at Robertson who stood with his eyebrows raised whilst tapping his watch?

'Yes.'

CHAPTER 61

He woke with the sweet smell of jasmine, the reminder that everything was not in vain, for he had loved. The very thought of that love made all that was happening trivial in comparison. They could take his neck, take his flesh and bones and do what they wanted, for the skin he stood in did not represent his life. His soul was full and armoured against whatever they thought they could do.

As a small gathering of policeman waited, one of them opened the barred doors to William's cell; William stood without resistance and said good morning to the men. They didn't return the compliment though, and the one with the keys spat at William, who wiped the spit off his face with his forearm.

The policemen and a few prison guards walked with him, a few in front and a few to the back. They joked in bad taste and taunted William as he walked his long walk…

His final walk.

One of the policemen looked at William as they walked, he smiled and started talking. 'Hey you, got to tell you this, ha-ha. You know one day, I remember reading a story by this guy. Can't remember who, but he worked with executions and so-on. Anyways, it was about a man who was going to be hanged to death, like you. The thing was this bloke wouldn't die; apparently the knot wasn't placed properly or something. But the funny thing was he kept passing out and then coming back to life to be hanged over and over. The description of it was absolutely horrific. I remember him describing how the guy vomited, but how the sick couldn't go anywhere. I don't remember the whole thing though, nor would I want to. It sounded *really* nasty. Just thought I'd share that with you in case you don't die quickly, just to let you know that death will come, eventually. You should pray for a quick death.' The man laughed even harder as the other policemen chuckled, the man turned to them. 'What do you lot think of it, hanging, that is?'

One of the prison guards behind William piped up, laughing as he spoke, 'Well, with that story you was just mentioning, I think that the sick would have just made it worse, burning in his throat. I also think I heard that the pressure makes your eyes pop out of their sockets. Nice…'

As the men ushered William through many doors and corridors, their taunting continued, but William didn't react; he just thought of her face, Lizzy's sweet smile, eyes, hair, smell, her laugh, and he smiled at the men as they kept up their cruel teasing.

Another policeman chatted away to William, his voice getting louder as William's blasé demeanour became all too apparent. 'If you broke your neck I would think it would be pretty fast, but then again, I don't think there is such a thing as instant death; you can get close, such as with a pistol, but I think most times you still feel something. Things may happen fast, but I still believe that you would feel a great amount of pain for even a split second before death.'

All the men joined in, giving their thoughts on death, pain and execution.

One guard with a ridiculous moustache seemed to have a stutter as he spoke, 'H-h-hey freak, you do-do-do realise you are supposed to t-t-t-tip the hangman? You got any coins?'

William stayed silent as he ignored the man, but couldn't help finding the man's stutter amusing and smiled a little.

'No? W-w-w-w-what you smiling at, you freak? Hey lads, he is smiling, even too stupid to know when to b-b-b-be scared! Oh dear, for the tips is v-v-v- very important. If you tip him, then he w-w-w-w will put the knot of the noose at the back of your neck and your neck should snap q-q-q-q-quickly. Then when he pulls the lever you will die instantly, not s-s-s-s-suffering. However, if you don't tip him...'

'Oooo, he'll be in trouble!' another guard laughed.

'Indeed he w-w-w-will... he will put the knot to the side of your neck. Then, when the lever is p-pulled, you will dangle and choke for several minutes, m-m-maybe m-more than ten or s-s-s-so before dying. How horrible!'

The policeman at the front of the bunch opened a door, there was a creak as the door opened and William knew by the smiles on the men around him that they had reached their destination. Breathing in and out slowly as he got his first glimpse of the stage of death, William tried to stay as composed as he could.

A man approached William in a hurried fashion and didn't even look him in the eyes; he pulled out a tape measure and talked to himself as he measured William height and waist.

'Right, let me see, height - over 6 feet; we have weight ... an average weight I'd say, so....that being said... I'd say....a drop of around....'

The man looked William up and down as he sized him up for the rope. 'Five feet, we need a five foot drop. Get the rope ready!' he shouted to an assistant who adjusted the rope on the contraption just a few steps away. The assistant proceeded to tie the noose around a sand bag. He looked at the man with the tape measure who nodded, the assistant pulled the lever and the trapdoor opened as the sandbag dropped. The two men nodded at each other as the guards, policemen and all who were in attendance seemed to clap.

'All's good,' snapped the man with the tape measure. 'Let's get him in place, then. We have around ten or so minutes, his person of religion is due to be here to read him a prayer, then we will carry the sentence out.' The man smiled then held out his hand to William.

It dawned on William that the man in front of him was not just some mere measuring man, he was the executioner himself.

'I have nothing to offer you, sir, I'm afraid,' William said as he shrugged his shoulders.

The executioner shook his head. 'That is fine, an offering will *not* make you any less dead, it may just take a while longer to get done.'

William sighed as they led him up the wooden steps. The rope swayed from side to side as he approached it. The policemen and guards made jokes with the executioner as William tried to keep calm, his mind repeating over and over, 'It's alright, it's alright. Think of Lizzy, think of Lizzy.'

He stood in wait for Father Fanshaw to turn up. He hoped he would turn up too; William felt that seeing a face he knew would make it all easier.

He just wanted to see a face that didn't hate him before he died.

CHAPTER 62

Lizzy wasn't granted permission to be present for the execution. It was an event only invited persons were permitted to attend. She wondered if she would have gone if she was allowed to do so, and she didn't truly know if she would have.

St. Christopher's Clock Tower which had been built by the fishermen in the area, was one of the tallest buildings in Barnes, and was situated about thirty or so yards from the main gates of the prison. Lizzy had spoken to a gentleman at the ground level and passed him some coins in exchange for her being able to walk the steps to the top floor. Her reasoning was for one purpose only…

As soon as the trapdoor activated from the gallows within the prison, there would be a bell rung three times. Three long morbid rings meant the order had been given - no reprieve, no last minute pardons, no miracles, it was the chime of death.

She stood on the top floor of the clock tower, waiting for some amazing intervention, waiting for Patrick Fenwick's promised pardon. He had sent a messenger to her instructing her to meet him at the tower after she had the paperwork sent to him regarding her estate, and surely enough, as the wind from the window blew her hair all over the place, Patrick reached the top floor to see Lizzy waiting by the window, overlooking the prison in dread of the three chimes.

'My dear!' he shouted as he got his breath back form the climb of the stairs, 'those bloody stairs are quite unforgiving! Great building this I'm sure you'll agree, ironic in some ways given the present circumstances. One building where people look for time, facing another where they'd give anything to avoid it! Ha-ha.'

She turned quickly. 'Enough messing around, Patrick, I trust the paperwork was satisfactory?'

'I think so, didn't check it!' laughed Fenwick. 'My little errand boy did not speak of any misgivings, why should I check it, I wonder? Ha-ha, no Anne, your sincerity is as predictable as it is foolish, still, my gain I guess! Ha-ha.'

Lizzy shook in fear, she felt faint as she read Fenwick's lying face. 'You did not get the charges dropped did you? You are going to let him die, aren't you?'

Fenwick couldn't control his laughter as Lizzy fell to her knees; her cries were loud and desperate as her tears fell like raindrops on to the rough, wooden floorboards. Fenwick stood over her and began to dance, and as he whistled a tune and waved the paperwork to her estate around the air like a soldier would with a flag to mark victory.

'I have a song for you, Anne, it's called 'stretch-a-neck'!' he laughed as he danced around the room and began to sing.

'Going to stretch his neck, we are.

We're going to stretch his neck,

Tie the noose so tight, we will

His feet won't touch the deck,

We'll beat him first, we'll make him thirst

And as we do we'll spit and curse,

Watch him suffer; we're going to stretch his neck! Hip-hip…hooray!'

Lizzy got up, her heart heavy in her chest, a despair of unimaginable pain like a hand tightening its grip around her very soul. She stood in front of Fenwick, her eyes a mixture of pain and vengeance. 'You pig!' she screamed as she flung her hands at him, clawing his face and pulling his hair.

It stopped him singing and dancing, that was for sure, and Fenwick struggled as he tried to fend her off. She hit him repeatedly and their fight moved around the room like some sort of violent dance.

He pushed her off for a second and as he did she ripped some hair off his already balding head, she showed it too him in her hands and threw it in the air as the wind from the window carried it outside into the gusty air.

His eyes squinted with hate, he had always loathed her. Right from when she married his brother and he would *always* loathe her!

'You, you tramp! You bloodsucking monster of a woman! You *want* to play like a man? You want to fight? '

Lizzy took off one of her shoes and kicked off the other to maintain balance. 'You are no man; you are a devil; you can do nothing to hurt me now, nothing!'

Fenwick casually unbuttoned his brown wool overcoat and neatly placed it on the floor, he then rolled up his sleeves and stood with his arms out, as he if was tackling a wild horse, he looked at her in with a real fury and nodded…

'Nothing?' he smiled, 'We'll see about that.'

CHAPTER 63

The Gallows, Barnes Prison, ten minutes before ten

The Reverend's presence was welcomed by William with a sigh of relief. They were allowed a few moments before the sentence was to be carried out and the Reverend stood in front of William with watery eyes. William could see his friend's hands shaking as they held a leather-bound bible.

The good Reverend opened his good book and William shook his head. 'Don't pray, don't, please.'

'Why ever not?' Father Fanshaw asked; whilst he fought back the tears as the tick-tocking of the clock on the wall nearby seemed to get louder and louder.

'I just wanted you here, so I could focus on a face I knew and loved. Thank you for everything, I know it must have been hard raising me after my father died, and I know over the past few years I lived somewhat of a reclusive lifestyle, but you know why. It was never that I stopped caring about you, it was just, they, the voices, they…'

'They got louder didn't they, William?' smiled Father Fanshaw. 'Ever since you were younger, I knew. I thought you had an imaginary friend at first! Then as you reached your teenage years, I realised you had found new friends; they showed you new ways to see things didn't they?'

'They did indeed, they taught me a lot of things, some of which I haven't even begun to understand. I heard them like I hear you now, and as they grew louder, more and more spoke to me. It was like I had to take care of them. At first I thought I was going mad…sometimes I still ask myself that same question, but I know what I know, father. If that makes me mad then…'

'You are not mad, my boy, you are special, you have a gift.'

Two men close to William came closer and Father Fanshaw started to panic a little, his voice shaking as he grew confused as to what to do. 'William…. it's happening, son.'

'I know Father, I know,' smiled William 'I am alright, take care of Lizzy for me, tell her I was smiling, will you? And tell her to find Azrael; she'll know what you mean.'

One man placed a white cloak over William's head and William winked at the father just before they covered his face with it. There was still some vision though; William could make out shadows of figures who were watching. He could see Father Fanshaw being led away and a man, probably the executioner stood in his place.

Tensing his own neck muscles, William wondered how long he could hang on once the trapdoor opened. He also wondered if he should fight it at all; he thought he should at least try and fight it. His mind was spilt, should he or shouldn't he?

Then he closed his eyes as a man chanted words he didn't wish to hear. He focused his mind on the last face he wanted to remember, Lizzy's beautiful smile, their amazing kiss on what was now the best day he had ever lived. Nobody could take that away – ever.

He felt the noose around his neck, whoever was controlling it fastened it tight and William gave a slight cough as they did. He then wiggled his head a little to try and ease the ropes grip, it didn't budge but he at least felt he could breathe again.

He heard some shouting, and wondered if it was aimed at him, he listened again…

'I said … any last words?' a voice shouted harshly.

'Guess it was aimed at me, then,' thought William.

He opened his eyes; he looked around at the many shadowy figures through the white cloak…

'Reverend Fanshaw, tell her one more thing…'

'Anything,' Father Fanshaw shouted, 'anything William!'

'Tell her 'Mortuus est Momentaneum.'

Father Fanshaw fought back his tears as his lip quivered and his hands shook, he knew what it meant.

William tensed his neck muscles again and put his chin low down towards his chest as his breathing became heavier. The tick-tocking of the clock nearby seemed to get louder and louder, but then *everything* seemed to fall silent apart from the clock.

Tick-tock, tick-tock, tick-tock.

Then he heard something else…a loud howling noise, he wondered if it was in his mind but it certainly sounded real enough, William smiled and remembered his furry friend.

'Bye Azrael! Take care of Lizzy.'

The howling continued as the clock kept ticking.

Tick-tock, tick-tock, tick-tock.

Then suddenly the trapdoor sprung opened and William's body fell downwards in what seemed like slow motion. He heard the people who were there gasp and he also heard someone scream

'No!' There was another sound William heard as he fell and the noose tightened its deadly grip…

The sound was loud, the sound was unmistakable…

The sound was of bells ringing.

It was ten o'clock.

CHAPTER 64

Fenwick and Lizzy stared at one another. The wind from the large open window shot through the air between them and made dust on the old floorboards move along with Lizzy's black hair.

Fenwick wanted to strangle her, he wanted to feel his hands around her neck, he wanted to watch her eyes as he squeezed every inch of life out of her.

Then she would see what a man looked like, see what the real man of the Fenwick family could do, and see who the true Lord Fenwick was!

'You repulse me,' she whispered at him as he walked forward slowly towards her. He swung his fist at her as she ducked, and Fenwick fell over because of his over-extended thrust.

She saw an opportunity to run for the stairs and quickly darted towards them, but as she did Fenwick grabbed one of her feet which made her trip over, she hit her head hard on the floor.

Not knocked out, but certainly dizzy, she rolled to see Fenwick crawling towards her, she felt the back of her head with her hands as it throbbed, then she looked at her hands which were wet, her red fingers confirming that blood was trickling out.

Lizzy blinked her eyes, once, twice, three times, in an attempt to get back to her senses, but then Fenwick was on her again!

His hands surrounded her throat, she coughed and spluttered, and she kicked, wiggled and tried to scream. His face was as red as could be, his veins were clearly visible as they stood out on his temples like snakes. She could hardly speak, but she managed to mouth some words to him which he read…

'I hate you,' her mouth spelled out silently as she scratched Fenwick's face with her nails, drawing blood as she did.

Fenwick screamed out, 'Aghhh! Animal!' but Lizzy kept on scratching and wiggling as best she could.

Her scratching stopped; he felt he was almost there; her face was going purple like beetroot. 'Come on Anne, die, give up! Die!' he screamed, and just as he said that, her hands fell to the floor. 'Yes!' he screamed 'yes!'

But then a huge pain crept over him as he let go of her neck, the pain came from down below she had kicked him in between the legs, she rolled and gasped for air as she crawled away towards the window.

'You, you cow!' screamed Fenwick as he stood up holding his man-parts with his hands.

Lizzy had stood up too; she looked outside beyond the prison walls and hoped a miracle had happened as she slowly gathered her breath, she hoped William was safe somehow!

Then she felt Fenwick's hand on her again, she turned and screamed at him as he pushed her almost out of the window, she grabbed on to his ears as she realised if she let go she would fall out!

'Let me go! Aghhh, my bloody ears!' screamed Fenwick, as he feared Lizzy would rip his ears off.

'Then pull me in and stop hitting me,' she said as she took a quick glance outside. It was a long way down; she was now sat on the window frame with her legs inside the building and her top half hanging out as she clung on to Fenwick's ears.

They stopped struggling with each other, Lizzy's chest moved up and down in a mix of tiredness and apprehension of the potential fall behind her, Fenwick too, was out of breath and felt like he had no more fight left in him.

Her hair seemed to dance with the wind and Fenwick looked at her and wondered what it would have been like if she had been his.

Then a noise echoed through the air and travelled with the wind as fast and harsh as thunder, there were three hollowing sounds as everything seemed to fall still.

Lizzy's heart felt like it had sunk deep into her chest…

She looked at Fenwick…he looked at her; he smiled as he saw her mind register what had happened.

Her face seemed to give up all fight and her blank expression looked through Fenwick, as if he was not there at all. She pictured William's face smiling at her; she smiled back at him… as she let go of Fenwick's ears.

She kept her eyes closed as she fell backwards; the wind blew her hair back as the fall became faster and faster but it still felt like she was weightless as images of time spent with William flashed over and over in her brain . She smiled as she whispered soft words whilst picturing his face…she remembered when their fingers barely touched and she felt tingles all over her body, the way they shared a smile, moments, dreams, secrets, kisses…

'I will be with you soon, my love, I'm coming.'

CHAPTER 65

His neck tensed as if it were acting on its own with no command from William at all. It was a natural reaction, an instinct to survive from deep within his soul. He twisted and turned and as he did he felt the rope getting tighter and tighter, like his very life was in a vice and someone was turning the handle, slower and slower.

'Let go,' a part of William's mind screamed, while another part shouted, 'Fight!'

The witnesses to the execution stood with hands over mouths as they watched William's legs kick the air in desperation for something to land on.

He felt like his head was heavy, like his eyes were about to pop out. His arms were beginning to feel numb and his legs felt like two anchors, pulling him down towards the depths.

He thought of Lizzy's eyes again, her smile and as her image floated through his mind his eyes began to close as his body twitched.

The people who were watching looked at each other nodding, as if they knew Williams's body was giving up.

The sounds were faint now; he could hardly hear any of the spectators. He could however, hear the rope swinging and the tension his weight was causing it and he could still hear his friend, Azrael.

Were the howls real or were they in his mind?

Then suddenly, as everything fell silent, he felt his legs touch something. Was it the ground? Was he alive, or was it the path of death on which he was about to walk?

Everything went black.

No images, no bright light, no sweet angels singing, just a deep chasm of black.

Suddenly, a sensation, suddenly he felt water; his eyes flickered and fought his eyelids so they would open.

Something was happening!

Then, a huge gush of air hit his lungs like a wave hits the sea. He breathed in and out, quickly and deeply and his body rose up in the air; his fists clenched and he screamed as he realised he was alive.

The lids of his eyes opened as his breathing calmed and he saw people before him. Everything looked fuzzy at first, like the way things looked underwater, the sound was muffled too, like the way he heard people outside his room when they were visiting the grave yard. Then as the vision and sound slowly cleared, William saw human eyes looking at him.

There were two sets of eyes in particular, eyes he recognised.

'William, William!' Robertson screamed as he slapped William's face.

Looking at Robertson blankly, William didn't respond as his body shook and his eyes looked all around.

'Dear William, answer if you understand, please,' cried Father Fanshaw, who turned to Robertson and whispered, 'I fear you may have been too late, it looks like there's damage to him.'

He felt wet; really, really wet, but the drops of water that fell down his face were soothing to William as he bowed his head and composed himself to speak.

'There is no damage, I am alive, but I ask why? Why do I live?'

'Get back, get back,' shouted Robertson as he moved the people who had gathered around like vultures, all wanting to be in on the events for the sake of curiosity and the right of town chatter.

Father Fanshaw sat beside William, he took William's wrists, which were still bound by chains, and raised them in the air as he screamed at one of the guards. 'Free this man at once! At once I say!' William had never heard Father Fanshaw scream in anger like that, not to *anybody*. The guard rustled around for his keys and tried two or three before finding the right key to unlock William from his chains.

William stood up as the people around gasped and whispered, for this was much drama for the little town of Barnes, a drama which would undoubtedly have bits added on here, there and everywhere for entertainment of course. Nevertheless, the event would live long in the memory for most, no matter how it was told.

Standing in what felt like another dream, William looked down at his wrists and saw the marks that the chains had left. He then felt his neck as it burned from the noose. He blinked over and over as his eyes returned to normal; he held out his palms and looked at them as people talked all around him. He made two fists and tensed them hard as he breathed slowly in and out.

He relaxed his fists and looked up at Father Fanshaw. 'Why? Why am I saved?'

Father Fanshaw smiled at William and passed him some water from a dirty glass which he wiped with his sleeve as he passed it over. William didn't care about how clean the glass was and gulped the water down like he had been in a desert.

'This man here,' Father Fanshaw said as he pulled Robertson forward from the crowd he was trying to keep back, 'He saved you, William. He found out the truth; you have a full pardon from Judge Stanbury - signed and sealed. Tell him, Constable Robertson; tell him what you have done.'

Robertson looked coy but happy all the same. 'I just did my duty, Reverend, no more no less,' he said as he held out his hand for William to shake.

William shook it and smiled with relief. 'Thank you, sir.'

'I'm just sorry I didn't get here sooner. Was up all night compiling evidence, items, a case,' Robertson said quietly, then he cleared his throat, smiled and looked at William as he turned to address the people in attendance and spoke with conviction as his voice got louder. 'A case which people might be keen to know now orders the arrest and questioning of one Patrick Fenwick.'

All around the people chatted and some of them even wrote down Robertson's words.

Robertson looked back at William. 'Can you walk, lad?'

'I'll walk out of here, that's for damn sure,' answered William with a stern look. 'So how did you do it sir? How did you do all that in one night?'

Robertson simply smiled as he patted William on the back. 'With guile, the right questions, and some gentle persuasion. You are totally free, William, free to walk with your head held high; there will be a *full* public apology, and a few people eating their words I would think too. Now, let me escort you out of here so Father Fanshaw can get some ointment on that neck of yours, it looks sore, lad.'

'Feels sore,' smiled William, 'still, better sore than broken, eh?'

'Eh, indeed,' laughed Father Fanshaw as the three of them walked out of the gloomy room.

As the three of them left the prison, Robertson and the Reverend explained the events in detail, how Robertson came running into the room waving the pardon and screaming at the guards to save William from death. How they emptied glass upon glass of water over William's face to wake him up, and the relief of everyone in the room when he did wake.

It surprised William to hear of the guards walking away nearly sobbing at the cruelty they made William endure, and how people booed them and threw things at them. Apparently Robertson even joined in and shouted obscenities which were not in his usual character.

They laughed and joked as they walked, and Robertson and Father Fanshaw felt overjoyed at the sheer luck and timing with which things had happened. They both knew though, that it was how it should be, it was a wrong that just had to be righted; it *had* to be.

Deep down Robertson in particular knew that he couldn't have lived with himself if William had died, so there was no choice really.

Justice *had* to prevail.

The feeling of the outside air touching his face as they exited the prison made William feel free. He still had aches and pains but insisted to both Father Fanshaw and Robertson that he wanted to walk into town.

They had just reached the outside of the prison grounds, and as the guards let the three of them out it started to rain.

The rain fell harder and harder and Robertson pulled his jacket over his head. 'Trust you wanting to walk William; we should get a ride into town.'

William had always enjoyed the rain, but the feeling of it after going through his ordeal made it even better. The pitter-patter of fresh water hit his hair and rolled down his face and he giggled as Father Fanshaw and Robertson ran off ahead in search of shelter. It was then up ahead, William saw a small crowd had gathered. He wondered if it was people wanting to question Constable Robertson about the warrant for Fenwick's arrest, after all, good news travelled fast in Barnes.

His steps in the rain quickened as he saw Robertson and Father Fanshaw talking to the crowd next to the big old Clock Tower. The Reverend turned and looked at William, and then back to the crowd. William wondered if there was something wrong as the Reverend disappeared back into the huddled mob.

He was not far away now, about twenty or so yards. William's clothes were soaked as the rain turned from fine pitter-patter to a full-on downpour. He wiped his eyes, trying to catch a glimpse of either Robertson or Father Fanshaw, when suddenly Robertson pushed his way out through the array of people as if he was trying to get away from something.

'Is everything alright, sir?' shouted William with one hand aiding his voice at the side of his mouth.

'Get back! Get back William; you cannot be here, get back lad!' Robertson screamed as he ran towards William.

'Whatever could be the matter?' thought William as Robertson raced towards him as if he was going to tackle him.

William stopped in his tracks as Robertson reached him. Robertson used both hands to stop William walking, by placing one on each shoulder.

He looked like he had tears in his eyes.

'William, oh my god, William,' he said as his head dropped to William's chest.

'Whatever is the matter, sir?' William asked in concern. 'Please, are you alright? Can I help? Where is the Reverend? What has happened?'

Robertson's words escaped him; he just looked at William and shook his head as the rain fell down his face. There was a loud shudder of thunder which was accompanied by a crackle of lightning.

William looked up to the rain-filled grey clouds, and it looked like the sky was angry. He looked back to Robertson, confused. He searched Robertson's face, his eyes were most definitely teary, a thing which was most unusual for the usually calm Robertson. He looked at Robertson shaking, but it was not from the wet of the rain, something else, something really bad, must have happened.

Robertson took his hands off William and moved his mouth but he could not seem to form any words.

'What, sir? What is wrong? Talk to me.' said William.

But then William looked at Robertson's hands, they were not their normal colour; William took Robertson's hands in his own and inspected them as Robertson tried to pull them away.

They were the reddest of red, red as a rose, red as Lizzy's lips even…

William looked Robertson in the eyes and he feared something terrible had happened.

The hands were red and covered in blood.

Robertson tried to keep William away, but the truth of the matter was no man could hold William on his own, he was simply too strong. William knocked Robertson aside as he eased by him and ran towards the crowd. Fearing the worst, William pushed and pulled people away as he made his way through the cluster of onlookers.

He fell to his knees and screamed an animal's scream, the people nearby jumped back, scared by the volume of William's haunting wail.

'I think she's gone, William,' cried Father Fanshaw who was also on his knees in tears. 'She's gone.'

'No!' cried William as he carefully cradled her head on his knees. 'I won't allow it!'

Carefully holding her head, William could feel how saturated her hair was by the blood, and then he saw it running down his wrists onto his arms then on to the ground as he watched her eyes, hoping for some sign of life, something, anything.

Lizzy's pretty face was blank as the rain fell on her cheeks and made the blood run down her face. William tried wiping some blood away from her eyes as he cried.

'Lizzy, dear Lizzy, don't leave me, please don't leave me all alone. We did it, we beat them, together we beat them, please don't leave me alone, please!'

Her eyes flickered for a split-second, but William caught the movement. 'Lizzy!' he whispered.

'STAND BACK!' shouted Robertson who had seen her eyes move too. 'Where is this doctor we have called for?'

'Lizzy-Lizzy-Lizzy,' whispered William as he saw her eyes move again; her lips moved too, but again it was hardly noticeable.

'My love, I am here I am alive, I am with you, I love you.'

He could see her lips moving a little, but William couldn't hear her, he turned to the people and gritted his teeth 'Get away! Get away!'

The crowd stepped back in fear; they could see the ferociousness in his eyes. William turned back to Lizzy; he could see her trying to speak so he leant his head close to her and positioned his ear near her mouth. Her skin was cold, and as he listened to her try to whisper her words he could smell the sweet smell of jasmine as the slightest sounds touched his ear like a feather.

'My love, my William, I love you,' she whispered as the relentless rain hammered down on to the ground.

Quickly lifting his head, William looked at her eyes and sobbed as he told her 'I love you, I have only ever loved you, will only ever love you.'

Her lips made a little crook at the side in an attempt at a smile; her eyes slowly blinked and she whispered again, 'don't be afraid, William, don't be afraid.'

He could feel her tremble slightly and look beyond him. He wondered what she looked at and looked behind himself but there was nothing there, he looked back to her. 'Lizzy, Lizzy?'

Her eyes focused back on him and this time her lips managed a smile. William felt as though his heart would burst as he saw the thing he prized most, then she whispered again, 'Mortuus est Momentaneum.'

The tears from William crashed down as hard as the rain as he heard the words loud and clear, he watched her slip away as the light from her eyes vanished like his tears in the rain.

William heard a single crack of thunder pierce the skies as he wept in despair. Some of the people nearby sobbed too, for all who knew or knew of Lady Anne, or Lizzy as she was known by those closest, loved her.

All but *one*…

CHAPTER 66

How does one cope with loss? Many have asked the same question throughout time. Educated men and women will try and put certain theories forward, try and rationalise it. It is all too easy to talk about loss and give comfort when you have not felt such loss yourself, for those of us who have experienced true loss know, there is nothing to be said, or done, that will make the person who grieves feel any better.

Death is not rational.

There are some who say they 'dreaded the day' a loved one was going to die, or 'couldn't imagine such an awful thing.' Whether dreaded or not, it comes to us all, and nothing prepares you for it.

Nothing can, or ever could.

For William Rathbone, he was in one of the many stages of grieving…denial.

The world as William knew it had become a hollow and insignificant place. Life made no sense anymore. His senses were numb; for days after her death he did nothing, nothing at all. He hardly ate, he hardly slept, and he was in that dark state only a grieving person knows. He wondered how he could go on, if he *should* go on, and *why*, why he should go on. William also questioned whether Lizzy would come to him, like the others did of Deadville. Would she speak to him, would he get to take care of her? Or did she go to the other place? The place where souls rested? He was so confused and part of him wished for her soul to be at peace, whereas the other half selfishly wanted her voice to call out, 'William!' He hated that he was so selfish, but he couldn't help it, he would simply give *anything* to hear her voice one more time.

He had so many questions, but didn't have any answers.

Meanwhile, the word had spread through Barnes like wildfire that Fenwick was a wanted man, and not only for the conspiracy regarding William. The caretaker from the clock tower claimed he heard Fenwick attack Lady Anne and flee straight after. There was a public outcry for the capture of Fenwick and his estate was seized by the law until further notice, He was wanted for murder. William was seen as a victim, and the powers that be read out his full pardon in full view of the folk of Barnes. The pardon was read out by Judge Stanbury himself in the Market Square; afterwards, he announced his retirement due to 'on-going medical concerns.'

He got off lucky, and he *knew* it.

William never attended his pardon; he refused to speak to anyone and everyone. He wasn't interested in work, he wasn't interested in life.

Nothing mattered anymore.

The day of Lizzy's funeral was the only time William came out of his room, even during the day the most physical thing William would do was to open the door at mid-day when Father Fanshaw brought him bread and soup; he refused breakfast and supper. He only ate to keep alive, and he wasn't even sure he wanted to do that.

The day of Lizzy's burial, William stepped out of his room to attend. He felt dozens and dozens of eyes on him but didn't acknowledge any of them.

William just watched as the coffin was lowered. He listened to the cries of people he hardly recognised.

'Who are they? What are they doing here?' he thought. He wanted them to leave, so he could be with her, alone.

Father Fanshaw and Constable Robertson offered their condolences, but William just held his blank stare.

Father Fanshaw feared he had lost William, but Robertson aired caution and tried to remind the Reverend that it was still early days. That William was in a place *he* knew from personal experience and should not be rushed in his grief. Father Fanshaw knew Robertson was right, it was just he loved William like a son, and it made him sad at both how hard William was taking it, and his own inability to soothe William's pain.

A few days after the funeral Father Fanshaw had just returned from a trip into town, he needed groceries so had taken an early morning stroll in an attempt to avoid the morning rush. Upon his return he caught a glimpse of William beside Lady Anne's grave.

William wasn't talking; he just sat cross-legged with his hands covering his face. Father Fanshaw walked over and when he reached William he placed a soothing hand on his shoulders.

'I'm here my boy, if you need me' Father Fanshaw said as he patted Williams shoulder.

'I know', William answered.

It was the first time William had spoken to anyone. Father Fanshaw placed his sack of goods on the ground and William could see a few apples roll out of the bag along with some carrots.

'You are losing your apples,' smiled William.

'Nothing new there, lad, I feared you were too!' joked Father Fanshaw.

Raising his eyebrows, William wondered if he even had them to begin with and chuckled at Father Fanshaw's effort at trying to spread some sort of minimal cheer.

'I just can't believe she's gone,' William said as he stared at Lizzy's headstone.

William looked like he felt awkward as he spoke, 'Who prepared…everything? Who, you know…?'

Father Fanshaw sighed as he sat up close next to William. 'Look, I'm going to get all dirty, sitting on the grass with you.' He smiled 'But today, I'll make an exception,' he said as he added a wink. 'The thing is, dear William, you wouldn't talk to any of us, so you see I had to bring a few others in to help out. I assure you, though they took the most intense care of her. You saw her coffin, it was lovely, and all the flowers were truly stunning, as were the words people spoke about her. Can you remember the words people spoke about her, William? Or is it all still kind of misty?'

As he nodded William sighed again, 'Misty. Definitely misty, it's like this past week I haven't been in my own body, when people have spoken to me I've heard them but I haven't, does that make any sense?'

'Makes perfect sense, my boy,' said Father Fanshaw as rubbed his hand hard on William's back. 'Don't make any excuses for grief, my son, for all is understandable. You are going through a truly horrid time William, horrid indeed. But I will say that time heals; you will never forget, but you will learn to live with it.'

'But what if I don't want to?' asked William.

'You have to,' Father Fanshaw replied sternly, 'You just have to.'

William looked at Father Fanshaw and shrugged his shoulders before changing the subject 'Who paid for it all?'

Father Fanshaw looked uneasy and William could see that he was stalling for an answer.

'Who?' William asked again, sharply.

Father Fanshaw held out his palm calmly. 'Listen, William, there are things we need to discuss, I was waiting for the right time.'

'What things?' asked William.

'Well, very early on the morning before … what happened. There were things happening William; proceedings of an absolute necessity, things which were all in aid of getting you free. I, as well as Constable Robertson and Lady Anne, were involved in events that were all combined in the desperate attempts to save you.'

'I don't understand? How does this have anything to do with…?'

'Hear me out,' Father Fanshaw interrupted. 'One of the things Lady Anne was asked to do, by…Fenwick.'

William's face automatically frowned. 'Don't mention his name to me.'

'I am sorry,' Father Fanshaw said cautiously. 'I am sorry. He offered Lady Anne a proposal, in a nutshell he wanted all she owned, Woodworth Manor and all its contents, all her money, everything she had. It was all to be part of an exchange for your life William. She was willing to trade it all… happy to trade it all.'

'Oh no,' William sighed, 'Surely it must be voided now, surely with the new information at hand it does not stand?'

'It was a legal contract, William, it *must* stand, and it was signed by Fenwick's legal man. All of Woodworth Manor including the attached Lordship was the deal.'

William stood in disbelief and looked at Lizzy's headstone, 'Lizzy.'

'She did it for love, William, she did it for love. But there was one thing Fenwick didn't count on,' smiled Father Fanshaw.

Turning to Father Fanshaw, wondering what made him smile, William raised his hands up in question. 'What?'

Father Fanshaw looked to his immediate left and right and motioned William to come closer with his finger, 'Here, come here,' he whispered.

William moved closer. 'What?'

'Fenwick didn't count on the cunning of an old man.'

Still confused, William looked at Father Fanshaw. 'I don't understand.'

'Early that morning, William, Lady Anne and I conjured up a plan. She was more than willing to give up everything for you. But then she had a thought; she really wanted to surprise you, and it just so happened her planned surprise would have aggrieved Fenwick greatly. Surely, he has heard by now, for it's all over town.'

'What is? Really, Reverend I'm not making sense of this,' William said as he shook his head.

'Stay with me,' the Reverend pleaded. 'I, a Reverend, a man of the cloth, so-to-speak, committed my first crime, and for a handful of coins, I coaxed one of the pick-pockets from old Dagger Lane to slyly pick the lock of Manley Legal. Once we were in, the task was simple. Now the deeds of the deal were already written, there was only one thing needed, Lady Anne's signature, which she planned on scribbling down later in front of the solicitor in her most careful way, but what also happened was the change in name of the benefactor. I tell you now William, Lady Anne smiled and laughed as she thought of it, she was so pleased. Her plan was simple, what she did, was replace Fenwick's name on the middle of the document with yours, she simply crossed his name out and wrote in 'William Rathbone', then she turned to me and smiled as she said, 'Lord William!' It made her so happy. I was afraid and worried that the solicitor would spot it, but the papers had been drawn up the day before and were rolled into a scroll. When we returned a few hours later, the solicitor merely unrolled the scroll a few inches, with your name not visible, and asked for Lady Anne's signature, she scribbled it down with the most serious of faces. The solicitor sealed the scroll with his marked wax stamp, and sent it off with an errand-boy. My guess is Fenwick didn't check it, as it was registered the very next day. So William, you are now Lord William Rathbone! And in answer to your initial question, technically, you paid for all this. I hope you don't mind but I acted as your guardian and signed for the cost. Constable Robertson witnessed it too.'

William fell back on the grass; he looked at Lizzy's headstone and back to Father Fanshaw. 'She was so great, never thinking of herself. I thank you for the words on her gravestone, and thank you for burying her here, in this part of the graveyard.'

'I knew you wanted her beyond the east wall, William, that's why I did it.'

CHAPTER 67

Having begun to accept the reality of his loss, he started to ask more questions and, unknown to William, he was beginning the healing process. He was becoming stronger and the denial was beginning to fade. But as he proceeded, all the feelings he had denied began to surface.

Now to avoid confusion, his state of mind wasn't getting better, but in saying that, things were certainly becoming clearer. He was having ideas, ideas on what he would do next.

He was in a different stage of grief now…

One he would embrace…

Anger.

William was more than willing to feel the anger, but more than that he wanted to share it, and direct it to its rightful destination. The more he felt it, the more he wanted to unleash his wrath. Underneath his anger was a deep wound nothing or nobody could ever heal.

'Learn to live with it.' That's what Father Fanshaw said and William was more than happy to oblige.

Anger could be used as strength, William knew this, and he also knew it could eat him up, but that was not something he cared about. His anger needed to be let loose, needed to be fed, and only one thing, one man, could feed it. That man was Patrick Fenwick.

Having taken a walk to his new estate, the magnificent Woodworth Manor, William walked slowly around the house. It was supposed to be his new home but how could it ever feel like home when the person who could have made it such wasn't there anymore? He walked the rooms and could still smell her, the scent of jasmine still hung in the air.

He couldn't move in yet, he just wasn't ready. So after he left Woodworth Manor he thought he needed some company.

He hadn't spoken to any of them in days, and knew that they would be able to at least understand how he was feeling. He made his way to the graveyard on foot and once he got there, walked quickly into his quarters and made a small cup of tea. William also brought out his tobacco and his pipe and got himself comfortable in readiness for his chat.

He lit his pipe and inhaled the pleasant feeling, he exhaled slowly and then sipped a little of his tea.

He looked around and everything seemed so still, so quiet. 'At least the rain has eased off a little,' thought William.

He waited, but nobody seemed to be talking, so he thought he'd try to get a response. 'Morning all, I know some of you may feel a little lost for words, maybe awkward at knowing what to say? Don't, I just want to chat, just want to hear friendly voices.'

Still there was no answer.

'You know, my friends, I could really do with a chat, has anyone seen Azrael?'

Everything was still quiet.

William was angry now and stood to his feet. 'Well thank you very much, all of you, thanks a bunch! All the time I have spent listening to you and you can't be there for me!'

Turning as if he was about to leave, William looked back, specifically at Mr Higgingsly's grave. 'Well I'm going now, really, I'm off, don't expect me back today.'

He walked a few paces and turned back again. 'Seriously, people, I'm going out for the day' he focused his attention on another grave now; surely she would talk to him. 'Old Peggy, you there? Peggy?' William sighed, 'You too? Alright, alright, guess you must be all…resting or something today? I feel pretty silly you know, talking to the air. People are already saying I'm crazy! Look I'll be back tomorrow, see you all soon.'

Nobody said goodbye back to William and he marched away to the gates, talking to himself in the process. 'I can't believe it, giving me the silent treatment, why? What have I done? Or not done? I have always been there for them haven't I?'

William wasn't sure where he was walking to; he half-expected one voice at least to yell 'Stop,' or something back in the graveyard but to his disappointment it never came. His legs seemed to want to walk. He didn't know whether or not it was all the time he had spent alone and cooped up in his room or that he just needed to be outside, either way, he walked.

He walked and walked and then he even surprised himself - he had walked into town. He found it strange in the town; people were tipping their hats to him, people he didn't know. It was like he was well known for a different reason now.

Well-known for escaping the noose maybe? It was a fame William didn't plan to bask in at all.

He still nodded at those who tipped their hats as he walked the cobbled streets into the market square and beyond.

He thought of Lizzy, and of the pretty things she used to show him that she would buy at the market and how excited her face would be. He missed her; he missed her so very much.

He wanted to see her face, he wanted to smell her perfume, and he wanted so desperately to kiss her again. Then he thought he could do at least one of those things, he could smell her perfume, and so he headed to Woodworth Manor, it still felt strange that the place was now actually his. He walked and tried to fight his tears. He started to feel overwhelmed by feelings and tried hard to walk and not cry, but his tears had other ideas.

He felt so vulnerable as he walked and people looked at him, watching him in his despair.

'Just keep walking,' he thought. 'You'll be away from them soon.'

Then just as he got within thirty or so yards of Woodworth Manor's gates, an old woman walked by him, she wore black like she was in mourning herself. She had red hair and a dark green lace scarf, William only slightly glanced at her, he was trying to avoid eye contact with anyone.

Suddenly she stopped him with her hands and she spoke very softly to him. William though, just looked at the ground, his tears still rolling down his face.

She carefully placed her fingers underneath his chin and tried to raise his face to her, 'Look at me, you are crying, here take this.'

William looked up again and to his amazement it was not an old lady at all.

Was he going mad? Were his eyes playing tricks on him?

'Er…good day ma'am,' William said as he noticed she was holding out a green silk handkerchief for him with her other hand.

'Take it,' she said straight-faced.

Taking the handkerchief, William wiped his eyes with it. 'I am so sorry, thank you,' he said and attempted to give the handkerchief back to her.

But she would not have it back.

'No you keep it,' she said.

William looked at her, there was something strange about her, like he knew her face but could not place it. She only looked in her mid-twenties, and William felt confused as to how he could have seen her as an old lady just a few moments ago.

'Do I know you?' she asked him politely.

'I was thinking the same thing, ma'am, but no, I don't believe so,' he answered.

'You have suffered a great loss, William,' she smiled.

'How, how do you know my name?' William asked in shock.

'It was a guess, is that really your name? Oh I do surprise myself, I think you just look like a William that's all.'

She then leaned forward to William as she held her hand close to her chest. 'What *are* you?'

Stepping back in defence, William wasn't sure what she meant. 'Er…good day, ma'am, I have to go, thank you again,' he said as he hurried off towards Woodworth Manor.

The lady watched William walk briskly off to the grounds of Woodworth Manor and then shut the gates firmly behind him.

'No William,' she smiled. 'Thank you.'

CHAPTER 68

The long days seemed to turn into weeks, and then the weeks seemed to turn into months. Before William knew it, it was November.

Winter was well and truly underway; there was a carpet of snow all over Barnes, snow on the roads, on the rooftops, and on the graves.

William had just moved into his new home at Woodworth Manor, he thought maybe a change of scenery would do him good; it didn't.

William felt as low as ever, he would occasionally take out some of Lizzy's dresses and wrap them in his hands as he fell asleep. He could still smell her perfume on them. It wasn't much, but it was something, a reminder of her, and he would take anything he could get.

He would wake some days and not want to get up. He had good days and bad days. On the good days he still helped Father Fanshaw by digging the graves and helping out in the grave yard. But on the bad days he didn't get out of bed and didn't speak to a *soul.*

He didn't speak to a soul, not one, and that fact was another thing which ate away at him.

He found it ironic that all the years when he wondered how it would be if he were normal and the voices went away, he sometimes begged for the voices to stop. Sure, he accepted them freely when he got older but when he was younger he used to get really scared. Now, when he needed them the most, the voices had vanished.

He wondered if he had lost his mind back then; he wondered if he used to be crazy, and now somehow had maybe reached a state of sanity.

Father Fanshaw had given him something from a bag that he had found which had belonged to Lizzy. He thought she must have put it down at some point and forgotten about it. Then with all the commotion that happened it must have been knocked over and hidden.

The Reverend had stumbled across the bag and found inside a present with a bow wrapped around it, so he handed it to William.

William loved it, it was a small brass telescope and Lizzy had even had his initials, 'WB' engraved on the side of it.

When the snow came in November, William walked to the forest beyond the graveyard every other day and used his telescope to look towards the large hills and landscape beyond the trees at the back of the forest. Secretly he hoped to catch a glimpse of Azrael, but it seemed he had long gone too.

William just hoped that wherever Azrael was, he was alright and unscathed by the men who tried to capture and kill him the night he was arrested.

The forest looked beautiful covered in the white blanket of winter and William thought that even if Azrael was out there somewhere, he would never spot him, not with his white and grey furry coat which was the perfect camouflage, particularly in the snow.

Images were still coming to William when he was alone, and the images were ones which were not welcome.

Patrick Fenwick's face seemed to haunt him and William was growing sick and tired of seeing it.

He could still picture the man's hateful smile.

Robertson had tried to keep William up-to-date regarding the hunt for Fenwick, but nobody had seen him. It was as if the man had vanished off the face of the earth. Even a handsome reward bore no fruit, not a single piece of information had been handed to the police.

CHAPTER 69

It was just a normal Friday. William had dug two graves on a rather cold morning. Stopping for a break, he headed into his old quarters and made a cup of tea. He gripped his hands around the cup in an attempt to warm up his cold fingers as he sipped his drink.

As soon as William took his first sip, he thought he heard something. He dropped the cup and it smashed as the sound got louder, then all of a sudden the door to his quarters which he had left open smashed shut, making William jump in the process. William stepped back, the sound was strange, like the sound was carried on the wind that crashed against the house and danced around the graveyard to its own melody.

Then it hit him, it was the sound of a piano! He ran outside and spun around trying to home in on where the sound was coming from and, as he let his ears guide him, he realised he was walking towards the east wall. Picking up pace as he headed towards Lizzy's grave he smiled as he got closer. 'My love, I'm coming, I'm coming,' he screamed. Just as he got a few feet away a branch from a tree snapped and almost hit him, William fell backwards on to his back-side. He wondered if maybe she didn't want to see him, but why?

Was he reading too much into this? It was winter after all, and branches did snap in winter. Was he merely clinging onto signs that meant nothing? William got up again, and wiped the snow off his trousers and coat. He walked forward, wondering if it was just chance that the branch decided to break at that specific moment. He took two steps forward and another branch snapped.

'What?' William screamed to the sky, 'What are you trying to tell me?'

Taking whatever hint he was supposed to take, he walked away and back into the house. William's head spun as he questioned his own sanity and sat on the bed. Then something flew towards him … it was his old envelope opener, a very sharp, envelope opener.

It narrowly missed his foot as it stuck in the ground like someone had thrown it with force.

William knew the wind couldn't do that, nor a draft of any kind.

He stood and asked again, 'whoever is there, if there is *anybody* there, tell me what you want, I will help you.'

Again, as in the many silent months before, there was no answer.

He thought it sad he had seemingly lost his gift, and now he missed it more than ever. He would have given anything to talk to Lizzy like he had with the other spirits for so many years. But he knew that part of his life was over.

He just hoped that wherever the spirits went that they were happy and free, he hoped it was someplace better.

It had been a testing day, and as the weather seemed to be getting worse William thought it best he stay in his own quarters that night. He nipped in to see Father Fanshaw who seemed over the moon that William was staying, and as William spoke with the Reverend briefly, he thought that maybe he should make more of an effort with the living. So with that in mind, William promised that he would stay for breakfast the following morning. But for the time being he just wanted to sleep a night in his old bed.

After putting some thick logs on the fire, William fluffed his pillows and made himself comfortable.

It seemed that in no time at all, William had fallen into a deep sleep.

It was the first night William had dreamt in a long time, and the dream was achingly beautiful.

There were images of Lizzy in the many different coloured dresses that she loved so very much. He remembered the days they spent together, he remembered such joys he shared with her … the jokes she made when she taught him chess and he couldn't play it properly; the loud laughs she had when William made a fool of himself. He thought back to one day when it had rained in the forest and she took his hands and taught him to dance. Then there were flashes of when she played the piano. He remembered her turning to him and smiling as she played Beethoven's Moonlight Sonata.

In one quick instant he woke, panting for air. His brain was in gear ever-so-quickly as he realised the weird sound he had heard earlier was indeed like that of a piano, notes from a piano.

Then he put the notes together in his head slowly, and as he did, he worked it out…

'That's it,' he cried out loud, 'it's Beethoven, it's Lizzy!'

He wondered if he had not, in fact, gone mad, and Lizzy was actually trying to get some sort of message to him, what *was* she trying to say and how would he respond?

William had a renewed hope that maybe, just maybe, something or someone was trying to contact him. All the little hints pointed to Lizzy, he just hoped it was true.

A few days passed, and nothing happened. No signs at all, no whispering sounds on the wind, no branches falling or knives flying towards him, no nothing.

William was low again, it was early in the morning and he had been sat at Lizzy's grave for hours just talking to her in hope she would respond.

But she didn't and he felt truly lost.

William sat on his knees and placed his palms on her headstone. His tears fell to the ground as he spoke, 'Death is momentary, that was what you said! Mortuus est Momentaneum! But how can that be true when you have left me for good? Everything's awful; everything's so very horrible now you're gone. The birds haven't sung since you left, the trees don't move like they did; the clouds are grey and horrid, it's like the sunshine won't come out because you're gone. The flowers all died, replaced by weed after horrible weed. Even the dead won't talk to me anymore. Azrael has vanished, everyone's gone. They've all gone Lizzy! I'm wasting away without you, my soul feels scattered and broken, I walk the dark forest and my legs seem to seize up like they have no life in them. My heartbeat feels laboured like there's no point to it all. I know now, I know you aren't coming back. I cherish the time we spent together, my love, I will always cherish it; even though I don't think we were given a fair chance, it's just *not* fair. I keep having bad thoughts too, bad thoughts I try to fight but they come back at me like angry wasps. They still haven't found…him, yet one of the policemen I know was involved in Fenwick's evil still wears a badge. *Ravensdale* is his name. I keep wondering if I at least punish one of them will it ease my pain. I am so confused, my love. I don't know what to do.'

William stood and kissed Lizzy's gravestone…'I pine for you, I yearn for you, I ache for you.' Then he slowly walked away.

As he walked a sudden feeling came over him, and it was not one that he had felt often.

Now a 'fit of rage' is, by definition an unplanned outburst of uncontrollable anger, a fit of rage that implies a loss of control.

Now William wasn't exactly sure whether it was rage or revenge he had in mind, but what he felt was definitely somewhere between the two.

With clenched fists he walked, his brain taunted by smiling, evil faces, evil faces that needed punishing, and there was one in particular he yearned for…

Fenwick, oh how William wanted him!

Time seemed to flash by and suddenly it was getting dark, William didn't feel right. Something was wrong, but he didn't know what. He felt dark, and was ready to do dark things.

Looking down he noticed his boots were now covered in worms, spiders and centipedes, but it didn't bother him at all, he smiled in fact. 'They must pay, somebody must pay,' he said out loud.

There was a crack of thunder, and William smiled again; he loved the thunder, it seemed to know how William felt sometimes, almost like an ally.

He looked to the sky like he knew it. 'Yes,' he said to it. 'Yes.' He nodded. The rain poured and he let it drench him as his thoughts twisted in his mind.

Someone needed to pay.

His eyes felt like they were on fire, and moments later, he realised he was surrounded by black ravens.

They seemed to be everywhere. There were some on Higgingsly's grave, a few on Thomas's headstone, one on Old Peggy's, a few on Maureen's, as well as on Lord Fenwick's and Pick-pocket Sam's ... they were everywhere!

It seemed they were in a circle as they focussed their eyes on him. He felt almost hypnotised by their gaze, as strange voices whispered, 'Do it - kill, kill, kill, kill!'

The voices where everywhere and William felt dizzy as they got faster and louder. 'Kill-kill-kill-kill-kill-kill-kill'! The ravens all started to squawk in unison and the noise was piercing like chalk screeching down a blackboard. William tried to cover his ears to the wretched noise but it pierced right through him as if it was coming from inside his mind.

Images came to him like he was being told to do something; Ravensdale's face flew through his mind as the voices rattled on...

Kill!

Kill!

Kill!

Suddenly William felt he wasn't in control anymore, his mind was numb and he walked towards the tool-shed. As he opened the door some bats screeched past him into the night, the night which was so very dark, so very black, black as coal, black as a bat, black as the grim reaper's waistcoat.

Black as a raven

There was only one tool that William wanted; his spade. The tool he knew, he trusted, it always got the job done. As he picked it up he saw his reflection in the cracked window of the shed; he had been meaning to fix that window forever. Standing in an almost sleepwalking state, he looked at his reflection and saw a different version of himself. His hair was still black, but blacker; his skin was still pale, but paler and his eyes were still deep, but deeper than ever before. Then as he looked at his darker version, he noticed shapes behind him. He didn't turn like he usually would have for he had no fear, only darkness.

Some weird and shadowy things seemed to be pulling him backwards, yet he stood still, they looked like black sheets that formed the shape of things which were a mix between men and creatures, some vivid yet unknown pack of soul-possessing parasites.

He watched as they pulled the darker version of him away and the reflection disappeared into the unknown, then he turned and headed out of the shed, his spade gripped firmly in his angry clenched hands.

In no time at all, William was digging. He dug deeper and deeper in some sort of frenzy and all the while the watchful ravens circled and flew around him as if they were waiting for something. Finally, the hole was dug; it was perfect, more than enough room for what was needed, more than enough room for a coffin.

More than enough room for a body.

William seemed to lose his state of consciousness almost, yet he saw what he was doing in flashes, as the rain fell on him and swept through the night air with its friends the thunder and lightning providing the music and the light respectively.

William loved music and the rhythm of the dark night enticed the darkness of his soul to dance to its tune as he dropped the spade deep down in the hole and started to draw with his finger.

His finger drew a circle, round and round and round it went, then he drew a star inside it as the thunder cracked in what seemed like an acceptance of his markings. Then suddenly, the squawking went crazier than ever, William covered his ears again as the ravens flew away. He looked up at what was going on and saw a man standing over the grave, the man was wearing a long overcoat, probably to protect him from the rain. As the ravens departed, the man was shouting 'Get away, go, go back to hell!' He waved what looked like a book to them.

William recognised the coat, it was his! Then he recognised the book; he recognised the voice and then the man, it was Father Fanshaw!

Father Fanshaw looked down at William; he looked furious as he shouted past the noise of the rain and the thunder, 'Whose grave dost thou dig?'

Seeming to drift off again, William raised his eyes slowly with a dreary looking face and smiled at Father Fanshaw, but Father Fanshaw knew it was not William's smile.

'William, whose grave dost thou dig?' he repeated, but William just stared at him with a sinister smile the Reverend had never seen on William's face before. Jumping down into the hole with William, Father Fanshaw shook William over-and-over. 'Come back to me, William, come back to me!'

Leaning his head towards Father Fanshaw, William kept his frightful grin and then picked Father Fanshaw up into the air with one hand by the collar of his overcoat. He hung there, suspended and helpless under William's grip; his strength was too much for any man. 'Don't do this, William; this isn't you, come back to me, please! William, please come back to me. She wouldn't want this … remember Lizzy, remember love? This isn't you, please don't let me watch helplessly again as another person I love rots in front of me by doing the Devil's will. Please William, you must remember her!'

Lowering Father Fanshaw ever-so-slightly, William's face seemed to change right in front of Father Fanshaw and he could see light returning to William's eyes. 'That's it, William,' he shouted, 'Come into the light, come to me. Think of Lizzy, think of her love for you. She *loved* you; she loves you *still* in heaven. She loved you *because* you are good, you're good William!' he said as William lowered him more and more and in a few seconds, William dropped Father Fanshaw and immediately collapsed onto the hole's wet and muddy ground.

His senses seemed to come back to him, although they did so slowly. As they did he saw Father Fanshaw opposite him covered in mud and out of breath.

'Goodness gracious, my boy, that was close,' smiled Father Fanshaw as William returned a smile that was not laced with hate, much to his relief.

Together they sat, for hours, sharing memories of the past, and struggles of the present. Father Fanshaw knew he didn't have to explain what had happened to William's father; he *knew* William knew. Instead he tried to focus on the present and convince William to spend more time with him, so that eventually with a combined great effort, whatever demons or bad spirits wanted William, they would be cast out forever.

William agreed wholeheartedly. He wanted to manage his darkness. He wasn't stupid though, and he knew and accepted fully, that every man had some darkness.

We *all* have it there and no matter what we do, we cannot fight it away completely. It lies dormant inside us all, patiently waiting in our soul's asylum, for that *one* day when we need it. There's a little darkness within all of us; search your souls and I'm sure you will find a little deviant you've left behind one of the forbidden walls of your mind.

So William wasn't alone in having his dark side, not at all…

It was just that he had a little more than most.

CHAPTER 70

The next day William woke with the sun staring down at him through the window in his quarters. He had slept very well but had woken feeling tired, he stretched his arms out as he gave a loud yawn and then got out of the bed.

As he put his clothes on and washed his face he could still see some of the bad things that had appeared to him the night before in his mind's eye. 'Calm down, calm down, b-r-e-a-t-h-e,' William told himself over and over. 'What can I do? Where can I go? I have to take my mind away from these terrible thoughts.' he walked outside into the sun and then past Mr Higgingsly's grave, 'You're no help either!' he snapped.

It came to him, an idea that he knew without doubt could calm him down. So off he headed to Woodworth Manor, or as he called it now, 'home.'

Once he got there he kicked off his boots and walked the polished wooden floors into the piano room. He closed his eyes and smiled as wonderful memories of Lizzy turning to him over her shoulder as she played, reminded him of how sweet life could be.

'Focus on the good things' his mind told him as he remembered *that* night in every detail: little candles all around, watching the flames move like they were dancing to her tune. He thought back to how the wind came through the window and tickled his arm giving him goose bumps. He remembered what she played, and as he sat down there was Lizzy's music book.

He wanted to try and play the tune. 'Come on, do it,' a voice inside him said. He closed his eyes and remembered how she taught him the language of song. He opened his eyes and remembered her simple but effective tips as his fingers seemed to brush against the keys like someone was moving them for him, but nobody was, it was all him, and before he realised it he was playing the Moonlight Sonata. He couldn't stop, the sweet sound of the music filled the room, and echoed all around, it was like there was a wave of music that had got in through the door and filled the whole house.

He smiled and laughed as he played the last notes, out of breath, panting in disbelief. He wasn't done there; he wanted to smell her perfume too. So he ran upstairs like a child playing a game, smiling from ear-to-ear, for the first time in a long time. He walked across the landing; he almost felt like he was intruding, and he called out 'Hello,' knowing full well he was the only person in the house; after all, the house *was* his.

There were many bedrooms, but William saw a door which appealed to him more than any other, as something which Lizzy once wore hung over the door. It was a silk scarf with a flowery pattern on it. Once he reached the door, he softly touched the scarf and in an instant, flashes of her wearing it came to him. He pulled it and put it to his nose and breathed in.

Jasmine...

Opening the bedroom door with the scarf in his hand, William looked around and guessed this must have been her bedroom. The room felt strange, there were still some clothes hung over a beautiful oak dressing table. There were still pairs of shoes on the floor as if Lizzy had just kicked them off. The room had her presence, yet was so obviously deprived of life; the silence was a stark reminder of what had happened.

Sitting on the bed which William almost sunk into, he wondered what it would have been like to wake in the room with her on a sunny day … to see her smiling as the birds hummed their morning hymns.

His eyes wandered around the room and then something else caught his attention. It was in the shape of a book on a little bedside table within reaching distance, so William picked it up and looked at it. The front cover of the book had a few different coloured butterflies printed on it, yellow, orange and pink and William smiled at how it was definitely her. Opening the book without a thought of what it might be, William read the first page and dropped the book on the bed, being all too aware he shouldn't be doing what he was doing.

The first page had two simple words, 'My Diary.'

As William sat there with his conscience giving him a stark slap, he stared at the diary and looked around; he knew it wasn't the right thing to do. It was an invasion of privacy to read someone's personal thoughts and William knew it.

'No, I am not reading it, that isn't fair,' said the proper part of William's mind, while the more inquisitive side of it screamed 'Read it, read it, read it!' His hands reached out for it again, but he pulled them back and placed the diary back on the little table. William had only taken a few steps towards the door when he heard something; he turned to see what it was and saw the diary had fallen to the floor.

Had it fallen? Had it been pushed?

He wondered if Lizzy was trying to tell him something, but then wondered if it was his mind's own way of justifying reading it. 'No, no, I have to go,' he thought as he left the room and headed downstairs in a hurry.

'No-no-no-no! I can't do it, I just can't. Why am I even thinking it?' William thought to himself as he got to the front door and put his hand on the door handle.

Once he had opened the front door a strange feeling came over him, like an irresistible pull, a pull towards something. It was like his inner voice was saying 'Get back in there, now!'

Was it a sign? Was it Lizzy's way of telling him he needed to read something in the diary?

Something, that was exclusively for his eyes and his eyes alone?

Who was he to argue?

Within seconds of his mind's intervention, William found himself running back inside and up the stairs.

He opened the first page and noticed the diary dated back a few years; he wasn't going to look through everything, as he felt it wasn't his business. It felt wrong enough looking in the first place, so William decided he would only look from when they first met and skipped to April, 1892.

The pages seemed to turn themselves as William read various entries in the diary. Looking at Lizzy's beautiful handwriting, with even more beautiful words gave William a smile he thought had died with her. It made him truly happy to read how excited she was, to know she was as lifted as he was when they first met. She had written questions to her diary, questions such as…

'Does he love me? Or does he just want a friend? Is all this pure kindness he shows real? Can it be real?'

William laughed so hard at other things she had written, He laughed so hard he put one hand over his mouth, almost in disbelief…

'I taught William chess today,' she wrote 'and I am utterly convinced that William took a piece when I was not looking! Though I must confess I didn't mention such an accusation, for if I am to be honest, I wanted him to win, and some part of me finds the devious side of him so alluringly charming.'

It was if she was always one step ahead of him, indeed it was true that William had taken a pawn in their game of chess when she had looked the other way, but he was convinced on that day that he had got away with it. It made him smile to know that she knew.

William read further entries, and all of her words were so very positive. She had written about her first meeting with Azrael, and how amazingly tame and beautiful he was. She wrote about the time he got her to close her eyes in the forest, when William taught her to truly hear it in all its wonder. She wrote how her heart skipped a beat when they danced together in the rain, and of how she felt lost in his arms when they kissed.

He reached the last few entries in the diary; his smile was like a cat with a saucer of milk. He was so jubilant, and then he read the last few words…

It was dated the day before she died...

'William, this note is for you. I write this knowing that things are scary, you face an unimaginable horror. But I hope, and I beg with all I am that you can be saved. There is a good chance you will never read this letter, but I would still get it to you, even if… Enough of that! What I want to say, what I want to write may well be for my own selfish needs; to pour my heart out maybe? It's just I have never known another like you. How wrong they are about you, how wrong they are! If only they could see. You have the warmest of hearts that they cannot see, but they are blind William, blind as bats. They mock you, but the joke is on them, you are a beautiful man. The days since I have known you have been the happiest times of my life. I feel we have so much in common, my love, for I have always felt I have never truly belonged to anything, to anyone even. I always felt out of touch growing up, like no person ever really understood me. I could never be interested in any potential suitors for marriage, they all bored me. When I married Lord Fenwick I made a mistake, we were friends, nothing more than friends. I naively thought that maybe being a 'Lady' would give me purpose and responsibility that I would thrive on, but I found the company of such circles both tiresome and undoubtedly fake. It was not until I met you, William, not until I met you that I knew. I knew from the first moment my eyes met yours in the graveyard that day. You brought simplicity to what I thought to be the most complicated word in life. That word is 'love', and with you it wasn't complicated, wasn't hard, it was just there. As plain as day, I tried to fight it, and I lost. I *gladly* lost and will be thankful for that the rest of my life. I am so proud of you, my love, so proud of the man you are, and so proud you are mine. There is none like you, there could never be such, you are my life now, and I will be with you always.'

Tears rolled down William's face; they were a mixture of grieving tears, and happy tears, for how could one not be touched when one you love so dear says the words your heart has secretly craved for?

It was like he had peeked into her soul; the words she wrote made his heart ache, but also made him appreciate the time he had spent with her. After all, that's all anyone can do isn't it?

He had known real love, what is better than that? People can get married, people can have indiscretions … *many* in some cases, but do all feel real love? It is a question that those who don't have it would wish to avoid, but William knew; deep down he knew.

The fact William knew that his and Lizzy's love was real from the deepest part of his heart, was worth more than anything, *ever*. If he didn't live a day more, he knew he had lived when he was with her, and no matter what happened in the future, he would always have his memories, and not one person or one thing could ever take them away.

After putting the diary in his pocket, William thought he would relax in the garden and reflect on the last words Lizzy had written. A swing outside which was in perfect line with the sun looked particularly appealing, so William sat, relaxing, even occasionally swinging a little bit. The words Lizzy had written had hit him hard, but in a good way. Although he was still very much in the grieving process, William had a new sense of optimism, which was born out of the feeling that life *could* in fact be wonderful. It wasn't in hope of one day finding another, for the thought didn't even enter his mind. His new hope of a good life, and trying to continue was that on the whole, people *were* good and life could be good. A new sense of realisation filled his brain, William smiled at the thought and ultimately, William thought that his love for Lizzy was to be celebrated. That when people die, they stay with us. By talking about them we keep them alive, we keep them around us. We remember advice, laughs, tears and unique moments between two people that can never be duplicated or reproduced with another. The moments we share are ours and ours forever.

William smiled to himself as he noticed the sun going down. It was getting late and he thought he would take a nice walk back to his other home and have some supper with Father Fanshaw. The sky dimmed, and William nodded to himself as he thought of words spoken, words written, words said.

'Death is a moment,' thought William. 'But she'll always be with me.'

CHAPTER 71

The walk back to his beloved graveyard was a long one, but nice all the same. William felt that the night looked so inviting when there was thick fog such as the one before his eyes as he walked the cobbled streets of Barnes. The street lantern's shades of yellow were pleasing on the eye as they became visible when William got close. The night was quiet, which William found odd as it was not too late.

Or was it? William hadn't actually checked the time before he left Woodworth Manor and wondered if he had simply lost track. Abandoning the worries of hours and minutes, he kept on walking at his own pace, and as he did he wondered where his friends might have gone to.

Had they gone to Heaven? Surely not to Hell? Did such places even exist? Having done so much soul searching William wasn't sure what he believed in. He hoped there was such a place as Heaven, and believed if there was, that Lizzy would be up there, playing piano and teaching chess to the angels.

The idea made William smile.

The real theories William had weren't so different from anyone else's though; William had come to believe that Heaven was one's own perception of it. That if you loved, let's say, a beautiful garden, flowers and such - that's where you would go, to the most beautiful garden there could ever be… one of unimaginable beauty , one beyond words. Or it could be that someone liked to ride horses? If so, then William's idea was that that person would find the most amazing stallion some place where the fields never ended, and they would ride and ride and ride.

William hoped his friends had gone to such places, that Mr Higgingsly, Old Peggy, all of them, were in their own personal heavens, and loving every minute of it.

But the truth of the matter was he still missed them, even Higgingsly's whining, the squabbles he had to try and sort out, it didn't matter. Friends are friends after all, and even though William could only hear them, it mattered not, for he cared about them all, and silly as it may have seemed, he felt like a father figure to them, like it was his responsibility to make sure they were all right.

But now that he didn't have that job any longer, the graveyard seemed such any empty place.

'Still, got to move forward,' thought William with his new-found positive attitude 'let's go cook Father Fanshaw some food,' his mind added. He wanted to spend more time with Father Fanshaw; he thought he owed it to him.

The fog had eased somewhat as William opened the gates to the graveyard. There was a light coming from the Reverend Fanshaw's kitchen and William felt relieved that he was home. William picked up pace in his walk towards the door but couldn't help giving an acknowledging nod to the graves as he walked past, there were still no voices, but William smiled as he remembered other times when he had returned to the graveyard and one of the dead would shout for attention, 'William, William, where have you been?' Mr Higgingsly would often say if he had some sort of gossip or urgent matter that needed attention.

After opening the front door, William wiped his shoes and took off his coat.

'Hello?' William called as he walked into the kitchen, but Father Fanshaw wasn't there.

The kitchen was the only room with a light on and William wondered if Father Fanshaw had decided to have an early night.

'Surely not,' William thought, as he looked at a clock on the wall which only read 8.30 in the evening. So William walked to the bedroom. The door was open so William had a quick peep; Father Fanshaw wasn't in there. William scratched his chin. 'Where could he be at this time?' he wondered as he also thought, 'I need a shave' as he felt his whiskers. William hadn't had a shave for a while and he was definitely in the early stages of owning a beard.

Walking away from the bedroom William looked in all of the rooms before returning to the kitchen; it was then that he saw a glimpse of something; he quickly shut his eyes and shook his head hard.

He stepped back, shaking his head saying 'No, no-no-no!' out loud.

Pausing for a moment, he knew he *had* to look. There was a small pot on top of Father Fanshaw's stove, which wasn't lit.

Slowly stepping towards the pot, William cautiously took another look, and he feared his first thoughts were correct. His eyes sent the message to his brain as he moved even closer to it, explaining that the crimson puddle of despair which surrounded a small pink looking object was in fact real.

It wasn't a meal Father Fanshaw had prepared, but it was some sort of meat, with a bone still in it, the bloodied thing was human.

It was a finger, a bloody finger, which from the look of it was fresh.

Taking a closer look inside the pot, William noticed something underneath the finger. He reached his hand into the pot and picked up the finger as his face tensed up, he placed the finger on the dining table nearby and picked up what was underneath.

William's own fingers were now covered with blood as he lifted the wet paper, which was partially red with blood, and held it to the light. William read something which had been written on it…

The words didn't explain too much, they didn't need to…

'I'm in the forest now let's finish this before I finish your friend.'

William knew what was going on, and he knew what this meant.

It was Fenwick, he was back…

Back for his revenge.

CHAPTER 72

Shaken, but not in full panic, William knew he had to think fast, so he quickly grabbed a large kitchen knife from the rack of kitchen utensils and ran out of the house.

His mind was going crazy as he sprinted through the soggy, wet soil. He wondered if he was going to be too late. Was Fenwick's intention to kill him? William assumed it was, why else risk all by coming back into a town where he was a wanted man?

This was Fenwick's climax, and William knew there was only one way it would end...

With his death, or Fenwick's.

The trees of the forest looked different at night. During the day one would marvel at the many shades of greens which were complimented by wild flowers and one could believe the forest had a heartbeat of its very own ... it seemed so alive. At night however, the forest was a different place altogether. The trees stood as tall as they did in the daytime, but they seemed to be higher, as if one could not know where the trees ended and the sky began.

Ravens flapped their wings as they shot past in the air, as if ready for witnessing death. Owls called out as if they were warning William of what the dark forest had in store, deep within the blackened bark and bushes.

His legs had moved faster than he thought and, in what seemed like no time at all, William was within the forest's grip. Trees surrounded him, everything was black, and the only light came from the nights mist as William slowed down his pace.

Things were quiet, too quiet, and as William moved each foot forward it seemed like the little twigs his feet snapped made a noise like a clap. The slightest noise became the loudest noise, like the forest was trying to give his position away to whatever, whoever lurked in waiting.

There was an eerie stillness, and as William stood still he felt a weird tingling sensation all over his body. There was most definitely a presence, a dark presence, but William was wise enough to know that fear of such a presence only feeds it, makes it stronger.

There was no way he was going to feed such a spiritual troll.

He needed to make the first move, he knew whatever waited for him probably wanted him to move first, like it was all some sort of dark game.

For the second time, thoughts of Lizzy teaching him chess came into William's mind like a guide. She had told him to imagine it was a battle, and to take them to the deep dark forest where things didn't make sense, where things didn't add up, until ultimately the pathway of escape would only be wide enough for one.

Deciding he was in control, William embraced the darkness around him, he needed it to be his ally, so he took the initiative.

Staying still for a second behind a tree, William called into the night with conviction.

'The forest is mine, Fenwick; you have chosen the wrong battle ground.'

William's voice soared amongst the trees and a colony of bats quickly flew over his head as if even they were scared of his intentions. As the bats disappeared into the night, William's ears registered a sound, and he knew it was the sound of his enemy; he heard whispering but couldn't make out the words.

Quickly and quietly, William tip-toed to another tree and stayed behind its cloak, hoping to hear something else.

'Come on, Fenwick,' thought William. 'Show yourself.'

More sounds invaded the night as twigs snapped in different directions…

Were there more than one out there? Maybe Fenwick had let Father Fanshaw go free? If that was the case, then he needed help for he was bleeding!

Coming out from his position of stealth, William moved into the clearing which was triangular and in the middle stood his enemy.

Fenwick was all that was bad about man, and the loathsome being stood in the centre of the clearing with an even more twisted look than usual, which was a feat on its own for the tyrant of Barnes.

Holding a large knife to Father Fanshaw's throat and a wooden bat in the other hand, Fenwick seemed to still bask in his over confidence, as if everything was already decided, like the victory had been claimed without the battle.

Reverend Fanshaw looked scared, and William hated seeing his good friend's eyes wide with such terror. The Reverend did nothing but good, and as their eyes met William nodded to him in reassurance.

Father Fanshaw said nothing, but he knew that William was going to unleash something; he could see it in his eyes.

'Let him go,' William shouted as he walked towards Fenwick.

'That's enough, freak,' smiled Fenwick as he pressed the blade closer to Father Fanshaw's windpipe, 'not one step further'

Coming to a halt, William raised his arms in the air, 'Let him go Fenwick, your quarrel is with me. This man, is innocent, he bears you no harm.'

Fenwick's madness started to rear its ugly head and as he spoke his voice was shaky. He screamed in William's direction, 'He is leverage *Rathbone*! My bait! For how else was I to meet with you? You, *Lord* William Rathbone! What a joke! Yes, I heard. Well this finishes tonight! I can't even set foot in the town, my town! You and your do-gooder friends have seen to that, conspiring and conniving against me!'

'You brought it all on yourself, Patrick,' said William softly, 'I had no cause to hurt you; you bore *no* significance to me at all. Even when you tried to have me killed – you did your very best for me to be disgraced and hung - you couldn't stop there, you had to take her too. That's where you made your mistake, Fenwick. The moment you touched her was the moment you may as well have dug your own grave; because that is where your bones will go after tonight. Your soul, however, will not have it that easy, it will be torn apart by the agents of the dead, over and over for eternity, and you will know in your suffering mind that it was caused by my hands. I am here to end you, Fenwick.'

Fenwick seemed baffled by William's words and pulled on what little hair Father Fanshaw had as he held the knife tight against his skin. 'End *me*? Well aren't you the optimist? I would say given your current predicament, that the plan you harvest in what little brain you do have, seems somewhat flawed. How do you expect to get to me without hurting you dear friend who is, if you haven't noticed, under my knife? You see you haven't thought the plan through have you? That's what I do you see, I have plans.'

William sneakily took a step forward which Fenwick didn't react to. 'But why kill Father Fanshaw? There is no need, this is our vendetta Fenwick, come and get what you want, come and get me.'

'I'm not going to kill him,' laughed Fenwick. 'He just happens to be an integral part in how I get my life back. You see, after I kill you, slowly and painfully, that no-good busy-body friend of yours, Robertson, is next. Then the judge, and whoever else stands in my way. I will get Father Fanshaw here to vouch for me, and I will somehow buy a judge, clear my name, and then take the estate that is rightfully mine. It's all part of my plan, and so it will be done, I promise you, I'll get away with it all, and your body will rot in a hole for good, like everything else you have ever loved.'

'You won't get away with this,' snapped William, 'for what's done in the dark always comes to the light. I swear you will pay, for even if I die here tonight, I swear I will be back, I would set the world on fire if it meant killing you.'

William tried to take another sneaky step forward, but then realised that Fenwick had seen him do it, as Fenwick smiled. Fenwick took the knife off Father Fanshaw's throat and threw it onto the grass nearby, as well as his bat. This was William's chance, and he had to go for it!

But as William got ready to pounce he felt something behind him, he saw in Fenwick's smile that something bad was going to happen as Father Fanshaw screamed out, 'William, no!'

Before William could turn he felt an abrupt pain in his shoulder, he looked down to it and a sharp tip of silver was protruding through his shirt as a trickle of blood followed, William felt cold as he heard Father Fanshaw crying out his name.

'Shut it' barked Fenwick hitting Father Fanshaw over the head with the wooden bat he had picked back up. The blow knocked him out cold and his body fell to the floor like a sack of onions.

William watched the blade's tip leave his shoulder as whoever had put it in twisted it on the way out. It hurt him, of that there was no doubt. But William knew he could not dwell on pain, he had to endure it.

As quickly as he could William turned as the blade left his body and he saw another face of evil. It was Ravensdale and his hand was in mid-thrust with a knife aimed at William's heart.

The blade flew forward guided by the wicked policeman, but just as its destination was about to reach its life-ending target, William reacted with a life-saving move to stop the blade with his palm, the knife went straight through. Ravensdale slung his other arm, his left, towards William in an attempt at a punch which hit William's face hard, but William took it and grabbed Ravensdale's left wrist, twisting his arm with ease as he cocked back his hand with the knife still in it, William head-butted Ravensdale…

Once, twice, then again and again until Ravensdale's nose was broken and flat. Falling to his knees, Ravensdale looked stunned and wobbled as he knelt before William.

Pulling the knife out of his own hand, William felt the cold blade scrape bones on its way, but he didn't wince. His eyes stayed fixed on the man who was supposed to protect people from the Fenwick's of the world. William held the blade, up in the air as Ravensdale looked up at him.

'Go to hell,' whispered Ravensdale as his head swayed in dizziness.

'You first,' replied William as he threw the knife away and grabbed Ravensdale's by the windpipe. He stood Ravensdale up through sheer strength, like a human puppet, then lifted him up a few feet in the air before crashing his head onto the ground.

William felt the man's neck break in his hands, as blood trickled out of Ravensdale's nose and head.

This was only part of the blood William's inner-self demanded. It was the currency of vengeance, and now he wanted to fill his pockets.

Having being so caught up killing Ravensdale, William quickly turned to see where Fenwick was, but it was too late, it seemed as soon as he turned he felt a large thud against the side of his head.

The dull clout caught William hard and he fell to the floor; he rolled around, dazed and confused and could see Fenwick laughing. 'You see! I always plan ahead!' laughed Fenwick.

William could see Father Fanshaw up ahead about twenty yards away and hoped he wasn't dead.

Maybe this was how it all ended; maybe he and Father Fanshaw would travel the final journey together? As William struggled to his knees he got dizzy again and fell back to the floor, his shoulder and hand were bleeding and his energy was so low he felt he could hardly move. His inner voice yelled 'Come on, get up, you can do it' and with every ounce of life he had he got to his knees as he watched Fenwick walk away towards Father Fanshaw.

'I'm not leaving you, don't worry boy, just retrieving my knife,' laughed Fenwick as he picked up the blade and held it in the moonlight.

William's eyes caught sight of the knife and he shook his head as he spat some blood onto the ground. 'Always need a weapon, don't you? Wouldn't you rather do it with your bare hands, give me a fair chance?'

'Fair? Ha! Sorry, Rathbone, that word is not part of my vocabulary. Now see this instrument of death I wield, see it! For this is going to open you up, William. This will not be quick; I am going to rip the intestines out of your stomach and strangle you with them. I am going to stab out your eyes, chop off your ears; I will cut you to shreds by the light of this beautiful moon.'

The moon shone bright, and as Fenwick seemed to walk to William in slow motion there was suddenly a series of loud unearthly sounds that stopped him in his stride.

The first sound seemed to shake the very ground William and Fenwick were on, like some unholy rising growl from the midnight blue sky, coming down with an intention of pure violence.

William usually enjoyed thunder, but he had never heard anything like the sound that seemed to shake the forest to its roots. Even the trees looked afraid as they stood still; neither a branch nor leaf trembled in the night's motionless air.

Knowing when nature was giving a hint, William followed his environment by staying perfectly still as he waited on his knees…

William stayed silent and still, still as a statue.

The loud thunder continued and Fenwick laughed, 'Quite scary that, for a moment! But don't you worry, I'm coming.' He smiled as he raised the knife up and took a step towards William.

It was then that the second sound came; it was a haunting howl that made William's whole body feel like it was covered in goose bumps. Even the air rushed into William's nose and into his lungs as if it were afraid, all the while sending shivers through his body, from his head to his toes. It made him jerk a little as his eyes searched the forest through the mass of trees for a sight of what made the sound, although he wasn't sure he wanted to know.

Fenwick stopped again with the knife in hand and stared at William. 'My god, what *is* that?'

Knowing the night had come alive … knowing that there was more to things than what could be seen, heard or felt, William smiled at Fenwick, even though for all he knew, whatever lurked, whatever was coming their way. Whatever was angry could be after the two of them.

'The demons seem to be on the prowl, bar the doors.'

Fenwick shook in fear as the howling got louder and louder, as if some wrathful apparition was using its own language as a threat of things to come.

'What do you mean by 'demon'? You are mad! Mad I say! That graveyard surely was your asylum; you should be locked up with chains around you saying such things!'

William's eyes looked straight at Fenwick's as the howling and growling continued. 'Then what are you waiting for, Fenwick? Finish it! But I think you know; I think you are beginning to see…'

The sound of the thunder became more and more unsettling as it hit again and again like a fist from the sky, and after a few more roars of great intensity, it found allies in the rain and the lightning which illuminated the angry sky above.

'See what?' screamed Fenwick through the night's anger, 'See what?'

Just as Fenwick asked his question, the dark trees which surrounded the clearing lit up.

A congregation of colours entered the night's blackness. There were little round lights, advancing with a sinister silence that made Fenwick freeze as he gripped his knife with all his might.

William saw the lights too, but he wasn't afraid; he thought the lights were so pretty, whatever they were, whatever they were here for. He loved the dark greens, the yellows and the ice-blues, he thought they were beautiful.

The colours grew closer and closer as the thunder ceased its attack on the forest, like it had given the order now and whatever approached was there to carry out the command.

'Oh my God, oh my God!' screamed Fenwick as his mind verified what the little round lights were…

They were eyes.

Lots of them.

The eyes doubled, tripled and before Fenwick knew it, the eyes surrounded both him and William.

'We are done for; done for. I tell you!' Fenwick screamed

Ignoring Fenwick's futile cries, William observed as the eyes revealed to whom they belonged.

The eyes belonged to wolves, *a pack*, of wolves.

William was amazed as he watched them prance gracefully out of the night's shadows and close in. William knew they stood no chance at all if they were attacked, so he stayed on his knees in acceptance of his fate and closed his eyes.

'What are you doing, you freak? We can work together, try and fight them!' yelled Fenwick as he kept his knife close to him; all the while watching the wolves move slowly closer.

'I'd rather be ripped apart by these creatures than stand side-by-side with you, Fenwick, but go ahead, fight them, see where that gets you,' laughed William still closing his eyes.

'If I am to die, then I will make sure I kill you first!' screamed Fenwick starting to sprint towards William.

Just as Fenwick started his run of murderous intent, a single howl rang out followed by the sound of something moving fast. William opened his eyes and watched Fenwick run at him, He didn't move as it all seemed to happen in slow motion. Something was behind Fenwick, but what? William couldn't see. Were the wolves coming to devour them both? Had Fenwick's run startled them into attack, or was it more simple… were they just hungry?

'Die, you wretched rat!' screamed Fenwick as he got to within a few feet of William. Fenwick's eyes had a malevolent edge and as William stared into them for the briefest of moments he saw what true ugliness was … it was hate wrapped in skin, violence with bones, a heartless heart which could never know love. To William, Fenwick was already dead, whether his heart beat or not. Fenwick lunged with lethality that craved a fatality and as his knife moved forward in the night air William waited to make his move. He waited for that spilt-second when the knife was almost touching his skin, so he could knock Fenwick off balance and counter the evil scoundrel accordingly.

It was then that the night revealed its intentions.

The intervention was as swift as it was brutal…

In a flash, the colours of the beautiful eyes made themselves seen as William gasped.

First, two sets of eyes followed by two sets of teeth bit deep into each of Fenwick's shoulders, stopping him in his deadly pounce. The knife instantly fell out of his hands as he screamed in pain. He fell to his knees and the wolves held him there; blood ran down his neck and body as he wriggled.

Two more wolves slowly growled like they were brewing their anger; the quiet before the storm- the still before the crash, the thrill of the kill. They bit into Fenwick's legs as he bellowed even harder. The sound tore through the night and back again to the point where it began, and William knew that the shriek was filled with anger, fear, pain and hatred towards his inevitable fate.

Rising to his feet, William watched in disbelief. Why hadn't these wolves attacked him, were they guarding him? Could it really be so?

Feeling it strange that the wolves simply held Fenwick in suspension, when they had the means and power to rip him limb from limb, William waited wondering what to do.

'Should I run? Wait? Do I take advantage of Fenwick's peril and finish him?' thought William as he watched Fenwick wriggle and listened to him moan in agony.

Then, as if in an instant reply to his inner thoughts and questions, an old furry friend appeared. William's eyes lit up as he took steps towards him and fell to his knees in a joy that made his eyes fill up.

'Azrael, Azrael!' called William as he cuddled the magnificent beast.

Azrael's tongue hung out as he licked William's face, William looked into Azrael's eyes and he thought the beautiful eyes looked sad for a moment.

'Come here, boy,' laughed William as he hugged and kissed Azrael.

'What about me?' screamed Fenwick as he looked on helplessly. 'Never mind hugging a bloody mutt, help me you imbecile, help me!'

Turning to Fenwick, William shook his head. 'Help *you*? No, I can't, I'm sorry Patrick.'

Fenwick tried to wiggle a little but the wolves bit down even harder, making sure Fenwick knew his place as he yelled out again 'Aghhhh! So, so you are going to kill me? I'm a person you know. Do you see? I'm being killed, I say! You are killing me!'

'I do see, Patrick,' nodded William as he stroked Azrael's neck. 'I see all; I see what beckons for you - wings of darkness, black as night, flapping towards you. Feathers burned by the wrong you have done; attached to a figure of might that has one purpose. While I know this means the end of your life, I feel a hollow sadness, but I also feel free. I feel the end approaching fast for you now, taking you to a sea of graves and lost souls. I see the Angel of Death, and it wants you.'

Azrael looked at William before it slowly walked a few steps away, pointing its nose to something. William looked and Azrael's eyes lit up as it knew William had seen what it wanted him too.

It was Fenwick's knife; it shone in the moonlight like a beacon. William could feel Azrael's eyes staring at him in anticipation, as if they were saying 'Go on, William, kill him! You have him, finish him!'

William picked up the knife and Azrael panted with excitement. Fenwick screamed out 'No, no! This is murder! How does that make you better than me?'

William knew Fenwick was right; William wasn't a killer - dark around the edges perhaps-but he wasn't cold blooded. He would only kill when he needed to, not when he wanted to, and to William there was a huge difference.

'I can't, Azrael. I'm sorry,' smiled William as Azrael's eyes stared into his.

'Ha-ha! Good boy, William, good boy indeed! Now get these wretched creatures off me before they tear my arms off, now, I said, now!'

William sighed as thoughts of Lizzy's smile ran through his brain. He turned to Azrael and nodded, then to Fenwick, 'I said I wasn't going to kill you, Patrick, but for these hungry fellows, I cannot speak.'

Azrael's eyes lit up as if Fenwick was the biggest, juiciest steak from the butcher's.

William looked in awe at his mighty friend's eyes lighting up with excitement.

The eyes were stunning, beautiful, adorable, lethal.

Quickly, in some sort of acknowledgement to William, Azrael howled into the night, and the other wolves who watched followed suit. It was like a deathly choir calling into the darkness in perfect tune.

William nodded again to Azrael, before turning his back to Fenwick.

Azrael stopped his howl; he stared at Fenwick and bared his teeth, as their eyes stared into each other's.

William walked away slowly, to check on Father Fanshaw as the sounds invaded his ears. He heard the screams, he heard the howls.

He heard the wolves' death frenzy.

CHAPTER 73

Many months had passed and it had fast become winter again. During the months after the night that Azrael took Fenwick, a lot of things changed in Barnes, and a lot of things stayed the same. That's just the way life goes.

Everything changes, everything stays the same. People live, people die, and no matter what anyone says, no matter what anyone does, nothing can change it, you accept it and try to move on.

Not that they will ever be forgotten, not at all. There were days when William thought he had the grief beaten, but the truth is, nobody ever beats grief, it's always there and always will be. The trick is accepting it, learning to live with it.

Learning to live with something abnormal wasn't new to William; after all, he had learnt to live with his darkness, his strange gifts. Yet just as he had come to embrace his darkness and control it, his dark gift didn't seem to work any longer and was replaced by grief, a new monster. Having felt many different things, in the real world and otherwise, William had had his fair share of frights and lucky escapes, but for William, grief truly was the worst feeling in the world. Any person that knows it knows that it takes over your life and just when you think it's gone, a huge wave crashes over you and it all begins again.

Grief is a pain deep inside, a wound to the soul that is incurable by any doctor and immune to any medicine. It is emptiness, loneliness, hurt and anger all rolled into one. But the worst thing is…it never goes away.

On some days William woke in the morning feeling like he just wanted to crawl back under the covers because when he slept he forgot about it, and then when he woke, *it* woke.

Morning!

That is how grief is, it has no mercy, no concept of timing and if you let it, it will consume you.

For William Rathbone, there was no way he was being consumed by a second type of darkness, no way at all.

One helping of darkness was more than enough.

So, when he needed to cry, he cried. When he needed to talk, he talked and during the months after Azrael's grizzly feast. William began venturing out into town more. He even spoke to the odd person here and there and he really felt it helped.

The Reverend Fanshaw had recovered and he and William never really spoke of the night the wolves came. Father Fanshaw had an idea what happened, but the truth was he didn't want to focus on the bad things. They were both alive, he and William, and the way Father Fanshaw looked at things was that now he would do his best to not just have William content with digging graves and eating, for that was just existing; he was going to push William, share the gift of this extraordinary man with as many people as he could.

He managed to get William to venture into town daily for his groceries, with the excuse that he was getting old and needed the help, which was a white lie of course. Father Fanshaw even asked William to go to specific shops where he knew the shop owners were lovely people and chatty, that was what William needed.

William needed his faith in people to be restored. He needed to see that on the whole, people *are* good.

Taking a walk to the forest was now something William did every other day, come rain or shine, or as it was, thick snow. William would walk to the forest, *his* forest as he liked to call it, and he would whistle three times.

That was the code, his and Azrael's code.

Some days Azrael would not show, some days he did. On the days he did William would play games with Azrael and talk about Lizzy.

On this day, Azrael hadn't showed. William was fine though, he sat on the log near where Lizzy came to him the day he was chopping firewood. He replayed scenes from a time that seemed long gone, but forever close to his heart. The memories made him happy, they always did.

This was William's quiet time, his time of thought and reflection. He knew what Father Fanshaw was doing, sending him out on errands in an attempt at making him be more sociable and it made William happy to let Father Fanshaw believe he was being sly, though the thought amused William as the words Father Fanshaw and sly just didn't seem to mix.

It was all fine, William didn't mind talking to people in small doses, and nobody could doubt his effort to at least try and interact with people, but the simple fact was he still needed his alone time.

It was all a learning curve, William knew as well as anyone that nobody was truly alone, and the fact that humans were social creatures was a reality he had to accept; as long as the people he met understood he couldn't just transform himself overnight, nor did he want to. His personality just needed a little tweak here and there.

In the winter, the forest was a cold and wearisome place. The trees were bare and the wind whistled through the branches. William sat on his log, smoking his pipe in peace as he looked up at the sky and snow-filled clouds through the silhouette of branches. When walking into the town he heard people complain about the winter, but William liked it. He enjoyed the different colours the winter had to offer, the shades of white, brown and grey. Underfoot the leaves formed a soggy mass that made his feet feel funny as his boots sunk slightly into the ground. Walking in the forest made William long for the warmth of logs on the fire at home, he just wished he could have experienced the joy of Lizzy's company around such a fire and he closed his eyes for a moment imagining the two of them wrapped in a fur blanket, watching the flames.

Opening his eyes to the reality of frostbitten trees, William stood and slowly walked back to the graveyard. Even though he was officially a 'Lord' now, and the owner of a giant estate, William asked if he could continue his duties, which of course Father Fanshaw had agreed to.

But William had been offered another job, which he was considering. A friend of Father Fanshaw, who lived out of town, had visited and saw how hard William worked when he dug; he offered William a job outright. William wasn't sure but said he would give the man an answer in a week.

It was the last day of that offer until expiry and William was torn as to whether he should take it or not. Usually William wouldn't have given the proposition a seconds thought, for he loved Father Fanshaw and everything in the town reminded him of Lizzy. The main reason was he had lost his gift, and wondered if he went out of town for a while, got his mind off things, that maybe his gift would return. Then he could come back and hope that he could speak again with his one and only true love.

He was willing to try anything

His boots left big footprints as he trudged through the snow, and as he got back to the graveyard he thought he would give the new job a go. He had to, his mind was still all over the place and he thought a change of scenery would do him good, if only for a month or two.

Looking at the many graves, where he once sat and chatted for hours upon hours, made William appreciate the gift he once had, but also sad at losing it. William always thought that if people knew of his gift they would be terrified, as he once was when he first heard the voices so many years ago. But William also knew, without any hesitation, that those very same people who would be terrified at such a prospect would give anything to talk to a person they had lost whom they loved with all their heart, for who can deny complete and utter love?

William nodded at his old friends' graves as a goodbye, he felt sad he couldn't say it to them anymore but hoped they were all happy, wherever they were.

Father Fanshaw was in town and William thought he would catch up with him and tell him the news. He had actually encouraged William to see another town; after all, William had lived in Barnes all his life.

Looking around the graveyard towards the east wall, William knew he only had one more goodbye to say…

Lizzy's head stone had not lost its newness, not like the many others which had deteriorated at the hands of the weather.

William knelt down in front of it, his knees crushed the snow underneath them and felt wet, but he didn't care. He stared, not at the grave, but at what seemed like a faraway past, a sparkling time, replaying every word spoken, every smile, every kiss.

Tenderly, as if worried he might disturb it somehow, William reached out one finger and caressed the stone. 'Hello, my love, I'm here,' his voice whispered in the cold relentless wind.

William read the words on the grave again 'Mortuus est Momentaneum' and smiled thinking the only reason he knew what it meant was because she told him.

Lizzy told him *so* much, taught him so much; about life, about everything.

'I am going on a trip, my love,' William said as he watched his breath hit the cold air. 'I don't know when I will be back. This place, this town even, just isn't the same anymore. It doesn't feel like home.'

A single tear escaped from his eye and ran down his face as he brushed it away without thinking.

Gulping for breath as he continued, he almost felt like he was betraying her by leaving. 'I just have to go, my love, I have to!' He covered his face with his hands. 'Oh, I don't know what I'm doing if I'm honest, I guess I am just trying to live. Every day is just another day without you. Azrael is good by the way; he has many friends it turns out. He comes to see me on occasions when I walk the forest; I sometimes wonder if he has a cat for a relative as he brings me gifts, he brought me a dead rabbit not so long back. Oh well, so long as he doesn't bring bits of humans to me, I guess he means well! Our favourite policeman Robertson continues to thrive. He told me he was promoted the last time I saw him near the fruit market. Word is Fenwick up and vanished with his accomplice Ravensdale … if only they knew. Father Fanshaw, he's doing well, but makes me do his shopping, thinks I'll make new friends.'

William laughed at the thought and looked at the grave as if Lizzy herself had laughed. 'Yes, me, making new friends, a funny concept I have to agree. I am playing the piano, every day in fact, not as good as you but I think over time…just kidding, my piano fingers are like lightning, they never strike the same place twice! Sorry, an old piano joke for you; it's awful I know. Oh, I would say that my chess is getting better though, I beat Father Fanshaw, gave him a good big and fat checkmate I did, he was most displeased.'

Williams's eyes stared at the stone, he knew how to say goodbye but the words wouldn't seem to come out.

'Nobody talks to me anymore, you know, and I'm not talking about people, wouldn't be bothered by that at all. I mean, well you know, *my friends*, it seems they have gone some place my voice doesn't travel. I know that's how things are *supposed* to be in reality, I do *know* this, but I ask myself countless times, why was I given such a gift for it to be taken away? Why, with all the spirits who whispered in my ears, wasn't I allowed just a few moments with the one person my heart has fully opened to, why?'

Standing to his feet, William felt if he didn't move now he never would. Turning away for a second with the intention of leaving, William cried and spun back around; he knelt again in the deep snow and hugged the grave like it was Lizzy, like he was desperate to never let it go.

'I have to go now, I will always love you. I am yours forever, my love, if you ever need me; all you have to do is call my name. Goodbye, my love.'

His lips felt cold as they kissed the stone. He stood back up as the snow started to fall again and turned to head out of the graveyard, for how long he didn't know.

His tears seemed to make him walk oddly, as if he were drunk. He felt like he couldn't walk straight as his feet took one step after another in the deep white snow that crunched underneath his boots as he walked through it. William stared at the snow as he took his staggered slow steps and wondered how something could be so soft and gentle to the touch by hand but crunchy and hard and unforgiving underfoot.

Out of the blue, as William's nose felt numb through the weather's hard bite, he picked up a scent…

It was jasmine.

Immediately as the scent tickled his senses, it was like all presence of time had stopped. William's tears were the only things moving in the graveyard and then they too halted mid-way down his cheeks. Then he heard it … and the voice was as clear as day…

'*William…*'

Printed in Great Britain
by Amazon